Tania Carver is the pseudonym for the husband-and-wife writing team of Martyn and Linda Waites, who have written four internationally bestselling titles in the Brennan and Esposito series. They live in Hertfordshire with their two daughters. Martyn also writes under his own name.

THE
DOLL'S HOUSE

TANIA
CARVER

sphere

SPHERE

First published in Great Britain in 2013 by Sphere
Reprinted 2013 (twice)

Copyright © Tania Carver 2013

The moral right of the author has been asserted.

*All characters and events in this publication, other than those
clearly in the public domain, are fictitious and any resemblance
to real persons, living or dead, is purely coincidental.*

A CIP catalogue record for this book
is available from the British Library.

ISBN 978-0-7515-5052-8

Typeset in Plantin by M Rules
Printed and bound in Great Britain by
Clays Ltd, St Ives plc

Papers used by Sphere are from well-managed forests
and other responsible sources.

MIX
Paper from
responsible sources
FSC
www.fsc.org   FSC® C104740

Sphere
An imprint of
Little, Brown Book Group
100 Victoria Embankment
London EC4Y 0DY

An Hachette UK Company
www.hachette.co.uk

www.littlebrown.co.uk

THE
DOLL'S HOUSE

PART ONE

ELECTRIC FUNERAL

1

Everything was perfect. Just like she had imagined it. Yearned for it.

And she knew that *he* wanted it too.

The butterflies in her stomach made her tingle and shake. She tried to ignore them, or at least enjoy their nervy, shivering anticipation, and gave the living room one final inspection. She saw a speck of dust or a curl of fluff on the carpet that may or may not have been imaginary and bent down to pick it up. Holding it between thumb and forefinger she walked into the kitchen, put it in the pedal bin, knocked any dirt residue off her fingers and smoothed her skirt down, the material crackling beneath her fingers, electric, removing any creases. Everything had to be perfect. Including herself. *Especially* herself.

A quick check of the pans on the stove in the kitchen – everything simmering away nicely, the extractor fan humming, the windows lightly misted with the homely fog of cooking – then back into the living room for yet another look round. She crossed to the sofa, moved a cushion, repositioning it slightly. Then moved it back again. She didn't need to, knew it was just nerves. She stood back, admiring. Everything was as she had pictured it, the best it could be. But then it should be. It had to be. She would only be doing this once.

And she would have no second chance.

The room was open plan; the living room at one end, the dining area at the back of the house. The cushions had been plumped up, placed in exactly the right spots on the sofa and armchairs. The room had been stripped, decorated, painted. Then cleaned, dusted and accessorised. Everything was in its place. She turned to the dining area. The table was laid out as she had wanted it, as they had both agreed. The crockery and cutlery, the tableware and place settings, even the covers and tie-backs on the chairs all matching and co-ordinated. It looked beautiful.

Beautiful.

She smiled. Felt something stir within. A ripple ran through her. Pride, she thought. Pride that her feminine skills and womanly ways were to be appreciated by someone at last. Someone special. *Very* special. She could have cried but it would have spoiled her make-up.

She hadn't just waited a long time for this evening; it was the culmination of a lifetime. She held out her hands, ignored the shaking and admired her nails. They had been professionally rendered the day before. Glossy acrylics, French-manicured, shaped and buffed. Costly, but worth every penny. Shiny and strong, they felt like they were more a part of her than her real ones underneath. Just like everything else, in fact. She smiled at her own joke, giggled. Then stopped. Remembered what all this was for. And hoped he would appreciate it.

He would. She knew he would. She wouldn't have gone to all this trouble if it were otherwise. Wouldn't have made the effort for him. When they had first spoken to each other she had thought he sounded promising. Better than all the others. Not a fantasist, a time-waster. Something more real about him. Honest about his intentions. And when they met for the first time her hopes had been confirmed. He'd touched her,

4

nothing serious, just stroking her arm, and there had been a definite spark, an exchange of energy as a frisson of electricity passed between the pair of them, jumping both ways. They looked at each other when it happened. And they knew. She had found him. The man she had been waiting for. Mr Right. And she was just perfect for him. He had found his Miss Right.

She had been looking for him for a long time. She had thought she had found him on a few occasions. It had gone from nervous curiosity to a huge yearning to find not just anyone to fill the emptiness but the right person to make her complete. But the times before had just been false dawns. So many that she had started to despair of ever finding anyone. The patterns had become depressingly familiar. She met quite a few men but most didn't interest her. Or there wasn't a great enough spark. The few that she did find something in common with she would see again. And that would usually lead to a relationship.

The sex was always significant, and she enjoyed it, but that wasn't the most important aspect, she told herself. She enjoyed the closeness that came from being with someone. The intimacy. And of course being accepted for who she was. Once that happened she would work hard to make sure it developed into a relationship. She would encourage her partners to share things with her. Their hopes, their dreams. Their fantasies. And in turn she would do the same with them. For the most part it would be fun. She would try to kindle the spark between them and they would find themselves moving on from just sharing to acting out those fantasises. She thoroughly enjoyed that. Then, when they had come to know each other really well, their inhibitions cast aside and her fear of rejection diminished, when she felt secure enough to say anything and be sure they weren't going to run, she would tell

5

them her ultimate fantasy. The one that would make her life complete.

And then her would-be perfect partner would turn out to be just like all the others. Not always straight away. Some would hang around, try to accommodate what she wanted, force themselves to want it too. But it would never work. So they would start to find excuses for not seeing her. Work appointments. Family commitments. They would still come round for sex when they were in the mood, and she would always give them what they wanted in the hope they would stay, but it was never enough. They wanted some of her but they couldn't take all of her. And gradually they would leave her, bit by bit. Excuse by excuse. Every single one. Every time.

It would leave her devastated, heartbroken. Back to square one and bereft. The unfulfilled fire would still burn within her, giving her the strength to try again. He must be out there somewhere, she would think. He must be.

And she would start looking once again.

Now her quest had brought her to this one. Things had started the same way, progressed from a spark to a flame to a fire. It was going well. Very well. And very quickly. So well she had felt able to tell him of her ultimate desire. And he didn't run away. Didn't call her names or feel repelled by what she told him. He just nodded. Smiled. And told her *his* ultimate fantasy.

And that was when she knew she had found him. Her perfect man.

She checked her watch. The butterflies fluttered once more. Bashing their beautiful wings against her raw nerve endings. He was due any minute.

She gave one last look round the living room, one last look round the dining room. A quick check of the kitchen. She didn't want anything to spoil it. That would be awful.

She looked down at her hands once more. Still trembling. Only to be expected. She had every right to be nervous. She was about to embark on the proudest, most beautiful, most perfect moment of her life. She was going to become who she had always dreamed she could be. The doll's house was still in the corner of the living room. The one she had played with when she was little, had taken with her everywhere she had gone. She thought of the hours she had spent with it, losing herself in the lives of the dolls, wishing she could live there permanently, become one of them. She looked up, caught her reflection in the mirror over the fireplace. Smiled.

She had a very pretty smile, even if she said so herself. Mostly when she looked in the mirror, especially when she didn't have any make-up on, all she could see were her sad eyes. Sad and depressing. Because she knew what was behind them and hated it, always avoided looking at them. But with her make-up on she was a different person. One who could smile at herself, properly smile, because she saw the person she had always imagined herself being. The person she now was.

'You're beautiful,' she said. 'Beautiful.'

The doorbell rang.

Her breath caught in her throat. She looked round again. Smoothed down imaginary wrinkles in her dress, gave the room one last check. She took a deep breath. Another.

And, her heart hammering in her chest, the butterflies trying to escape, went down the hall to open the door.

Smiling as brightly and as widely as she could.

PART TWO

PARANOID

2

'Jesus Christ, is she . . . smiling? Just what we want before Christmas.'

The lead forensic scene investigator's voice carried from the middle of the living room to the hallway. Detective Inspector Phil Brennan made to move inside. An arm thrust across his body, restraining him.

'Not yet,' said the voice attached to the arm. 'Maybe you do things differently out in the sticks, but we follow the rules here.' Then a cough. 'Sir.'

Phil looked at the speaker, aware that other eyes, down the hall, were on him too. Detective Sergeant Ian Sperring carried an extra ten years and an extra twenty-odd pounds compared to Phil. Plus an open dislike of authority, especially when it came in the shape of a younger superior officer from outside the area.

Well this is working out, thought Phil, the note of sarcasm directed towards himself. He wondered whether to say anything, to give DS Sperring a reminder, gentle or otherwise, about who was in charge of the case and respecting the chain of command. Decided against it. They were working. They needed their energies for the job in hand.

But it wouldn't be forgotten. Just dealt with later.

The two men wore regulation hooded blue paper suits and booties, second-skin latex gloves. Despite the December cold, Sperring was red-faced and sweating in his. They were both impatient to be allowed in. Phil craned his neck round the door frame again. Just the glimpse of what he saw both stunned and sickened him.

'Call me when you're ready,' he said, turning and heading outside.

A white tent had been erected around the doorway, lit from inside. Blue plastic sheets had been staked and placed to stop onlookers and news crews peering in. Beyond that, yellow and black tape marked the perimeter of the ordinary world

The location wasn't important. No matter where he went, it was always the same. When a murder was committed, it opened a doorway from the ordinary world to the nightmare world. And those doorways could appear, he had discovered throughout his career, anywhere and everywhere.

The house was cold enough, but outside was freezing, the Birmingham winter being particularly harsh.

Birmingham. Of all places. Phil had never imagined he would end up working here.

It was eight months since a deliberate explosion had killed Phil's father and almost killed his mother and himself. Eight months since he had come out of a coma. Eight months since his daughter's abduction and his wife's fight to get her back. Eight months. A long time to think about where he wanted to go, what he wanted to do with his life.

But still. Birmingham.

'You know, maybe we should get away for a bit,' Marina, his criminal psychologist wife, had said one night in July as they sat on a bench outside the Rose and Crown pub in Wivenhoe. They were squeezing what they could out of the brief summer. Phil was, uncharacteristically, wearing a baseball cap, as his scars were still a little vivid, his hair not yet grown enough to cover them. Their young daughter, Josephina, was with her grandmother for the evening. They had both decided they needed to talk.

Three months had passed by then. Their wounds, physical, mental, emotional and spiritual, had been patched up but were still fragile. Sudden, unexpected movements could and did split them open again.

At first they hadn't talked about what had happened, not in depth. They hadn't been able to articulate it; like soldiers sharing a horror of surviving war, the experience had shell-shocked them into silence. But gradually, over time, that had changed. They needed to do it and had found a way. To Phil and Marina it was like learning a new language; different and unfamiliar, yet evolving into forms expressing and communicating hurt, loss, rage and guilt.

Once they had reached that stage, they had both received counselling, separately and together. Just as they had learned how to talk and communicate once more, now they relearned how to walk, readying themselves to move on. But recently Marina had been distracted, like something else was on her mind, something she couldn't discuss with him. And now, first asking Eileen to look after Josephina, she had decided they should go to the pub to talk. Phil, with some trepidation but no choice, had gone along with her.

'A holiday,' he had replied, somewhat relieved. 'Good idea.' That was what she had been up to, he reasoned. Booking a holiday. Keeping it from him as a surprise. Yes. That must be it.

'Yeah ...' Marina put down her gin and tonic, leaned across the trestle towards him. The lowering sun made a golden halo around her mass of dark curls. Phil never tired of seeing that. Hoped he never would. 'That would be good. Help with your convalescence and all that. But I was thinking something a bit more . . . long term.'

Phil shuddered inside. *She's leaving me. Next she'll tell me that she can't look at my face without being reminded of what happened.* He said nothing. Waited for her to continue.

'You gave me the idea,' she said.

Phil frowned. 'Me?'

'Yeah,' she said. 'You said you were dreading going back. Walking into the office, the whole team staring at you, wondering how damaged you were, whether you were still up to it.'

The halo around Marina's head disappeared, the sun hidden by a cloud. 'Let's not—'

'You said so yourself. Even told that police counsellor you were sent to.' There was an undercurrent to that statement – clearly Marina thought the job should have been hers. She continued. 'How everything around here reminded you of what had happened, and that you couldn't shake it off.'

Phil said nothing. There was nothing there he could disagree with.

Marina sat back, drank. The alcohol gave her the courage to speak her mind. 'It was the same for me. You know that. Worse in a way – I haven't got a job to go back to. I can't rejoin the police as a psychologist, DCI Franks made that perfectly clear.'

'What about Essex? I thought the university would have you back. Jump at the chance, your old mate there said.'

She shrugged, her face in shadow. 'Yeah, well, my old mate doesn't hire and fire. And the ones that do, well . . . maybe they thought that after everything that's happened, the notoriety, having me there, my name, might attract the wrong kind of student.'

14

'They tell you that?'

'Not in so many words. Just in the spaces between the words.' She looked around at the harbour, the pub, the people, as if she wouldn't see any of it again. Or not for a long time. 'Still, they're not the only university in the country ... I've been headhunted.'

Things fell into place for Phil then. He felt relief at understanding, apprehension at what she was about to say next. 'Where?'

Marina paused before speaking. 'First, I should say it's a good job. Very good. Good money, level seven. Lecturing in psychology. Senior position.'

'Where?'

'Birmingham.'

Phil stared at her. 'Birmingham? But—'

'Yeah, I know. I said I'd never go back after the childhood I had there. But everything's changed. I've changed. And none of my family are left there now. Thank God.'

'But Birmingham ...'

'It's like a new city now. Hardly anything left of the old one. A good place to make a fresh start.'

Phil paused before speaking. 'With me?'

She reached across the table, took his hand in hers. 'Of course. I wouldn't want to go without you. Or Josephina. We're a family. A team.' She smiled. 'So what d'you say?'

'This would be permanent?'

'A year. At least. Probationary period. Just so they can be sure that, you know, my name doesn't attract the wrong kind of student.'

'What about me?'

'Get a transfer. A secondment.'

Phil stared at her. 'And end up in Ops or Traffic or plain clothes or something? Or stuck in the office, desk-jockeying.

15

I'd want to go into Major Crimes. Front-line work. It's what I'm good at. What I know. What I am.'

'Well, with your arrest rate and commendations it shouldn't be too difficult. Think about it.'

He did.

And surprisingly, it wasn't.

3

'Birmingham.' Standing on the doorstep in the cold night air, saying it aloud, still didn't make it any more real. 'Birmingham.'

'Ready when you are, DI Brennan. Boss.'

Phil turned at Sperring's voice. The DS had caught him talking to himself and was staring at him, thoughts of a less than complimentary nature behind his eyes.

Phil felt himself reddening. 'Just reminding myself where I am, DS Sperring.' Once he'd spoken, he felt angry with himself. Despite his age, Sperring was a junior officer. Phil didn't need to explain his actions to him.

'Whatever works for you, sir.' Sperring, face passive but clearly unimpressed, turned and went back into the house.

Phil turned to follow and stopped. He became aware of his breathing, listened to his body for pain, tightness. He had always suffered from panic attacks, even before the explosion. A lot of police at his level did – more than would let on, he had discovered. It went with the job. When they hit they were excruciating and debilitating. And back on front-line duties, in charge of what looked to be a major homicide, heading up a team that didn't know him and, if Sperring was anything to go by, didn't trust him, this would be the perfect time to get one.

He hesitated, breathed deeply, told himself everything was OK. His occupational therapy had been good and his psychological tests had been solid and consistent. He had been given a clean bill of health. He was fine, fit. Ready to go. His physical scars would heal. His stomach lurched.

It was the mental ones he worried about. How much had the explosion, the coma really taken out of him? What was still buried inside? What had he forcibly contained within himself in order to return to work?

There was only one way to find out.

Checking his chest for those familiar tightening bands and finding none, he looked at his hands. They weren't trembling too much.

I'm ready, he told himself.

Ready to push everything else to the side: the pain, the uncertainty of the previous few months, the horror of the months before that. Operations. Convalescence. Doubt. Cruel doubt, building from nagging to consuming to outright fear: that he would ever be whole again, fully functioning as a man, a husband, a father. That he could ever come back to work, ever regain the respect of a team, ever be as good as he had previously been.

Yes, he said. *I'm ready*.

Ready to step into that nightmare world once more. To take control. Listen to the ghosts, honour the dead.

Ready.

He hoped.

He stepped inside.

The hallway seemed even brighter after the dark outside. Squinting, he reached the living room. 'What's the state of play?'

Detective Constable Nadish Khan, standing beside Sperring

in the doorway, turned to him. Short and sharp, with enough cockiness and self-composure to power a small town. He flicked a thumb inside. 'You seen that film *Seven*?' he asked.

'Yes,' said Phil, slightly confused.

'Proper old-school stuff. But good, you know? Brad Pitt. That old black guy who always plays the clever one.'

'Morgan Freeman,' said Phil. He gestured to the corpse. 'What's that got to do with . . . '

'Well, you know how they did it, so you got these proper horrific crime scenes, but you only get glimpses of them, you know; someone's standing in the way, that kind of thing? And it leaves you to put the rest together in your head?'

'Yes . . . '

'And you know how your imagination works, how what's in your head is worse than what's actually there?'

'Yeah . . . '

'I've just seen glimpses. And I hope it's my imagination.'

'That bad.'

Khan nodded. 'Pretty much.'

'Joy,' said Phil.

'Anyway,' continued Khan, 'Jo Howe's just finishing up.'

Phil peeked in. Jo Howe was the leading forensic scene investigator. A short, round, middle-aged woman. She was just straightening up from the body. Phil glimpsed the corpse behind her. Cold, rigid. He saw blonde hair, a pink party dress, like a child's idea of what an adult would wear. Howe moved in his way again and his glimpse was gone.

She shook her head. 'God . . . '

'You ready for us yet?' Phil called.

'Thought I was. Just one second . . . '

Phil looked down the corridor, out into the night, back to the living room. He shivered. The house seemed about as cold as it was outside.

It was an ordinary house in an ordinary boxy housing estate just off the Pershore Road on the fringes of Edgbaston. Built fairly recently, gated, and at odds with the larger, older Edwardian houses it was nestling between, the estate seemed to have won a competition for how many tiny houses could be squeezed into as small a space as possible.

'Who called it in?' Phil asked Khan.

'Community support officer,' the DC replied. 'Neighbour reported that the house had its lights on day and night, and no one ever went in or out.'

'Very civic-minded.'

'Gated community, innit? Thought something must be up.' Khan smiled. 'Neighbour said they'd seen a thing about cannabis farms on the telly. Thought it was one of them. Thank God for public vigilance, yeah?'

Phil nodded. Khan's accent – young, street yet Brummie-inflected – took some getting used to. 'Yeah. In this case, anyway. Who owns the house?'

'Rented,' said Sperring, hearing the conversation and cross-ing to them. 'A letting agency operating just off Hurst Street. City Lets.'

'We know who the tenant is?'

'Glenn McGowan. Moved in a couple of weeks ago. Short-term let. They had no one over Christmas so they let him take it. Said he wouldn't want it for long.'

Phil gave a puzzled frown. 'How d'you know all this?'

Sperring's face was impassive. 'Phoned the agency before I came here and remembered the conversation.' His voice matched his face. 'I'm police. It's what we do.'

Khan, Phil noticed, looked slightly uncomfortable at Sperring's words. Phil weighed up whether to challenge him or not. He decided this wasn't the right time. Concentrate on the investigation.

'Glenn McGowan. What do we know about him? Anybody contacted him yet?'

'Not yet,' said Sperring. 'We're looking into it. He seems to have done a runner.'

Phil looked into the living room. 'Don't blame him.'

Jo Howe gave the all-clear. Phil stepped into the room. 'Come on,' he said. Sperring and Khan followed him.

'I'm Phil Brennan, by the way,' he said to Jo Howe. 'New DI with the Major Investigation Unit. SIO on this case.'

He was sure he heard a disparaging remark from Sperring's direction.

Jo Howe introduced herself. 'What a lovely way to meet.' She was small, cherubic, with a face more suited to smiling than frowning. She wasn't doing much smiling at the moment.

'So,' he said, 'what have we got here?'

She stepped back.

'Look for yourself.'

4

The first thing Phil noticed was the smile. Wide and taut, fixed and immobile. Like the Joker from *Batman*, he thought. Or one of his victims.

The woman's face was overly made-up, with not a square centimetre of natural skin showing through, creating a barrier between decomposition and the outside world. Her eyes were highly coloured and elaborately lined, with huge false eyelashes. Her lips were shining bright red, her face powdered and pale, her cheeks almost as rosy as her lips.

'Well overdone,' said Jo Howe. 'Make-up like that can be seen from space.'

Phil kept gazing at the face, transfixed. 'She looks like a doll . . .'

Once he had thought that, he couldn't get the idea out of his mind. He looked at her body. The make-up was consistent with her clothes. She was dressed like a doll too. Her dress was pink gingham with puffed meringue shoulders, in at the waist then out in a pleated skirt with ruffled white netted underskirts beneath. Her legs were covered in pink nylon, her shoes heeled and pink. Long pink satin gloves covered her forearms.

'Is the pathologist here yet?' asked Phil.

'On her way,' said Khan. 'Shouldn't be long.'

'She'll have her work cut out with this one,' said Sperring.

Phil stood back, still studying the body. She was sitting at a table laid for dinner. One arm was frozen in mid air, finger and thumb pressed together. A teacup lay on its side on the table nearby as if it had been dropped or fallen. He clocked the table.

Two place settings. And properly done: matching crockery, correct cutlery. Knives and forks for the first course on the outside, working inwards; plates and bowls in the right order, wine and water glasses at the side of the settings.

'Check . . . ' Phil heard his own voice. It sounded like it was coming from the wrong end of a telescope. 'Check those glasses for DNA.'

He looked again at the body. The pink gingham and the white underskirt were splattered and stained a dark blackish red around the hem. He reached out a latexed hand, lifted the skirts. The pink stockings underneath were similarly coloured. He lifted them further.

'Jesus Christ . . . '

She wore no underwear. And where there should have been genitals there was just a gaping hole.

Sperring and Khan knelt down beside him, looked also.

'Aw, fuck . . . ' Khan turned away, stood up.

Sperring kept looking. Phil watched his new DS. He was focused on what was in front of him, eyes hooded, expression once again impassive. Trying to be detached, Phil thought. Reacting and responding like a professional. Phil couldn't fault him on that, at least.

'What d'you see?' he asked, kneeling next to the DS.

'No blood,' Sperring said. 'Or very little. Cleaned away. Or drained.' He peered in closer. 'Minced flesh. God. But neatly cut. Well, considering what's been done to her.'

Phil let the skirts drop, straightened up. Sperring did likewise.

'Hold on,' said Khan.

The other two turned. Behind them, the junior officer was swaying, eyes flickering. His face had turned bone white, as if he was suffering from a sudden deficiency of melanin.

'Not in here,' said Phil. 'Locard's exchange principle.'

Khan nodded, straightened himself up. Phil knew he wouldn't want to faint at a crime scene, where he could contaminate or destroy evidence.

'I'm just . . . ' Khan turned, left the room.

A look of amusement crossed Sperring's face, then it returned to its usual unreadable expression.

Phil waited until Khan had gone, then looked round the room and back at the body, trying to take it in as well as its surroundings. He glanced at his hands. They were shaking. Not wanting to go the way Khan had, especially not in front of Sperring, he turned away, gulping in air quickly, forcing his body to steady itself. This was his first test since coming back. He had told his superiors he was ready, that he could cope. Now he had to prove it.

He sucked down more air, focused his mind once more. Turned back to study the body, the layout. He looked down again.

'Legs have been tied to the chair.' He glanced at Sperring. 'What does that tell us?'

'Staged? Left like this for a reason? From the lack of blood, the cutting wasn't done here.'

'Right,' said Phil. 'And that hand? The thumb and finger together? Must have been holding that teacup.'

'Rigor?' said Sperring. 'Never seen it like that before.'

'Me neither. Jo, get your team to check through the rest of the house. Look for blood, a murder scene. I don't think he carried her too far; it should be in here.'

She nodded, did so.

Phil went back to looking at the body, trying to put himself in the victim's place. Unconsciously, his hands began to move. He found himself miming her actions, imagining what he would do if he had been in that situation. He put his hands up to his neck.

If someone was cutting me, I'd have fought. Tried to pull away. But I didn't, so . . .

'She was placed here, yes.' Phil spoke aloud. 'One arm is down, the other . . . ' He looked at the fallen cup, the rigid arm. 'Here. Staged. And she's smiling . . . ' He moved round to the other side of the table, bent down to get into her eye-line. 'Smiling towards here . . . '

'Whoever did it must have sat there,' said Sperring. 'The other side of the table.'

'Romantic little dinner party. Lovely.'

'Didn't go quite according to plan.'

Phil stood up, looked round the room once more, back to the dining table. Chair covers with tie-backs, table runner, matching crockery. All the same colour, all pink. He moved in close, examined the crockery. It looked new. There was something on both sets of plates. Red and brown lumps; congealed blood as sauce.

'We'd better get that analysed,' he said. 'I wouldn't want to even speculate on what it is.'

He turned once more, looked round the rest of the room. The living room was open-plan, all one big space, the kitchen off to the side. The walls were a light shade of pink, the carpet darker. The furniture was covered in throws of differing shades of pink with both matching and complementing cushions. There were even a few pink stuffed animals dotted around the place. It all looked new, fresh. Clean.

He crossed to the wall the sofa backed on to. Leaned in close, smelled the wall. Turned back to Sperring.

'How long did you say this house had been rented out for?'

'Couple of weeks, something like that. Short-term let, they said.'

Phil nodded. 'This wall's just been painted. Very recently.' He knelt down. 'The carpet's new too. Still shedding the pile.'

He moved slowly through the living area, careful to walk lightly, not to disturb any potential evidence. The sofa had been sat on; the throw and cushions reflected that. He looked closer. More than just sat on: lain on.

He straightened up. Looked back at the dining area. Tried to piece together what had happened. Back at the living room. A TV sat in one corner, DVD player underneath. A few DVDs were piled neatly at the side. He checked the spines.

A couple of Hollywood blockbusters, a bit of Formula One and some unmarked ones that looked home-made.

'Let's get those checked out,' he said.

Something else in the room jarred. He realised what it was. No Christmas decorations. No tree, not even a small plastic one. But there were cards on the mantelpiece. He opened them, began reading.

Happy Christmas, Glenn, love Ted, Elizabeth and kids.

Merry Xmas, Glenn, love Aunty Vi. Followed by a selection of kisses.

He checked over some others, found the same kind of greeting to the same sole person. Glenn. No woman's name.

He found a large one, picked that up. *To Glenn*, it said in blue felt tip followed by a printed greeting and a jumble of mismatching signatures. A works card. He checked the company name: Allard Tec Ltd, Coventry. Made a mental note, replaced it.

At the far end of the room, by the window, something

caught his eye. He crossed to it, knelt down. A doll's house. He turned back to Sperring, back to the doll's house. No FSIs around. He touched it carefully, opening the front.

It was fully decorated. He glanced round once more. The toy living room was a miniature facsimile of the real one.

'Is that a doll's house?' asked Sperring, coming to join him.

'It is,' said Phil, eyes still searching it. 'But it's empty.'

'No doll,' said Sperring.

Phil looked at the body sitting at the table.

'Apart from the one over there,' he said.

5

The doll was in his pocket. He kept putting his hand in, touching it as he walked, unable to help himself. Stroking her hair, smoothing down her tiny pink gingham dress. Running his thumb gently along her smiling face, over her nose and eyes, the plastic indentations caressing his skin, making it tingle.

She had looked so lonely sitting on the shelf, in her pink dress and little pink shoes, her smile red, wide and blank, that he couldn't leave here there. And he couldn't stay in either, he had to go out. So she had to go with him.

Now he walked down Hurst Street in the city centre, the muted techno thud pounding from the bars and clubs matching his footfall, matching his heartbeat. Plugged into the city, alive with it.

His hand in his pocket all the time, stroking.

He had always done that. Even when he was a boy. If there had been something he found exciting, that obsessed him, he would take it with him wherever he went. Carry it round no matter what he was doing. Especially books. He could remember going clubbing with a copy of Thomas Harris's *Silence of the Lambs* in his pocket, taking it out and reading a chapter in the strobe-lit darkness if there was no action happening before him, being transported to a world of serial killers and then looking up, disappointed to find that, no matter who was looking at him, giving him the glad eye, reality was mundane alongside it. Before that it had been Robert Bloch's *Psycho*. Sometimes he didn't read it; just took it out to stare at the lurid cover painting depicting a blood-dripping blade reflecting a pair of mad killer's eyes. He could stare into those eyes for hours. And had done. Many times.

And now he had the doll. And he couldn't stop touching her.

He stopped and looked round. Breathing in the smells of stale beer and cheap fried food on the cold night air, feeling the thump and hum of the music penetrate him down to his bones. He was humming with electricity, like an overhead cable. If someone touched him, sparks would fly from his fingertips. If he held someone, pressed his fingers against them, he could burn them. He could incinerate. That was how powerful he felt. He carried life and death within him.

There had been questions afterwards: *What was it like? What did it* feel *like? Was it as good as you thought it would be?* And he had answered honestly: *No*. Shock and surprise had greeted the word. He had continued. *It was better*.

He stood still. People moved all round him, flowed like a human river. He ignored them. His hand on the doll in his pocket, reliving the experience.

Everything about it had been exquisite. From the time he turned up on her doorstep to leaving with her doll, the whole thing had been perfect. Gentle and loving. Just like they had both agreed. Her smile as she greeted him. Then the foreplay. Then deep, intense loving. Exploring her body. Playing. There was a moment when he thought she would back out, crumble. Not have the courage to go through with what she had agreed to. What she had said she wanted to do. That had angered him. He was ready just to take the blade and slash. See what she made of that. Or rather, what it made of her. But he hadn't. He had been controlled. He had explained, put her at her ease. And it had all been fine after that.

He had gone to work with the drugs, just as they had agreed. Then the blades. Cutting slowly, expertly. Clinical and precise, like the internet tutorials had shown him, but also tenderly, lovingly. Then the meal. He could still taste it, still summon up the aromas, the flavours. He felt he always would. It was the best thing he had ever eaten.

She had been too weak to eat hers. Despite his best efforts, she had started to slip away. He had placed her where she wanted to be and waited. And watched. Eventually, with a final kiss and a smile for him, she had gone.

But not before she thanked him. For making her dreams become reality.

Something had happened then. At first he had thought it was an illusion, a fantasy. His mind playing tricks on him. But the more he thought about it, the more he decided it was real. When she had finally slipped away, her soul leaving her body, her mouth had opened and out had flown a beautiful, brightly coloured butterfly. He had seen it. And eventually he worked out what it meant. Her body was just the chrysalis, the husk. The butterfly was her beautiful soul, finally freed. And he had done that for her. He had made that happen.

The exquisiteness of the moment had moved him to tears as he cradled the doll in his arms and cried and cried.

Once he had regained control of himself, it had been a simple matter of honouring her wishes, arranging her how she wanted to be left. He should have left then. That was what they had agreed on. But he couldn't. When he saw her sitting there, the doll in her doll's house, just like they had both wanted, her perfect apotheosis, he couldn't bring himself to leave. He just wanted to stay there with her, not let go, cling on to the special time they had spent together, relive every moment.

So he had done. Revisiting the places they had been, reliving the experiences they had shared, eating once more from her plate. And then, when the memories were used up and there was nothing left but the doll before him, he had settled down and slept.

When he woke, it was light and he was still lying on the living room floor. At first he didn't know where he was or even *who* he was, but his memory soon returned. Though he didn't know how long he had been there or what day it was. His first impulse had been to run, but he had stopped himself. That would have been a stupid thing to do. He would wait until dark, then leave as quietly as possible. He looked at the doll. Until then . . .

When he had left, he had taken the plastic doll with him. He wished he could take the whole doll's house, put her in her proper place, where she belonged, but it would have attracted too much attention. The neighbours might have thought he was a burglar and called the police. And that was the last thing he wanted.

Once he had left, there hadn't been a single second he didn't wish he was back there, reliving the whole experience. He had wanted to climb on to the roof of the tallest building in the city and scream about what he had done, over and over and over. But he hadn't. Just contented himself with his memories.

For now.

'Arcadian.' He blinked and found himself back on Hurst Street once more. The voice that had spoken had been his.

That had been happening more often: zoning out, getting lost in his thoughts and memories, not knowing where he was when he returned. It didn't worry him. He had just lived

31

through the most extreme, most beautiful experience of his life. Only natural he would want to relive it.

He recognised where he was now. Outside the Arcadian. An apologetically eighties collection of bars, restaurants and clubs, though he knew the real meaning of the word. Of course he did, he wasn't thick. Arcadian. A resident of Arcadia, the most perfect paradise ever. He smiled. Thought of his doll. She was his Arcadia. He was the Arcadian.

He became aware of men all around him. All shapes, all sizes. All looking for the same thing. Some stopped, their eyes roving up and down his body, smiling, nodding, gesturing. He didn't return any of their looks. He had thought coming here would be a good idea. Meet someone, go off with them, feel the friction and burn of their body against his. But the doll in his pocket just reminded him of what he had done. Who he had become. He had the power of life and death. Electricity, not blood, coursed through his body. Compared to those around him, he was a god.

But he had to go somewhere. He didn't want to go home alone, so he walked, stopped at a pub. The Village Inn was festooned with rainbow banners, a poster on the side advertising it as the city's number one cabaret venue. There was a long line of airbrushed images beneath, the faces wigged and made-up but none managing to hide the essential masculinity beneath.

None were nearly as beautiful as his doll had been.

Not Arcadian, but they would have to do. It would be like going back to eating kebabs after dining on filet mignon, but he knew that their friction and burn, their pounding, their need to stave off loneliness would be better than nothing. For now.

Caressing the doll once more, he opened the door and went inside.

Singing the body electric.

6

'**D**earie dearie me.'

The pathologist had arrived. She stood at the doorway, suiting up. Tall, slim, long hair pulled back into a ponytail. How apt, thought Phil. By her accent and bearing she seemed more at home on a horse than with a corpse.

She smiled at him. 'Esme Russell. You must be the new boy.' She sounded like she had never mispronounced a word in her life.

Phil introduced himself.

'Welcome aboard.' She crossed to the body. 'Now, what have we here . . . '

'No one's touched her,' said Sperring. 'Been waiting for you, Esme.'

'And so you should, Ian, so you should. Right.' She stood over the body. 'Dearie me. Something she ate disagreed with her?'

'You tell us,' said Sperring.

Crime scenes were always horrific. And those that attended them often hid their revulsion with sardonic gallows humour. The alternative being to break down in tears or throw up. It was something Phil had never subscribed to. Laughing, for whatever reason, disturbed the scene, blocked the signals, the instructions that the ghosts were sending, made them angry. And he didn't want that. He carried enough angry ghosts around with him already.

'You boys can run off and busy yourself with whatever it is you boys do.'

Phil shared a look with Sperring, who moved towards the hall. 'Let's have a look upstairs,' he said. 'We'll leave you alone, Esme.'

'Hardly that.' She turned to the body, already engrossed.

They left the room and started up the stairs. They reached the landing, both treading warily in case they disturbed any potential evidence, hands not touching walls or banister, feet making as little tread as possible. Phil looked out the window. Uniforms were going door to door, talking to neighbours, trying to build up a picture of the mysterious Glenn McGowan. TV vans and journalists were waiting ready to pounce behind the barrier. Phil had to shield his eyes from the glare of the arc lights.

'Day fourteen in the Big Brother house,' he said with a terrible Geordie accent.

Sperring didn't reply.

The redecoration downstairs hadn't extended upstairs. It was slightly shabby. Clean but not cared for. A typical rental property.

Something on the landing caught Phil's eye. He knelt down. Studied the carpet. Took his iPhone out, switched on the flashlight.

'Ian, what d'you think that is?'

Sperring knelt down alongside him. Looked where Phil indicated. The carpet was a nondescript brown, tough and hard-wearing, but dotted about were areas of darker discoloration. The DS unfastened his paper suit, reached into his pocket, took out a pair of reading glasses. Peered at the marks once more.

'Blood, I reckon,' he said.

'Me too,' said Phil. 'Let's get Jo and her team to take a look. Do a luminol test.'

He straightened up, looked round the landing, deciding which room to try first. It was hived off into three bedrooms, each one smaller than the last, and a bathroom.

'I'll start here,' he said, entering the smallest bedroom.

Sperring moved off to one of the others.

The room held a laptop, desk and chair. Some empty shelves on the wall. A racing car calendar had been pinned up. Phil checked the dates. The last entry was 10 December, the previous Friday night. It had a big star scribbled on it. There was nothing planned beyond that.

He left the room, moving into the main bedroom. It had a bed, two side tables and a wardrobe. All in variations of brown and beige. He opened the wardrobe. A couple of suits, some jeans. A few plaid shirts. T-shirts, socks, underwear. An empty canvas holdall on top of the wardrobe. Nothing remarkable. He left the room for the bathroom.

It was small, feeling crowded even with just Phil in there. He looked round. The showerhead was lying in the bath, curled like a long metal snake. There was something around the rim of the tub.

He knelt down, examining it closely. Dried blood. Watered down but not totally washed away. He checked the shower curtain. The same. It had been streaked a pinkish-brown colour in parts. The wall behind the bath too.

Phil felt that familiar tingle. This was the crime scene. He was sure of it.

He stood up again, scrutinised. The bathroom looked clean apart from that. Trying to leave as little trace as possible, he carefully opened the mirrored cabinet on the wall. It was divided in half. On one side was shaving equipment, aftershave. Men's moisturiser. Toothbrush and mouthwash. On the other side were more feminine things. Make-up. Removing pads. False eyelashes. Depilatory cream. Phil noticed the halves weren't equal. The female side was fuller, overpowering the male side.

Glenn McGowan hadn't lived here alone, he thought.

He closed the cabinet door but didn't move. He'd missed something. He turned, open the door again. Saw it.

Two people, but only one toothbrush.

Maybe she just visits, he thought. Leaves her stuff here. He looked again. Awful lot of stuff . . .

He closed the cabinet door, left the bathroom.

'Think I've found the crime scene,' he said to Sperring. 'Bathroom.'

Sperring nodded. 'Come and look at this, sir.'

Must be important, thought Phil. The older man had forgotten to be sarcastic.

Sperring was in the middle-sized bedroom. Phil entered. It couldn't have been more different from the main one. It was a miniature version of the living room. All pinks and frills. Curtains and matching duvet and pillowcases. Pink walls, pink carpet. Sperring was standing by the wardrobe. Phil joined him, eyes widening. It was full of women's clothes. Dresses, skirts, blouses. Mostly pink and frilly like the dead woman downstairs. But in amongst them were others. Fetish wear. PVC. Rubber. Uniforms. He pulled out the drawers. Lingerie ranging from filmy and wispy to industrial and constraining. Another drawer yielded restraints, bondage material. The bottom drawer held sex toys. Phil took one out, held it. It was a huge black plastic phallus, about the thickness of his forearm.

'Sex toy,' said Sperring, clearing his throat.

'Doesn't look like there's much fun involved,' said Phil. He replaced it, closed the drawer. Turned to Sperring. 'Well.'

36

'Well indeed, sir.'

Esme called them. They made their way downstairs.

'Looks like we've got a deviant sex killer on our hands,' Phil said to her. 'We'd better find Glenn McGowan as soon as possible.'

'That's why I called you,' said Esme. 'I think I have.'

'Where?' asked Sperring.

Esme pointed to the body, held up a blonde wig.

'There,' she said.

7

'Dear Christ . . . ' Phil discovered his voice.

'Indeed,' said Esme Russell.

Phil looked from the pathologist to the dining table tableau to the blonde wig and back again. 'But what is . . . ' Questions formed and fizzed in his brain quicker than he could articulate them.

'If it's answers you're looking for,' said Esme, 'then I'll have to disappoint you. Lot of work to do on this one.'

'Glenn McGowan . . . ' Phil took in the scene once more. 'Transvestite. Murdered while . . . eating? Or before?'

'Hard to tell. Of course, it may not be him. He may have done the murdering and run.'

'Possible,' said Phil. He thought of the bathroom upstairs. Two identities, one toothbrush. 'My gut instinct says this is Glenn McGowan. But I'll keep an open mind.' He looked again at the artfully arranged body.

'We've got our work cut out for this one,' said Esme.

'Yeah . . . Time of death? Any idea?'

'He's been here a few days. The house is cold. Whoever did this turned the heating off before they left. Knew the body would keep longer.'

Phil breathed deeply. 'How long before you can do the post-mortem?'

Esme shrugged. 'Week before Christmas? Don't know what it's like in your neck of the woods, but it's our busy time. The lonely and the skint top themselves, hypothermic pensioners freeze to death, binge-drinking teenagers think they're super-heroes ... they all come out of the woodwork.'

'Cameron's Britain,' said Phil.

No one answered him. Everyone looked away.

'Right ... ' He felt uncomfortable, reminded once again that he didn't belong here. 'So ... time scale?'

'As quick as I can. But ... ' Esme gestured to the body, 'there's a veritable smorgasbord to be going on with, so don't expect anything soon.'

'Smorgasbord. Right.'

'Including what's on those plates. But get your boss to bump this up in importance and you'll have your answers quicker.'

Esme's eyes twinkled as she turned back to the body. Phil, thinking how all pathologists were the same, made his way out of the house.

The street was cordoned off, the outer barrier keeping prying eyes away. Reporters had gathered beyond that point, telephoto lenses in position, waiting for one of the team to give something up. Beside them, members of the public craned their necks to see what was going on. Unable to believe how their own unremarkable street had become the focus of something so dramatic. Phil had been at the centre of enough crime scenes to know what they would be experiencing. And it would be conflicting: horror at discovering that the place they had regarded as a safe haven was just as terrifying as the places they imagined they were seeking refuge from; relief that it was happening to one of their neighbours and not themselves. And the illicit thrill of vicarious deviancy, as they wished for the crime to be the most depraved, salacious and titillating they could imagine because it made for better gossip. Phil had seen enough to know that the imagination of the general public was something to be very frightened of. Because that was who he cleaned up after every day.

As he was removing the blue paper suit, Sperring came alongside him.

'What now? Sir?'

'Now?' echoed Phil. 'We plan what we're going to do next.' He shivered, flapped his arms about him, but it was no good. He could feel the cold penetrating through his clothes, right down to his bones. 'But not here,' he said. 'Too bloody cold.'

'I know somewhere,' said Sperring.

He walked towards the barrier. The crowd parted for him. Phil bobbed along in his wake.

8

Just over five minutes later, Phil was sitting in the lounge of the Edgbaston Tap, an old, low, sixties red-brick box of a pub on which a contemporary facelift had been attempted. Phil didn't care about the decor. He was just pleased to be somewhere warm.

On entering, Sperring had taken charge. He had flashed his warrant card to the landlord, asking for privacy and for any journalists to be kept away. A couple of uniforms were standing by the door to do just that. Phil, again, hadn't challenged him.

He sat down with Sperring and a very pale-looking Khan. His new team. He felt their eyes on him. Still sizing him up, still – in Sperring's case, at least – finding him lacking. He had to win them over. He had to inspire. He had to lead.

'OK,' he said, huddling with them round the table, 'let's gather, let's pool. I like my team to put together their first impressions while they're still fresh in our minds. It's the way I've always worked. I've found it helpful.'

Phil noticed that Sperring's eyebrows had risen at the mention of the words *my team*. Khan looked between the pair of them, seemingly wanting to go along with Phil but glancing at Sperring as if waiting for the older man to give him the go-ahead.

Sperring gave an almost imperceptible nod. Phil noticed. 'DC Khan,' he said. 'You first.'

Khan took out his notebook. 'House-to-house hasn't given us much yet. Most people didn't even know there was someone living there. They saw someone moving stuff in, carpets and that, but thought it was being rented again.'

'He must have decorated,' said Phil. 'Thought everything looked new.'

'Apparently it was rented to students before that, but the neighbours complained about the noise. Gated community an' all that, so the letting agency said they'd only rent to professional people in future.'

'And Glenn McGowan was a professional man?'

'City Lets had references for him from his employer,' said Sperring.

Phil remembered the Christmas card. 'Allard Tec?'

Sperring checked his notes, nodded.

'We'll talk to them. Coventry, according to the Christmas card. We'll also need to look into his background, friends, colleagues. And we'd better do a check with prisons and hostels, see if any known deviants have recently moved into the area.'

'Apart from McGowan, you mean?' Khan laughed. Sperring's mouth lifted, eyes twinkled.

'Very funny. We still have to make sure it's him. And there were other Christmas cards in the house,' said Phil. 'We need to find out who they were from. How well they knew him, what their relationship was. He must have given an address when he rented the house; the letting agents should have that. We've got to find out everything about him, get some lever into his background. Also those DVDs by the TV.'

Khan gave a snort. 'Not the only TV in there, was it?'

'Hilarious,' said Phil, his face demonstrating that it wasn't.

'The DVDs. The home-made-looking ones. They had no labels, no names. Also the laptop in the box room. See what that can tell us. He's a man of mystery.'

'We'll set up a mobile incident room in the street, keep the door-to-door going,' said Sperring. 'Someone might come forward. I'll get the techies to check on local CCTV as well. Car number plates, see if anything's been recognised.'

'Elli's got some new computer software thing she wants to try,' said Khan. 'Some Venn diagram thing.'

'Elli's the team's resident geek,' said Sperring, his tone of voice showing his opinion.

'Every team's got one,' said Phil. 'Let's see if we can identify some kind of pattern to his life, where he went, what he did, who he knew.'

'If he liked dressing up,' said Khan, 'he'll be down Hurst Street.'

'What's there?' asked Phil.

'Gay quarter,' said Sperring, voice neutral. 'Bars and clubs. Every city has one.' Stressing the word *city*, reminding Phil he only came from a town.

Khan giggled. 'Bender Central. Shirtlifters' paradise.'

Sperring's lips curled in amusement. Phil's didn't.

'If that's the case, we might need someone to go round those bars, see if our victim was known there. I don't condone homophobia on my team, DC Khan, so I wouldn't laugh if I were you, because going down there might be your job.'

Khan stopped laughing. Sperring's face was unreadable.

'There's something else,' said Phil. 'Something we haven't mentioned.'

'What?' said Khan, his voice betraying a sulky edge.

'The doll's house,' said Phil.

'So what?' said Khan, masking his anger at Phil's earlier words. 'It's a doll's house. The bloke liked to dress up as a girl.

Probably liked playing with girls' toys as well. Bet he's got a bedroom full of Barbies.'

'He's got toys up there,' said Sperring, smiling unpleasantly, 'but they're a bit more grown up than Barbies. Bit bigger, too.'

Khan laughed. 'Saw that. Take it down Hurst Street with me. Might open a few mouths.'

'Open more than a few mouths,' said Sperring.

He and Khan laughed, heads back, cackling. The laughter died away. Sperring looked at Phil, who hadn't joined in. His eyes were hard, challenging. Khan's eyes jumped away, wouldn't meet Phil's.

Phil held Sperring's gaze, unblinking. He knew he shouldn't, knew he should rise above what his junior officer was doing, but he couldn't help it. He had to put him in his place.

'Do you have a problem with me being in charge, DS Sperring?'

Sperring kept his face impassive. 'Me, sir? No, sir.'

'Good. Because we have to work together here. This case is the very definition of what the Major Investigation Unit should be dealing with, so we're going to be in the goldfish bowl. We have to get a result. And the only way we're going to do that is if we pull together and respect the chain of command. Are we all agreed on that?'

'Absolutely, sir.'

'Good,' said Phil. 'As long as we're all clear.'

The other two nodded. Phil looked round the room, breathing hard. While his head was angled away from them, he felt Khan smile. He was sure Sperring had winked at him.

'The doll's house,' said Phil, turning back. 'Did you look inside?'

Khan shook his head. Sperring nodded.

'A perfect copy of the living room of the house. But no doll.'

Sperring shrugged. 'So?'

'So that's a massive clue. That's telling us something.'

'What?' asked Khan.

'I don't know,' said Phil. 'That's what we have to find out. It's not random, not accidental. It was there for a reason. We have to find that reason.'

'There was no doll,' Sperring repeated.

'No,' said Phil. 'Either . . . I don't know, maybe the victim thought one wasn't needed, he was going to take the place of it himself.'

'Maybe the killer took it with him,' said Khan.

'Very good,' said Phil. 'Maybe he did.'

Sperring leaned forward, eyes lit by amusement. 'Maybe we should bring in a psychologist, sir. Know any good ones?'

He's read my file, thought Phil. *He knows about my wife, what she does*. He felt angry at that.

'I do, yes,' he said. 'I know an excellent one. And if we need her, we'll call her. We could also do with a couple more officers, too.'

Sperring's face was once again impassive. 'Belt-tightening, sir. We all have to do more with less, as our masters tell us.'

'And you know that's bullshit,' said Phil. 'We'll just end up doing less with less. But in the meantime, we've all got jobs to do. So let's go and do them.'

They rose from the table, Sperring and Khan leaving first.

Phil breathed deeply. Wished he had his old team alongside him.

And his wife.

9

'**O**K?'

Marina Esposito turned, barely able to make out the other person's voice over the din in the restaurant. It seemed to be one large Christmas party, the diners mostly drunk or on the way, the waiting staff stretching their smiles. Joy Henry was sitting on Marina's left, glass of wine halfway to her lips, a smile of concern on her slightly flushed face.

'Yeah,' said Marina, looking at her own glass of wine in front of her, wondering whether it was half full or half empty. 'Fine.'

'They're a good bunch, aren't they?' said Joy, continuing before Marina could answer. 'Friendly.' She leaned in closer, the wine taking her balance away slightly. 'Not stuck up like some of them lecturers can get. Especially psychologists.' She took another mouthful of wine. 'Not you, obviously.'

Marina didn't take offence, just sipped her own wine. San Marco was an upscale Italian restaurant in Birmingham's city centre. Mostly popular with – if the photos on the walls were any indication – footballers and their WAGs plus visiting actors, it was tonight playing host to the Birmingham University psychology department's Christmas party.

Noise levels were rising as people graduated from cocktails to first, or even second, glasses of wine. School was out for everyone in the restaurant, and the coming of Christmas just heightened the feeling of escape as the alcohol reddened faces and dissolved inhibitions.

The end of Marina's first term working in Birmingham. She had enjoyed it more than she thought she would. The city was still familiar enough for her to know her way around but different enough to give her the frisson of being somewhere new. Ghosts had been laid. Time had healed. For the most part.

Occasionally she would find herself walking along a street, admiring the new buildings, getting lost in the architecture, then turn a corner and be punched by a memory from her past that had been waiting to ambush her. The feeling would soon go but leave ripples, echoes within her. Reminders that she would never fully be rid of her past.

But the work had engrossed her. She hadn't realised how much she had missed it. Teaching, meeting students, chatting with fellow academics. And all in a safe, controlled environment. Part of her missed the thrill of police work, but doing this her life wasn't in danger, she didn't work every day and she got home at night to see her husband and daughter. She found it a trade-off worth making.

And she enjoyed the company of her colleagues, had even made friends with one or two. Joy, the departmental administrator, had steered her well. Given her the lowdown on who to talk to and who to avoid. Marina had thought at first that she would feel, to borrow a phrase Phil often used, like Jimi Hendrix in the Beatles, but they all seemed fine.

As if on cue, her phone trilled. A text. She checked it:

Out on a murder case. Could be a late one. Josephina's still with Eileen. Don't wait up. Hope you have a good night. Love You. Pxxx

She texted back:

Love you too. XXX

A murder case. And there it was, that familiar thrill. Get in there, find out what had happened, who had done what and why. She took another sip of wine. *Let it go*, she thought. *Not my concern any more.*

'That your husband?' asked Joy, turning away from a young, handsome PhD student she had been chatting to.

Marina nodded. 'On a case. Be home late.'

Joy's eyes widened. 'Exciting.'

Marina shrugged, trying to play it down. 'Not really. Just work.'

Joy was still looking at her. Marina knew the look, had expected something like this. Everyone in the department knew her background but no one had asked about it. *This must be it*, she thought. *The night the inhibitions come down and I'm expected to fill them all in on what they read in the papers and saw on the news.*

Suddenly she wasn't enjoying herself so much.

At that moment, the empty seat the other side of her was abruptly filled. Marina turned.

'This seat taken? Thought not.'

The man's voice was deep, resonant. Trace of an accent she couldn't immediately place. She took him in. Tall, his hair longer than was fashionable, but he managed to pull it off, sweeping it back and letting it hang down. His chin and cheeks had matching stubble. He was one step short of medallion man, his shirt open at least one button too many, his jacket expensive and designer but creased. Like he was used to the best but didn't have to make an effort with it. As she opened her mouth, he smiled at her. And that was when she noticed how beautiful his eyes were. Deep green, like sparkling wooded pools on a summer's day. Even without Joy's introduction, she knew who he was.

'Don't think we've met,' he said, extending a hand. 'Hugo Gwilym.' His voice was commanding, authoritative. The hint of accent she hadn't been able to identify she now spotted as Welsh. He was used to being listened to, like a politician or a mesmerist.

She found herself taking his hand. 'Marina Esposito.'

'Oh, I know who you are,' he said, shaking her hand lightly. The gesture was a very sensual one. 'I know all about you.' Another smile. His eyes crinkled appealingly at the edges. She saw the shots of grey hair in amongst the black. It gave him a rakish, piratical air.

Marina felt herself reddening. She was aware of Joy's eyes on her. 'Oh,' she said, then mentally chastised herself because she couldn't come up with anything better than that.

Hugo Gwilym. Marina had heard of him but not met him until now. The star of the department, of the university even, a psychologist who had parlayed an academic career into a media one. He had started writing articles for specialist journals, then hopped up to the broadsheets. Courted by publishers, he had brought out a couple of pop cultural psychology books. They in turn opened the door to TV interviews, which he finessed into regular appearances as a talking head on news and cultural programmes. He had even been a guest panellist on *Have I Got News For You*. He was ambitious, controversial and famous. And if the campus rumours were true, enjoying everything that fame brought.

Marina had read his work. She hated it. Disagreed with every point he made. A controversialist, a populist, a cynic.

But, close up, with lovely eyes.

He smiled again, reached for the wine bottle, filled up her empty glass.

She put her hand out to cover it. 'No, I'm—'

'We're here to enjoy ourselves. Don't worry.' He leaned forward. 'Mind, out with this lot you need to drink as much as you can.' He sat back. Looked at her. 'The famous Marina Esposito. Been looking forward to meeting you.'

'Famous?' She felt herself reddening again. 'I'm not the one with the media career.'

'True.' He took a mouthful of wine, closing his eyes as he swallowed, making even that gesture seem sensual. The wine gone, he opened his eyes once more, fixed them on Marina. 'But you've got the experiences. First hand. You've *lived* what I just write.'

'Believe me,' she said, taking a drink without realising, 'I would have been happier to have just written about it.'

He waved his hand, dismissively. 'Whatever doesn't kill you makes you stronger, and all those old clichés.'

'I don't believe that,' she said.

'No?'

'No. Whatever doesn't kill you might not make you stronger. It might harden you. But it's more likely to weaken you. And probably kill you eventually. Slowly.'

He gave her another crinkly-eyed smile. 'I'm glad I made the effort to turn up now. I like a woman with spirit.'

Oh fuck off, she thought, and turned away from him. She felt a restraining hand on her forearm. She turned back.

'Everyone has the right to die. Everyone has the right to choose their own death, to determine it, don't you agree?'

'That's the shittest chat-up line I've ever heard.'

He put back his head and laughed. Then looked at her, green eyes alive. 'My new book. I'm researching it at the moment. Voluntary euthanasia. I believe it's morally wrong to punish those who want to die. And those who assist them shouldn't be found guilty of murder. I'm sure you agree.'

'Are you?'

He leaned in closer. 'My research has thrown up some fascinating stuff. Really fascinating. Stuff you wouldn't believe. I didn't.' His eyes locked with hers. 'I'd really like your opinion on it. *Really*.'

Marina was dark-haired and olive-skinned, her Italian roots showing in her features. She dressed well and, in her late thirties, had a good figure. She had seen off more than her fair share of unwelcome attention over the years, and was about to do the same to Hugo Gwilym. But something in the intensity of his words, his gaze, made her stop.

'Why me?'

He frowned as if the answer was obvious. 'Because you've been there. You've *seen* it. You've stared into the abyss.'

'Oh please.' Marina had had enough of him. She made to move away once more. Again she felt a restraining hand on her arm.

'You're the only reason I came here tonight. I want to spend some time with you. Get to know you. I think we could . . . hit it off.' He kept his hand where it was, made no effort to move it.

'I've read your work,' Marina said, staring at his hand like it was a spider.

Hugo Gwilym smiled, gave a mock bow of his head. 'I'm flattered. Thank you.'

'I didn't agree with a single word of it.'

He froze. For a second or two something dark passed behind his eyes. Quickly – but Marina caught it. He soon replaced it with his smile. 'We really are going to get on, you and I. I can tell.'

His hand fell from her arm. Slowly, trailing as it went.

Marina stared at him. 'I'm married, you know.'

'Absolutely,' he said, taking a mouthful of wine.

'Talk to my husband. He's done more abyss-staring than I have.'

'Perhaps. Eventually.' He put his glass down, stared at her. 'But it's you I'm interested in. You I want to talk to.'

Clearly, she thought. *I should go. Talk to someone else, even.* But she stayed where she was.

Hugo Gwilym refilled her wine glass. Marina allowed him to. He raised his, toasted her, staring at her all the while like a hypnotist. She returned the toast.

'Now the night has become interesting,' he said.

10

Keith knew. As soon as he saw the house on the news, he knew. Even with the white tent in front of it, the blue sheet at the side, the glimpses of police going in and out, it was unmistakable.

It was the death house.

He sighed, causing pain to stab at his chest. He closed his eyes, rode it out. Waited until it had subsided, then returned to watching the TV. The reporter was standing in front of the house, heavily made up and bundled up against the cold. Fighting the urge to be somewhere warm in order to deliver a story that she hoped could make her nationally famous.

'Details are still emerging at this point,' she was saying in reply to a studio-bound anchor, the wind taking away her breath, 'but it's understood that the house had been rented over the Christmas holidays to a single man. It's still not been disclosed whether the body found inside is him or not.'

That was all he needed to see, to hear. It set his pulse racing, pushing the blood round his body quicker. Hastening his death by a few seconds.

Seeing this on the news, with police and reporters, made it all real. Brought it home to him. What he had done, what he was going to do, what he had *agreed* to do. And of course, what was going to be done to him. No. It wasn't a game any more, an abstract idea. It was real. Deadly and real.

Kelly chose that moment to enter the living room. He looked away from the TV, caught her by the doorway. The lurch in his stomach had nothing to do with his illness. She was beautiful, no doubting that. Beautiful but hard. Like a marble Rodin sculpture. She saw him watching, ditched the hardness from her features, expelled the hatred and distaste, turning on her sympathetic face before reaching him.

Good girl, he thought. *What I'm paying you for.*

Or what you think I'm paying you for.

'What you watching?' Her voice was as annoying as ever. With its doomed attempts at refinement, at forcing her West Midlands accent into shapes it wasn't naturally meant to be in, it sounded like she was mouthing elocution exercises while gargling coal.

'The news,' he said, the words tiring him, his breath wheezing out.

'Shouldn't watch that,' Kelly said, taking the remote from his lap and walking away, knowing he wouldn't be able to follow, and even if he did would be too weak to fight her for it. 'Gets you all excited. And you don't want that. Remember what the doctor said.' Her voice sing-song and patronising.

Keith nodded. 'Yeah.' *Bet* you *remember what the doctor said.* No sudden shocks. No excitement. With what his body had been through, it could be fatal. Surprised she hadn't given him more shocks. That was what he would have expected.

But he had a surprise for her. A real big shock. He just wished he could be there to see her face when she got it . . .

Kelly flicked the remote at the TV. The channel changed to a late-night quiz show. Smug comedians making snide remarks about everyone and everything, the audience laughing like it had been pumped full of nitrous oxide.

He hated it. She walked away, leaving it on.

Bitch.

'And put some lights on, Keith ...' Before she left the room, she switched on the overhead chandelier. He winced from the sudden glare. He hated overhead lights, had done since childhood. And she knew that, had done it deliberately. He couldn't bear them to be on in any room he was in. He blamed his parents for that one.

He could remember one night when he was six years old, hearing noise from downstairs, a horrible wailing sound, and getting out of bed to investigate. He found his mother in the living room, the next-door neighbour with his arms wrapped round her, his wife by his side. His mother was screaming, breaking down before his eyes. She had always seemed like such a capable woman. He was terrified seeing her like that.

His mother saw him and grabbed him, clutching him to her. Then she told him.

Your dad's dead. Car crash.

And started wailing again. This time, he joined her.

The one thing he remembered, the one thing that stuck in his mind from that night, all the way into his adult life, was the overhead light. Shining down at full strength like an unforgiving, unrelenting desert sun. And he had hated them ever since.

Now here he was, sitting in his own living room, his chair wheeled in front of the TV, looking down at the tucked-under tracksuit bottoms, empty from the thighs down, where his legs used to be. The overhead light blazed down, reminding him that there was more than one way to die.

'Can you turn the ... the TV back ... I was ... was watching that ...'

No reply. She could hear him. He was sure of it.

She came back into the room. He noticed that she was dressed up. Spike heels, short, clinging dress. Full hair and make-up. Her pulling gear. What she had been wearing when they first met. His heart sighed once more.

'Where ... where you going?'

'Just out,' she said, putting her earring in place. 'Broad Street with the girls. The Basin.'

'It's ... late ...'

'I know, but it's the only time I get to see them. It's just one night. For Christmas.'

He felt anger rise within him. Anger he was too impotent and weak to use. He knew where she was going, who she was meeting. If not the names, then the type. A younger man. A fitter man. A whole man. A man who wasn't about to die.

'So you're leaving me ... alone ...'

A flicker passed over her features. It could have been read as guilt, but he knew better. Fear. Even now she couldn't make him unhappy. *Especially* now.

'I won't be long. I promise. Just a Christmas drink with the girls. Honest.' She waited, breath held, while he made his mind up.

'I can't stop you, can I?' he said eventually.

She smiled out of relief, then crossed to him and gave him the smallest and most careful of kisses on his cheek. Her perfume hit his lungs harder than mustard gas. He began coughing. She straightened up and left, fluttering her fingers, making promises not to be late. The coughing eventually slowed, then stopped altogether. He swallowed back blood. Felt it run down his throat.

He looked down between what remained of his legs. Saw the plastic rectangle in his crotch, mimicking his impotent penis.

56

At least she's left the remote, he thought. *That's something*.

Keith flicked the channel over but the news had rolled on. Men were fighting in the Middle East now. He turned the TV off. Tried to relive what he had just seen.

The house. The body. *This is it*, he thought. It wasn't a game any longer. It was for real. And all because he'd talked to that university professor about his bloody stupid book. Funny how one thing could lead to another. From that to this. He tried to smile, but another bout of pain racked his chest, making him cough up more blood. He didn't swallow it down this time; instead he spat it on to the beige carpet. He looked down at it. Dark against light. Like blood on snow.

He managed to get himself back in control. Closed his eyes. Not long now.

I just wish I could be there to see the bitch's face, he thought. *When it happens*.

11

From the outside, it looked like an old Gothic school-house with its red-brick exterior and leaded casement windows, chimneys and crenellations. Inside had more than a whiff of it too, with dark wood-panelled walls and doors, exposed heavy metal pipework and shiny worn floor tiles the colour of old blood. The rooms would have been big, echoing halls if the twenty-first century hadn't invaded and subdivided with its plasterboard and glass offices, its laminate cubicles and workstations. Computers, phones, internet, TV all installed and working, keeping the old ghosts at bay, helping the new ones find rest.

It was the home of the West Midlands Major Incident Unit.

The building was an annexe of the main central police station on Steelhouse Lane. With its grey stone front and heavy wooden double doors, the station looked to Phil like a 1950s Hollywood version of a medieval castle. Both buildings were a far cry from the late eighties beige brick urban prison architecture of Southway station that he was used to in Colchester.

Inside his office, Phil held a mug of what he had been informed was tea but looked and felt more like the weather outside. Cold and grey. He hadn't taken to Birmingham. Or his new team.

He had finished late the previous night, but not too late – overtime hadn't yet been signed off. They had done what they could, Sperring accompanying Esme Russell and the body to the mortuary for the post-mortem, Khan heading home. Phil had followed suit.

He had been exhausted but unable to rest, tired but wired, the way he always was at the start of a new investigation, potential leads and avenues of investigation fizzing and popping in his head. So he had phoned Eileen, checked Josephina was OK and set about getting a drink, trying to calm himself down. Marina wasn't in. He remembered she was attending the department's Christmas party and wasn't expected back early, so he settled down with his bottle of beer, Wintersleep playing softly in the background. They were living in Moseley village, a suburb of Birmingham between Edgbaston and Balsall Heath that consisted of huge old Edwardian houses, thirties semis and well-established plane trees along the pavements. Many of the large houses had been divided up into flats, attracting students from the nearby universities, as well as lecturers and academics, which gave the centre of the village a relaxed, bohemian air. Marina had described it as a big-city suburban version of Wivenhoe, minus the river, and Phil had laughed but agreed with her.

Marina still wasn't back when, a couple of hours later, he turned off the CD player, dumped his bottles in the recycling bin and went up to bed.

She was settling in to their new surroundings much better than he was. He was sure she was starting to realise that. She would come home from work energised, sharing anecdotes and stories about her day, laughing as she retold them. He kept silent, having nothing to share with her except the discomfort and unease he felt at his own team and the doubts and uncertainties he had about taking charge once more. He didn't want to burden her, spoil the obvious enjoyment she was experiencing at her new job, and consequently could feel himself drawing away from her as he tried not to infect her with his darker moods. It wasn't the healthy thing to do, he knew that, but it was the way he dealt with things. Everything would pick up now he had a major investigation to run. It had to.

It had to.

He took a sip of the tea, grimaced and stepped out of his office into the main workroom of the MIU. The doll's house had been removed from Glenn McGowan's rented house the night before. It had been forensically examined overnight and now stood at the side of the murder wall in the briefing room. It was large, wooden, Georgian in design, old. The front wall hinged open. Inside, the majority of the rooms had been laid out in period design. Judging from the peeling wallpaper and the dust collecting on the miniature furniture, it had been done some time ago. The one exception was the living room. It had been recently decorated to match that of the room in which they had found the body – Glenn McGowan, it had just about been confirmed – the night before. Freshly papered pink walls, new furniture. As near to a small facsimile as could be achieved, even down to the crockery on the table.

The only thing missing was the doll.

Phil heard noise behind him, looked up. His superior officer, Detective Chief Inspector Alison Cotter, put her head round the door.

'There you are, Phil. Morning. Got a minute?' She turned and walked towards her office. Phil put down his mug and followed.

DCI Cotter's office was adjacent to his. Bigger and better

decorated, it also showed signs of permanent occupancy. Family photos, books on the shelves. Personal souvenirs and mementoes. The opposite of Phil's office.

Cotter sat down behind her desk. She was in her mid forties, red-haired, with pale skin that glowed inwardly with the kind of vitality regular competitive exercise gave. The squash tournament trophies on the shelves showed how successful she was.

Phil sat down. The photos on Cotter's desk were angled towards her. Phil knew who they were of. Cotter's wife, a defence barrister, and their son. She was out and proud, and anyone who had a problem with that would, Phil imagined, feel the business end of a squash racquet. He could imagine Sperring's opinion on having a lesbian for a boss.

'So,' said Cotter, leaning back, sipping the same anonymous grey liquid from her mug that Phil had attempted to drink, 'I hear you caught a live one last night.'

'Yeah,' said Phil. 'This could be big.' He didn't have to go into detail. He knew she would have read up on it.

'Any clues? Leads? Anything to go on?'

Phil shook his head. 'Nothing yet. I just put my head round the door to see if there were any updates, but no. Khan's co-ordinating the door-to-door, collating all that. I'll get him to run down any CCTV there might be too. Sperring's following chain of evidence with the body for the post-mortem.'

'And you?'

'I'm going to do a bit of legwork this morning. Pay a visit to the letting agency, see if I can find out something about our deceased's background. Then his place of work. Try to track down any family, friends, see what we can do.'

She gave a professionally rehearsed smile. 'Good. Glad you're on top of it.'

'I am,' he said and stopped.

Cotter leaned forward. 'But?'

'But . . . I could do with more staff. More bodies on the ground. I'm used to working with a bigger team on a major inquiry.'

'So am I,' she said, her features darkening. 'But this is out of my hands, as you know. We're being reformed. Having our waste trimmed. Streamlining efficiency. Becoming leaner and meaner. Doing more with less.'

'And other euphemisms for having our operating budget removed,' said Phil. 'I didn't vote for them.'

'No,' said Cotter, lifting an eyebrow, 'I don't suppose you did.'

'I'm sure this one'll be upgraded,' said Phil. 'The media'll get hold of it. It's too big for them not to.'

Cotter frowned. 'Maybe not. There's no angle. No cute victim. They might leave us alone to do our job.'

'We've got a dead mutilated transvestite. They're not going to let this one lie.'

She sighed. Gave up on her mug, placed it on the desk. 'Leave it with me. Let me see what I can do.'

'Thanks. I appreciate it.'

She nodded. Looked straight at Phil. 'How are you getting on, Phil? Taken to your new surroundings yet?'

He didn't know what to say. He was sure she had seen he wasn't happy, wasn't fitting in. 'You'll have to ask the team,' he said.

She smiled. It didn't reach her eyes. He guessed from that look that she already had asked them. 'We're very pleased to have you here. You come highly recommended. Excellent record. A little unconventional, perhaps, but you get results. And Gary Franks is an old friend of mine. I trust him. If he says you're good, you're good.'

'Let's hope so,' said Phil.

'Yes,' said Cotter. 'Let's.'

Phil sensed the meeting was at an end. He rose, left the room, ready to get to work. 'If you could think about some extra bodies, I'd be very grateful.'

'I'm sure. We need a result on this one. Let's make sure we get it.'

Walking out, he felt less reassured than when he had gone in.

12

Marina had chased her hangover away long enough to get out of bed, make herself a coffee and get back in with the morning papers. Josephina had spent the night with Eileen and she was enjoying the first lie-in she had had for several weeks. She was under the duvet, an old Natalie Merchant album on the bedroom CD player, the mug of hot coffee to her lips, when her mobile rang.

She placed the coffee on the bedside table, picked it up. Her first thought was: Eileen. *Something's happened to Josephina.* But she dismissed it from her mind. She could be forgiven for thinking like that after everything that had happened recently. Her second thought: Phil. Catching up with her, wishing her a good morning since they had missed each other the night before.

The night before. She shuddered.

She checked the phone's display. It was neither of those. It was a number she didn't recognise. She answered.

'Hello?'

'Good morning.' The voice overly cheerful, a redcoat at a holiday camp chivvying up the late sleepers.

Oh God, thought Marina, *a sales call*, and made to hang up.

'Not up and about yet, Marina? Shame on you. Glorious day, you're missing it.'

She stopped, finger poised above the button. She knew that voice. It took her a few seconds but she placed it. Hugo Gwilym.

'Hugo?'

'Who else would it be?' He gave a chuckle. That was the only way she could categorise the sound – a chuckle.

She looked round the room, confused. It somehow felt wrong hearing his voice in here. This was her and Phil's room. Private. She felt stupid and a little ashamed for thinking it, but it was almost like an invasion.

'How . . . What are you calling for?'

'Just wanted to say thank you. For last night.'

She said nothing. Waited for her memory to come back.

'You can't remember last night?' Another chuckle, deeper this time, heavy with meaning. 'I can.'

'Course . . . ' Could she? Her memory flashed back. What was he talking about? What had happened? She tried to order events. The details were cloudy. She was sure she hadn't drunk that much. She tried to think. The dinner. Everyone talking, laughing. Then Hugo arrived. Smarming all over her. She could remember glances and looks from the rest of the table, not all of them approving. Had she done something wrong? She didn't think so. They had chatted. Well, argued was a better word. He had explained his theories, she had rebutted them. Then . . . nothing. It all became hazy from there on.

She looked round the room once more. Her clothes were piled on the chair in the corner where she had taken them off before getting into bed. She could barely remember that. Or how she got home.

Her face reddened, her heart tripped. How much had she

had to drink? Not much. A gin and tonic before the dinner, a couple of glasses of red during. Nothing after. Her colleagues were still pretty new – she didn't want to make a fool of herself in front of them so she had been moderating her intake. And then ... nothing. Until she woke up.

'Good,' he said. 'Wouldn't want to think you'd forgotten me.'

She had no idea what he was talking about or what had happened, so she said nothing.

'Speechless? Not like you. You are still there, aren't you?'

'Yes, yes, I'm still here.'

'Good. Thought for a minute you'd nodded off. No chance of that last night, though, was there?'

She had to say something. 'What ... what d'you mean?'

'Last night,' he said, an irritable edge to his voice, as if it was beneath him to explain. 'I mean about what happened last night.'

'What did happen last night?'

Another laugh, more like an explosion this time. 'Well that's an insult, I must say.'

Marina's head was spinning from more than just the alcohol residue. 'Just ... tell me what happened.'

'You know what happened. You were there.'

'Humour me. Pretend I wasn't.'

Another noise – an intake of breath, a snort, she couldn't be sure – then a sentence started and quickly halted before she could make out what he was saying. 'We ... had fun.'

Her stomach flipped over. She thought she was going to be sick. 'What kind of fun?'

'What kind d'you think?'

Suddenly Marina's skin was too hot for her body and she felt like she wanted to claw it off. Her head spun again, her breathing fast and irregular. It was how what she imagined one of Phil's old panic attacks felt like.

'I ... I ...'

Another chuckle. 'Two I's. Very egotistical. But I like that in a woman.'

'I ... don't know what you're talking about ...'

'Oh come on, don't be bashful. Don't try and pretend it never happened. We're all grown-ups here. Deal with it and move on.'

Marina said nothing.

'Until the next time.'

'What? What are you ... I can't even remember the last time. There's not ... there's not going to be a next time.'

'Would you like to meet for lunch? I'll pay.'

'Aren't you listening to what I'm saying?'

'I am. And I'm asking you to lunch today. And you're going to say yes.'

'Oh, am I?'

'You are.'

'Why?'

Another chuckle. 'Because I'm a much better psychologist, and a better reader of people for that matter, than you give me credit for. And because you won't let this go without seeing me. For whatever reasons you think you may have.'

Marina said nothing. She could hear her breathing, the blood pumping round her body, hot and fast.

'All right. When and where?'

He told her. 'And don't be late. I can't abide that.' The words carried an undertow of threat. He hung up.

Marina flung the phone on the bed. Looked around the room, taking in the walls like a zoo animal trapped in its cage.

She took a mouthful of coffee. It was still hot. It tasted cold.

Then she ran to the bathroom and threw up.

13

Maddy could feel it. Knew it was there without even looking. Still. It hadn't stopped coming, wouldn't stop. No matter what she put there to stem it, absorb it. Every time she moved her body she could feel that it hadn't stopped, that it was only waiting. A reminder of what she had done. An admonishment.

In blood.

The tears had stopped long ago. She had cried so much, let so much hurt and pain come screaming out of her body that it left her feeling physically tired. Once the tears and snot had dried on her face she could have just curled up and slept. And she would have done, if she hadn't been feeling so depressed, so bereft. So empty inside.

That was almost a joke. The kind *he* would find amusing.

Acid curdled in her stomach at the thought. Of the joke. Of him. Of what she had done to herself. Of what she had let him do to her.

She sat in her bedroom, afraid to leave, afraid to talk to the rest of the house. They would want to know what was wrong with her and she wouldn't be able to tell them. She had sworn not to, one of the first things they had agreed. That he made her agree to. And she had kept her word, not told a single soul. Not even Ami, her best friend. Ami might have suspected, guessed something was going on when Maddy was being secretive about where she was and who she saw, but she had managed to get round it. And Ami wasn't the kind to go prowling and prying. So Maddy sat in her room, surrounded by her own things, her tokens and talismans brought from home, her photos and fetishes picked up along the way. Her attempts to accumulate her few possessions into a lodestone she could navigate her future life from. Instead she found herself clinging on to them, like the survivor of a shipwreck grasping any flotsam and jetsam, desperate not to be swept away.

She sighed, looked down at her legs, her groin once more. The slight bulge in the front of her jogging bottoms. She knew she shouldn't look, but she couldn't help it. Like picking at a scab and not letting it heal properly. Slowly she pulled her jogging bottoms out, away from her body. Looked down. Her underpants held the slight bulge of the damp pad against her skin. She pulled them away from her body too. Checked the pad.

Blood. Fresh.

She took her hands away quickly, letting her clothes snap back. She was still bleeding.

She felt her body shake, convulse, as another wave of tears threatened to overtake her, sweep her away from the makeshift raft, cast her adrift into nothingness.

'I can't . . . can't do this . . . ' The words a whispered invocation between sobs.

It had all started so well. Too well. He was handsome, dashing. Charming. All the clichés her old self would have hated to hear her new self using. But he was different from all the others she had been out with, the clueless boys who strived too hard and missed the mark, just children playing at being men. He had swept her away from them, away from her friends. He had given her a glimpse into a world she knew about but had never been admitted to. Sophisticated, grown up. He had welcomed her into that world, told her she belonged, that he would guide her, shape her, make it hers. And she had let him. Because he had done something else for her too. Something none of the previous fumbling boys had even managed to do. Made her feel like she was the most important person in the universe. In *his* universe.

How could she not fall for him?

And now this. Her insides scraped out, an unending stream of blood between her legs. Like her life was running out of her. And a broken heart. No phone calls. No texts. No DMs on Twitter. Nothing. Like she'd been put back in her own world. Dumped. Hurt.

Alone.

She wasn't naïve enough to think that the baby would have bound them together, made them a family. He didn't want that and she was in complete agreement with him. She didn't want a baby, not even with him. Or at least, not yet. She wanted him. To herself. Just him. And now she didn't even have that.

Another wave of despair built up, threatened to crash against her. She couldn't stand for that to happen, couldn't bear it. She looked round the room, once her sanctuary, now her prison, where everything she saw, touched, smelled reminded her of him. Her muscles, tired, aching, flexed, spasmed. Her body convulsed as the tears hit, started again. She threw herself to the floor, jamming her fist in her mouth, eyes screwed tight closed.

'Stop ... make it stop ... make it stop ...'

Her feet hammering lightly on the floor, wanting to get it all out of her but not wanting the rest of the house to know what was happening.

The rest of the house. Maybe she should call Ami. Tell her what had happened. Give her the whole story. The secret affair. The mad lovemaking. The baby. The abortion. All of it. Tell her. *She's a friend, a best friend, let her be a friend.*

Maddy's hand snaked out to grab her mobile, fingers ready to call. She pulled herself to a sitting position, held the phone in front of her. Saw the photo. Him. And her. Smiling, happy, laughing. Looking into each other's eyes, sharing a joke. The best joke in the world, from the way her eyes were shining, her head thrown back. Taken by a student at a party who probably never guessed, didn't realise what was happening, what they actually meant to each other.

She stared at the photo. And put the phone down beside her. Carefully cradling it, as if the image might fade and along with it the memory.

She gazed at the image until the phone switched itself off, the screen going black. She sighed, felt another wave of tears about to hit.

No. Not this time. She couldn't bear another bout, the bleeding, the pain. She had to do something. Make the pain stop. End it. Take it away. For ever.

She got slowly to her feet, her stomach twisting and cramping as she did so, reminding her of what she had done, and started looking around the room, rummaging through drawers, boxes. She knew they must be there somewhere. She knew she hadn't loaned them out. She found them. Something her mother had made her take to university. Encouraging her to make her own clothes rather than waste money on buying them.

Dressmaking scissors. The blades razor-sharp.

She sat back on the floor, opened out the blades, held one of them along her wrist. The bigger one. It would cut deeper, quicker. That was all it would take, just a quick swipe of the

71

blade along her wrist, a few seconds of pain as the metal dug deep into her flesh, as she pressed it down to the bone and moved it backwards and forwards. Then the same with the other wrist. Then . . . nothing. No pain any more. Ever again. Just peace. Rest. Nothing.

Blood began to well underneath the blade as she held it down. She felt the metal burn as it went in. Tears were rolling down her cheeks, mingling with snot. She heard herself blubbering, crying, made out words of apology, prayers for herself and her mother.

'Sorry . . . sorry . . . '

She tried to push the blade in further. That was all it needed, just one more push . . .

Maddy threw the blade across the floor. It skidded under the wardrobe, lay still. She put her injured wrist up to her mouth, kissed the blood away, looked at the wound. There was barely anything to see; it had hardly broken the skin.

She sat with her back against the wall, feeling the blood trickling between her legs, along her wrist. *The bleeding girl. That's who I am.* And a coward. Who couldn't even kill herself.

She thought again of that word. *Coward.* No. That wasn't what she was. She had stopped her suicide attempt not because she was afraid of dying, even though that was probably true. She had stopped because in that moment, just as the blade was about to slide through her flesh, she had thought of something else.

Make him pay. Make him sorry.

She stood up, wiping the back of her hand along her face. Heading for the shower.

Maddy was going out. She had someone to see.

14

When Phil Brennan showed his warrant card, the receptionist tried on several expressions before she settled for surprised – yet totally innocent – interest. And in those few seconds he knew exactly what kind of company he was calling on.

City Lets was based in an old office building on the fringes of Chinatown and the ungentrified portion of Digbeth. The area had been officially rebranded as Southside in an attempt to make it hip, urban and edgy. But this part of it had resolutely refused to play along. Part of Birmingham's once ubiquitous square poured-concrete architectural heritage, it looked like what they had imagined the future to be sixty years ago. Now, squatting in the shadow of the undulating metal curve of the new Selfridges building and the rejuvenated Bullring, the building looked old and crumbling, a monolith to a lost religion.

'I'd like to see Ron Parsons,' said Phil, putting his warrant card back in his jacket. The waiting room was old and shabby, dotted with several chairs nearing the end of their lives and two large wilting pot plants at opposite corners. A large man, bearded, wearing a plaid shirt and reading a paper, sat in one of the chairs. He put the paper down as Phil approached, became interested. The receptionist was old, large and tired and looked like she had come with the building.

'He's—'

Phil didn't give her the chance to come up with an excuse. 'It's to do with a murder inquiry.'

Her eyes widened. The bearded man picked up his paper again, pretended to look at it.

'In one of your properties.'

He was ushered straight through.

At first glance Ron Parsons seemed as anachronistic to his trade as the office block was to the rest of Birmingham. An overcoat and trilby hung on an old square wooden coat stand. The desk he sat behind was of a similar vintage; so too were the shelving, box files and filing cabinets. The walls were nicotine yellow, showing either a disregard for the smoking ban of the last decade or a disinclination to give the room a coat of paint. From the smell in the air, Phil knew which one it was.

The only piece of modernity in the room was a sleek, shiny black laptop on the desk. Parsons looked up from it, gestured.

'Please, take a seat, Detective ...?'

'Detective Inspector Brennan.' Phil sat. The chair creaked.

Parsons nodded. 'We had a call from one of your lot yesterday. Woman, I think. Hard to tell these days.' His voice was working-class West Midlands marinated in years of unfiltered cigarettes and whisky. Quiet but authoritative. A boss's voice. 'Said there'd been a murder at one of our properties.'

'That's right. Falcon Close, just off the Pershore Road. You probably saw it on the news.'

Parsons's eyes were flat glass. Opaque, not transparent. 'I don't watch much telly. Apart from the football. And the boxing. I'm not a news person. But your young woman said as much. So I expected a call today.'

'And here I am.'

'Here you are.' He slowly closed his laptop screen, gave Phil his full attention. 'What is it you want to know, Inspector Brennan?'

'Just a bit of background about your tenant.'

'What d'you need?'

'Whatever you've got. Where he's from, what he does for a living, who his referees were, his family, anything at all.'

Parsons raised his eyebrows. 'Anything to oblige.' He leaned back in his chair as if making to stand up, then thought better of it. Instead he pressed a button on his desk intercom. 'Cheryl, can you come in a minute, please, love.'

The heavy, tired receptionist made her way inside. Stood in the middle of the floor, waiting. The look she gave Parsons told him she had been called away from some vital UN business so it had better be important.

'Can you get everything on the Falcon Close property, please. Last tenant.' He turned to Phil. 'You just want the last one? Any more?'

Phil was about to say no, but something stopped him. That wasn't the question he'd been expecting Parsons to ask him. And because of that, he changed his answer.

'Just the last six months, please. That ought to do it.'

A look passed between Parsons and Cheryl. It was gone almost as quickly as it appeared, but Phil caught it. Unfortunately he couldn't read it well enough to know what it meant.

'Six months?' said Cheryl.

Phil smiled. 'Please. Printouts would be good.'

Cheryl went to work. But not before, Phil noticed, Parsons gave her the nod to do so.

'So,' said Parsons, once the receptionist had gone, 'what brings you here, Detective Brennan?'

'Murder, Mr Parsons.'

Parsons smiled, slowly shook his head. 'I mean, you're not from round here. That's not a Brummie accent I can hear.' He frowned. 'What is it, London? Essex?'

'Colchester,' said Phil. 'Just moved here.'

Parsons spread his arms expansively. 'Welcome to our humble city.'

'Thank you.' Phil leaned forward, hoped the chair wouldn't collapse completely. 'Did you know Mr McGowan, Mr Parsons? Have you met him?'

'The dead bloke? No, not at all. I'm not usually in the office, Inspector. I'm only here today because your officer told me I could expect a call. I like to do my bit to help our boys in blue. And girls, I suppose. Wouldn't want to be sexist.'

'Would anyone here have met him? Spoken to him?'

'Might have done, but might not. Most of the business is done on the internet these days. See us on a website, click, done and dusted.' He gave a near-mournful look at the closed laptop.

'So you deal with mainly residential properties? Commercial?'

'Mainly residential. Mostly students around the university, Snaresbrook, Balsall Heath, those sorts of places. And contract workers coming into the city on fixed-term leases. Also short-term lets, DSS, asylum-seekers, that kind of thing. Better than a B and B, eh?'

Phil nodded. Old-school slum landlord type, he thought. Straight from Central Casting.

'The Falcon Close place used to be let to students. Neighbours didn't like it. So we aimed it more at professional types. Coming here to work, short-term lets, that kind of thing.'

'How short-term?'

Parsons blew out his cheeks. 'Depends. Obviously if

workers are on a contract we try to be flexible. Take it on a month-by-month basis.'

'And how long was Glenn McGowan's tenancy agreement?'

Parsons shrugged. 'A month? I don't know. You'd have to check. Ah. Here we are.'

Cheryl appeared with a file of papers. She handed them over to Phil. Again a look passed between her and her boss; again Phil couldn't read it.

'Thank you,' said Phil, standing up. 'Well if there's anything more you can tell me about Mr McGowan . . . '

'All in there, I should think,' said Parsons, 'But you might want to give his wife a ring.'

Phil frowned. 'His wife? We haven't tracked down a wife.'

'She phoned here earlier. Managed to find our number. Needed him to sign something or other. Wanted to know where he was.'

'And did you tell her?'

Parsons shrugged. 'Not my job, mate.'

'Her phone number's in with the rest of the stuff,' said Cheryl. She put her finger on top of the file. Phil noticed how well-manicured her nails were. Blood red. She saw him looking and smiled. There was something hungry in the smile. Suddenly she didn't look so tired after all.

'I'll see myself out,' said Phil.

The bearded man put down his newspaper and watched him go. Phil's phone rang as he made his way down the concrete staircase. He answered it, stepped into the street. Hurried away in response to what he heard.

Unaware that Cheryl had joined the bearded man watching him at the window.

15

Phil almost ran into the room. 'I got here as quick as I could.'

Sperring, sitting on a chair, looked up from reading the *Daily Mail*. 'It's all right. Our pal's not going anywhere.' He went back to his paper, ignoring Phil.

Phil stood there trying not to bunch his hands into fists. 'So what are the findings?' No response. 'Obviously if you think it's more important to find out how gay Kosovan refugee benefit-scroungers are coming to take your job and undermine your way of life, you just keep on reading.'

Sperring gave a last glance at his paper, folded it and stood up. 'You're very funny. Sir.'

Phil didn't rise to it. 'The post-mortem?'

Sperring, disappointed not to be having a confrontation, said, 'This way,' then turned and walked off along the corridor. Phil followed.

The halls of the mortuary were like every other mortuary Phil had been in. Bare and cold. He heard occasional snatches of pop songs and radio jingles as he walked, incongruous bursts of life that just made their surroundings all the more deathly. At least that was how he felt. He had never been comfortable with this aspect of the job.

'So where were you when I called?' asked Sperring.

'I'd just been to the letting agents,' said Phil.

Sperring grunted.

'Apparently Glenn McGowan had a wife. We can give her a call when we've finished here. I've got some files about the house too. Letting agreements, that kind of thing.'

'Give them to the juniors. Got to earn their keep somehow.'

'There's something else,' said Phil. Sperring didn't reply. Phil went on. 'The boss of the letting agency. Something about him. Red flag.'

'Yeah?' Sperring couldn't have sounded more uninterested if he'd tried.

'Yeah. Name of Ron Parsons.'

Sperring stopped walking. Turned to face Phil. 'Ron Parsons? You sure? Older guy, suit and braces type. Trilby.'

'There was a trilby hanging up in the office. He was wearing the braces.'

'Jesus bloody Christ. There's a name from Jurassic times. Ron bloody Parsons.'

'Who is he?'

Sperring opened his mouth as if about to tell all. Before he could, something flitted across his eyes. 'Long story. All you need to know is Ron Parsons is as bent as bloody fuck.'

Before Phil could say anything else, Sperring stopped in front of a heavy industrial rubber and plastic door. 'Through here.' He opened it, and let it fall back on to Phil as he walked through. Phil managed to catch it before it connected with his face. He followed Sperring into the room.

White-tiled walls, angled cement floor with drainage channels and gratings. Stainless-steel body-shaped beds. And on several of the beds were plastic-sheet-covered bodies. The cutting room.

Esme Russell, wearing her blood-smeared work clothes,

79

entered from her office at the far end of the room. 'Good morning, gentlemen,' she said, smiling.

'Very cheerful,' said Sperring.

'That's because you're here, handsome,' she said, laughing.

Sperring, Phil noticed, reddened.

She turned to Phil. 'Well,' she said, 'have we got something interesting for you.'

'Good interesting or bad interesting?' asked Phil.

'Depends what you make of it. Come on.' She walked along the rows of bodies, coming to a stop before the final one in the row. 'I bumped this up. I know I said I couldn't, road accidents and all that, but once I'd got it back here and taken a good look, I thought I'd better.'

'Why?' asked Phil.

She pulled the sheet back. 'See for yourself.'

16

The Arcadian had tried to make the doll feel at home. It wasn't the same as where she had been, that beautiful doll's house he had taken her from, but he had tried his best with what he could afford. He put love into it. And he had to admit, he was pleased with the result.

The house was plastic, cheap, the furniture likewise. He had spent the morning in Toys R Us and going round charity shops until he had enough. The furniture didn't match but it was mostly pink, which was important. Hers had been pink. It wasn't pristine like hers had been: some of it was old and worn, chewed-looking in parts, but he tried to ignore that. The walls were pink. And the doll looked happy in there, like she belonged. That was the main thing.

He stood staring at her. For how long, he didn't know. He zoned out. He had heard that builders did that, stood and admired the work they had done. Not looking at any part of it in particular, just staring. Seeing it, seeing through it. That was what he was doing.

He imagined that she was talking to him, telling him about her life. Thanking him for putting her in the house, not letting her go. He remembered the butterfly he had seen when she had died, beautiful, iridescent, and then the smile on the doll's face. He knew what had happened. It was so obvious. She was thanking him in that smile. And telling him something else: *Take the doll. Give her a home. She's me now. And she's yours. I'm yours*.

She sat at her chewed table, teacup in hand, smile etched permanently in plastic. Perfect.

He shook his head, blinked. It brought him back to reality.

The previous night came to mind. And the elation he had felt at placing the doll in her house escaped out of him. He had entered the bar wanting to make contact. The friction of flesh, the frisson of fucking, the release. He knew he wouldn't recapture the high he had experienced with the doll, all smiles and butterflies and pure Arcadian pleasure, but he had to try. Or at least settle for the next best thing.

He had stood in the bar, hand in his pocket stroking the doll's beautiful blonde hair, looking round. The men were all shapes and sizes, but he felt they had one thing in common: they were staring at him. At first he didn't like that, felt naked, exposed. But he gradually became accustomed to it, drew strength from it, even. It gave him the power to choose.

Except there was no one there he wanted to choose.

The drag artist was up on stage, miming to some old pop song, and the audience were whooping it up. But the Arcadian didn't like it. The drag queen was doing the actions to the lyrics in the song, but not very well. She overexaggerated any subtlety the song had, telegraphing her gestures as if she wanted them to be seen several miles away. Her make-up matched her actions. Like a Kabuki or Noh actor. Not like a genuine woman. Not like his doll.

He smiled to himself. Oh yes. He knew Kabuki, he knew Noh. He wasn't thick. He was an educated man. Educated.

There was nothing the drag queen had that he wanted. He checked the others at the bar. Men made up as women. He stared at them. Imagined his doll in their place. Imagined doing to them what he had done to his doll. Getting them alone, loving them for what they were, then showing them how they could be so much more. Giving them their dream. Taking out his knives and sculpting them into real women. He imagined doing that to all of them. Each and every one. Just standing there, staring. His hand in his pocket caressing the doll, his other hand sculpting with a non-existent knife.

That was what they all wanted, he told himself. The Arcadian to work his magic on them. That was what they were all there for, why they had come out for the night. Secretly they wanted to meet him, have him take them home. Make them into the best they could be. And maybe they didn't realise it. Maybe he had to show them. Give them what they wanted, what was best for them. Even if he had to subdue them, tie them up in order to do it. They would thank him for doing it. All of them.

He had stared at them so long, his imagination working all the while, that he zoned out again. When he blinked himself back to reality he was aware that the drags weren't looking at him any more. In fact they were looking anywhere but at him. He became aware of his hand in his pocket pressed against the doll, the doll rubbing his erection through his trousers. That must have been the reason why. He didn't care. But he couldn't stay there. So he had left the bar, gone home.

And that was when he thought of the idea of his own doll's house.

Now he sat, curtains closed against the harsh winter daylight, staring at his doll's house. It was perfect. The doll, the house, everything. He was amazed he hadn't thought of it earlier. Small and controllable, yet also noticeable. But something about that wasn't right. Something didn't fit. He stared again at the house, trying to work out what it was. And then he had it. So obvious he didn't know how he hadn't thought of it earlier.

There was only one doll.

She was lonely. She needed company. Someone to talk to. Someone for him to talk to. He had to plan ahead. Work out who she would like to live with her. The house could become a diary. Each doll a memento of his work. Yet more than that: a repository for the butterfly. A home for souls. With him all the time. He could talk to them, listen to them. Live with them.

He sighed, crossed his legs. Pondered.

What to do about it, what to do . . .

He could go back to the bars again, like he had done last night. Entice a drag home and set to work.

Maybe. But that didn't appeal so much. Part of the fun in creating the doll had been the build-up, the anticipation. The preparation. He was ready to do another one, no doubt. But he would have to do it right. Picking up someone random held too many variables. All he could see was the ways it could go wrong.

No. He had to do it better than that.

He thought some more.

The answer came to him. So simple. So perfect.

He looked at the doll in her house and smiled. 'Not long now,' he said. 'You're going to have some company . . .'

17

The body on the stainless-steel table was almost unrecognisable from the one Phil had seen in the house the night before. It had been wiped clean of make-up, the nail varnish removed from the fingers and toes. The face held none of its previous doll-like features. It had bloated up purple, the eyes and tongue protruding. The bloating was spreading to the rest of the body.

'I had to start quickly,' Esme said. 'The house was so cold – on purpose, I expect – that it had preserved the body to a degree. But as soon as we moved it and a change of air hit it, it began to putrefy. Stage two now. We've managed to stabilise it in here, but the damage has been done, I'm afraid.'

'What have you got, then?' asked Phil. 'Time of death?'

'Difficult to say because of the cold. The body's decomposition has been deliberately slowed.'

'Why?' asked Sperring.

'Either to stop us guessing when it was done,' said Phil. 'Or . . .'

'Or what?' said Sperring.

'Or there's another reason we haven't discovered yet.'

'Well,' said Esme, 'that's your job. I'd put time of death – and remember, this is only a guess – at somewhere in the last two weeks.'

'You can't be more specific than that?'

'I can run some more tests, see what shows up, but it'll take time. The cold's stopped the decomposition.'

'If we trace the victim's movements, come back with a timeline, could you fit it around that?'

'I should think so.'

'Good. What else have you got?'

'Well.' Esme shook her head, continued speaking with an enthusiasm Phil found slightly disturbing. 'There is so much going on here that you could give this body to trainees and students. If they spotted everything they'd all get A stars.' Another smile. 'Lucky for you boys I *did* get an A star.'

They waited for her to go on.

'Where to start? Lividity. Good a place as any. He died in the chair we found him in. But the injuries leading to his death were done elsewhere.'

'And the body was moved,' said Sperring.

'Indeed. And judging by the fact that there is no evidence of shifting lividity –the blood hadn't started to gather anywhere in his body before he sat down – I'd say he was still alive when he got to the chair. But his blood levels are well down.'

'Cause of death?' asked Sperring.

Esme pointed to the mutilated area in the corpse's groin. Discoloration had given it the appearance of rancid mince. There was nothing left to identify it as human. It was almost desensitising to look at. Esme's words provided the right context. 'That. Mutilation. His genitals were removed. There's no evidence of cauterisation, so we can assume that the resulting blood loss would have led to his death.'

'Signs of sexual activity?' asked Phil.

Esme gestured to the mutilation. 'Be my guest. If you think you can find anything. Whoever this was has done a very thorough job.'

'Professional?'

Esme frowned. 'I don't think so. But a very enthusiastic amateur.'

Phil glanced at Sperring. From the look on his face, he guessed the older copper was wishing he was still sitting down the corridor with his *Daily Mail*.

'We had a look in the bathroom in the house,' said Phil. 'The CSIs are still checking it out but we think that's where the mutilation was done.'

Esme nodded. 'Very probably. But that still throws up some questions.'

'Was the victim conscious when this was done to him?'

'The first question. And a very good one, Ian.'

Phil glanced at Sperring once more and was surprised to find him blushing again.

'The answer is yes. As far as I can make out, the victim was fully aware this was being done.'

'What about painkillers, anything like that?'

'We won't get the tox reports back for a few days, so we won't know. But judging from the look of some of those internal organs, the shape of the liver, I'd say there was something in his body. Just not sure what yet.'

'Something to induce paralysis?' said Phil. 'If the killer wanted him alive when this was done, as seems likely, then maybe look for traces of, I don't know, Rohypnol? Something like that. I'm not trying to tell you your job, Esme, I'm just attempting to get my head round this.'

'As are we all. No offence taken. Obviously I've asked for that to be done.'

'Thank you. We think that after the mutilation in the bathroom he was taken downstairs,' said Phil. 'We found cleaned-up blood on the floor.'

'The perpetrator was strong, then. Must have had to carry him.'

'So let's get this straight,' said Sperring. 'He was chopped about upstairs in the bathroom, then brought downstairs and sat at the dining room table. All when he was alive and dressed like a . . .'

'Doll,' said Phil.

Sperring shook his head.

'That's about the size of it,' said Esme.

'Anything else?' asked Sperring. Phil noticed he was turning as pale as the wall tiles.

Esme's eyes lit up. 'Oh yes.'

'I don't like the way you said that,' said Phil.

She laughed, slightly embarrassed. 'I don't get out much. Please forgive me. When you mostly deal with drunks and car crash victims as I do, being given something like this is like Christmas.'

'Lucky you,' said Phil, unsure if he was joking or not.

'Indeed.' She crossed over to a trolley behind them, returned holding a piece of wire.

'What's that?' asked Sperring, looking like he was dreading the answer.

'It's what was in the victim's arm and hand,' said Esme. 'It's how he was able to hold the teacup for so long.'

Phil and Sperring exchanged glances. 'So,' said Phil slowly, gathering his thoughts as he spoke, 'the teacup was posed deliberately.'

'Looks that way,' said Esme. 'The wire was inserted post mortem, I'd say. Or at least after the mutilation had been done. The drug, I would think, was administered before-hand to induce paralysis.'

'But . . .' Sperring stared at the wire. 'Why?'

'It was a tableau,' said Phil.

Sperring shook his head. 'Still haven't answered the question.'

'And there's a question neither of you have yet asked.' Esme had a gleam in her eye. Phil knew that to a member of the public her enthusiasm might have seemed inappropriate, but to someone else in the job it was a positive sign. It meant she was doing what she was paid to do. And taking pride in it.

'Probably for a reason,' said Sperring, with the look of a man who wished he could be anywhere else.

'Yes. You boys might be squeamish about these things. And I can understand that.'

'What d'you mean?' asked Phil.

'The mutilated genitals. Where are they?'

'Oh God,' said Sperring.

'Good question,' said Phil. 'We assumed we just hadn't found them yet.'

'You're right. You haven't found them yet. I have.'

Sperring and Phil shared a look. For the first time Phil felt united with his fellow officer.

'I did an analysis of stomach contents,' said Esme.

'Here we go . . . ' Sperring turned away. Phil waited.

'And there they were.'

Sperring turned back round. 'You mean . . . he's eaten his own cock?' He almost gagged on the words.

Esme nodded. 'And there were no signs of trauma, no indication of force-feeding. So you know what that means? He did it willingly.'

'What?' said Phil. 'Ate his own genitals willingly? Or did everything willingly?'

'The latter, I'd say.'

Phil said nothing. He could find nothing to say.

Sperring ran from the room, hand over his mouth.

18

Keith had been dreaming of summer, of warmth. He had been running. In the woods, the breeze light against his skin, sunlight dappling and stranding through the tree trunks. He looked at the woman in front of him. He could remember her. She was so young, so pretty. So happy to see him. She smiled at him. He returned it. And never wanted that moment to end. That perfect moment.

Keith opened his eyes. And found he had pissed himself.

He was still in his chair from the previous night, still propped in front of the TV in the living room. He looked round. Listened. Heard nothing. He was alone in the house. Kelly hadn't returned.

Keith knew she wasn't just being quiet. She was incapable of that. When she was in the house she would always have the TV on, or the radio playing some inane pop music, or her iPod going. Or she'd be on the phone to one of her equally gormless mates. Never silent for one second. She wouldn't be sitting reading or doing a crossword. She was too thick for those things.

He saw the girl from his dream again. Perfectly formed once more, in his mind's eye. Smiling. Happy to see him. Making him feel good about her, about himself. Giving him hope. He sighed, his chest hurting, but not as much as his heart.

That was Kelly. The girl he had met in a nightclub, just a chance encounter, had turned his world upside down. Made him happier than he had ever thought possible. But that was years ago. Before everything that happened happened. Not the Kelly who lived here now. She was a different person. A lesser person. A wholly despicable person.

And a bitch that hadn't come home.

The dream had reminded him of what things used to be like when they were good. When she used to look at him like she did that time in the woods, with the sun on his skin, the breeze on his face. The girl in the summer dress in front of him, running, teasing, making him follow. Giggling, her dress falling from one shoulder. Giving him the promise of what pleasures awaited when he caught up with her.

He remembered it so well. Revisited the memory often. He *had* caught up with her. Tickled her to the ground. Laughing and squirming they had gone down in a happy heap. Then, once on the ground, the branches crackling beneath them, the leaves and moss warmer and more inviting than he would have imagined, they had looked into each other's eyes. Their mouths had met. Then their hands. Then their bodies. Then . . .

A key in the door.

He opened his eyes, turned. It was her entering. He knew by the clack of her spike heels on the polished wooden floor of the hall.

Keith looked down at his lap once more, saw again the stain on the front of his tracksuit bottoms, felt the cold material against his skin, smelt the acrid tang of urine. He was ashamed of himself. Whatever she was, whatever she had become, he didn't want her to see him like this.

Kelly came into the living room. Stopped dead.

'Oh,' she said. 'You're . . . '

'Still here,' he said. 'I fell asleep in front of the TV.'

He tried to move the chair away from her line of vision, but it was too late. Her eyes had darted to his lap. She had seen what had happened. The curled lip, the expression of distaste on her face told him that more eloquently than words could have done. He felt his face reddening from the shame. Wanted to scream, to cry out, to . . .

He wanted his legs back. His body. *His life*.

'So where've you been, then?' He asked the question to stop the depression overwhelming him, knowing that there would be a new kind of depression hitting him soon, depending on her answer.

'I just . . . It was late. And I couldn't get . . . so I stopped at Debbie's.' She looked away from him, clearing her throat as if to dislodge the lie. Unable to even believe it herself.

'Come . . . over here,' he said. He knew that was asking for trouble, knew it was only going to make the pain worse.

She came nearer, looked down at him. 'You've . . . '

'Pissed myself, yeah. That's . . . what happens, isn't it? That's what happens when you go . . . go running off and, and . . . leave me.' His breath coming in short, ragged gasps, each one seeming to tear a strip off his insides.

'I'll . . . ' She looked downcast. 'I'm sorry. I'll . . . ' She made to move away.

'Stay . . . here.' His voice, although weak, still carried some of its old authority.

She did as she was told.

He noticed that she was still wearing her coat, despite the heat in the house. In fact, she had it pulled up around her throat.

He knew what she was hiding. 'Take your coat off,' he said.

Her hand went quickly to her throat, alarm in her eyes, but the coat stayed where it was.

'Take your coat off,' he said again.

Still she didn't move.

'It's . . . hot in here. You should . . . should take it off.'

He stared at her, looking deeply into her eyes, making sure she looked into his. This wasn't like his dream. They weren't the same people any more. When he looked into her eyes now, he didn't see love, or joy. Just calculation and resentment. Fear that things might not go the way she wanted them to. And lurking somewhere at the back, hatred. Of what he had become and what she had allowed herself to become. Of what she had to do to get what she wanted.

It almost made him smile.

'Take . . . it . . . off.'

Reluctantly, but seeing she had no choice, Kelly removed her coat, placed it over her arm. Keith stared at her. Saw what he wanted to see. Felt acid gather in his body.

'What's that?' he said, pointing to her neck.

Her hand jerked upwards, covering her skin.

'Take your hand away.'

'I'm just . . . '

'I said, take . . . your hand . . . away.'

She did so. He saw the discoloured skin. The dark bruise of a love bite. She opened her mouth to speak.

'Don't,' he said. 'Just . . . don't.'

She stood there mutely, her eyes trying to communicate telepathically how sorry she was.

'Get out of my sight.'

She knelt in front of him, ignoring the smell, the stain. 'I'm sorry, Keith, really I am. I didn't mean to, I just . . . He . . . '

'Just . . . fuck off.'

The tears came then. Not for him, he knew that. But

because it looked like her money was disappearing over the horizon, never to be seen again.

She had no idea how true that was, he thought.

'Please don't cut me off,' she said. 'Please don't ... when you've, when ... I don't know what I'll ... ' Her hands fumbled at the waistband of his joggers. 'Here, I'll ... ' Her hand was inside them then, the look of distaste on her face replaced by one of desperation. She lowered her head, eyes closed.

He put his hands on the wheels, turned the chair away from her. The movement sent her sprawling on the floor. He saw straight away she wasn't wearing any underwear.

He wheeled himself away, kept his back to her. Eventually he heard her get to her feet, walk quickly out of the room. He heard her go upstairs, sobbing.

Anger welled within him. It built, then came crashing down.

This is it, he thought. *This is the time. No more fucking about.*

He wheeled himself over to his phone, picked it up, dialled a number he knew from memory. Quickly, before he could change his mind. The call was answered.

'It's me,' he said, his voice rasping and harsh, like it was costing him a lot to speak. 'Keith Burkiss.'

'Yes, Keith,' said the voice. 'What can I do for you?'

Keith took one last look around the living room. Then down at his own lap, his useless, broken body.

'Do it,' he said. 'Let's do it now.'

19

The Green Man was huge, looming; it looked like it could fall at any minute. Or come to life and walk away. Marina always stared at it, she couldn't help it. A huge statue made of stone and augmented with vegetation, the extravagantly horned forty-foot figure towered over everyone and everything in the area. His features wild, his body overly muscled, the statue rippled with a pagan energy that was simultaneously stimulating and terrifying, a reminder that no matter how humanity tried to fool itself, comfort itself in the belief that it was the dominant species, there were much stronger forces on the planet that needed to be treated with respect and fear.

Or that was how it made Marina feel. But now, taking her place at a table in a coffee house opposite the statue, she knew there were other things – and people – to be feared. Much nearer to home. And much more real.

The Custard Factory was part of the ongoing gentrification of the Digbeth area of Birmingham. Originally the area's Bird's custard factory from which it took its name, it was now home to a thriving community of artists and designers, media and charity organisations, with vintage clothes and furniture shops, record shops, bars, cafés and restaurants. Marina found it achingly hip but not uncomfortable.

'Hello.'

She turned. Hugo Gwilym appeared from a shadowed alcove beside the till, walked towards her, pocketing his phone as if just ending a call. He smiled, sat down. She looked at him. Sunlight from outside the café hit his face full on. He squinted against it. Caught in the bright glare and without the previous night's make-up ministrations of a TV studio, his features looked older, more worn, dissolute. His skin carried his life's history of various alcoholic and narcotic abuses like a road map. He gestured back to where he had come from.

'Can we . . . ?'

'What?'

'Go and sit over there. The light's too bright here.' He made to rise.

'Here's fine for me,' said Marina, refusing to budge.

Gwilym sat back down again. Marina felt a slight thrill at the little victory but something dark and ugly flapped across Gwilym's features. He clearly wasn't used to being answered back. 'Suit yourself.' The tone of his voice said anything but.

'So,' said Marina, struggling to keep her voice level, not betray the anxiety that was churning inside her, 'you wanted to see me.' She kept her back stiff, hands folded in her lap. She didn't want him to see how much they were shaking.

'Of course I did. Only natural, considering . . . ' His features returned to their familiar setting. He smiled.

'Considering what?' she said, throat dry.

He leaned forward, head down, voice low, conspiratorial. Back in control now. 'Considering what we shared last night.'

Marina felt her heart thudding in her chest. Her head was light, vision spinning, spasming. 'What . . . what did we share . . . ?' She had thought about his words over and over on the way there. What he had implied, what he had said. There could be no doubt what he meant.

She had had sex with him.

The thought had made her physically sick and the feeling still hadn't gone away. In fact it had intensified. The thought of having sex with him was abhorrent enough, especially when she couldn't remember doing it. But something niggled at her. Something that wasn't right, that didn't fit. She had tried to pull it from her memory on the trip into town, but it was no good. Nothing came back to her. Just a sense of unease that something bad had happened. Something awful.

He didn't answer her straight away. He just smiled once more.

Marina hated that smile. It was the smug smile of a bully, of someone who had got away with so much, had gone unchallenged for so long they no longer had any self-doubt. They felt they could get away with anything.

'We talked,' said Marina. 'That was it.'

Another smile, showing his teeth this time. 'Let's order.'

'I'm not hungry.'

'I am.' He gestured the waitress over, told her what he wanted. She looked at Marina, expectant.

'I'm not hungry. Just water.'

Gwilym studied the menu. 'She'll have the same as me.' He smiled.

The waitress looked between them.

'I'm not hungry.'

'She'll have the same as me.' He turned to her. 'You can't not eat anything. Especially after the amount you drank last night.'

Marina's head felt like it was about to explode. 'Whatever.'

The waitress hurried away. Gwilym turned to her, a look of smug triumph on his face. He had managed to get his own way again. He leaned back, comfortable. In control.

'So. Last night.'

97

'Did you fuck me?' Marina sat back, surprised by the words she had spoken and the vehemence with which she'd expressed them.

Gwilym seemed surprised also. His eyebrows rose. He laughed. 'Well. I never suspected you possessed such directness.'

'Just tell me.'

Another smile. She felt like a half-dead mouse being played with by a cat's paw. That, she suspected, was what he wanted her to feel. His tone, when he spoke, was mocking. 'We had a ... dalliance, yes. Quite enjoyable. Can't you remember?'

Marina felt the world around her tunnelling in then out again. A Hitchcock *Vertigo* trombone shot. Her stomach lurched and she thought she might throw up again. She breathed deeply, tried to get her body back in control.

'No,' she said. 'I can't remember. I've only got your word for it.'

'Well I assure you, Marina, I am a man of my word. I wouldn't lie about something like that.'

She felt like she had been cast adrift from her life, like this was all happening to someone else. She looked round the café, saw Gwilym, her own reflection in the glass. This was real.

'What ... what happened?'

'You were in a terrible state after the restaurant, so I escorted you to a taxi. You couldn't stand up, so I thought it best to take you home. But once we got into the taxi ... ' He laughed. 'You were a tiger. Oh yes.'

Marina said nothing. Gwilym continued.

'Couldn't keep your hands off me. Pulling at my shirt, my trousers. I mean, I don't know what the taxi driver thought. Seemed a very devout, religious man. A Muslim, judging by all the paraphernalia hanging in his cab. Bet he'd never seen anything like it.'

98

'So . . . what happened?'

'I took you back to mine.' She stared at him, eyes wide. 'What else could I do? You made it quite clear what you wanted to happen.' He held his hands up, shrugged. 'How could I resist?'

'So we . . . slept together.'

'Well, there wasn't much sleep going on. You got what you came for, then I called a cab. And off you went.' He sat back, gave another smile. 'And here you are. Back for more.'

20

'Just wait till you see this.'

Her full name, Phil knew, was Detective Constable Elina Ghosh. But he, like the rest of the team, called her Elli. She was short, didn't look like she hit the gym much, in her late twenties and Asian. Her naturally dark hair had been coloured with streaks of deep pink and red, and her ears, lips and nose bore indentations caused by removed jewellery. She pushed the MIU dress code as far as it would go, wearing T-shirts advertising bands and games Phil had never heard of – today's said *It's On Like Alderaan*, with the 'On' being a cartoon Death Star – plus jeans and boots that Judge Dredd would have been proud of. He liked her. He recognised something of his own attitude in her.

He and the rest of the MIU team were gathered around her desk, DCI Alison Cotter on his left, Sperring to his right, Khan next to him. The lower ranks were behind them. Phil was aware that there were more bodies in the briefing room than had been there previously. Clearly West Midlands Police were taking the investigation seriously.

'What have you found, Elli?' asked Cotter.

She glanced round, her eyes gleaming with the kind of triumph only geeks knew, Phil thought. Then she turned back to what was before her. Glenn McGowan's laptop was open, the screen glowing, columns of incomprehensible letters and numbers scrolling down before them.

'It wasn't easy,' said Elli. 'Password-protected, firewall, the lot. With that level of security I was worried that he might have left a few spikes or booby traps in place. You know, to wipe the hard drive if you didn't give the correct command. Luckily, he hadn't. Still, he was good. Very good. But . . .' She put her hands together, pushed them out from her body, flexed her fingers back until they cracked. She smiled. 'I'm better.'

She put her hands on the keys and the screen changed to something more recognisable. A desktop, files stacked down the left-hand side, wallpaper in place. Phil studied it.

'Marilyn Monroe,' he said.

A photo montage of the dead Hollywood star took up the entire screen. Smiling, laughing, pouting. Looking gorgeous.

'Girl of his dreams,' said Sperring.

'Or the girl he dreamed of being,' said Phil.

'I've had a look around,' said Elli. 'I thought he might have hidden some stuff away. But he hasn't. It's all here. All you could want, and more.'

'Let's see, then,' said Phil.

Her fingers moved quickly over the keys once more. 'There's work stuff on here, files, documents. Routine stuff. Boring stuff. But . . .' She pressed more buttons, waited for another file to appear. It was marked AMANDA. 'Here,' she said.

'Amanda?' said Khan. 'His name was Glenn. Why didn't he call himself Glenda?'

'Think about it,' said Phil. 'Would you want to be called Glenda?'

Khan sank back into silence.

Elli clicked the file open. Thumbnails of photos filled the screen. She clicked on the first one, set up a slideshow. They showed a tall, awkward person dressed as a woman. Wearing a sleeveless summer dress, arms hairy and tanned up to his T-shirt line, unsure what to do with his limbs, what position to put them in, the posture of a long-distance lorry driver in drag. Heavy, inexpertly applied make-up, unconvincing wig. And the eyes: staring into the camera like a rabbit in the headlights. Almost paralysed with fear.

'This looks like our man,' said Sperring.

'It is,' said Elli. 'Keep watching, they tell a story.'

The first few photos were all the same. A man they took to be Glenn McGowan dressed in women's clothes, posing uncomfortably for the camera. The next section showed him draped over a bed in a black basque, suspenders and stockings, trying to look alluring.

'Don't fancy yours much,' said Khan, sniggering.

A couple of other officers joined in. Phil didn't.

'I've clicked through all this,' said Elli. 'He's put some of the best ones on his Flickr account. But I think it's worth going through them all to follow his progress.'

Glenn McGowan was beginning to display more confidence in his female persona and the photos reflected this. His make-up improved, became subtle, more feminine. More doll-like, Phil thought. He also sported a selection of wigs, different colours and lengths depending on the clothes he was wearing and the mood the photos were trying to convey. Patterns emerged: short blonde wigs and brightly coloured dresses for sunny housewife-type shots, usually taken in kitchens or gardens; long dark wigs, low-level lighting and full silk underwear for sultry boudoir bedroom ones. Short dark wigs and tight-skirted business suits for office photos. Long blonde wigs and sequinned dresses for party-girl shots that, judging by the similarly made-up and dressed people in the photos, had been taken at transvestite bars and nightclubs. Again, Phil was drawn to the eyes. There was none of the earlier fear or reticence in them now. Glenn – or Amanda – was full of confidence and what seemed like the joy of living. Or the joy of living as a woman, thought Phil.

'Looks happy enough,' said Sperring, echoing his thoughts.

'He does,' said Phil. 'But I wonder what he felt like when he had to take the party dress off and go back to being boring old Glenn?'

'You sound like you want to give it a try,' said Khan, sniggering once more.

Phil stared at him. Khan quickly broke eye contact, looked away. 'Sorry, sir,' he mumbled. Phil turned his attention back to the photos.

'Here we go,' said Elli, laughing. 'Brace yourself, boys ... '

'Oh, for fuck's sake,' said Sperring, eyes on the screen, unable to hide his displeasure.

'Language, Ian,' said Cotter.

'Sorry, ma'am.'

From the tone of his voice, Phil doubted he was.

The next set of photos showed Amanda enjoying the intimate company of other transvestites. They had neither the carefully staged quality of the earlier pictures nor the sense of fun and abandon from the party shots. What they did have was an intense carnal quality. Amanda, head back, eyes closed, looked like she/he was lost in the moment. Borne away by pleasure.

'Disgusting,' said Khan, looking round at his fellow officers for support for his views. 'I mean, 'snot right, is it? Doing that. It's just ... ' He looked again at the photos. 'God ... shouldn't be allowed to do that. Disgusting ... '

103

'You know, they do say,' said Phil, still studying the screen, 'that those who are most violently opposed to something are the ones who secretly wish they could do it.'

It took a few seconds for Khan to realise what he had said. The laughter of fellow officers told him. He turned to face Phil, anger on his face.

Phil stared at him. Khan backed down, reluctantly returned to looking at the pictures.

'Are there any more?' asked Phil.

'A few,' said Elli. 'Things take an interesting turn next. Those were just the warm-up shots. Hope you've got strong stomachs . . .'

The setting for the photos changed. The backgrounds became stark, more industrial. Dungeon-like. Amanda was now dressed in bondage gear. Apart from one obvious physical characteristic, Phil noticed, she was looking more feminine than ever. There seemed to be no trace of Glenn McGowan whatsoever. From the positions she was in and what was being done to her, she was totally submissive.

The first few pictures showed some fairly innocuous mild S&M activity as Amanda was tied up, spanked.

'*Fifty Shades of Grey*'s got a lot to answer for,' said Sperring.

The images soon intensified. Amanda – apparently willingly – was depicted undergoing torture. Nipples and upper body first, then legs. Then they became worse, when they reached her anus.

'Oh Jesus,' said Sperring, turning away. 'Broken bottles? How can he . . . ? Jesus . . .'

Phil felt like joining him, but forced himself to keep watching. He soon wished he hadn't. Amanda's penis was shown being tortured in varying degrees of pain. Nettles first, then barbed wire, then even razor blades.

'I think we've seen enough,' said Cotter. 'Turn it off, Elli.'

She did so. They all turned away from the screen. No one spoke.

'Thoughts?' asked Cotter.

'He must have really come to hate himself,' said Phil. 'Or at least hated the male part of him.'

'I think that was quite evident from those last few photos,' said Cotter.

'Like he was daring himself to cut his own penis off,' said Phil.

'Please,' said Sperring, disgust in his voice. 'Do you have to?'

'You think these are bad,' said Elli, grimacing, 'wait till you see the DVDs.'

21

Marina was speechless. So many emotions rushed around inside her. She felt numb.

'No . . . ' she managed to say, 'no, I'm not.'

Again that smug smile. 'Oh, I think you are.'

Marina made to stand up. Her legs wouldn't support her. She slumped back down in her seat. 'I'm not . . . not going to do anything. I can't even remember what happened.'

'You were well out of it.'

'So you took advantage of me.' Her voice hardened, anger behind it.

'Hardly. I couldn't stop you. What winks and fucks like a tiger?'

She looked directly at him, confused. 'What?'

He repeated the question.

'I . . . don't know.'

He winked at her. Then laughed. Marina felt her face reddening. Burning, in fact.

'That's what you said to me last night. In the taxi. Then your hands were all over me. So I hardly took advantage of you. In fact it took nearly all of my strength to hold you off until we got back to mine.'

Marina sat there, stunned. 'I don't believe you. You're lying.'

He sat back. 'I thought you'd say that. So I brought along a little bit of proof.' He reached into his jacket pocket, took something out, laid it on the table between them.

With horror, she realised it was a pair of her panties. The ones she had worn last night. She quickly grabbed them, stuffed them into her bag.

The waitress chose that moment to arrive with their food and drinks. Marina knew she was being scrutinised and felt doubly ashamed and embarrassed.

'You said I could keep them,' Gwilym said with a blithe wave of his hand as the waitress set down plates, 'but I'm not into all that. Trophies and stuff.'

The waitress hurried away, her expression saying she couldn't wait to tell her colleagues about what she had just seen. Gwilym looked at Marina's plate. 'Tuck in.'

She sat staring into nothingness while he ate and drank heartily.

'Oh, meant to say,' Gwilym said between mouthfuls, 'thanks for the conversation about my book last night. Really appreciate your comments.'

Marina said nothing.

'That was something else I wanted to talk to you about. As one professional to another. You've taken a contrary stance to me on my theories, obviously; you made that clear last night. But I meant what I said. I really do want to talk to you about your ... experiences. What you've been through, the things you've faced. I think we could have a lot in common.'

'Really.'

'Yeah.' He began gesturing, warming to his theme now, his food forgotten. 'I mean, some of the things I discovered when I was researching the new book you would not believe. The lengths people will go to. You remember what I said last night? About voluntary euthanasia?' He didn't wait for her to reply. 'You wouldn't believe some of the stuff I've turned up.'

'Wouldn't I.' Marina just wanted to get up and leave. But she couldn't bring herself to do it. She felt that if she did, something even worse would come out of Gwilym's mouth.

'Doubt it. Even you, chasing your serial killers and the like. There's almost a cult of death out there. People wanting to die, encouraging their own death, wanting to participate willingly in it. They go looking for their murderers, invite them in to their lives. Invite them to kill them.' He laughed. 'Isn't that incredible? And of course that throws up the most fantastic moral dilemmas. Is it really murder? Or only assisted suicide?' He shook his head. 'I'm sure you would be interested in that.'

Yes, she thought, *I would be interested in that. If you hadn't just told me I'd slept with you and not remembered it*. She said nothing.

'We'll talk about it at length.' He wiped his mouth with his napkin, reached a hand across the table for hers. She recoiled from his touch. He smiled, like it was all part of a game. 'We will.'

'No,' said Marina, finding her voice. 'We won't.'

'We will.' His voice quiet but insistent.

She managed to stand up. Her coffee cup wobbled in its saucer, spilling undrunk coffee over the table. 'We won't. Because this is the last time I'm going to talk to you.'

'I don't think so.'

She grabbed her bag, fumbled, dropped it. Bent down to pick it up.

'Sit down.'

'No. I'm going.'

'Sit down.' His voice was stronger this time, more authoritative. She looked at him. His green eyes were shot through with a hard, steely cast. There was power behind them. Power that could inspire fear.

She sat down.

'That's better. We are going to see each other again. Because I want you to help me with my work. And also . . . ' His hand snaked across the table once more. It found the back of hers, began stroking. Too tired to fight, she made no attempt to remove it this time. He gave a victorious smile. 'Also, I want to get to know you better. Much better . . . '

'There you are. I . . . I knew you'd be here.'

Gwilym quickly withdrew his hand. Marina, startled as if out of a trance by the voice, looked up. A woman stood there, early twenties. She would have been pretty if her face wasn't red and puffy from crying and her hair had been washed. She looked distraught, teetering on the brink of a breakdown. She was holding one bandaged wrist with her other hand.

Gwilym spoke. 'Maddy. What are you doing here?' He looked at Marina. 'One of my students.'

'I'm . . . I'm . . . ' She looked between Gwilym and Marina, obviously wanting to say something but not wanting to do so in front of a stranger.

'It's all right,' said Gwilym, indicating Marina. 'She's a friend.'

Maddy, clearly distressed, nodded. 'I'm . . . *bleeding* . . . still . . . '

A look of concern came over Gwilym's face. 'Oh dear. Are you . . . are you OK?'

She shook her head, hand to her face, attempting to stop the next bout of tears.

He stood up. 'I think I'd . . . ' He gestured to Maddy, looked at Marina. His voice dropped. 'She's been in a bad way. She needs . . . a lot of help.' A lascivious smile crept on to his features. 'I'll call you.'

'No,' said Marina. 'You won't.'

He moved in close to her, angled his body away from Maddy so she couldn't see his face, hear his words. They were for Marina alone. 'I will. And you'll answer. And you'll come and see me when I call. Because if not . . . '

'What?'

'Well, I doubt that your PC Plod hubby would want the world to know what a little slut wifey is . . . '

He turned back to Maddy, a kind, solicitous expression in place once more.

Marina turned and almost ran from the café.

22

'DVDs?' asked Phil. He spoke with all the enthusiasm of a man contemplating root canal work. 'Do we have to?'

'I've had to suffer, I don't see why the rest of you shouldn't,' said Elli.

'Are they . . . are they like that?' Sperring could barely look at the screen.

'I just looked at a few of them,' she said. 'Pretty similar.'

'We'd better go through them,' said DCI Cotter. 'Or someone should. Let's work this in shifts.'

'I think we should pay a visit to Glenn McGowan's wife,' said Phil. He was aware of Sperring's instant, and not at all pleasant, attention. He turned to him. 'Coming with me?'

'D'you need to do that now?' asked Cotter.

'The photos show pretty conclusively that Glenn McGowan's our victim. We'll have to get his wife to do a formal identification. But I'd also like to have a talk with her first. See if she can throw some light on their relationship, what led to him leaving home, setting up here. See if there's anything she can tell us.'

'Right. We'll get a car to bring her in.'

'I think it might be better if Ian and I go,' said Phil. 'Talk to her where she feels comfortable, before the circus starts up around her.'

Cotter nodded. 'Good idea. Off you go. I'll get a family liaison officer down there first. Prepare the way for you.'

'Appreciate it. Thanks.' He turned to DC Khan. 'Nadish, can you get started on the DVDs? Thanks.' Then back to Sperring. 'Come on.'

Sperring followed Phil out. Khan staring after them, looking less than happy.

'Thought you were just trying to get out of looking at the DVDs,' said Sperring as Phil drove down the M6, Warren Zevon issuing lightly from the speakers, singing about how *life'll kill ya*, following the sat nav to the address they had been given for Julie McGowan.

'Yeah,' said Phil, 'doing a death message. Always the easy option.'

'Wonder if they shared frocks?' Sperring laughed as he spoke. 'Maybe he looked better in them than she did. That's why she threw him out.' More laughter.

Phil didn't reply. Sperring stared at him, then turned away, gazing out of the window, lips curled like he had something bitter in his mouth.

'Look, Ian,' said Phil, not taking his eyes off the road, 'I know you have a problem with me. D'you want to get it aired, here and now, when there's just the two of us? Just so we can get on with things.'

Sperring said nothing.

'So what's the problem?'

Sperring gnawed his lower lip, deciding whether to answer or not. And if so, how much truth to put behind it. Phil kept at it.

'You don't like having me as a boss, do you?'

'You want me to be honest, sir? No. I don't.'

'Right. Any particular reason? Something I've done?'

More lip-chewing, then, 'You shouldn't have been brought in in the first place. A spare DI position should have been filled from within the team.'

'And you think you should have got it?'

'Why not? I've put in the years, I've given good service. I put in for it but they gave it to you.'

'And that's why you don't like me.'

'One of the reasons, yeah.'

Phil found he was gripping the wheel tighter than he needed to. He also noticed his speed was creeping up. 'Any others?'

'We don't trust you.'

'*We?*'

'The lads in the team. You're . . . not like one of us.'

'You mean I'm not some unimaginative *Daily Mail*-reading, misogynistic, homophobic twat?'

Sperring didn't answer.

'Well get this straight, Ian. We might not see eye to eye on things. You might not like me. You might think I'm a *Guardian*-reading liberal. I don't care. But we're on the same team. *My* team. And we've got to work together. Understand?'

Sperring tried to shrug. 'Sure. Whatever.'

'No. Not whatever. It means we put aside what we might think of each other. It means you don't piss about or rock the boat or try to undermine what I say or the way I do things. It means you're either on my team or you're not. Got that?'

Sperring gave a mock salute. 'Yes, sir.'

'Good.' Phil realised that was the best he could hope for from his DS. Not for the first time or, he imagined, the last, he wished he had his old team back with him.

They drove the rest of the way without speaking, Warren Zevon the only thing to puncture the silence.

113

23

The Firebird. Stravinsky. It was playing in the Arcadian's head. Soon it was playing in his living area, too. As loud as he dared, balancing attracting attention to himself with outwardly expressing the joy his soul was experiencing.

And the joy was for one reason only. He had his next victim all lined up.

The voice had spoken and he had listened. Guided him and he had followed. Or he would follow. Soon. He was preparing. Getting his tools ready. Deciding on his approach.

That had been the most thrilling thing so far. The anticipation. The preparation.

This one was going to be different from the last. Very different. Far away from the other one, both psychologically and geographically. When he'd realised that, his soul sank with disappointment. He almost called it off. But he didn't. And the more he thought about it, the gladder he was that he hadn't done so. Because the more he allowed the plan to percolate through his consciousness, coalesce inside his head, the more he grasped how he could make it work.

The trick, he thought, would be to find enjoyment in it even though it wasn't what he would have done given the choice. To find satisfaction while doing a thorough job, but –

and this, he felt, was the important thing – to show he could be professional too. Yes. That was it. That was what he would do.

He had read interviews with film directors saying the same thing. They would do one personal project, one for the studio. One personal, one for the studio. Alternate, like that. That was what he would do. The doll was his personal project; this one would be his in-house studio job. He would bring the same degree of care and attention to it, of planning and preparation, of execution.

He smiled at the unintentional pun. No, maybe it had been intentional. He smiled some more at his own cleverness.

He would use this as a calling card. To let them know he was serious. That he could turn his hand to whatever was required. Because it was all very well doing what he had done with the doll. But that was all passion, desire. With this one he had to show detachment. There would be no time to savour his handiwork like last time. It would be a quick in-and-out job. He had wondered whether he was up for that and had actually hesitated in considering whether to do it.

But he had decided yes. Yes. Definitely yes.

It was to be a man this time. Nothing special about him, not like last time. Something else for him to be disappointed at. But after thinking it through, he had soon overcome the disappointment.

'Gives it a . . . degree of symmetry,' he had said, and he was pleased with that response. Showed he wasn't biased, sexist. The phrasing showed his erudition, too. Never a bad thing.

And there was something else. Something practical to consider. This wouldn't link him to the doll's death. Apart from the end result, there would be no similarities. By not sticking to the serial killer's usual signature, he would run rings round the police. How brilliant.

The Arcadian felt a delicious shivery thrill run through his body. He smiled once more, checked his tools. Heard the music both inside and outside his head.

The Firebird. It wasn't just a piece of music to him. No. It was more than that. He knew all about it. Hadn't just listened to it, but had researched it as well. He remembered a music teacher at one of the schools he had briefly attended telling the class that music was understood through intelligence. The rest of the class had ignored him, went on listening to whatever pop shit was in the charts that week. But the Arcadian had listened. Started listening to classical music. Going to the library, getting out CDs. Then getting out books to go with them, ones talking about the composers' lives. Reading them while listening. Trying to understand what made them come up with the music they did in the way they did. He didn't always get it, didn't always understand. In fact, if he was honest, he hardly understood at all. And that made him angry. That made him think he wasn't intelligent, that he wouldn't be able to appreciate the music, that he was just like the rest of them. So he persevered. Kept on listening, kept on reading. Made himself understand, made himself enjoy it.

And now he loved it. He knew everything about it. Everything. Even the Polonsky poem *The Firebird* was based on.

'And in my dreams I see myself on a wolf's back,' he recited aloud, 'Riding along a forest path/To do battle with Kaschei.' He smiled, into the music, the moment. 'In that land where a princess sits under lock and key/Pining behind massive walls./There gardens surround a palace all of glass;/There Firebirds sing by night/And peck at golden fruit . . . '

He spread his arms wide at the final few lines, as if expecting applause. But only the single doll in the doll's house looked back at him.

116

Kaschei. The Immortal. The Deathless. He could only be killed one way. By capturing his soul. And that was well hidden. In a needle which was in an egg which was in a duck which was in a hare which was in an iron chest which was buried under an oak tree on the island of Buyan. If the chest were to be dug up, the hare would run away. If it was caught, the duck would escape from it and fly away. If the duck was caught, though, Kaschei was in trouble. Because then they could crack the egg and take out the needle. And if that was broken, he would die.

He looked at his doll's house. His doll, sitting there looking perfectly happy. He thought of the butterfly. Smiled.

'We don't need to go to all that trouble, do we?' he said to the doll.

She stared at him, smiling. Unblinking.

'You're getting some company soon,' he said. 'A gentleman friend. Would you like that?'

The doll kept smiling.

He looked at her sitting all alone. Although she had him for company, it couldn't be much fun. All those empty chairs in empty rooms. He felt the overwhelming urge to provide her with company, to fill the house with other dolls.

He checked his tools once more.

'And I will,' he said aloud. 'Soon.'

24

The house was small, boxy, in a curling crescent of other small, boxy houses. It looked like a place where if dreams didn't necessarily die, they were comprehensively contained.

'So, er, you didn't have any, any idea he was, you know, your husband, dressing up in, like, women's clothing?' Sperring was leading the questioning. Phil wanted to show there were no hard feelings. But Sperring was uncomfortable and he was letting it show. Phil took a sliver of unprofessional satisfaction from that.

The woman sitting opposite them looked like she was in shock. Eyes wide and staring, red-rimmed from the ghosts of tears. Face so pale it could have been bleached. Expression blank, like she had suffered so much pain it had left her numb. Phil recognised her reactions; he had given the death message to relatives before. But that didn't mean it ever got any easier.

Kimberley Penman, the family liaison officer, sat on the other armchair in the room. She had broken the news to Julie McGowan before they had arrived. It had gone down as well as could be expected. Which wasn't well at all.

Julie McGowan managed to make eye contact with both of them for a few brief seconds, then looked away. 'I don't ... It's like ... I'm being punished. I just ... just don't understand ...'

Sperring sat back, looking physically exhausted. He gave Phil the nod. Phil leaned forward, voice low, eyes solicitous. 'We know this is a difficult time for you, Mrs McGowan, Julie, but if there's anything you can tell us, anything at all that might give us some clue as to why your husband ... that might have contributed to your husband's state of mind, please tell us.'

Julie McGowan looked like she was about to burst into tears once more, but she stopped herself, shook her head. Her hands unconsciously twisted a paper tissue into fluttery, powdery pieces. 'He never told me,' she said. 'That he used to like dressing up. And then ...' she sighed, 'I found out. Came home early, caught him doing it.' Another sigh. 'Almost a cliché, isn't it?'

'But you stayed with him,' said Phil, keeping eye contact, 'didn't you, Julie? You stayed with him. Tried to work it out.'

She nodded. 'For the kids. I started thinking it was my fault. I was doing something wrong, failing in some way, that it was my fault, I was being punished ...' Another sigh that threatened to turn into a sob. She controlled herself. 'But then I realised no, it wasn't me. It was him. And I tried to understand, to let him go out to his ... things. Clubs and that. I tried.'

'Did you think he was gay, was that it?' Sperring chipped in. Phil stared at him.

'I ... I hoped not. But ... I don't know. He said that when he was Amanda – that was his name for, for that – when he was Amanda, he thought like a woman. Felt like a woman. So ...' Another sigh.

She fell into silence. Phil glanced round. The house looked ordinary. Stiflingly so. Department store furniture and decoration, nothing out of the ordinary, nothing too different. At least on the surface. But he knew, after years of doing this, that there was no such thing as normal. The fact that he was here was testament to that.

'Your husband moved out,' he said. 'When was that?'

'About . . . I don't know. A year? Something like that? A year ago.' She put her head back, thought. 'Yes. Just after Christmas last year. This would have been the kids' second Christmas without him . . .'

A sob threatened to choke her up. Phil kept questioning, keeping her focused.

'Where did he go, d'you know?'

'He . . . he rented a flat.'

'Here? In Coventry?'

She nodded. The tissue came in for more punishment.

Sperring leaned forward. 'So why did he move to Birmingham?'

She looked straight at him. 'I don't know. We weren't . . . He didn't tell me everything.' She sighed. 'He was slipping away by then. I'd almost lost him.' Another sigh. Another twist of the tissue. 'I've sent the kids to my mother's,' she continued. 'God knows what's going to happen to them when they go back to school, what the other kids'll say . . .'

'Kids can be cruel, Julie,' said Phil, 'but they're resilient. Keep that in mind.'

She nodded. The paper tissue disintegrated further.

'Was there anyone he mentioned, any name that sticks out?' Phil asked.

She said nothing, lost in her own world.

'Someone in Birmingham he might have moved to be nearer to?'

She looked up. 'There was that university thing he was doing.'

Sperring and Phil exchanged a glance. 'What university thing?' asked Phil.

'A book that some professor was doing. He wanted to speak to . . . ' she gestured, throwing the tissue around, 'you know. People like Glenn. Ones that were . . . '

'Transvestites?' asked Sperring.

She nodded. 'That. And others. Ones that . . . weren't right. Deviant psychopathology, Glenn said.' She gave a bitter laugh. 'Said it was going to make him famous.'

Phil frowned. 'How come?'

'Because it was that . . . him. That professor from the telly. The handsome one. Always got plenty to say. You know the one.'

'From Birmingham?' asked Sperring.

Julie nodded.

'Hugo Gwilym?' said Sperring.

'That's him,' she said.

'And he was interviewing Glenn for a book? What kind of book? Case studies?'

'You'd have to ask him that.'

Phil made a note. 'We will.' He frowned once more, leaned further forward. 'Would there have been anyone else he might have moved for? To be closer to? It seems quite drastic to go all that way just to be in a book.'

'There . . . ' More tissue abuse. 'I didn't . . . didn't want him to talk about it. Didn't want to know. There might have been.' Grief and revulsion were fighting for prominence on her features.

'Can you tell us who? Give us a name, even?'

Julie sighed, steeling herself to revisit unpleasant memories. 'I found him on a website one night, a website for . . . for people like him. He was talking to men. Other men like himself, but also men who . . . who liked that kind of thing. Who met transvestites for sex.'

'Any names?' asked Sperring.

121

She shook her head. 'I . . . No, I . . . ' She looked up. 'One. Yes. Ben, I think he called him. Ben. Yes.'

Phil had his notebook out. 'Ben? Last name?'

Julie almost laughed. 'This is the internet. Lucky to get a first name. And even then it might not be a real one.'

'We've got his laptop,' said Phil. 'Would we be able to find this Ben through the website?'

She nodded. 'He never used a password. Always kept it open. Like he wanted me to find it. Like he was doing wrong but was too weak to stop. Like he wanted to be punished because of it.'

'And he met this Ben, did he?'

'A few times. It was one of the main reasons I asked him to leave. Not just because of what he was doing to me and the kids, or the fact that I couldn't get my head round it, but what he was bringing back into the house. What he was picking up from these . . . people.'

'D'you know if it was just the one?' asked Sperring. 'Were there any others?'

'There were others. But Ben was the main one. Apparently they always met in a bar on Hurst Street in Birmingham. Or a club, some club he went to round there.' She paused. Looked down at the tissue. 'Was . . . was it . . . D'you think it was this Ben who killed him? He was murdered, wasn't he?'

'He was,' said Phil.

'How . . . Did he suffer?' Her voice sounded like it had been dropped from a great height.

'He . . . ' Phil didn't know what to say.

'He went peacefully,' said Sperring. 'I don't think he suffered.'

'Thank you.' Julie McGowan nodded.

Phil looked at Sperring, surprised by his tact. The DS didn't make eye contact.

They stood up. The FLO did likewise.

'This is . . . I'm sorry,' said Phil, 'but could we ask you to come and make an identification of the body? As next of kin it should be you, I'm afraid.'

She nodded without speaking.

'Thank you. Kim's your family liaison officer. Would you like her to come along?'

'If you like,' Julie said, looking up. 'But to be honest, I lost my husband ages ago. This is just . . . confirming he won't be back.' The tissue was no more.

They left the house in darkness.

25

The door was locked, bolted. The curtains drawn, the blinds closed. Marina wanted to keep the outside world as far away as possible. Just her, in the house, alone with her thoughts. Her fears.

And what fears. She had gone straight home without picking up Josephina from Eileen. Let her grandmother enjoy her company for a little longer. She had been shaking so much she could hardly drive, her hands barely able to grip the wheel. The car had wandered into the wrong lane on the Belgrave Middleway, and only the angry horns of fellow drivers pulled back her concentration. And all the while Gwilym's words rang round her head.

I want to get to know you better. Much better ...

I doubt that your PC Plod hubby would want the world to know what a little slut wifey is ...

I brought along a little bit of proof ...

She felt inside her jacket pocket. Her panties were still there. The touch of them triggered off something inside her and she ran into the bathroom, retching. She bent over the washbasin for what seemed like ages. Even though her body was empty, her stomach still kept spasming, trying to expel every bit of unpleasantness, vileness from her.

Eventually it stopped and she looked up, gasping, at her face in the mirror. She didn't recognise the scared, tousle-haired, mad-eyed woman staring back at her. She looked like she had aged a decade since leaving the house that morning.

She splashed on cold water, towelled herself dry. Kept her face in the warm, soft fabric for as long as she could before reluctantly taking it away. She stared into the mirror. The water hadn't improved her features. She still looked the same.

She threw down the towel, went into the bedroom. With the doors secured tight and the blinds and curtains closed, she lay down on the bed, curled into a foetal ball, tried to block out everything else and think. Let her training kick in, not give in to her emotions. Easier said than done. She closed her eyes. Breathed deeply.

Last night. The dinner. Sitting round the table, making polite conversation. She was still finding her feet with her new colleagues, sussing out who was an ally, who an enemy, who could be trusted, who couldn't, who could be cultivated into a friend . . . then Hugo Gwilym had arrived.

She tried to focus, concentrate harder. Relive every part of the conversation, every gesture. Try to work out just how much alcohol she had drunk.

Answer: not much. Two glasses of red. That was it. Or as near to that as she could remember. Maybe her glass had been topped up by the serving staff and she hadn't noticed, but it wouldn't have been much more than that. Apart from Hugo, she thought with a shudder. He had been intent on filling her glass. But she hadn't let him. Not too much. She had been determined not to get drunk. She was still on her best behaviour, didn't want to embarrass herself in front of her colleagues. Didn't want them forming a negative impression of her.

Her colleagues. Maybe one of them could shed some light on what had happened.

She took her phone from her bag, scrolled through the contacts until she found the right one. Joy Henry. The departmental administrator. She had been sitting on Marina's other side for most of the evening. She would be able to help. Marina dialled the number. It was picked up.

'Joy? Hi. Marina.'

She was answered by a groan. 'Oh God . . . what time is it?'

'It's . . . afternoon, I don't know. Are you OK?'

'Didn't make it in to work today. Feel rotten.'

'Right.' Marina paused, unsure of how to continue. Joy took the choice away from her.

'You enjoyed yourself last night.'

The words caused Marina's stomach to turn over once more. 'Did . . . did I?'

'Can't you remember? No, neither can I much. Except . . .'

Marina steeled herself, fearing the worst. Joy's voice dropped low.

'You know that PhD student? Guy, the cute one?'

Marina knew him. And of Joy's attraction to him.

'Well,' Joy said, her voice now a whisper, 'he's still here. Didn't go home last night.'

'Oh. Good.'

'Promise not to tell?'

'What? Yeah. Promise. Course.'

'Good. Knew I could rely on you. What happens at the Christmas party stays at the Christmas party, doesn't it?'

Another shiver ran through Marina. 'What, what d'you mean?'

'Just what I said. I can keep a secret if you can.'

'Do you . . . do you have a secret to keep about me?'

Joy laughed. 'Well, you seemed to be getting very friendly with Hugo . . .'

Marina's stomach flipped once more. She felt like she was going to be sick again. 'We were just . . . talking. Arguing, mainly.'

'That's how it starts, isn't it? Insults. Means you really like each other. But don't worry. I won't tell.'

Marina wished she hadn't made the call. 'Joy, when I left, did I seem . . . I don't know, exceptionally drunk to you?'

'No idea. When did you leave?'

I can't remember. She wanted to say that but, realising how bad it sounded, stopped herself. 'I . . . didn't check the time.'

'Well I didn't see you go. I might have left before you. I was a bit drunk and a bit preoccupied with . . .' her voice dropped again, 'you know who.'

'Right.' Marina sighed. It felt like a dying breath. There was a pause.

'Have you got some gossip, then?' asked Joy. 'You and Hugo?'

Marina didn't know what to say, how to answer. 'Let's . . . let's speak soon,' she said. 'Enjoy . . . enjoy yourself.' She hung up.

She threw the phone on the bed, flung herself down next to it.

She felt like she knew less than before she had made the phone call. She couldn't call anyone else without her actions seeming suspicious. And Joy had had no idea. Though she probably did now.

Marina felt she had made the situation worse.

Tears began to well behind her eyes. Of anger, of frustration, of self-pity.

She thought once again of the previous night. Came up with a blank.

127

Had she willingly had sex with another man? Really? The recent trauma that she and Phil had been through had necessitated a move away. Could it have also triggered something in her subconscious? Led to behaviour like that, behaviour she couldn't remember?

She had to find out what had happened, what she had done. What had been done to her. Had to. Even if the answer wasn't the one she wanted to hear.

She lay on the bed, curled into a foetal ball, riding out the waves of tears, wondering what to do next.

Feeling so alone. So horribly, guiltily, achingly alone.

26

Maddy should have been feeling better. She had met him, confronted him, talked to him. But the feeling of joy, or at least euphoric release, she had expected from hearing him say the right thing, tell her that everything was going to be OK hadn't happened. She didn't feel any different. If anything, she felt even more anxious.

They had left the café, walked up to the Bullring, where his car was parked. She had wanted to come back to her room, bring him with her, talk in private, but he hadn't allowed it.

'I don't think that would be a good idea,' he had said, driving away from the city centre, his hand on her thigh. 'Not straight away. You might feel a little . . . depressed there.'

She had wanted to argue with him, tell him that she felt depressed everywhere, but if there was somewhere she felt even a little bit comfortable and safe it was in her room. She had wanted to explain that if they talked there, she could draw strength from being with her own things, that she wouldn't feel bullied into saying or doing something she didn't want to. She tried to say all that but felt too weak, too exhausted to make her points clearly. 'It's OK,' she had said finally, too tired to explain further, 'the others won't mind you being there.'

'It's not that,' he had replied, voice all warm and solicitous, like he was looking out for her best interests, 'Really, it isn't. It's just you I'm thinking about. What's best for you. How I can best help you. Do the right thing.'

He had paused while his words washed over her, and she had drawn what strength she could from them.

'They know then, do they? The rest of your house? They know about us?' His hand was gone from her thigh. His voice no longer held its previous warmth.

She shook her head. 'No,' she said, 'they don't. Or if they do, I haven't told them.'

'And they know about ... what's happened to you? What you've done.'

Her stomach flipped at the words. *What I've done. What I've done ...*

Another shake of her head. 'I didn't tell anyone. Honestly. You told me not to. You told me I should only talk to you. And I did.'

This seemed to calm him somewhat. He smiled at her, replaced his hand. Squeezed. 'Then don't worry. It'll all be fine.'

'Who was she?' asked Maddy.

He turned to her, his eyes narrow, unpleasant. 'What d'you mean?'

'The woman you were with. Who was she?'

'Didn't you recognise her? She's another lecturer. A work colleague. Why?'

'Because you were looking at her like you used to look at me.'

'What?' He laughed. Maddy didn't. 'Bollocks. I work with her. That's all. And besides ... ' he squeezed her thigh again, 'why would I want her when I've got you?'

She saw the look in his eyes and knew she couldn't argue

any more. She tuned out again, thinking about his eyes, his words, trying to order her thoughts, her emotions. They drove the rest of the way in silence. When she looked up again, the car was coming to a halt in front of his house. She had been there before, plenty of times. She had been so impressed the first time she had walked in. An old house but with modern designer furniture. Sofas and chairs and cabinets and lighting all looking like they had come from the best catalogues. Shelves full of books. The kind of place a person the BBC did serious cultural documentaries about would live in. 'Who lives in a house like this?' she had said to herself the first time, in that irritating voice belonging to the host of a quiz show that used to be on when she was little. 'Someone with intelligence and culture and taste and money,' she had replied. And she had congratulated herself for being there with him.

But the sheen had gone now. The furniture was out of date by a few years and looked it, the sofas worn and stained, the cabinets chipped, the lighting mottled and dull-looking. Even the books no longer represented the thrilling collection of knowledge she had first thought. Now they just looked old and stuffy, dust-coated and never touched. Just there for show. *To impress people like me*, Maddy thought. The air was still, both oppressive and depressing. It felt like nothing happened here.

Or nothing good, anyway.

'Make yourself at home,' he said, taking off his jacket and throwing it over the back of a chair. She sat down on the sofa. He came and joined her, passed her a glass. She looked at it. Dark amber liquid swirled. It smelt faintly medicinal.

'What's this?' she asked.

'Drink it. Do you good.'

She sniffed it. Grimaced.

'Down in one,' he said, sitting next to her, eyes on hers, waiting for her next movement.

She looked from him back to the glass, put it to her lips, sipped.

'Down in one,' he repeated, voice slightly harder now. 'You'll feel the benefit that way. I promise you.' His voice softer that time.

She looked to the glass, back to him. Unsure and clearly not wanting to do it, but also unwilling to disappoint him, even after everything that had happened between them. She tipped her head back, put the glass to her lips, closed her eyes. Gulped down as much as she could.

Immediately she was coughing, gagging. It not only looked medicinal but tasted it too. And it burned, really, really burned. She felt it stripping away her insides. Like she had put the stuff she used on her legs and bikini line inside her body.

'Good girl,' he said, and took the glass from her. Immediately it was replenished. 'Here, have another one.'

She shook her head, hand still at her throat. 'No . . . '

'Go on,' he said, filling it even higher this time. 'It'll help. With the pain. Make you feel better. It will. Trust me.'

He handed it to her. She took it. Again she didn't want to drink it; again she felt that she had to. She closed her eyes once more, tipped her head back, poured it down.

She coughed, but not as much. It burned, but a little less.

'That's it,' he said, 'you're getting used to it. See? It's good for you. It helps. Sometimes things that seem unpleasant at first, well, you just have to persevere, don't you?' He put his hand on her thigh. 'We'll get there in the end.'

She lay back against the sofa. The room was spinning now, pitching rapidly and swirling. She felt the same way she had when she had smoked a joint. Hot and nauseous. She had hated that feeling, never touched it again. This was the same.

'Not used to drinking?' he asked.

'Not ... not like this,' she said. 'Just wine, usually.' She frowned. 'What ... what is it?'

'Just a little cocktail of my own invention,' he said. 'You'll get used to it.'

She nodded. Or at least she thought she had nodded.

'Now,' he said, voice once again warm and solicitous, hand still on her thigh, 'how are you feeling?'

The conflicting emotions seemed to be dropping away inside her mind. Things seemed to be easier. 'Good,' she said.

'Glad to hear it,' he replied, and moved in close to her.

She put her head limply on his shoulder, snuggled into him. All the things she had wanted to say to him were dropping away. She smelt his cologne. She loved the smell of his cologne. She felt his arm around her. She loved his arm around her.

'You're still bleeding?' she heard him say.

She nodded. It seemed like the right answer.

'That's only to be expected,' he said. 'It'll soon pass. And then ... ' he pulled her even closer, 'you'll be good as new.'

She nodded. Yes. That made sense. *Good as new*. She closed her eyes.

She felt – or thought she felt – his arm tighten its grip on her. She felt – or thought she felt – his hand moving up her thigh. Part of her wanted to tell him to stop, that she had come to talk to him, that she had important things that needed to be said. That she had to get up, go. But the other part of her, the part that was affected by what he had given her to drink, just wanted to relax. To feel the comfort of his embrace.

'It's all right,' he was telling her. It sounded like his voice was coming from the end of a long, dark tunnel. 'You did the right thing. And everything's going to be OK ... '

She felt his hands on her again. Her lips curled. She didn't know if it was a smile or a grimace.

And then she felt nothing.

133

27

Keith Burkiss was alone in the house. He couldn't describe – even to himself – how he was feeling.

This was the end. He knew it. And he drew strength from that, power, to a certain extent. Or as much power as he could muster under the circumstances. He might not be able to live, he thought, feeling the pain in his chest and looking down at where his legs used to be, but he could certainly control how to die.

Money doesn't matter, his old man used to say, *as long as you've got your health*. Keith had always thought his old man was soft in the head to choose that as his personal mantra, a snivelling excuse for not working harder and being more successful. And his old man had died young when that other car had smashed into his. So what did he know?

After he died, his mother started saying it too, as if chanting the words could bring him back to life. It didn't. He stayed dead. But it gave Keith something to think about. Something to modify into his own mantra: *Money buys you everything*.

He looked down at his legs once more. Felt a tide of bitterness rising within him. Hoped it wouldn't trigger another coughing fit. It didn't. He just about managed to stave it off.

Cancer and diabetes. A hell of a double whammy. And his

doctor, the expensive fucker who was supposed to stop this kind of thing from happening, said it was his own fault. Smoking to excess. Drinking heavily. Eating a horrendously self-indulgent diet and taking no exercise whatsoever. Keith had complained. Said he didn't do anything different to other men, friends of his that he did business with and went drinking with. The doctor had shrugged. Genetics still played a large part. And ignoring the advice of all his regular health check-ups over the years. That just made Keith angry. But since he couldn't blame himself, he took it out on the doctor. And the doctor just struck him off his books, private patient or no private patient. Keith's first thought had been to try and find another one. But he didn't get round to it. He came to a decision instead. If this was the way he was, then this was the way he was. There was no point in changing things; just bring it on.

And he had done.

He wheeled himself over to the window, looked out. The house was huge, Edgbaston opulent. Set well back from the road in its own grounds. He had been proud of that when he first moved in, pleased he had made something of himself, his life. Now it just felt like a huge private prison. Luxurious, but still a prison.

He listened. Nothing. Good. Kelly was out. He had told her to go. She had looked at him suspiciously, narrowing her eyes when he told her he didn't mind if she went into town to meet friends. They both knew what they were really talking about. What kind of friends she was going off to meet. She made some attempt at pretending to care for him, not wanting to leave him on his own, but he just waved her off. He couldn't bear to hear any more of her lies. Eventually, not believing her luck, she thanked him and got ready. Left the house.

Left him alone once more.

She was his second wife and he used to love her. Totally, unconditionally. Like life itself. Now he couldn't believe how stupid he had been, how naïve. She was just his trophy, his midlife crisis made real. A nightclub pick-up elevated to mistress to wife. Nothing more. Not the love of his life. Just something he was supposed to have when he reached a certain age and a certain status, like the Bentley and the house. Something to show off with. Something that said he had made it. She knew that. Had known it straight away. Unfortunately, Keith had only recently realised.

The first time he met her she had looked stunning. Half his age at least, but he didn't care. He wanted her, had to have her. She was in the club with friends, all dressed to the nines, all in sex-predator mode. And she latched on to him. He had thought at first that she actually liked him. His looks, his jokes. He was even stupid enough to think he aroused her. But there was only one thing he had that did that. If he had been a long-distance lorry driver she wouldn't have given him a second glance. However, if he had been a long-distance lorry driver he wouldn't have been able to afford a private booth in the VIP section of the club for himself and his friends, and he wouldn't have been drinking champagne at three hundred pounds a bottle. There was the aphrodisiac.

She told him her backstory. A poor, underprivileged kid from Druid's Heath, using whatever talents she had to better herself. It struck a chord within him. He wanted to take her under his wing, protect her, love her, give this beautiful woman an equally beautiful life.

After that the story had been pretty straightforward. The old wife was divorced, given a fair amount of money to cover her bitterness, and the new wife moved in. She was a terrible cook and never cleaned the house, but he forgave her that. It wasn't why he had married her. She made him feel like a sex god in the bedroom, an enthusiasm he now knew was faked but which made him feel good about himself. And when he took her out, he knew all his friends were staring and wishing they had her. Keith got a huge kick out of that.

Then the health problems started. And Kelly wasn't quite so supportive any more. She began going out without him, seeing friends he'd never heard of. Spending more and more time away from him but still expecting him to pay for it. Eventually she left him, said she couldn't cope. And that was when he saw her for what she really was, and what an idiot he had been for her. The hurt curdled, the bitterness increased. She asked for a divorce. He gave her one. But made sure her settlement was next to nothing.

And when she realised she had got nothing, back she came, contrite and apologetic and ready to play happy families again. He had pretended to welcome her back. But he was wise to her now. He knew what she was doing. Help the crippled ex-husband, remarry him even, get the lot when he goes.

She did nothing to help him. She regarded him with barely disguised revulsion. He had watched her from his wheelchair, losing first one foot then the other, then his shins, then his knees as the diabetes took control of his body, then his lungs and liver as the cancer stepped up to stage four. He had seen how she behaved. The secret phone calls that she abruptly cut off if he was around. The unguarded looks she gave him when she thought he wasn't watching her. The trips out with 'the girls'. He knew what she was doing. He knew how much she hated him. How she was just waiting for him to die so she could take his money, his house and his cars, and install whoever she liked to replace him. And all the things Keith had spent his life toiling for, the life he had built for himself, would be given to someone else.

Well, he wouldn't allow that.

He had talked to his solicitor, got his will changed. She would receive nothing, but he told her she would get everything. And the stupid cow believed him. He had smiled at that, laughed even.

Blissful revenge.

He tried to think what he could do with the money, since he had no children, no natural heirs. At first he thought about giving it to charity, but that would just be a waste. Then he thought of doing nothing with it. Eventually he came up with the idea of giving it to the university, creating a professorship in his name. He knew that would seriously piss her off.

He just wished he could be there to see her face.

He turned away from the window. This was it. It was really happening. Now. Tonight. His last night on earth.

He still didn't know how he felt about it. Still hadn't decided. Part of him wanted to rage against the dying of the light, as he had read somewhere. The rest of him, or rather the little of him that was left, just wanted to let go. He was tired. He wasn't living. He was just dying slowly.

He pointed the remote, put the TV on. *The One Show*. The anodyne, unthreatening presenters were speaking politely to the studio guest, the crew behind the cameras laughing as if it was the funniest thing they had ever heard. He switched it off.

He didn't want his last memory to be of *The One Show*.

He felt he should write something, say something. Make some statement, share the truths he had discovered from his time alive. But he couldn't think of anything.

He wondered about God, the afterlife. He had never believed in it and thought it was a bit late to start now, but just in case, he closed his eyes, and, hedging his bets, tried to say a prayer. Nothing came.

So he just sat there. Waiting.

28

'Well, that was nice. So what have we got next, then?' DC Nadish Khan laughed as he took the DVD out of the tray, replaced it with another one. It didn't disguise his shaking hands.

The woman sitting next to him didn't respond. Her features were blank as she made notes in her pad.

'Dunno about you,' said Khan, 'but this isn't how I normally spend Friday evenings.'

She put her pen down, looked directly at him. Lips curled into a smile. 'You sure about that?'

Bitch, he thought, grabbing the remote and stabbing Play. He sat back to watch the next DVD, angry. Not just with himself but with his new boss. Brennan had given him this job deliberately. And that pissed him off big time.

Yes, it was deliberate. No doubt about it. He had seen the look on Brennan's face the previous night when he had made a couple of comments about gays. Nothing nasty, just the usual stuff. Banter. Sperring had laughed, but then he was a good bloke. Brennan, however, had made it clear that he didn't appreciate what he'd said or think it was funny. Still, thought Khan, he could have been going door-to-door down the gay bars on Hurst Street. Something else Brennan had threatened him with. So considering the alternative, sitting here watching filth might be getting off lightly. At least he wasn't out in the cold.

He looked at his fellow officer sitting on the chair next to him. *Cold enough in here with her*, he thought. Detective Constable Imani Oliver put down her pen, watched the screen.

Khan didn't like her. If he was honest, he didn't like black girls at all. Just a personal preference, he always said; their skins were too dark for him to fancy them. And their features not pretty enough. He liked something a bit lighter and finer. But even he had to admit Oliver had a well fit body. Cracking tits and a great arse. Face wasn't all that much, though, the usual wide nose and big lips, but he might forgive that, if he had to. I mean, who looked at the mantelpiece when you were stoking the fire?

Not that he thought he would ever get to shag her. Her arse and tits might be great; it was her personality that turned him off. Typical black girl. Uppity. Always plenty to say for herself. Not all of it complimentary. Certainly not to him. He used to answer her back when she started giving it lip but stopped after a while. He was sure she was the type to cry racial harassment. He knew, from experience, that her sort always did.

This was the third DVD and Khan was starting to get used to them. He checked himself – get used to them? Jesus. He hoped he would never find the kind of thing he was watching normal. Guys dressed as girls, *behaving* as girls, while other guys treated them as girls. It turned his stomach. And not only that, but some of them looked really convincing. Would make him think twice before picking someone up in Gatecrasher, that was sure. Well, maybe.

They were all of Glenn McGowan, dressed up, calling himself Amanda. And the first two were home-made. Or rather amateur, not professional. They had been filmed with a static

140

camera, pointed at the end of a bed. The victim himself had come into shot, walking round after switching the camera on, then lain down on the bed waiting for another transvestite to join him.

'Make-up looks a little inexpert,' Oliver had said. 'Same with the clothes. I reckon this is an early one, before he got the hang of it. What d'you think?'

Khan had agreed with her. Not just because he thought she was right – which he did – but because it saved him looking at the screen too much.

The sex had been perfunctory. Ordinary, even. Just two blokes getting it on, if you took away the clothes.

He had caught Oliver looking at him out of the corner of her eye, smiling.

'What?' he asked. 'Why you looking at me?'

'Just wondering,' she said, as if giving the matter some serious thought.

'Wondering what?'

'Well, you know how men like to watch two women together?'

Khan sensed a trap but knew he had to agree. 'Yeah . . . '

'I don't think this is much different.'

He sensed himself reddening. Suddenly the room felt hot. 'What d'you mean? This isn't . . . isn't like that. This is . . . ' He looked at the screen. 'God . . . '

She shrugged. 'They're dressed up, stockings, suspenders, the lot. Wigs, make-up. Some of them make more convincing women than some women.'

'So?'

'I think that's what men go for. The dressing up. It doesn't matter who's inside, as long as they've got the right kit on.' She turned to him, smiling. 'Don't you think?'

He didn't know how to answer.

'Bet you've looked at this kind of stuff before,' she said.

'No I haven't. It's . . . fucking perverse.'

'Really? Come on, you're a man. You can't tell me you haven't been trawling through the internet looking for something to get yourself off to and fancied something a little different. Bet you have.'

Again he said nothing. Just went back to looking at the screen. With another added layer of discomfort.

The second DVD had been similar to the first. The only difference being in the severity of some of the sexual acts. An unmistakable tone of sadomasochism had crept in, with Amanda on the receiving end of some increasingly brutal punishment.

That's not sex, thought Khan. *I don't know what it is, but it's not sex.*

Amanda's partner was male, hooded and wearing leather. No help at all.

This new DVD was different to the others. He spotted that straight away. Perhaps not up to professional standards, but certainly not amateur. There was more than one camera, for a start, one for long shots, one for close-ups. And Amanda – he was referring to her like that now – was much more professionally made up.

He leaned forward. 'Hold on . . . '

Oliver caught his serious tone. 'What? What is it?'

'Look,' he said.

She did so. The screen showed Amanda dressed exactly the same as she had been on the night of her death. But there was more to it than that. The room on screen was the living room they had discovered Glenn McGowan's body in. Amanda was going to the door, letting someone in.

'Ben,' he heard her say in a parody of a woman's voice, 'what a surprise. Come in.'

A man stepped into shot. Only visible from the shoulders down.

'Fuck,' said Khan. 'Can't we, I dunno, can the techies let us see his face?'

'We might see it later,' said Oliver. 'Keep watching.'

They did. The newcomer was ushered in, Amanda talking all the while about what a thrill it was to have him for dinner. The camera followed as they went to sit on the sofa. Ben's head was in full view.

'No we've . . . Oh.'

He had a thick head of jet-black hair, obviously a wig. He also wore heavy facial hair and sunglasses.

'He looks like a seventies porn star,' said Oliver. 'I bet that's deliberate.'

'Shit,' said Khan. 'Thought we had him there.'

They kept watching.

'So what d'you think?' asked Oliver. 'Is this it? Are we watching Glenn McGowan's last night on earth?'

'I . . . don't know . . . '

He didn't. But he had that copper's tingle he always got when he was on to something. He knew this would be one film he would watch all the way to the end.

29

The Arcadian had the plans of the house in his head, memorised. All he had to do was get inside without being seen or recognised.

No problem.

He had spent his life hiding in plain sight. Going about his business without anyone aware he was actually there. He knew that the best way to not be noticed was to just be ignored. He didn't dress flashily, behave outrageously. He had made a study of ordinary people and knew how to behave like one. Still, after tonight his work was going to receive more recognition, so he had to be prepared for that. But he couldn't draw attention to himself. No matter how much he wanted to. How much he wanted to shout from the rooftops about what he was doing, how brilliant he was. He had the dolls. He would tell them about it. They would have to do.

For now.

The street was full of big houses. All hidden from view by huge hedges and fences, all made unreachable by electronic gates, sensors, motion lights and alarms. Physical dividing lines between the haves and the never-will-haves. The Arcadian could smell the money. It even made the air feel different. Richer, more rarefied. And something else: fear. Like he had no right to be there, breathing it in.

He smiled. He had every right to be there.

He placed a gloved hand on the gate. It swung soundlessly open. Giving one more look around, checking he hadn't been seen – he hadn't, the street was deserted – he stepped over the threshold.

A thrill of anticipation ran through his body. Almost sexual. He loved it, that rush before the job. Even a relatively quick one such as this. It was still the same, the expectation then the commission. Then reliving it afterwards. The perfect cycle.

But he had to concentrate now. Focus on the job in hand. Because if this went wrong, there might be no afterwards.

He walked slowly up the gravel driveway, trying to stay out of the pools of light cast by the ornate faux-Victorian lamp-posts that lined the sides. Even in the semi-darkness he could see that the driveway wasn't well kept, weeds reclaiming the stones.

He reached the house. Looked round, listened. Nothing. There had been barely any vehicle or pedestrian activity on the street; back here it seemed like he was out in the country. There was no sound from inside the house either. Just a dim light coming from behind the curtains in the huge bay window on the left. He stood before the front door. Large and imposing, old, heavy wood. He placed a gloved hand on it. It opened.

Just as he had been told.

He stepped inside. The hallway was in darkness, but he could make out shiny, glittering features. A huge chandelier overhead, gold sconces and gilt frames on the walls. Black and white tiled floor covered by a faux-leopardskin runner. Money but no style, he thought.

Not like the doll's house. She had real style. Real class. Or the part she had decorated did.

145

Light framed a doorway to the left. He put his hand on the handle, turned. Entered.

The room had the same type of decoration as the hall. Opulent but tasteless. And the same lax attention to upkeep as the driveway. It had been turned into a downstairs den: a bed ran along one wall, oxygen cylinder next to it, an easy chair over to one side by the huge TV. Shelves of DVDs behind it, the spines brightly coloured and football- or car-related.

And in the centre of the room sat what was left of a man in a wheelchair.

The man looked up. No surprise on his face, just exhaustion. 'You're here, then,' he said, looking him over. 'Thought you'd be . . . I don't know. Taller, something.'

The Arcadian stopped moving, took the man in. His lack of legs was the first thing he noticed, the remaining stumps clothed in filthy tracksuit bottoms, folded under, stained at the crotch. A similarly discoloured T-shirt covered his shrunken torso. From the contours of his body he looked like a large man who had lost weight but forgot to tell his body. Rolls of stretched, useless skin lay around him like creases in a baggy sweatshirt. He was unshaven, his hair unwashed, his skin the colour of a rotten egg yolk. He smelled of death, even though he wasn't yet dead.

The Arcadian thought back to the doll, the hours of fun they had had together, the consummation, the execution . . . then looked at the pathetic, stinking figure before him. This wasn't going to be fun at all.

'Come on, then,' the lump before him said, 'get it over with. Haven't got all night.' He laughed at his own joke, which caused him to cough, which caused him to retch blood into a filthy handkerchief.

The Arcadian's first response was to turn round, walk out. This wasn't what he wanted. Wasn't what would make him happy, give him fulfilment. Then he remembered what he had agreed to. Be professional. Put his skills and training into practice. Even if the thought of touching the lump revolted him.

He moved closer, breathing through his mouth to avoid the smell.

'Just be quick,' said the lump. 'Although to be honest, I doubt you could give me any more pain.' He held up a jar of pills. 'Morphine. This is the stuff, this is. Do what you like. I won't feel it.'

The Arcadian said nothing, thought hard. He had toyed with methods of death over and over in his mind. Some flamboyant, some mundane. He hadn't allowed himself to settle on any particular one, telling himself he would be adaptable, fit whatever felt right into the situation at hand. But now, staring at the stinking cripple, he was at a loss.

'You can throw some stuff around if you like,' the cripple said. 'Make it look like a robbery.' He shrugged. 'Dunno. Up to you.' He fell silent again, looking into his lap, then back up, straight at the Arcadian. 'I'm scared. Please, I . . . I'm scared. I . . . ' He sighed. 'Just do it. Please.' He closed his eyes, braced himself, as if waiting for a punch.

The Arcadian looked round. Something to hand, he thought. Something in the room. Make it look less premeditated, more opportunistic. A statue, ornament to bring down on his head or face . . . no. Too much mess. Too much transfer of DNA. Something . . .

A cushion. A pillow. Yes.

He walked over to the bed, picked up the pillow, crossed back to the cripple, who opened his eyes.

'Oh. Right. This is . . . this is it, is it? This is it . . . '

He placed the cushion over the cripple's face. The cripple struggled, coughed. The Arcadian pushed harder.

It didn't take long. The cripple had hardly any life left in

147

him. The Arcadian dropped the cushion on the floor, looked at the cripple. Head back, eyes open, mouth wet with saliva and blood.

But no butterfly. No soul.

The Arcadian felt angry then. Cheated. This wasn't right. This wasn't what was supposed to happen. There was no euphoria, no catharsis. No release. Like building up to an orgasm but being denied it. Not right. Not right at all.

He let the anger build, then waited for it to explode. To manifest itself on the room. Ornaments were thrown at walls, pictures and photos torn down and hurled against cabinets, smashing. DVDs were pulled from shelves, furniture upended. The cripple was thrown from his wheelchair on to the floor.

Eventually the Arcadian's anger was spent. He stood in the centre of the room breathing heavily, surveying the damage. It looked like a break-in now.

He turned, ready to go. His disappointment like a stone in his stomach. As he reached the doorway, he stopped.

'Keith? Keith? The front door's open, are you OK . . . ?'

He looked round, tried to find a hiding place. No time. Just hid behind the door. Waited.

The door opened. In walked a blonde woman dressed like a footballer's wife. Her cloying perfume masked the stench of the cripple. His first response was to wait until she was well inside the room, then try to get past her, run out. But the plan didn't get that far. Because as soon as she entered, she turned, saw him. She opened her mouth to scream and he was on her. He held her tight, arm round her throat, gloved hand clamped tight over her mouth. There was no way he could just escape now.

As he held her, he smiled.

Perhaps he would have some fun tonight after all.

30

Maddy opened her eyes to find herself walking. She looked round, surprised and startled at where she was. A residential street in Selly Oak, not far from the university campus. Not far from her home. But it was dark. And the street was deserted. And freezing.

She checked herself. She was dressed, still wearing the same clothes as when she had left home earlier in the day. To go to the Custard Factory and confront Hugo.

Hugo. The name hit her brain like a flash of lightning.

That was where she had been, the last thing she could remember. At Hugo's house. Telling him about her problem. Trying to get him to understand. How upset she was. What she felt for him. Maddy tried to remember. To fill in the blanks, work out what had happened.

She had been sitting on the sofa alongside him. He had offered her a drink. Then . . . nothing. Until now.

She stopped walking, shocked. She checked her watch. Nearly midnight. God, that meant she had lost . . . hours. How many? She had no idea. She felt panic rising. What had happened to her? What had she been up to?

She tried to think it through chronologically. Keep calm and be methodical.

Sitting on the sofa at Hugo's place. A drink. Then . . . nothing. No, not nothing. *Think, think* . . . The drink was strong. It hit her head straight away. Made it spin, made the room blur in and out of focus. She had lain back against the sofa, her body heavy, her head too big to support. She tried to keep her eyes open but her eyelids refused to co-operate. Her arms, legs wouldn't move.

So she must have slept. That was it. Slept. But that wasn't right. If she had slept, why had she woken up walking along a street near her home?

So she hadn't slept. Then what had happened?

Maddy stopped walking, closed her eyes. Replayed what memories she could. The last thing she remembered seeing was Hugo's face. Right next to hers, smiling. And . . . something more. His hands. *Yes.* His hands . . . on her thighs . . .

Her eyes opened again with another jolt. *Oh God.* Hugo's hands on her thighs. What had happened? *He wouldn't have . . . No. Not Hugo.*

Her legs were shaking as she hurried along. She tried to remember more details, but her memory wouldn't work. The blackness wouldn't shift, allow her access.

She had to get home. As fast as she could. While she was walking, she took out her phone. Punched in Hugo's number, put the phone to her ear. It rang. Her blood pounded, her heart skipped in double time, twice for each ring of the phone.

Come on . . .

The phone kept ringing. Maddy was holding her breath.

Answer . . . please . . .

Ringing and ringing. Then a voice telling her that the person she was calling was unavailable and to try again later. She called again. Got the same thing. And again. The same. She put her phone away. Kept walking. Shaking from more than just the cold. Anxiety eating through to her bones.

'Oi! Oi!'

Oh God . . .

The voice was behind her. Her heart, already trip-hammering, went even faster. That was all she needed. Some drunken nutter on the street. She felt in her handbag for the rape alarm that the university had supplied. She usually carried it when she was out at night, but it wasn't there. Left at home because she hadn't expected to be out this long.

Shit . . .

She kept going.

'Oi! Wait!'

The voice was getting nearer. Maddy had almost broken into a run.

'Maddy! Wait!'

She stopped. Turned. A young man was hurrying towards her. About her age, tall, dark-haired. Smiling. Dressed like a student. Did she know him? He knew her, apparently.

She moved into the beam of the nearest street light, making sure she was well lit, and waited for him to approach her. Still unsure of him, her hand inside her handbag. Her fingers curled round her door keys, making sure the jagged edges were sticking through her knuckles. Just in case.

He reached her. Stood next to her. Out of breath but smiling.

'Hi, Maddy. Thought it was you . . . '

She just stared at him. He frowned.

'Ben,' he said. 'Remember? Mike's friend? Who's seeing Abby? American studies Abby?'

'Oh,' she said, 'Ben. Yes . . . ' He obviously knew her, but she still couldn't place him. And it was impolite to say so, so she would just have to pretend until it came to her and hope he didn't notice. 'Hi. What are you . . . Where're you off to?'

151

He shrugged. 'Just going home. Been down the Bristol Pair with the others. They were heading off into town to Snobs but I didn't fancy it. What about you? You been out?'

'Yeah,' she said, not wanting to tell him anything until she had worked it out for herself at least. 'Yeah.'

'You live round here, don't you?'

Oh God, she thought, *he's probably been to a party at our house and I still can't remember him.* 'Yeah, that's right. Just off Coronation Road.'

'Right,' he said, nodding. 'Thought so.'

They stood in silence beneath the street light, their breath fogging the night air.

'Listen,' he said, looking round. 'Bit dodgy being out here on your own. Never know who you'll bump into. Shall I walk you home?'

She flinched as he said the words. He caught it.

'Oh no,' he said, 'I just meant . . . ' He shrugged, his voice dropping. 'It's safer with somebody with you, that's all.'

'I . . . I don't want to put you out. Out of your way.'

He gestured behind him, the way he had come. 'I'm only ten minutes back that way. Not putting me out at all. Plus I'm making sure you get home safe. That's all.'

Her fingers began to uncurl from the key ring, her hand slipped out of her handbag. 'OK, then. But I'm very tired.'

He frowned.

'I'm . . . just going to go straight to bed.'

He laughed. 'Do what you like. As long as you get home safely.'

She looked at him again under the street light. Maybe there was something familiar about him. Maybe she could remember him after all. Mike's friend. Abby. Right. She'd just had a bad day, that was all. A bad few days. Didn't mean everyone was a nutter. Or out to hurt her.

She thought of Hugo. Sighed. Felt that familiar sink of depression in her stomach.

'You OK?' he asked, concern in his eyes.

She looked up. 'Fine,' she said. Hugo could wait until tomorrow. He would have to. 'Let's go home.'

They walked off down the street together.

31

The house was in darkness when Phil let himself in.

He put his car keys on the kitchen table, his bag down by the side. They hadn't been there that long and already he was establishing patterns of behaviour, getting used to the new routine. He had read somewhere that human beings were pre-disposed to find routine in everything. He remembered an old crime novel he had read, years ago, in which a man left his family and job and went to another city to set up a new life. When the private detective found him, he had established a new family and a new life. Routine had taken over.

He shook his head, wondered why his mind had thought of that, opened the fridge door. There were half a dozen bottles of beer on their sides. Routine dictated that he would take one, sit down and use it to help him to dial out work, dial in the family.

Except it was very late and the rest of the family were in bed.

He closed the fridge door, made his way upstairs. He thought of having a shower, decided against it. He was dog tired and it might wake him up, then he'd never sleep. And tomorrow, when he went to talk to Hugo Gwilym, he would be half asleep and might miss something. Given the level of scrutiny he was feeling from the rest of his team, that wouldn't do.

Hugo Gwilym. Phil had heard of him, knew of his media profile, but nothing more specific than that. And he knew Marina was working alongside him at the university. She hadn't mentioned him, except a few disparaging offhand remarks, but he wanted to talk to her about him. If she was friendly with Gwilym – which he doubted – there might even be a conflict of interest and he would have to step down as SIO. If that happened, he could just imagine what the office gossip would be like. And how much further his standing would slip in the eyes of the rest of the team.

He made his way slowly up the stairs, using the flashlight from his phone, so as not to wake the other two. He put his head round Josephina's door, saw his daughter fast asleep, clutching her favourite soft toy, Lady. It was disgusting, filthy and ragged, but Josephina and Lady had been through a lot together, so neither he nor Marina minded her hanging on to it.

A quick visit to the bathroom, then into bed. Marina was lying on her side, eyes closed, breathing steady. He moved slowly round to his side, careful not to wake her, got undressed and slipped in beside her. Setting the alarm on his phone, he closed his eyes.

He had thought he would lie awake most of the night, working out the case in his mind, but he was so tired and, if he was honest, relieved to be engaged to this degree once more that he went straight off to sleep.

Marina had heard Phil come in. She knew his pattern: the door opening, the keys on the table, the fridge door. She heard the fridge close again, heard him make his way upstairs.

And her heart flipped.

She should talk to him. She knew that. Share what had happened to her.

But what *had* happened to her? She couldn't remember. She had spent all day trying to relive the previous night. Over and over in her mind, replaying every single second that she could remember until she wasn't sure what was real and what she was imagining was real.

Had she been raped? Or had it been consensual and she was so out of it she hadn't been able to remember? And if so, if she had been so out of it, wasn't that just date rape? Not if what Gwilym said was true. That she had wanted it, instigated it. She wished she could remember. Or at least part of her did. The rest wanted it never to have happened.

She heard Phil on the stairs. Opening Josephina's door, checking she was OK. Routine. Then the bathroom door. She quickly lay on her side, closed her eyes. Pretended to be asleep.

She knew it was cowardly, but she didn't know what else she could do. She couldn't talk to him about it. Not now, perhaps not ever. And that made her feel even worse inside.

She heard the toilet flush, the bathroom door close. And then Phil was in the room, making his way slowly round the bed. A considerate and decent man. One of the few she had met. Partly why she loved him so much.

He got into bed next to her. She didn't move in case he realised she was awake.

She needn't have worried. He quickly got himself settled and his breathing changed. She knew he was asleep.

Marina lay there, physically so close but emotionally miles away from her partner, feeling warmth from his body but so, so cold inside.

She didn't move all night.

PART THREE

HEAVEN AND HELL

32

There. That should do it.

The Arcadian stood back, stared at the doll's house once more. It still didn't look right. It looked wrong, unbalanced. And that didn't just niggle away at him when he looked at it; it burned. Inside. Even when he wasn't looking at it, he knew it was there, could feel it was there. He had wanted perfection. He had failed.

The blonde doll sat at the table where she always sat. Her new friend sat in an armchair next to her. And the Arcadian hated seeing him there.

He wasn't the one the doll should be with. One look told him that. The Arcadian had done what he could to make the new doll fit in. He had already prepared him before he had gone to the house, what he thought he should look like, be dressed in. His character built up in the Arcadian's mind, how he would complement the doll already there. But the reality was very different. The fat, legless slob he had discovered just wasn't right for the doll, not right at all. Not fit to share her house, not worthy of being her companion.

But he had to make do with what was there. The Arcadian had known this one would be different, accepted that. But he hadn't known just how different. How much of a disappointment it would be.

He looked at the new doll once more. It fell off the chair.

Anger rose within him. He wanted to tear it apart, throw it at the wall. But he didn't. He just picked it off the floor, plonked it roughly back down again, forcing it down, making it stay.

Maybe I shouldn't have cut the legs off, he thought. *But no. I had to. Because that was the way he was. And that's the way it has to be done.*

So he looked at the doll once more, mentally challenging it not to fall, threatening it with unspeakable tortures and punishments if it did.

It stayed where it was.

The Arcadian smiled. Relieved.

He thought back to the previous night. Shambles. Absolute shambles. But that was good in a way, he thought. That meant they wouldn't connect the two murders. He thought again, mentally corrected himself. Three murders.

The blonde woman. The only good thing about the previous night.

Killing the man had been most unsatisfactory. No release, no catharsis, nothing. No butterfly. But the woman, that was different. She had been more fun.

Once he had overpowered her – which was easy, because while she stood there in shock, mouth gaping open to scream, he was on her – he stood back, regarded her. Like a butcher deciding which cut would be the most succulent. No, not a butcher. A fishmonger. Because she wasn't meat, she was female. Smelt different, bled differently. And he had gone to work on her.

Maybe he had been angry with her and let it show. At least with her he had found his catharsis, his release.

No butterfly, though. Or at least not that he had noticed.

And no doll for her either. Yet.

The Arcadian didn't like women. Never had. The woman who was supposed to have been his mother hadn't been particularly maternal. And because of that he had nothing but hatred for her.

But he also had reasons to be thankful to her. Because if it hadn't been for her, he would never have found his true calling, his real identity.

He couldn't remember his father. He must have had one, but his mother never talked about him, or if she did, his description changed every time. Sometimes he was tall and bald, sometimes short with blond hair. It was only later that he realised what a whore his mother was and that his father could have been any one of a number of men.

That just made him hate her more.

But one thing he did remember. He'd been little, sitting at home in their flat, rehoused again in a high rise in Rotherham, watching TV. His mother had come into the room. He'd known instinctively something was up. She was smiling at him. She never did that unless she was either drunk or about to hit him.

'Scott,' she had said, using his real name, his old name, 'someone's here to see you.'

She stood aside and let two men into the room. They were both smiling. He felt immediately suspicious. They didn't look drunk, so it must be the other thing. One of them stepped forward, handed him a present. A red fire engine.

'You can play with that in a while,' the man said, kneeling down. 'We're just going to have a bit of fun first.'

Up close the man had bad, uneven teeth and his breath smelled. The man stretched out his hands towards him. He looked up, fear and panic gripping him. He saw his mother take some money – big money, notes – off the other man, tuck it down her top and leave the room, closing the door firmly behind them.

161

Then they had fun with him. Their idea of fun.

No matter how much he screamed, how much he begged, his mother didn't come back into the room. Not until they were finished. And all that evening she just sat on her own, away from him, drinking. She cried at first. But the tears soon dried up.

That was the first time. But not the last.

And the fire engine was never played with.

That day was the end of his childhood and the start of ... something else. His journey to becoming who he was now. Who he could be.

After coming out of the YOI he had done time in for rape and assault, they approached him again. Not to use him any more. He was too old for that. They didn't fancy him. No. They wanted him to go recruiting. Find new young lovers, just like he used to be, that they could play with.

He didn't want to at first. Told them where to go, what to do with themselves. But they kept on at him. Reminding him of who had brought him up, the things they had done for him. And they *had* done things for him. Good things. They had given him days out, holidays. Bought him stuff, toys and clothes.

'We were your real dads,' the first one, Brian, had said.

And they had been, really. They had been good to him and he had even got used to Brian's rotten teeth and breath.

Along with a few other things.

He felt guilty when they said that. So he did what they asked. And it wasn't too bad. It was fun. He enjoyed it. They even let him join in himself.

Targets were easy. Young single mums who weren't too choosy. Who wanted to believe everything he said. Give a fake name and he was in. He had to fuck them, which was distasteful, but he just kept in mind what he was getting in the end.

162

And it worked. Always. Well, nearly always. If it didn't, just offer money. That usually did the trick.

But something was missing. He didn't feel right. So he left town. Overnight; there, then gone. Ended up in Birmingham. Stuck in the middle of the country. He liked that.

And that was when he set about making a new identity for himself. That was when he started becoming the Arcadian.

He continued the education had started in prison. Bought books about things that interested him. Went to places that he enjoyed. Found people who shared the things he loved to do. And things were good.

Then he heard his mother had died.

He lost it a bit then. Drinking, drugs, sex, violence. Horror and hatred. Hitting out. Hard. But it was no good. Still he saw her face everywhere. And nothing he took or did could take that away.

Eventually he was spent. Slowly he rebuilt himself. And as he did so, he told himself there would be some changes made. No one would ever hurt him again. In any way at all. In fact, from now on he would be the one doing all the hurting. He would enjoy that. And it would make him perfect.

The new doll fell off its seat once more.

He blinked, the sudden movement bringing him back into the room. How long had he stood there? He didn't know. He had phased out again.

The doll lay on the floor of the house. The Arcadian felt anger rise once more but controlled it this time. Tamped it down. Instead he went to the cupboard, rummaged around until he found what he wanted. An elastic band. He picked the doll up, forced the band round it. Tied it to the chair. He stood back, admiring his handiwork. Smiled.

That was what you could do, he thought. If you controlled

your anger. If you made yourself think. He was pleased with himself.

He looked at the doll's house once more. Still not right. But the elastic band was better. One thing missing, though. The woman. He checked his pockets. He had enough for a cheap doll. Because that was all she had been really.

He grabbed his jacket, left.

Determined to make some good come of this. Planning what he would do next.

33

Marina closed her eyes, put her head back, tried to relax. Willed the hot water to take away any dirt from her body, pain from her mind. Tried to think, rationalise. But all she saw was Hugo Gwilym's leering, grinning face.

She shook her head to lose the image, water droplets flying, and tried again.

Put the night in order. That was what she had to do. And not for the first time. It was all she had thought about since Thursday night, all she had done. Put the night in order. The restaurant. The meal. The drinks.

The drinks.

Marina was sure now that she had been drugged. She had no evidence to support the idea, not yet, just a feeling, a conviction. Gwilym must have slipped something into her drink at the restaurant. *Must* have done. She hadn't had enough wine to explain the awful headache the next day, the aching in her arms, legs.

The blackout. The total absence of memory.

Drugs. It had to be.

She ran her hands over her body, examining herself. She opened her legs, inspected the tops of her thighs, her vagina for any signs. Bruises. Abrasions. Redness or soreness. Signs that *he* had been there.

She had done the same thing the day before. Obsessively, compulsively, over and over, like Lady Macbeth trying to wash the guilt-staining blood from her hands. Hoping that her fears were as imaginary as that blood was.

She had found nothing. Any time, yesterday or this morning. Nothing. She knew what she looked like, what she felt like when she had had sex. And this wasn't it. She had investigated thoroughly and she was sure of it. Or she hoped she was sure of it. Hoped she wasn't deluding herself, clinging desperately to a false belief, ignoring the obvious signs because she didn't want them to be true.

No. There was nothing to show he had been there. *Nothing*. But still . . .

There was too much she couldn't explain. The trip in the taxi. Gwilym knowing too much. Her panties in his pocket.

Oh God. She was going to be sick.

She put a hand to the wall, steadied herself. Kept her eyes closed, breathed deeply. Waited until the nausea passed.

It did. Eventually.

Marina knew she should finish in the shower, towel off, get going. But she stayed where she was, the water running all over her. Just one more feel, one more investigation . . .

No. Still no sign. Nothing there.

Or she hoped that nothing was there. Because the alternative . . .

She shook her head, tried to shake Gwilym's leering face from it once more.

She still couldn't believe what had happened. How a simple dinner with colleagues had turned into a nightmare. She hated to use such a clichéd phrase, but there was no other way to describe it. That was what it was. Her life, in the space of two days, had become a living nightmare.

The enormity of what had happened played over in her

mind once more. Someone she had been talking to, someone she knew, albeit briefly, had drugged her and forced her to have sex with him. If that was what had happened. *Forced her to have sex with him.*

She knew the word for that all right. But she still couldn't bring herself to say it. Not head on. She would skirt round it, try to approach it sideways. She knew she would have to say it eventually. But if she did, if she admitted and acknowledged it, that word, that one little word that defined what she had gone through, then that was her life off in a completely different direction. One that could redefine not only her but all her relationships with everyone else she knew or met. And certainly with Phil.

Phil. It broke her heart not to be able to tell him what had happened. But she couldn't. Not yet. Not until she had it straight in her own mind. Not until she was ready to confront it herself.

She was scared of what he would say. Or even what he would do. She had played out every possible reaction he might have, spent the night lying there going over and over them. He might believe her, go after Gwilym. Hurt him. Kill him, even. And she wasn't sure she could live with him doing that, even though a part of her wanted him to. Worst of all, though, he might not believe her. Call her a slag and a slut, say she had asked for it, that it was all her own fault. That she had fucked someone else and was scared he would find out and this was how she covered for it. That was the reaction she dreaded most.

She shook her head once more, tried to clear it. To calm down. Think. Plan. Decide on a course of action.

Confront Gwilym. That was what she would do. Tell him she was going to report him to the university for what he had done. She thought again. Was that wise? Her career might be over if she did that. If she brought allegations against their star lecturer. Especially allegations she couldn't substantiate with evidence.

No. That wouldn't work. She couldn't do that.

But she had to do something.

Marina felt hands on her body. A quick, sudden movement, round her waist. She gasped, tried to turn, ready to fight. Lost her footing, slipped.

She screamed.

34

'Whoa, hold on ...'

Marina stopped screaming. The hands round her waist grabbed on to her, steadied her, stopped her from slipping. She managed to right herself, turned. Phil stood behind her, naked.

'Steady,' he said. 'I was just about to join you, but ...'

Marina leant against the wall, bent double and breathing hard, as if she had just made a dash for a bus she had no hope of catching.

'It's ... it's you ...'

'Course it's me. Who were you expecting?' Phil tried to laugh, but he could tell she was seriously spooked. 'What's up?'

'Nothing, I was ... I was miles away.'

'Right,' he said. 'Miles away. And nowhere good.'

She straightened up. Became aware of her husband looking at her naked body. Usually she enjoyed him doing that, responded to it, returned it. The way his lips curled into an appreciative smile at what he saw, his eyes brightening as his imagination began working. His cock hardening ...

But not today, not now. She didn't want him looking at her now. Not like this, not after what she had been through. The water hadn't made her feel clean at all. Water alone, she doubted, ever could.

She pulled the shower curtain in front of her, cutting off his view.

'Please,' she said. 'Just . . . just let me have some privacy . . .'

'OK,' said Phil, confused now. 'What's wrong?'

'Nothing.' She almost spat the word out in anger. Knowing it was a sure indicator that something *was* wrong, she tried to calm herself down. 'Sorry. I'm just . . . I'm not . . . just some privacy, please.'

Phil, clearly not happy and not understanding at all, picked up his dressing gown, turned and left the bathroom.

Later, she joined him in the kitchen. Josephina was still in her pyjamas, eating cereal. Phil was dressed and ready for work. For him, every working day was dress-down Friday. It was one of the things she loved about him. He had got away with that when he had a lenient boss; she just hoped the new one was equally tolerant.

There was no tailored jacket today, just his favourite old battered leather one. Levis and boots and a dark plaid Western shirt with pearl snap buttons over an old T-shirt. Not what the average MIU detective wore, she was sure, but what he wore.

And, her heart breaking as she thought it, he looked wonderful.

'Hi,' she said, hoping she sounded normal. Or at least casual.

He glanced at her, went back to what he was doing. 'I'm making coffee. D'you want some?'

She did. She sat at the table next to Josephina, started talking to her daughter. The normality of the scene made her inner turmoil even worse.

Phil sat down next to her. Looked at her. She flinched, looked away.

He passed her a mug of coffee. She took it; he put his hand on her arm. 'You OK?' he said, voice low, concerned.

She nodded. His hand felt simultaneously warm yet uncomfortable. She didn't want to be touched. By anyone. Not yet.

'Yeah,' she said. 'Fine.' Her voice aiming for breezy, missing.

She stood up, losing his touch as she did so. She walked over to the toaster, taking her coffee, her back to him.

'So,' she said, for something to say, 'you're going in today. Saturday's normally your day off.'

'Yeah,' he said. 'Big case. You've probably seen it on the news.'

'Haven't been watching the news.' Snappy again, jumping at him. She took a deep breath. Tried to calm herself down. It wasn't Phil's fault. He didn't deserve to be shouted at. She kept telling herself that.

'Yeah, this case,' Phil was saying. 'Can't say too much here . . . ' she knew he was referring to Josephina, 'but it's a biggie. In fact, there was something I was going to ask you. D'you know Hugo Gwilym?'

Her heart skipped a beat and her hand was in sudden pain. She looked down. She had spilt the mug of coffee she had been holding all over her other hand. Coffee pooled outwards on the kitchen work surface. She just stared at it.

'Marina . . . ' Phil rushed over to her, held her hand up, examined it. It was red, burning. 'Come here . . . '

He guided her towards the sink, turned on the cold-water tap, put her hand underneath it. He looked at her. She tried not to make eye contact.

'What happened?'

171

'I just . . . I spilled it. Knocked it when I went for, went for the toast . . . '

'OK.' He turned the water off, put a towel round her hand. 'That should be OK. I'll get this mess cleared up. You sit down.'

Like a sleepwalker she went over to the table, sat down next to her daughter.

'Did Mummy hurt herself?'

She looked at her daughter; Josephina's eyes were wide with fear and compassion. She managed a smile.

'I'm fine. Mummy was careless. Don't worry.'

She could see that the little girl wanted to believe her but was still wary.

'I'm fine. Honest. You keep eating your breakfast.'

Josephina, with some reluctance, did so.

Phil was wiping up the spilled coffee, using too much kitchen roll as usual. Marina opened her mouth to say something, but changed her mind. What came out was completely different.

'Why d'you want to talk to Hugo Gwilym?'

Phil put the sodden kitchen roll in the waste bin, wiped his hands. 'Well, his name's come up in the investigation . . . '

'How? In what way?'

Phil turned to her, frowning. 'Just . . . came up. That's all. Apparently he was researching some book and the . . . ' he looked towards Josephina, conscious that she was listening even though she was pretending not to, '*person* was one of the people he interviewed.'

'Is he dead, Daddy? This person?'

Phil and Marina looked at each other. Phil spoke first. 'The person, he's . . . been hurt. And I'm helping to find out who did it.'

'Not dead?'

Another look passed between them. Phil opened his mouth to speak once more, but Marina beat him to it.

'Have you finished your breakfast, darling? Why don't you go and watch TV in the living room?'

Josephina, deciding that that was more interesting than two grown-ups talking, got down from the table and ran out. Phil and Marina waited in silence until they heard the shrill cries of cartoons coming from the next room. Phil put his back against the workbench, folded his arms.

'What's up? What's wrong?' His voice was warm, but the trained police officer's interrogative wasn't far from the surface.

'I'm fine, I'm just . . . fine.' He was about to speak again but Marina got in first. 'So this guy who was killed knew Hugo Gwilym?'

'Looks that way. I just wanted to ask you about him.'

Her stomach roiled. 'What sort of thing?'

Phil shrugged. 'Do you know him, what's he like. That kind of thing. If he's a close colleague of yours, should I declare a conflict of interest and step away? You know. The usual.'

'No,' said Marina emphatically. 'No. I don't, don't know him.'

'Good,' said Phil. 'Because this looks like being a biggie, like I said. And I'm in charge. If I pull it off, well. West Mids may actually start to respect me. Or even like me.'

He smiled as he said it, but Marina knew there was some truth behind his words. She knew he hadn't been fitting in, getting along well. He had tried to cover it up, knowing she was happy in her work. And she loved him for that. But he wasn't good at hiding his feelings. And she hoped that wouldn't drive a wedge between them.

But she had other things to think about at the moment.

'Well, you're fine,' she said. 'No problems. I know him as

well as you do. Seen him on TV. Apparently he's a twat, though.' She spat that last sentence out with more venom than she had intended.

'Right. I'll bear that in mind.'

'So you're going to see him, then.'

'Yeah.'

'When?'

'I don't know. Maybe later today sometime. If I get round to it. Why?'

'No reason. Just wondered.' She stood up. 'OK. I'm off.'

'Where you going?' he asked.

'Dunno. Out. Into town, probably. Eileen's busy today. I'll take Josephina out somewhere.'

'OK. Well . . .'

She turned, left the room. 'See you later.'

Phil was left at the sink, watching her go.

'Yeah,' he said to empty air, 'see you later . . .'

35

Maddy opened her eyes to find another pair of eyes staring back at her. She jumped, gasped. And was met with a smile.

'You're awake. Morning.'

She lay still, letting her consciousness catch up with her body. Retracing the steps of the night before that had brought her here. She looked at the young man lying opposite her. Even with his hair tousled and his eyes half open he looked handsome. Better-looking than she remembered, in fact.

'Ben,' she said, groaning instead of adding anything else. She tried to move, but her body wasn't ready for that yet, so she lay flat on her back.

'That's me.' He propped himself up on one elbow, hand on his cheek, kept looking at her. Eyes crinkling attractively as he smiled.

She turned her head sideways. 'How long you been awake?' she managed.

'Not long,' he said. 'I would say I've been watching you sleep, but that just sounds weird and creepy.'

'*Have* you been watching me sleep?'

'Yeah ...' He laughed. It was a good sound, a positive one. Maddy joined in. 'But not inappropriately,' he said. 'I woke up but I didn't want to disturb you. And I didn't want to go creeping round the house. Your housemates might think I was a burglar. Call the police.'

'I'm sure they wouldn't.' She was still smiling.

'Oh.' He traced a couple of fingers slowly down her neck. Smiled as he spoke. 'Have a lot of men here then, do you?'

'No,' she said, pulling away from him.

'Sorry,' he said, withdrawing his fingers. 'Was only joking.'

She turned back to him. Saw sincerity in his eyes. Slight hurt at his words being taken the wrong way. 'I know.' She took his fingers in her own. Held them.

It had happened so easily, so naturally. After bumping into her on the street, he had walked her home. And that, she thought, would have been that. But standing outside her front door with someone who had seen the state she was in and not taken advantage of her, she thought she needed to do more.

'Would you like a coffee?' she had said. 'Sorry, that's a bit . . . but would you? It's cold and you've got to walk home. I've only got instant, though.'

He had laughed. 'Cup of tea would be nice.'

And that was what they had had. Tea and a couple of rounds of toast and Marmite. And conversation. Lots and lots of conversation.

'I feel like I've known you for years,' Maddy had said. 'Like I can just talk to you.'

'That a good thing?' Ben had asked.

'Yeah, course. It means things aren't difficult. They're good.'

'Great.'

They had kept talking. Or rather Maddy had. After what she had recently gone through with Hugo, there were things she needed to say. And it was better to say them to a complete stranger than to a close friend. Close friends cared. They judged. Strangers didn't care at all. At best, like Ben, they listened.

So it all tumbled out. The relationship. The affair. The sex. Then the abortion. And how she felt he had just abandoned her. As she said that, she had tried to hide her wrist so he didn't see the bandage. Then the confrontation in the café. The trip to Hugo's house. Then ... she didn't know. She thought perhaps Hugo had ... No. He couldn't have. She was just imagining things. Anyway, she couldn't remember. Her mind a blank until Ben had found her in the street.

'He sounds like a real fucking bastard,' Ben had said.

She nodded. And kept nodding. Soon, she found herself crying with Ben's consoling arm around her shoulder.

The kiss had come so easily after that. She couldn't remember who had initiated it, just that it happened. Like they were both thinking the same thing at exactly the same time. Their mouths had locked and she felt his tongue on hers, pulling and probing. She had clung to his warm, close body, feeling the yearning, aching emptiness inside herself, wanting to pull him in to fill her, warm her. In every way possible.

And he almost had done.

'No,' she had said.

He looked at her, puzzled.

'I ... can't. Because of what happened. I'm still ... not right down there. Not yet.'

Ben had smiled then. 'Right. Yes. I see. Well don't worry. We can still ... have some fun.'

They had. And she had loved it. The intimacy. Being desired just for being who she was. It was a long time since she had felt that wanted, that close to another human being. Not since ...

Hugo. Before things went bad.

'You OK?'

She blinked, reverie over. Ben was still lying next to her, looking at her, concern in his eyes.

'Yeah,' she said. 'Fine.' She found a smile, stroked his chest. He had a good chest. She stroked it some more.

'So what are your plans for today?' he asked.

'Dunno,' she said. 'Nothing planned. It's Saturday. Just chill. What about you?'

'Got a few errands to run, things to do. That kind of thing. But I'm free later . . . '

That smile. It got her every time. She returned it. 'OK,' she said. Then suddenly became aware of the situation. Of who he was, how long she had known him. 'Listen. I . . . I don't make a habit of this, you know.'

'Of what?'

'Of . . . ' She suddenly felt self-conscious, pulled the sheet over her naked breasts. 'This. Picking up men. Bringing them home. I don't . . . I'm not . . . '

His hand was back on her skin, stroking her once more. 'That's OK. I know you don't. I know you're not like that. For what it's worth, neither am I. And if you want to be pedantic about it, you didn't bring me home. I walked you home.'

'Right.'

She nodded, feeling much better. He was still smiling at her, still staring intently at her. She realised that she knew nothing about him. She liked him, but that was it.

'So how did you say you knew me? You told me last night. I've forgotten.'

'Oh.' He pulled his hand away. 'Yeah. Helen. Friend of Helen's.'

Maddy frowned. That wasn't right. 'Helen? That's not who you said last night.'

'No? Didn't I?'

'No. You said Abby. That was it, Abby.'

Something passed over Ben's features, too quick for her to catch. 'Abby,' he said. 'Yeah. She's housemates with Helen. Geology Helen, yeah?'

'And it's her boyfriend or Abby's boyfriend you know?'

'Hers.'

Maddy looked at him. He seemed to realise he had given a different answer to the previous night.

'Well,' he said quickly, 'used to be hers. But I think he's seeing Abby now. Sounds about right. You know what she's like. And Mike for that matter.'

Maddy said nothing. Mike. That sounded right, though. She did know Abby and Mike . . .

Ben looked at his watch. 'I'd better be off. Things to do.'

'OK.'

He turned back to her. 'But can I see you later?'

She didn't reply. He began stroking her again. 'Look,' he said, 'I know you don't know me. And you don't normally do things like this. And neither do I, for that matter, like I said. But I really like you. Really. And I'd love to see you again. Could I?'

Maddy felt herself weakening. Ben touched the bandage on her wrist.

'I'm not an angel,' he said, 'by any means. But I'd never do this to you. Never.'

She looked him in the eye once more. Saw nothing but sincerity. She smiled, feeling herself welling up.

'OK,' she said. 'I'd like that. Lots.'

He returned the smile. 'Good. So would I.' He kissed her, got out of bed. 'Sorry. Got to go. Said I'd help a mate of mine move flat.' He looked at his watch again. 'I'm already an hour late. Give me your number and I'll call you later, yeah?'

She did so. He kissed her once more, held her and then was gone.

She didn't move from the bed. She could still smell him, still feel the cooling warmth from where his body had been.

She smiled, her doubts about him allayed. Or at least pushed to the back of her mind.

She rubbed her wrist. Tried hard not to think about Hugo Gwilym.

36

Phil took a sip from his mug, grimaced. Incredible, he thought. Police officers could catch criminals and solve crimes. In their spare time they could run marathons, get rave reviews in amateur dramatics, write phone apps and computer programs. Even be gourmet chefs. But put them next to a kettle in a station house and they had a mental aberration. He had tried it from the machine and that was, if anything, worse.

He set the mug down on the desk beside him, knowing the sickly-looking pot plant in the corner of the room would be the eventual recipient of its contents, and looked round the room at the team.

His team, he thought, not *the* team. *His* team. It still didn't feel like that. He hoped it would at some point. Soon, preferably.

He tried to concentrate, but his mind kept returning to Marina. Something was wrong, he knew that much. And she wouldn't tell him what it was. That wasn't like her. Usually if something was wrong they would work through it together. Both of them. But she was pulling away from him, withdrawing. And not only did that upset him, but, if he was honest, it scared him.

Driving into work, with Sparklehorse's bruised and damaged love songs playing in the background, he had found his mind coming up with all sorts of theories. And each one led back to the same conclusion: he wasn't enough for her.

She was having an affair and couldn't bring herself to end things with him.

She had had an affair, felt guilty and wanted to tell him.

She was sick of him.

He didn't normally get like this. He was usually strong, could cope with whatever was thrown at him. But the events of the last year, nearly losing his life, moving to a different part of the country, not fitting in, doubting himself and his capabilities while Marina flourished, all conspired to bring him down. And now this.

He turned, back in the room, looking at the murder wall behind him. A photo of Glenn McGowan as he used to be. Then as his alter ego, Amanda. The progression in his journey was evident. Then a post-mortem photo, almost unrecognisable from the first two. Phil tried to blink the thoughts away. Compartmentalise them to a part of his mind where he could deal with them later. For now, he had a job to do. A team to lead.

'Good morning,' he said, looking at the assembled faces before him. 'Only thirteen more shopping days to Christmas. Thanks for coming in, and think of the overtime.'

A couple of polite laughs. He cleared his throat, continued.

'Glenn McGowan, where are we?' He turned to Khan. 'What have we got from the door-to-door?'

Khan looked at his notes. 'From what we've been given so far,' he said, 'we know that he kept himself to himself. That was the main thing that came up.'

'That's what they said about Dennis Nilsen,' said Sperring. That got laughs, including from Khan.

'It's that kind of estate,' said Phil. 'Small. Gated. Attracts people who want to be anonymous. Perfect for what happened.'

Khan continued. 'None of the neighbours noticed anyone else besides Glenn McGowan. Not coming to visit, anyway. Just dropping stuff off.'

'Like what?' asked Phil.

Khan went back to his notes. 'Furniture. Carpet. He had that delivered and laid about a week before we found him.'

'The pink carpet in the living room looked new,' said Phil. 'There must be a receipt for it somewhere. Let's see if we can trace it back to where it was bought from. He had it laid as well? Might be an idea to have a word with the fitter.' He nodded, indicating for Khan to continue.

'Neighbours saw a dining table going in, chairs. Some boxes. They saw McGowan carrying bags and boxes in too. Like he'd been on a spending spree. Or Christmas shopping.'

'Did he have a car?' asked Phil. 'Do we know where it is?'

A DC on the team, someone Phil didn't yet know the name of, answered. 'Ford Focus,' he said. 'We've brought it in to have it looked over. Nothing so far.'

Phil nodded. Khan continued.

'All this furniture and stuff was also about a week or so before we found him. Nothing after that.'

'Which leads us to thinking two things. It was well planned, and that's when the murder was carried out. Or the earliest date.' Phil looked at Khan. 'Thanks.'

The DC nodded, closed his notebook.

'We need to track down not just the carpet fitters but the furniture deliverers too. Get some photos of them, take them round the neighbours again. See if there's anyone of interest there or if we can eliminate them as suspects. See if that leaves us with anything.' He looked at Khan once more.

'Did no one mention anyone suspicious coming or going? Anyone who looked like they didn't belong there?'

Khan took his notebook out once more. *Boy's got a bad memory*, thought Phil. Not a good trait in a copper. He read down his notes. Shook his head. 'No one said. If they did see someone, they must have thought he was delivering furniture or something.'

'Thanks,' said Phil. He turned to Sperring. 'Post-mortem. We've spoken to Esme. Where are we with that?'

Sperring spoke without recourse to notes. *He's good*, thought Phil. *Whatever I think of him as a person, he's a good copper.*

'We're still only at the preliminary stage,' he said. 'And some of you know this already. So to recap. Glenn McGowan was murdered by person or persons as yet unknown. He had his genitals removed. This seems to have been done in the bathroom, and there are no signs of him putting up a struggle. This leads us to conclude one of two things. That Glenn McGowan was complicit in this, or he was drugged. Or perhaps both.'

He paused while the team grimaced, groaned and uttered a few expletives and oaths.

'My thoughts exactly,' said Sperring. 'He died, as far as we can tell, from massive blood loss caused by this mutilation. His body – and we have good reason to believe he was still alive when this was carried out – was then placed at the dining table, where he and his murderer sat down to eat. The meal was McGowan's own genitals.'

More groans, more expletives.

'They were found partially digested in his stomach. And there's more. His arm was wired so that his hand could hold a teacup.'

'Which leads us to believe the whole thing was deliberately staged,' said Phil. 'DNA results in yet?'

Sperring shook his head. 'Nothing yet. Our lad was careful. And we haven't managed to trace what drug was in McGowan's system when he died. Esme's still looking into it. We should know soon.'

'Anything else?'

Sperring continued. 'There are signs that McGowan had engaged in anal sex. Before death, at least. Wouldn't want to think he was weird or anything.'

That got a big laugh. Of relief, mainly.

'And I think,' said Khan, talking loudly to be heard over the noise, 'we might have got it on camera.'

37

They gathered round the TV screen. Khan smiled, looked round. Opened his mouth to say something.

'First one who shouts "Showtime!" is demoted to traffic duty,' said Phil without looking up.

Khan's mouth immediately closed. There was laughter at his expense. He clearly didn't like it. Phil smiled inwardly at that, then chastised himself for being so petty. Khan was young. He would learn. Hopefully.

The DVD started playing. It showed Glenn McGowan, dressed as Amanda, sitting on the sofa in his living room.

Sperring pointed at the screen. 'That's . . .'

Khan nodded, triumph in his eyes. Pleased he had something to show off about. 'DC Oliver and me watched this yesterday. We thought we were on to something. And we are, just . . .' he shrugged, 'dunno what yet.'

As they watched, there was a ring at the door. Amanda got up to answer it. A heavily disguised man entered and the two of them began to have sex.

'Has he come to read the meter?' said Sperring. 'Jesus. Looks like an old porn film.'

More laughter.

'That's what we thought,' said DC Oliver. 'We also thought

we were watching Glenn McGowan's last night on earth,' she added. 'But sadly we weren't that lucky. Sadly for us, that is.'

'You mean he's still alive at the end of it?' asked Sperring.

'Yeah,' said Oliver. 'That's what gave it away.'

They kept watching. The sex took a diversion into pain, Amanda the recipient.

'Watch here,' said Khan. 'The guy gets so into it that it looks like his wig's about to come off.' He froze the screen and pointed. They all peered in, trying to make out the colour and style of his real hair underneath.

'Dark hair,' said Phil. 'Same as the wig.'

'Gets better,' said Khan. 'You don't mind?' He fast-forwarded the action to another spot. 'Here.'

The disguised man had stripped off fully now. His body looked young, hard. The camera went between the two protagonists, trying to get as much action and reaction in frame as possible.

'There. Just . . . there. That.'

Khan froze the screen once more. There was a near close-up of the man's right arm. On the inside of his forearm was a tattoo.

'Looks like a twisted staircase,' said Cotter. 'Or the bars of a cage.'

'It's a double helix,' said Phil. 'Isn't it? Human DNA structure.'

The rest of the team looked at him. DC Oliver nodded, glancing at Khan. 'That's what I thought, boss. I made a sketch of it and checked it out. It is.'

'Good work,' said Phil.

Khan didn't look so happy.

'So he did it already in his living room,' said Sperring. 'What's this, then, d'you think, a dry run?'

'Doesn't look that dry,' said Khan, the picture still frozen, his back to the screen, addressing the group. 'Not when you see some of the stuff later.'

'Right,' said Phil. 'So this must have been after McGowan moved in. And after he decorated, by the looks of it. I don't suppose there's a date on the film anywhere?'

Elli shook her head. 'Sorry, boss.'

'Not to worry,' said Phil. 'We'll find another way in. If McGowan only moved into the house a couple of weeks ago, and he's been dead, I don't know, one week, five days, let's say for argument's sake, then he must have worked bloody quickly to get this place decorated and the camera up and running.'

'Something else,' said Imani Oliver. 'McGowan's in a pretty brutalised state by the end of this film. He's got wounds that must have taken some time to heal. Did the post-mortem mention them?'

'No,' said Sperring. 'Scars, yes. And fairly recent. But healed. Not wounds. Not the kind that would be still be around from such a short time ago.'

'Gets better,' said Phil. He looked at Khan. 'Do we need to watch this through to the end?'

'Only if you want to, sir,' said Khan, an insolent smile on his face.

'I meant is there anything else we can pick up from it?'

'Just one thing,' said Oliver. 'McGowan refers to the other man as Ben. We don't know if that's his real name or all part of the scenario, a role he's playing, but when he – she, sorry, says it, he stops and looks up. Like he's not happy.'

'So that would lead us to believe it's his real name,' said Phil. 'That also fits with something Julie McGowan told us. That her husband had been – as Amanda – seeing a man called Ben. Right.'

Show over, mercifully for most of them, they turned away from the screen. Returned to the usual briefing.

'OK,' said Phil. 'So where does this leave us? Well, we've got a name. Ben. We've got a tattoo of a double helix. I would imagine that would be quite distinctive. We need someone to check the local tattoo parlours. See if it was done in the city. See if anyone answers his description. Tall, dark-haired young man.'

'That should narrow it down a bit,' said Sperring.

Phil stared at him, but realised that the older man, for once, wasn't being facetious. Just showing his desperation.

'And the big one,' said Phil. 'He hasn't been in that house for long. How did he manage to film this in there and then for his wounds to heal before he did it all again, but fatally?'

38

The Arcadian was in the Bullring branch of the Entertainer. He thought he had got away with it. The phone call he received told him he was wrong.

He was standing there, the cheapest, blondest doll he could find in his hand, when he heard the voice. He immediately put the doll down, left the shop as quickly as he could. The mall was crowded almost to overflowing with pre-Christmas Saturday shoppers, all pushing and jostling for their own bit of personal space, forcing themselves and their bags through. It looked like a slow-motion riot.

Usually he enjoyed being among the masses. It made him feel different, superior. He wasn't there for the same things they were after. He liked to move through them, mix among them, unobserved, unnoticed, an invisible shark. But not today. Not now. Because the voice had spoken.

Ignoring the mass of humanity around him, he took himself off somewhere quiet – or as quiet as he could manage – and tried to concentrate. He found a passageway that led to toilets and stairs and stood there. Closed his eyes.

'You fucked up.'

'I . . . I . . . didn't . . . ' His voice sounded weak, even to his own ears. He hated to hear weakness, especially his own. It made him angry but there was nothing he could do about it.

'You did.' Strong, no arguing. 'You took the woman as well. You weren't supposed to do that.'

'No, no . . .' He was shaking his head as he spoke, knowing he would attract attention, starting not to care. This was important. More important than Christmas shoppers. 'I . . . She came in. When I was there. She wasn't supposed to.'

'So what did you do?'

He almost smiled as he said the word. 'Improvised.'

A sharp intake of breath. He didn't like the sound of that.

'But . . . but . . . I made it good. Made it look like a robbery. Threw some, some stuff around. Broke things. You know.' He recounted it as quietly – as professionally – as possible, making no mention of the rage he had experienced. That wasn't important. Not now.

'And left your DNA all over the place, too.'

The Arcadian froze. He had gone over this in his mind, time and time again since the previous night. He was sure he had left nothing incriminating behind. Sure of it. 'No,' he said, trying to pump strength into his voice. 'No. I didn't.'

'You sure?' It was clear he wasn't believed. 'Doesn't sound like it.'

'No,' he said shaking his head rapidly. 'No. I didn't. I swear I didn't.' He took a couple of deep breaths, tried to calm himself. Compose himself. Speak like a professional. One professional to another. 'I was controlled.' He swallowed hard at the lie. 'I made sure nothing of mine was left at the scene. Nothing.'

There was a pause. 'You sure?'

A sudden image came into his mind. The cheap blonde slut lying on the floor the way he had left her. The mess she had been in. And how he had wallowed in that mess. He swallowed again. Felt his fingers shaking as he held the phone. 'Yes,' he said. 'I'm sure. Definitely. Definitely . . . definitely

191

sure. Yes.' He nodded to emphasise the point. To convince himself of it, if not the voice on the phone.

Silence. He wondered if the voice had hung up.

The Arcadian felt he had to say something. His reputation was being eroded. He had to do something, say something to bring it back. To convince the voice that he was a professional, that he could be entrusted with jobs like the one the previous night. If he didn't, then his plan was in jeopardy. He was just another loser. Another sad wannabe.

No. That wasn't him. He was better than that. And he would prove it.

He took another deep breath. Then another. When he spoke, he modulated his voice so it was lower, slower. Calm and controlled. He had read in one of his self-help books that people responded better to slow, deep voices. Found them more trustworthy. That was what he would do now.

'There's no problem,' he said slowly, 'none at all. The woman complicated things, yes, no doubt, but, as I said, I did what anyone would do in the circumstances. Any *professional*. I improvised. There's no way it can be traced back to me. And there's no way they'll connect it with the doll.'

'The doll?'

'The last one.'

'Right.'

'As I said . . .' He paused, building up to the last part of his speech, 'no . . . trouble . . . at . . . all . . .'

The voice made a sound somewhere between a laugh and a snort. 'What you talking like that for? You on Mogadon or something?'

The Arcadian felt himself blush. No one made him blush. No one. 'Everything's fine,' he said, quick as he could.

'It had better be.'

'And the next one will be perfect too.'

But the voice had gone.

He stared at his hands. They were shaking. But not just from fear. From anger. From ... He didn't know. So many conflicting emotions.

He pocketed the phone and stood there staring straight ahead, seeing everything. Seeing nothing. The mall was playing the same irritating Christmas songs on a continuous loop that were always played at this time of year. He hated them. Each and every one. Didn't know how the masses listened to them. Well, he did. Because they were thick. Stupid. Because they knew no better. Not like him.

He thought back to what the voice had said. How it hadn't replied at the end. And his hands started to shake again. He had to have another one, he had to. If he didn't, he would just be back in the crowd. No better than the hordes in front of him. And that could never happen.

He blinked. Once. Twice. Felt tears well up. Kept them down.

'No,' he said, not realising he had spoken aloud. 'I can't. I can't. I've got ... There's things. Things I've got to do.'

He looked back at the toy shop. *Yes*, he thought. *Buy the doll. Go home. Everything will be all right when you get home. You're safe there.*

He walked towards the shop, knocking shoppers out of the way, not caring, not apologising. He had work to do. He was on a mission, a calling. He went back to where the doll had been. It was still there, right where he had left it. He wasn't surprised. What child would want that cheap piece of shit?

He picked it up, walked to the till, ready to pay.

And stopped dead.

There, on a shelf right in front of him, was a red fire engine.

He stood there staring. The years fell away. And there he

was, sitting in front of the TV in a flat in Rotherham, his mother pocketing the money, disappearing out of the door.

'No ... no ...'

He tried not to think of what had happened next, but his mind was set on a track it couldn't get off. He felt their hands on him again. Their breath. Making him ... making him ...

He tried to think of later, when he was out of the YOI, working for them. When he was in charge, when he wasn't being hurt. But he couldn't. All he could think of was that poor, sad, hurt little boy. The red fire engine.

The doll dropped to the floor. People were scared. He wondered why. Then he realised he had been shouting.

And crying.

He turned and ran from the shop.

Ran all the way home.

39

The briefing was continuing.

'Ben,' said Phil. 'Possibly a real name. Might be worth getting out into the gay community, the transsexual community, asking around the bars on Hurst Street for anyone with that name and a double helix tattoo.'

He saw a glance pass between Khan and Oliver. One looked decidedly happier than the other.

Elli was almost jumping up and down to be noticed. She wanted to go next. Phil gestured for her to stand up. With a clank of jewellery she did so. Phil noticed today's T-shirt: *Winter is Coming*. She'd got that right, he thought.

'Thank you,' she said, and scanned the team, clearing her throat. Her eyes widened and Phil spotted immediately the look of someone more used to spending time on their own or with digital friends and colleagues rather than with real flesh-and-blood people. Even the ones she worked with.

'Don't get too excited about the tattoo,' she said. 'That could have been a disguise. Like the wig and facial hair. If he was being captured on camera he might have wanted to throw us off the scent.'

The sense of deflation in the room was palpable.

'But maybe not,' said Elli, sensing the mood and trying to

bring the room back to her. 'I've got some new cross-referencing software that might help us. I'll give it a go.'

There was a silence as the team waited for her to explain what she would be doing, but Elli obviously thought she had said enough and was preparing to sit down.

'Can you run us through it?' asked Phil.

She cleared her throat once more. 'Yes. Of course. It's like ... it's a Venn diagram. It'll triangulate whatever set of facts we want to input. Such as ... well, in this case, for instance, that would mean ... ' She looked over at the screen. 'White male. Age twenties, thirties. History of violence. History of sexual deviance. Perhaps on the sex offenders register. Geographical location, somewhere round here. Not currently in prison. Start from there.'

'But not tattoos?' asked Sperring.

'Well that could be secondary data to input. Although I imagine most of them would have at least one anyway. Start with the first lot. It should give us a list. From that list we extrapolate further. Height, even. That's something he can't fake. Time out of prison.'

'All that's assuming he's known to us,' said Sperring.

'I think from looking at that,' said DCI Cotter, pointing at the frozen screen, 'it's probably a given. He'll have been on our radar in some shape or form.'

'Well, we can try all the variables we want,' said Elli. 'But I recommend we start with the holy triumvirate: sex offenders in one group, violent offenders in the other, work out who's not in prison and off we go.'

'How soon can we get a list?' asked Phil.

'With variables like that? Minutes,' she said. 'The more variables, the more specialised. The longer it takes.'

'Like a Google search for violent sexual deviants,' said Phil.

'Exactly,' she said, nodding.

'Great,' he said. 'Get on it.'

'May I?' She looked at Cotter for permission to leave the briefing. The DCI nodded. Elli went back to her desk, began tapping keys straight away.

Phil's attention was back on the team. 'Hugo Gwilym,' he said. 'What do we know about him?'

'The bloke off the TV?' said Khan, surprised.

'That's him,' said Phil.

'What's he got to do with this?' asked Imani Oliver.

'His name's come up,' said Phil. 'Not as a suspect, I don't think. Although of course we have to keep an open mind. Julie McGowan said that her husband was contributing to a book Gwilym was writing. Providing research, apparently.'

'On transvestites?' asked Khan.

'On deviant psychopathologies. That was the phrase his wife used. I just wondered if his name had come up for anything before.'

Negative head shakes all round.

'Wasn't there something about him a while ago?' said Oliver.

'In what way?' asked Phil.

'I don't think it came to much,' she said, 'and it certainly didn't get as far as us. But there was something, some allegation in the paper about him and a student? They'd had an affair? Something like that.'

Phil noticed Khan rolling his eyes at her words.

'Not illegal, though,' said Sperring, with what sounded like a note of regret in his voice. 'As long as she was over eighteen. You know what those university types are like.'

Phil was aware that Sperring was looking directly at him. He said nothing.

'You know what some of those students are like as well,' said Khan.

197

Some of the team laughed. But not many. And certainly not Imani Oliver, Phil noticed.

'I think we'd better pay him a visit anyway,' said Phil. 'OK. One last thing before we divide up the work for the day. Ron Parsons. He's behind the letting company that rented the house to Glenn McGowan. He sounds like he's got previous. And that makes him, to me at least, a person of interest. But he's before my time. Anyone care to enlighten me?'

There was silence round the room. Eyes found the floor suddenly interesting, shoes scuffed against table legs.

'No one?'

Phil noticed even Alison Cotter was reluctant to speak.

'He was a villain,' said Sperring, eventually. The rest of the team looked up, relieved that someone else had spoken. Even more relieved that it was Sperring. Their reaction gave the DS's words more weight, Phil thought.

'Go on,' he said.

'Back in the day, as the youngsters say now. A villain. But old-school. Had his fingers in everything going. Everything.'

Phil noticed DCI Cotter lean forward, open her mouth slightly as if ready to interject should Sperring keep going. He also noticed that Khan's face was reddening.

'Slum landlord. His letting agency is about all that's left of that. But all sorts. Drugs. Prostitution. Clubs. Extortion. Protection. Anything where he could turn a profit. Any*one* he could turn a profit from. Proper villain.'

'What happened?'

Sperring shrugged. Gave a glance to Khan that Phil wasn't supposed to spot but did. 'He got caught. Did time. When he came out, the parade had moved on. He was old news. And no one wanted to know him any more.'

The room seemed to breathe a collective sigh of relief. Phil was sure he hadn't imagined it.

198

'And that's all that's left of his empire?' said Phil. 'A letting agency.'

'It seems like it's legit, too,' said Sperring. 'Insult to injury.'

'Right,' said Phil. 'Thank you.'

Sperring nodded. Didn't make eye contact with anyone else in the room.

'OK,' said Phil, addressing the team once more. 'Let's divide up those jobs. Let's catch this guy. Ian, you're coming with me,' he added as Sperring was walking away, seemingly about to pick his own assignment. 'Back to school.'

'What?'

'Or at least university. I thought we wouldn't get on to this until this afternoon, but there's no time like the present. Let's see what Hugo Gwilym's got to say for himself.'

40

The front door opened. Hugo Gwilym stood there, smile in place for whoever it was, persona ready, not wanting to disappoint his public.

The smile wavered and fell away. Surprise replaced it. And apprehension.

'Hello, Hugo.' Marina stared at him, barely managing to suppress the hatred and hurt she was feeling. He smiled back, recovering quickly. His features smug once more.

'Can't keep away, eh?' He began to laugh, but stopped when he saw what was at the side of his front door.

A pushchair. With a child in it.

'This is my daughter, Josephina,' Marina said. 'I thought you might be less inclined to try something if she was with me. Move.'

Still looking at the small child, he stood aside numbly, allowing her to lift the buggy over the threshold and into the house. She pushed it down the hallway into the living room, stopped, looked around, taking in the room.

'Thought it would be like this. Your decor. Did a magazine do it for you a couple of years ago? "Handsome Psychologist Invites Us Into His Gorgeous Edgbaston Home"? Am I right, yes?'

He had reached the doorway and stood watching her.

'Yes, yes you're right.'

'And you just left it as it was, yes?'

'How did you know?'

She smiled. There was no warmth in it. 'I'm a psychologist. I read people. It's my job.'

Marina looked at Josephina, who seemed to be happy playing with Lady, her soft toy, in the buggy. She smiled at her daughter then returned her attention to Gwilym, crossing the floor to stand next to him, lowering her voice as she spoke.

'I know what you did,' she said, eyes locked on to his, waiting to gauge his reaction. She would know in the next few seconds whether she had been right. 'To me.'

He swallowed hard, tried to keep eye contact with her. Small beads of sweat had broken out along his hairline. *Either he's nervous*, she thought, *or he's been on the charlie. Or both*.

'What ... what I did. What did I do?' He tried to laugh, pitching for bravado, nonchalance. Missed.

'You know what you did,' Marina said, struggling to keep her voice low, steady. 'You drugged me. You *raped* me.' The word hissed at him. She didn't know if he had or not. This was the best way to find out. Saying it emboldened her.

He glanced nervously around at Josephina, back to Marina.

'What? You worried about me saying the word *rape* in front of my daughter? Is that right? Are those your limits? Is that how far your decency stretches? Not saying *rape* in front of children?'

She could feel her voice getting louder, her control slipping. She took a breath. Calmed herself. Focused again on why she was there. What she wanted.

'I ... I didn't ...' his voice dropped, 'rape you. That's ... that's a lie.'

'Then why are you so nervous? If you didn't do anything wrong, why are you sweating?'

As if noticing for the first time, he wiped his brow with the back of his hand. 'I . . . I'm not.'

'You are.'

'It's . . . hot. In here.'

'No it's not. And it's December out there.'

He was about to reply, but Marina cut him off.

'Look, Hugo, cut the bullshit.' She took a deep breath. Steadied herself for what she was about to say. 'I told Phil. My husband. You know, the detective?'

Hugo looked terror-stricken. 'You . . . told him . . . ?' He clutched his face in his hands.

Bullseye. Marina tried not to smile. 'Yes. I told him everything. As soon as I got home. And you know what? He believed me. That you drugged me, then raped me.'

Hugo looked suddenly like his own ghost. 'But I—'

Marina trampled over his words, trying hard to keep the sense of triumph from her voice. 'Yeah. I told him. And you know what he did? Guess.'

'I . . . don't know. Could you, could you please leave, now . . . '

'He took samples. Blood. Urine. Sent them off for testing. See what's still in my system. What d'you think of that?'

Gwilym looked like he was about to either disappear into nothing or just expire before her eyes. 'I . . . I . . . ' He glanced around as if expecting the house, his world to come crashing down around him.

Marina moved in close to him, face up against his. Her voice low, threatening. Like heat lightning rumbling nearer. 'So what was it, eh? What did you give me?'

His mouth worked but no sound came out.

'Did you slip it in my drink during the meal? All those glasses of red wine you were keen to pour for me? Did you?'

He didn't answer.

'*Did you?*'

He nodded quickly. Beads of sweat flew from him.

Marina nodded, her suspicion confirmed. 'Thought so. And then back here. To rape me. Isn't that right?'

He was about to agree but stopped himself. Shook his head. 'No,' he said, his voice as bleak as his features. 'No. That's . . . No. I'm not, not a rapist.'

'Oh yes you are, Hugo. That's exactly what you are.'

He tried to shake his head again but didn't seem to have the energy.

'How many others? Eh? How many? I mean, I'm sure I'm not the first. What about . . . ' She tried to think of the girl's name, failed. 'That girl in the café? The one who'd been crying, what about her? Had you raped her as well? Is that what she was so upset about?'

Her words seemed to shock Hugo out of his trance. 'No, I . . . That was . . . different.'

'I'm sure. Or at least I'm sure you think so. What if I find this girl? Track her down? See if she's got a similar story to me? What then, Hugo?'

He couldn't answer, seemingly in a trance.

'You're finished,' she said. The words were soft, almost whispered. Like a lover's caress. 'Finished, Hugo.'

She stood back. Smiled. She had got what she came for.

'Rapist,' she said. 'What are you?'

He looked broken, defeated. His mouth was open to answer.

The doorbell went.

Neither of them moved.

It rang again.

Gwilym seemed to snap out of his trance. He moved to the window, looked surreptitiously out.

'Oh God . . .'

'What?' Marina joined him.

'It's them? Isn't it? Them . . .'

Marina looked. Standing on the doorstep were two police officers. She recognised one of them.

Her husband.

41

'**M**r Gwilym?' Phil smiled, but not too much. Just in case. He introduced himself and Sperring; they showed their warrant cards. 'Could we come in, please? We'd like to have a chat.'

'Why? What d'you want?'

There was a tremor in Gwilym's voice and the fingers of the hand gripping the door seemed to be trembling. Phil also noticed a line of sweat along his brow. *Coke?* he thought. *Bit early in the day.* And then: *But he does work in media.*

'Your name's come up in the course of an investigation and we'd like to talk to you about it.'

'Why? What investigation? What . . . what d'you mean . . . '

Phil and Sperring exchanged surreptitious glances. This wasn't the greeting they had been expecting.

'Will I . . . will I need my lawyer?'

'I don't know,' said Phil. 'Have you done anything wrong?'

Gwilym didn't speak, but Phil was aware of the man staring at him intently. His lips were moving, eyes darting, like there was some kind of inner dialogue going on that Phil couldn't fathom but that nonetheless seemed to be directed towards him.

'It's to do with Glenn McGowan,' said Sperring.

Gwilym jumped, his face twitching as if he had just received an electric charge. 'Glenn McGowan?'

'You do know Glenn McGowan, don't you?'

'Glenn McGowan . . . ' Gwilym rubbed his chin, thinking, lips still moving, like he was trying to work out the probability for each possible way the conversation could go, anticipate them, have an answer prepared.

'Could we come in, please?' said Phil. He voiced it as a question but weighted it so there could be no argument.

Gwilym held on to the door as if he would be blown off into the path of a hurricane if he let go, but eventually relented and stood aside. They entered the house.

'In . . . in here,' said Gwilym, slamming the front door and pushing his way down the hallway so that he was in front of them. He opened the door to what Phil assumed was the living room, looking round it first as if expecting to be attacked. When it didn't happen he opened it fully, let them enter.

Phil and Sperring sat next to each other on the sofa, Gwilym opposite on an armchair. He didn't look comfortable.

'So,' said Phil. 'Glenn McGowan.'

Gwilym's face was almost blank. 'Yes,' he said. 'Glenn McGowan.'

'I presume you've heard the news,' said Phil.

Gwilym looked between the two police officers. 'News?'

'Glenn McGowan,' said Sperring, 'has met a sudden and untimely demise.'

'Wh-what?' Again his eyes darted between the two of them. His lips moved as if he was reciting an incantation at speed. 'What? Dead? He's . . . dead?'

Phil nodded.

Gwilym closed his eyes. 'He's the . . . Yes. The transvestite. Yes. Dead?'

Phil confirmed the fact once more.

'How . . . how did he die?'

'He was murdered, Mr Gwilym,' said Sperring, his voice no-nonsense and businesslike.

So I'm playing good cop, then, thought Phil.

'Murdered? Jesus Christ . . . ' Gwilym let the news sink in. The two officers studied his reaction. 'When?'

'I'm afraid we can't divulge those details yet, Mr Gwilym.' Sperring again. Not bothering to disguise the fact that he had taken a dislike to the man. 'I'm sure you understand.'

'Yes, yes, of course . . . ' It was clear Gwilym was just saying the words they wanted to hear. He leaned forward. 'But . . . could I ask what happened? How he died?'

Phil and Sperring exchanged another glance.

'Any particular reason, Mr Gwilym?' said Phil.

Gwilym's eyes held a curious light. Phil knew what it was: self-interest. 'I just wondered . . . '

'He died while dressed as his alter ego Amanda,' said Phil. 'We believe he invited someone into his home who then killed him.'

Gwilym's eyes widened. He smiled, almost laughed. 'And . . . and this is what you want to talk to me about? This . . . this murder?'

'It is,' said Sperring.

Gwilym did laugh then. A short, sharp burst. 'Ask away,' he said. 'Anything you like.' He sat back in his armchair, slapped his hands on his thighs and smiled, looking a lot more composed than he had done when he had answered the door.

Phil was beginning to take a strong dislike to the man. He had to make sure it didn't show. He was glad that Marina had had nothing to do with him. 'We'd like to know what your relationship was to him,' he said.

'My relationship? To Glenn McGowan?' Gwilym smiled as

if about to make a joke, then, correctly judging the reception he would get, decided not to. 'Well, he was . . . Let me think. Glenn McGowan. I interviewed him. Well, initially one of my assistants, my researchers did, but I followed it up.'

'Is that how you work?' asked Phil. 'Assistant first, then you?'

'Pretty much,' he said. 'I'd say it's standard practice. In my trade.' He smiled as he said that, trying to be self-deprecating but just making himself seem self-aggrandising instead.

'How does that work, then?' asked Phil. He was aware of Sperring looking at him, clearly unhappy with the way Phil was leading the questioning.

'Well, I decide on a theme for my new book. Start putting together ideas, threads, you know. Then when these have percolated somewhat, I draw up a list of the kind of subjects I want to interview. The kind that I think will prove or disprove – I like to have something to argue against – my theme, my hypothesis. These people will be representative of what I'm looking for but not clichéd examples.'

'And do any of them ever disprove your hypothesis?' asked Phil.

Gwilym smiled once more. He was on home territory now. In control. 'They may do. At first. But then it's my job to find other examples to refute their claims.'

'Or it's your assistant's job.'

Gwilym shrugged. *Whatever.*

'And then what?'

'Then they all go through an interview process with my assistants.'

'How does that work?' said Phil. Beside him, Sperring sighed.

Gwilym leaned forward, eager to talk about his favourite subject: himself. 'They're given a standardised list of questions to ask. The questions have been prepared by me and depend on what the subject of the book is, though some are fairly standard. You know, childhood, relationship with parents, formative experiences, how a subject's self-defining memories were formed, that kind of thing.'

'Right,' said Phil, nodding. 'And then?'

'Pretty straightforward, really. The interviews are taped, I watch the tapes. Or DVDs or whatever. Hard drives, I don't know. The footage. And from that I decide which ones I want to talk to further.'

'And you decided on Glenn McGowan.'

'I did indeed.'

Phil nodded, wrote something down, looked up. 'Where d'you get your assistants from?'

'What?'

'Your assistants. Where do you get them from?'

Gwilym looked momentarily taken aback by the question. It obviously wasn't the one he had been expecting. 'I ... Students, mainly.'

'Mainly?'

'Yes. Well, virtually all students, I would think. Yes.'

'Students that you teach? Or have taught?'

'Yes. Pretty much. Or ones who come to me and say they want to work with me, can I help them, that kind of thing.'

'So who would have been the assistant who interviewed Glenn McGowan? Can you give us a name?'

Gwilym was about to reply, but at the sound of a small child's voice coming from the kitchen he froze.

42

Marina's heart was pounding, her arms and legs shaking. She pushed her body up against the kitchen door, felt like she was about to have a heart attack or pass out.

The knock at the door, the ring of the bell.

Phil. This afternoon, he had said. Later. He was the last person she had expected to see. Or wanted to see. Especially after what she had said to Gwilym.

'I've got to go,' she had said.

'Why?' said Gwilym. 'Worried about what your husband will say?'

'No,' said Marina, thinking quickly, 'worried about what he'll do to you if he finds me here.'

'Oh. Well. You can't,' Gwilym had replied fearfully. 'I mean, yes. I want you to go. But you can't. The front door is the only way out.' He rubbed his chin. Usually so artfully stubbled, this morning it just looked unkempt.

'There must be a back way.'

'There is. But it leads round to the front.'

'They'd see me.'

'Yeah,' said Gwilym, eyes alive with hatred, voice spitting bile, 'they'd see you. And we wouldn't want that, would we? Hubby coming round and spoiling wifey's big moment.'

Marina ignored him. 'Then I need to hide. Where can I hide?'

There was another knock at the door, another ring of the bell.

Gwilym looked round. 'There,' he said, pointing towards the kitchen. 'Go in there. Close the door.'

'What if they want to come in? What if you need to get something?'

'They can't. I won't.'

They looked at one another once more. Co-conspirators in a play neither of them wanted to take part in.

'Quick. In there. Now.'

Marina had pushed Josephina, falling asleep in her buggy, into the kitchen and closed the door behind her. Stood with her back against it, heart pounding.

Everything had gone wrong. Quickly, in the snapping of fingers. Gone from good to bad. She'd had him. Exactly where she wanted him. Admitting he was a rapist. Then this. She'd known Phil was coming to see him but thought she would have had time to get there first. Clearly not.

She looked down at Josephina. The little girl's eyes had been getting heavy while she talked to Gwilym. The house was warm compared to outside and she was well wrapped up. She had been growing drowsy and now she was off. Good. That was one less thing on her mind.

Marina tried to get her breathing, her pulse under control. She pressed her ear against the door, straining to listen. No good. All she could hear were the voices, not the actual words. The door was old, heavy. Designed not to let sound pass through.

She sighed. She didn't have a clue what would happen next. Would Gwilym confess before Phil had even asked him anything? Break down and tell all? She doubted it. A thought occurred to her. She should have told him to do that. Thought more quickly and explained that that was why the police were there. To arrest him. And that if he confessed before they said anything, before they even accused him, he would be looked on more favourably. It might have worked. But the best ideas, as she knew, always appeared after the event.

She tried to listen again. No good. She thought of cracking open the door slightly, just a little bit, letting the sound through. Too risky; they might see the handle move, want to know who else was there.

So what? part of her brain said. Would that be so bad? Yes, said the other part. Because everything she had told Gwilym was a lie. And there was no way of knowing if Phil would go for it.

She sighed once more, checked Josephina. Still asleep.

She looked round the kitchen. It continued the theme of the living room – designer, a couple of years old – but didn't seem to have been used much. The pans hanging over the central island were dusty and untouched, the chopping boards relatively unmarked, the knives hanging on a magnetic strip above the hob had dull blades. A cursory look in the nearest two cupboards showed that Gwilym lived mainly on ready-made sauces and pasta. He might have been able to impress the ladies, but it certainly wasn't with his cooking.

Something caught her eye. On the draining board at the side of the sink were two glasses, both heavy-bottomed tumblers. One was empty; the other had a small amount of amber liquid left in it. And lipstick marks on the rim.

She crossed to the glasses, picked up the one with the remaining liquid, smelled it. Grimaced immediately. Marina was no whisky drinker, but that was terrible. Even peaty Scottish malts didn't smell as bad as that. She sniffed at it again. It wasn't whisky. Or brandy. In fact, she didn't know what it was. It had elements of both but something more, like a local tipple picked up on a foreign holiday that never got drunk at home and was left at the back of the drinks cupboard. There was something else in there too. A strong chemical aroma. Medicinal.

As soon as she thought that, she knew what it was. Not its actual chemical composition. But what it was meant to do. What Gwilym used it for. It was probably what he had given her at the dinner. Slipped it into her wine, let her drink it. His date-rape drug.

And he had used it on someone else recently.

She picked the other glass up, smelled that one. Whisky. Straight. No date-rape drug chaser.

Her heart was beating fast once more, but no longer in desperation. This time she was energised. Focused. She looked round the kitchen. What she wanted wasn't there. She started opening drawers, cupboards. As quietly as possible.

In her buggy, Josephina stirred. Marina stopped moving until her daughter went back to sleep.

She kept on opening drawers and cupboards until she found what she needed. Cling film. She carried the roll over to the lipsticked glass, pulled off enough film to give it an airtight seal, wrapped the whole thing up and slipped it into her handbag. She smiled.

'Gotcha,' she said.

'Is that Daddy's voice? Where's Daddy?'

She looked round. Josephina had woken up.

213

43

'Is there someone else here, Mr Gwilym?'

At the sound of the voice, Phil's eyes darted to the heavy wooden door at the back of the room.

Gwilym's eyes were wide, staring once more. 'No ... no ... there's ... No.'

'No one listening in to our conversation?'

Gwilym shook his head. 'No. Definitely not.'

'I heard a voice. A child's voice.'

'So did I,' said Gwilym, then smiled, trying to regain control. 'Must have been ...' He shrugged. 'I don't know. A radio next door? Perhaps I left it on upstairs.'

Phil stood up. There had been something familiar about that voice. 'D'you mind if I take a look?'

Gwilym stood also. 'I do mind, yes. This is my house, Mr Brennan, and I don't like people to just go walking round it without my permission. And you need my permission.'

Phil, sensing he would get no further, sat down again, resumed questioning straight away. 'The assistant's name. What was it?'

Gwilym's eyes widened. He too sat back down. 'Erm ... I can't remember.' He was taken aback by the sudden resumption of the interview.

'Try.'

'I can't, not off the top of my head. Is it important?'

'It might be. We would like a list of all the assistants who conducted interviews. Would that be a problem?'

Gwilym looked between the pair of them. There was something going on behind his eyes that Phil couldn't read. 'I . . . don't know. You'd have to speak to the university, not me. They hold those kinds of records. Yes. Talk to them.'

'We will,' said Phil. 'And we'd like to look at the tapes of the interviews too, please. Especially Glenn McGowan's. Do you have that?'

'Erm . . . at the university, I should think.'

'If you could arrange that, please, we'd be very grateful. So what was the book about?' asked Phil. Sperring, he noticed, was now looking round the room. 'Transvestites?'

'No, no. Not at all. No. Free will.'

'Free will?'

'Yes,' said Gwilym, leaning forward, gesticulating. 'Free will. Its concept and actuality in our society today.'

'And where did Glenn McGowan come into all this?' asked Sperring, with the tone of a man clearly wanting the interview to be over. 'Because he liked to dress up in women's clothes?'

Gwilym gave him a patronising smile. 'Not quite. Although the dressing up plays a large part in it. In Glenn McGowan's case, anyway.'

'You wanted to look at what would make someone want to live that way, pretending to be a woman, is that it?' asked Phil.

'Partly,' said Gwilym. 'Glenn McGowan was an extreme case, even amongst the transgendered community. He hated himself. Loathed and despised who he was. Or who he had once been.'

'The Glenn side.'

'The Glenn side. Very good, Mr Brennan. Exactly right. Very astute. Psychologically.' Gwilym locked eyes with Phil, gave a secret smile. It unnerved Phil slightly. Angered him. He tried not to let it show. Gwilym continued. 'Glenn suffered from a very extreme form of gender dysmorphia. He hated his body. Or parts of it. He wanted those parts taken away.'

'Which parts?' asked Sperring.

'The parts to do with his gender,' said Gwilym. 'His genitals.' He smiled, enjoying the reaction. 'Not as uncommon as you might think, you know. You'd be surprised how many extreme castration fantasies I've encountered over the years. I've even met some individuals who have gone through with it.'

'And that's what Glenn McGowan wanted?'

'Yes and no,' said Gwilym. 'He wanted much more than that. He was only happy when he felt nothing. When he was numb. He enjoyed living as Amanda so much more than living as Glenn. He was much happier doing that.'

'His wife might disagree,' said Phil.

Gwilym shrugged. 'Wives, eh?' he said, eyes glittering with that secret smile once more. 'You just can't trust what they say, can you?'

'She seemed pretty insistent when I talked to her,' said Phil, feeling his hackles rise.

'Oh,' said Gwilym, laughing. 'They're always insistent. Wives.'

Phil had been undecided before. But now he had made his mind up. He definitely disliked the man.

'So this book,' said Sperring, his eyes metaphorically on the exit. 'Free will, yes?'

'Yes,' said Gwilym, turning to him. 'As I said. But more than that. It examines how we have the right to live our lives as we want to. As we choose to. This might be despite – or

216

because of – the way society views those who want to do that. Who want to transgress. Deviate. Be deviants. It also examines – in detail, I might add – what lengths some of those deviants will go to to do just that.'

'Right,' said Phil.

'It also examines, through the case studies, the boundaries and barriers that those who want to live that way might – or do – encounter. Social, economic, moral, whatever.'

'So it's about living your life as you want to,' said Phil.

'That's right.' Gwilym nodded.

'And dying as you want to,' Phil said.

Gwilym became uncomfortable. 'Well, that was . . . that was part of the . . . that was one of the reasons behind the book. Of course.'

'Because Glenn McGowan was murdered, Mr Gwilym,' said Phil.

'Professor, actually.'

'*Professor* Gwilym. Murdered. We have reason to believe the murder was planned and premeditated. We also believe Mr McGowan freely invited his murderer into his home. And that he was complicit in his own killing.'

Gwilym was looking suddenly uncomfortable once more. 'I don't know what you're—'

'Suggesting?' Phil leaned forward. 'I'm *suggesting* that if you had prior knowledge that a murder was going to be committed, you had a duty to inform the police.'

'Otherwise you could be an accessory after the fact,' said Sperring.

'Exactly,' said Phil.'

Gwilym's face reddened. 'May I speak freely, Mr Brennan?'

'Please do. And it's Detective Inspector.'

'The people I have interviewed were all extreme cases.

217

Some were fantasists, happy to define their boundaries and live within them. One, as I have just discovered, actually went further than that. He acted out his fantasy.'

'So you knew about it?' said Phil. 'It was there in the interview?'

'Yes, it was in the interview. It was his ultimate fantasy. His ultimate desire.'

'So why didn't you—'

'What? Try to stop him? Talk him out of it? Why should I do that? Doesn't it negate the whole point of the book? Which is, of course, that we all have free will to do whatever we want to with our own lives.'

'Not reporting it was illegal,' said Phil. 'Not to mention immoral.'

'But that's the whole point!' Gwilym was off his seat, gesturing. Phil stayed where he was. Stared at him. Hard. 'What about those people who take their terminally ill partners off to Switzerland and help them to die? Is what they're doing illegal? Immoral? Is it?'

'That's a different issue,' said Phil.

'No it isn't,' said Gwilym. 'It's exactly the same. That's the whole point of the book. To stir things up. Shift attitudes.'

'Or manufacture controversy and shift units,' said Phil. 'If you want to be cynical about it.'

Gwilym stared at him. Anger in his eyes.

'We'll need to look at the book,' said Phil standing up. He looked directly at Gwilym. 'And we'll need that list of your assistants and researchers and access to the taped interviews as well, please.'

Gwilym stared back at him. 'I'm not sure I want to do that, Detective Inspector. Maybe I do need my solicitor after all.'

Sperring stood also.

'I'll see you out,' said Gwilym. He walked them to the door.

Phil and Sperring were crossing the threshold when he spoke again. 'Oh, I did enjoy having your wife the other night.'

Phil turned, stared at him. Gwilym had a smile of triumphant self-satisfaction on his face.

'What? What did you say?'

Gwilym's eyes widened. 'Your wife. Had her for dinner the other night. We're in the same department at the university. The Christmas dinner? I was with her.'

'Really?' Phil felt his hands start to shake, his anger build. He wasn't sure why. 'She didn't mention you.'

'I'm surprised. We had quite a time together. Goodbye, Detective Inspector.'

The words sounded like both an insult and a threat.

Phil walked straight to the car, started it up. He almost didn't wait for Sperring. He drove away not looking back.

He knew Gwilym would be standing there laughing.

44

Marina ran towards her daughter, terrified she would speak again. She knelt down beside her, held a finger to her lips. 'Ssh ...' Eyes wide, imploring.

Josephina, confused by her mother's reaction, did the same. Marina smiled.

'It's ... it's a game, sweetheart,' she whispered, as quietly as she could.

'Does Daddy know we're playing it? Where's the man? Is he playing it?'

Marina flapped her arms, tried to get her daughter to shut up. 'Ssh ... please, Josephina, you have to be quiet. Or it'll spoil the game. Right?'

Josephina, finger on lips, nodded.

Marina smiled, nodded. 'Good. Now you just sit there as quietly as you can, OK?' Relieved, she went back to the door, tried to listen.

Again, she could hear the tone of the voices but not the actual words. She tried to pick up what was being said. It was difficult, but she tried to work out rhythms and cadences and from them make educated guesses as to what the speakers were actually saying.

Gwilym was showing off with his knowledge. That, Marina

would have thought, was a given. This went on for some time. She heard Phil's voice once more and looked over to Josephina to check she still had her finger on her lips. She did. The little girl smiled, enjoying her game. Marina returned the smile but it didn't stay on her face for long.

She listened as intently as she could. There seemed to be some kind of argument going on. Or certainly the makings of one. Then she heard movement and stepped quickly away from the door.

But the movement was in the opposite direction. Phil and his associate – Sperring, she assumed, although she had never met the man – were leaving. Gwilym was showing them out.

She waited, breath unconsciously held, until the front door closed. Then let out a sigh of relief.

'You can come out now,' Gwilym shouted from the living room. 'Hubby's gone.'

She opened the kitchen door, turned the baby buggy round.

'Is the game finished?' asked Josephina.

'It is darling, yes.'

'Can we see Daddy now?'

'Not just yet, sweetheart. We'll see him later.'

She wheeled the buggy into the living room. Gwilym stood in the centre, hands on hips, like he was the lead actor in a bad play and this was the set.

'Well, that was interesting,' he said.

Marina said nothing. Not wanting to give herself away.

'Yes,' Gwilym continued, clearly too excited to keep quiet. 'Very interesting.' He crossed the room, stood in front of her. 'You lied to me. Didn't you? Lied.'

Marina tried to move the baby buggy past him and out of the room, but he blocked her path.

'Let me go, please,' she said.

'Oh, you can go,' he said. 'When I say so.'

Marina felt her hands shaking as she tightened her grip on the handles of the buggy. 'Let me go.'

He kept standing in front of her, unmoving. Marina, seeing she had no choice, pushed the buggy straight at his legs.

Gwilym screamed. Josephina looked back at her, confused and a bit scared.

'Mummy, you hurt him . . .'

'It's all right, darling,' Marina said, eyes locked on to Gwilym's. 'He's not a nice man. He deserved it.'

Gwilym barked a short, hard laugh. 'Coming here to my home with your stories, your accusations, telling me you've told your husband . . .' He waggled his finger at her. 'Naughty, naughty . . . Beware your sins will find you out . . .'

She moved the buggy round him. This time he let her go. 'Liar.'

She turned to him, hands off the buggy handles and on the front of his shirt. 'Yes, you bastard,' she hissed, voice low, 'I lied to you. And what did you do? You admitted everything. *Everything*. You crumbled and admitted everything. Rapist.'

'Oh really? Am I?' He leaned in close to her, his mouth to her ear. So close she could feel his breath, his lips almost kissing her skin. 'Prove it.'

'I will,' she said, pulling back from him. 'Don't you worry. I will.'

'No you won't,' he said. 'Because there's nothing to prove. My word against yours. You've got no evidence, nothing.'

'I'll get some. You can be sure of that.'

He shrugged. 'You won't. Because there isn't any. And there's something else, isn't there? Something you haven't thought of.'

Marina frowned. 'What?'

'You don't know,' he said. 'Not for definite. You don't

know if we fucked. Not for sure, I mean. I know you think we did, but you don't know, do you? You don't know whether I did it to you and you wanted me to, or whether you came on to me. Tiger.' He winked. Laughed.

Marina felt sick to her stomach.

'My daughter's over there,' she said, mouth dry. 'Mind what you say.'

Gwilym smiled. 'Of course. Wouldn't want her to know that Mummy's a nasty cheap whore, now would we?'

Marina saw stars dancing before her eyes. Red ones. Her hands bunched into fists.

'Careful,' said Gwilym. 'You don't want to do anything silly in front of your daughter, do you?'

Marina tried to compose herself. Breathed deeply. Gwilym stepped right up close to her, mouth on her ear once more.

'*Whore*,' he whispered.

She slapped him. As hard as she could, right across his face.

His hand to his cheek and eyes wide in shock, he staggered back, falling into a coffee table behind him, tripping over it and crashing to the floor. He stared up at her, eyes dancing with surprise and hatred.

Marina turned away from him. 'Come on, sweetheart,' she said to a horrified Josephina. 'Let's leave the horrible man on his own now.'

She pushed the buggy to the door.

'Bitch,' Gwilym shouted behind her. 'You've got nothing on me. Nothing.'

'We'll see about that,' said Marina.

And pushed her daughter out into the cold December day.

45

'**Y**ou've gone the wrong way. Sir.'

Phil looked across at Sperring, who, having spoken, had composed his features as impassively as possible. Phil felt anger rise within him.

'Yeah, I know I've gone the wrong way, thanks. If you didn't build every fucking square inch of this city out of concrete and make it look exactly the same as every other fucking square inch and put a fucking flyover and roundabout in the middle of every fucking road then I wouldn't go the wrong way, would I?'

Sperring said nothing. His head was angled away from Phil, looking out of the window. In the reflection Phil caught the look of surprise on his DS's face, along with wry amusement. He knew his outburst would be straight round the office.

Phil sighed. 'I'm sorry. You didn't need that.'

'No problem, sir.' Still not looking at him.

Band of Horses was playing. Phil was sure Sperring wouldn't like it. He didn't care.

Phil sighed again. Gwilym had rattled him. Making veiled but lewd comments about Marina, saying things that didn't tally with Marina's version of the events of a couple of nights before. And Phil had risen to it. Bitten back, even.

Unprofessional, especially in front of Sperring. But he hadn't been able to stop himself.

'So where am I now, then?' he asked.

'Ladywood.'

'Right. And I can get back to the office from here?'

'Course you can. Just follow the road round. I'll direct you. If you get lost.'

I'm sure you will, thought Phil. *And love doing it.*

He looked out of the window. Edgbaston, at the other side of Five Ways roundabout, had been a vast stretch of well-maintained houses sitting behind high brick walls on streets lined with mature trees. Gwilym's house had been one of them. But the other side of the roundabout, the area they were now travelling through, couldn't have been more different. On both sides of the road were stunted, warren-like estates of tiny red-brick boxes, managing to look simultaneously spread out and cramped together, separated by patches of bare, sparse ground. The whole place looked sullen, desolate.

'What did you think of Gwilym?' asked Phil.

Sperring turned, coming out of his reverie. 'Gwilym? An odd one. But these academic types often are.'

'Hiding something? Cagey?'

'Could be,' said Sperring. 'Worth looking into a bit more.'

'Yeah, I think you're right. Something about what he said wasn't adding up.'

Sperring frowned, as if deciding whether to speak. He did so. 'Can I ask you something, sir?'

Phil knew what he was about to say.

'Go on.'

'Cheers. What was all that he was saying about your wife? Sir. Gwilym. If you don't mind me asking.'

Phil hesitated. He did mind. And if it wasn't something that had a bearing on the investigation, he wouldn't talk about it.

225

Certainly not with Sperring, a man he couldn't trust. But he had to. If Marina had lied to him and was close to Gwilym, and if Gwilym became more interesting to them, then that would become a conflict of interest and he would have to declare it and step down from leading the investigation.

And if I do talk to Sperring, it might bring us to a better understanding of each other. He shook his head. He sounded like a teenager.

'I don't know,' he said. 'Honestly. I asked her about him and she said she barely had anything to do with him. She'd seen him around in the department but never really spoken to him, spent any kind of time with him. Always at a distance.'

'That wasn't what he was implying.'

'No,' said Phil, looking at the depressing landscape around him and wondering where he was. 'I didn't think so either.'

Sperring leaned in closer, as if the two of them were sitting in a pub and he wanted to keep what he was about to say private. 'She been different lately? Your missus?'

Phil didn't answer. His hands gripped the steering wheel harder; he pushed the accelerator down further.

'Bit off? You know what I mean. In my experience there's only one reason a woman – a married one, I mean – would play down knowing someone . . . You know what I'm saying? Happened to me. That's how I found out. Then it was bye bye, Mrs Sperring, don't think you'll get a penny out of me, you cheating bitch. And she bloody didn't. I made sure of that all right.' His lips curled into a cruel smile at the memory.

Phil slammed on the brakes. A roundabout had appeared before him. He smacked the steering wheel in frustration. 'Where the fuck do I go now?'

'Turn right. Heading into the city centre. You'll get the hang of it. If you're staying around here.'

Phil didn't reply. Just drove where he was told to drive.

Office blocks and towers appeared. Concrete loomed high on both sides of the road. Cars came at him, seemingly from all directions, knowing where they wanted to go better than him. Negotiating the underpasses and dual carriageways of Birmingham city centre made Phil feel like he was taking part in some futuristic, post-apocalyptic gladiatorial combat. Auto-geddon.

'You know you'll have to step aside,' said Sperring. 'If it turns out Gwilym was telling the truth.'

'I'm well aware of that,' said Phil, turning the steering wheel sharply to avoid a Fiat that had decided to change lanes, seemingly on a whim.

'Can I say something else?' said Sperring. 'Since we're, you know, speaking freely and all that.'

'Go on then.'

'The boy Khan. Nadish. He's a good lad. Got a lot of potential. I know you maybe haven't seen eye to eye and he's probably not the sort you get on with, but don't ride him so hard. Sir. He's not had an easy start but he's got all the mak-ings of a good copper.'

'Your protégé, is he?' said Phil, feeling the anger well up once again. 'That it? You're moulding him, grooming him for greater things?'

'He's a good lad, like I said. The kind of copper we need on the force. Here. In our city.'

'Right.' The traffic was backing up in front of Phil. He wanted to pull away, drive as fast as he could to match his quickening heart rate. Instead he slowed down, joined the queue. Kept his foot off the accelerator, but poised. 'What do you mean? He didn't have an easy start?'

'His old man was a copper,' said Sperring, weighing his words. 'Back in the day. He put up with all manner of shit. Not just from the kids on the street, but from other officers.

Paki. Wog. The lot. And he worked through it. Twice as hard as anyone else. He was hard, tough. He won respect.'

'What happened to him?'

Sperring paused before answering. 'The job claimed him. But he was a good man, before that. I was proud to know him then. And now I'm proud to know his son.'

'Very touching,' said Phil, still staring ahead.

Sperring turned to him. 'You know, you've come here with a lot of attitude. Plenty to say about how we do things wrong and how you'd do them different. How we don't respond in the same way as your team would respond. How we're not as good. All of that. We've put up with a lot from you. *I've* put up with a lot from you. You think I'm an old reactionary. A dinosaur. Don't you?'

Honesty time, thought Phil. Good. About time the air was cleared. 'Truth? Yeah. I think you are. But also, like I said, you're pissed off because I got the job you wanted. And you can't bear it. Every time I say something or give an order, you think it should be you. Isn't that right?'

Sperring glared at him. 'The traffic's moving. Turn right at the next roundabout.'

'I know,' said Phil. 'I know where I am now.'

The traffic eased. The car moved forward. Band of Horses sang about the slow cruel hands of time.

They reached the station in silence.

46

Everything in Maddy's house was looking suddenly better. Everything in Maddy's life was looking suddenly better. And she knew why. Ben.

It was only hours since he had left and already he had made a difference. Just thinking about him, how positive he had been, the way he had gently rubbed her injured wrist, the sincerity in his eyes. The flowers hadn't hurt either. A huge bouquet, lilies and gladioli and some tall, thick-stalked things with beautiful open petals that she didn't know the name of but that looked lovely. There wasn't a vase big enough in the house, so she had used an old rusting watering can she had found in the back garden. Now they were taking up most of her dressing table, and she had to say they looked gorgeous.

The card was standing next to them. *Thank you for a wonderful time. Can't wait to see you again. Ben.* And some kisses.

No one had bought her flowers before. Not even a tongue-tied teenage boyfriend spending his pocket money on things that grown-ups would buy to impress a girl. She'd never had one of them. She'd never had a boyfriend at all. Not a proper one. Not really. There had been boys during her teens, but they had mainly been friends. A few kisses and an exploratory furtive fumble after a school disco one night, but that was it.

Nothing more than that. Not before she had come to university.

Not before Hugo Gwilym.

Talk about in at the deep end.

She smiled. Hugo would have hated to hear her use such an obvious cliché. Maybe she should use them more often. As a tiny act of revenge. Her own little way of getting back at him.

But there were better ways. What was that about living well being the best revenge? Was that another cliché? Probably. In fact, definitely. But did it matter? She looked at the flowers once more. And smiled. No. It didn't.

Living well. Just twenty-four hours ago she hadn't wanted to be living at all. And she had the slashes on her wrist to prove it. But miraculously, in such a short space of time Ben had changed all that.

She took a shower, her head whirling, struggling to process everything that had happened. She was happy. She knew that much. She must be: even the normally scuzzy, freezing, mildewed bathroom didn't seem too off-putting to her.

Ben had come along at just the right time. Her knight in shining armour. Cliché alert! She smiled. Hugo seemed to recede further into the distance. How had she ever fallen for him? Because he was impressive. That was why. For one thing he was older than her, and because of her background she had always had unresolved father issues.

Her mother came from a good family, a good home. But she had a rebellious streak. When she was sixteen she had tired of the stifling family environment and the Cornish resort they lived in and ran off with her older surfer boyfriend. The rebellion didn't last long and she soon returned home. Broken and pregnant. The boyfriend disappeared.

It was hard for Maddy growing up knowing that she had been a mistake, an unwanted child.. Her mother had done her best, constantly reassuring her that even though she was unplanned, having her in her life had turned into a blessing. Rebellion over, her mother had settled down, trained as a teacher and married a local vet. Her stepfather took her in and gave her his surname. Maddy never liked him. She found him creepy and pervy. Looking at her in an unhealthy way once her body started to bud and grow. Her mother evidently agreed, as they subsequently split up. She was teaching at the local secondary school by this time and had become involved with another teacher. He was a kind, decent man and clearly loved Maddy's mother. He asked them to move in with him. They did so. Her mother was happy, Maddy was stable. She still had her stepfather's surname, but that wasn't a problem. It was just what she had become used to being called. She should have felt secure there, but something still gnawed at her.

She saw how happy her mother was, how she tried to make Maddy happy, and she tried to ignore it, but that didn't work. Just that one thought, one seed. It built and built, worming its way into her head, rattling round her brain, then bedding itself down, where it spat out its poison, setting off causal chains of events. One thought, one seed.

I'm not wanted.

As a baby, and now as a teenager, with her mother happy for once in her life. And from there the feeling grew, triggering ever deeper and darker spirals. That was when she was diagnosed with depression. When the antidepressants started. She was still struggling with it, still taking them at university. That was how she ended up studying psychology.

That was why she was fair game for Hugo Gwilym.

He had dazzled her, transfixed her with his radiance. She had thought he was the most wonderful person she had ever met. Tall, dark, handsome, intelligent, funny, charming. A media personality, no less. A celebrity. And best of all, he seemed interested in her.

She couldn't believe it at first, thought she must be imagining things. But no. It was really happening. He would bump into her in the corridor, remember her name. They had coffee, he asked her opinions on certain aspects of the course, what they were studying, and didn't laugh, didn't ignore her when she replied. He really listened.

Maddy Mingella, the unwanted child from Newquay, was smitten.

At first it had been brilliant. Drinks and meals out in bars and restaurants that she would not only have been unable to afford, but wouldn't have had the confidence to enter on her own. Hugo bought her clothes, gave her encouragement. She blossomed. On every level.

She had been a virgin the first time she and Hugo made love. And it *was* making love. Tender, slow and incredibly moving. Maddy had cried after she came, the emotion so overwhelming. Her life had become almost unreal, like something out of a fairy tale. It seemed like it couldn't get any better.

It didn't.

Hugo changed. They no longer went out as much. And when they did, he didn't bother to compliment her on the way she looked. He didn't listen to her opinions either, just seemed irritated that she had them. The sex changed too. Lovemaking was out. Sex was in. As rough as possible.

The alcohol increased. Drugs were added to the mix. Maddy hated the cocaine, what it did to her. Made her head spin, her heart palpitate like it was going to vibrate out of her ribcage. The vomiting afterwards wasn't pleasant either.

And then there was the missed period.

Hugo had stopped using protection. He didn't like it, he

said. Just got in the way. *We'll do without*. And Maddy, taken by surprise at the suddenness and forcefulness of his attentions, hadn't been able to take precautions. Result: one unwanted pregnancy and history repeating itself.

She had collapsed. Unable to cope, in pieces. And totally dependent on Hugo now. He had dropped her off at the clinic, given her money. Told her to get rid of it. She had done.

And then – nothing. No calls, no visits. No invitations to dinner or even for drinks. Like he had never met her. Maddy had never felt so unwanted, so alone. So bereft.

But that phase was all over. It would be like Hugo had never existed. Because Ben was here.

Yes, maybe he seemed a bit vague about who he knew, but she couldn't hold that against him. In the space of one night he had proved himself to her. And now the flowers. She was, she didn't mind admitting, smitten.

She finished washing herself. Checked her fingers. No blood. She smiled.

She got out of the shower, towelled herself dry.

Getting ready to meet Ben.

Getting ready to move forward.

47

The light was starting to fade. The daylight streaking through the windows of the MIU office, weak and dirt-filtered at the best of times, was slipping away. The overhead fluorescents were taking over.

Phil arrived at the office in a bad mood. Marina, Gwilym and Sperring couldn't have given him a worse day if they had got together and conspired against him. He wished he could have just gone home, spent some time with his wife and daughter. Relaxed. Enjoyed life. He remembered the way Marina had been when he left. He doubted that would happen.

Elli was waiting for him.

'Got the list,' she said, smiling.

He stared at her, mind still on the past, not yet on the present. 'List?'

'Local deviants. Cross-referenced and checked, like I said I would. Yeah?'

Phil shook his head, tried to dislodge his memories, bring himself back into the present. 'Right. The list. Yes.' He rubbed his face, his eyes. 'Sorry. Been a long day. A long few days.'

He looked at her. Noticed dark circles beneath her bloodshot eyes. Naturally brown skin turned pale. He knew she would have been staring at the screen all day, pulling down leads.

'For everyone.'

She nodded. 'You're not wrong there. So, you want it? I've broken it down geographically to make it easier for the assigned teams to work on.'

'Yeah. Thanks.' He took the proffered printout. Elli was still standing there, staring at him. She looked about ready to drop. Phil glanced at the printout. There was a lot of work there. Good work too, by the looks of it. He knew what she was waiting for. He didn't blame her. 'You've done a great job,' he said. 'Really. Great job. Appreciate it.'

She gave a small smile. 'Let's hope it works,' she said, nodding, taking the offered praise.

'You been doing this all day?'

'Mostly. Imani – DC Oliver – and me have been going through the DVDs. What larks.'

Phil clocked the look that passed over her face. The dark things flitting behind her eyes. 'Find anything?'

'Apart from the fact that he was a grade A sexual deviant? A few things. May take a bit of finessing to make them into something.'

'Such as?'

'Well, the acts are bad enough. I mean, some of them. Some of them aren't too bad. You know. *Fifty Shades*, and all that. Open mind, consenting adults. Not a crime.'

Phil looked at her. Was she blushing? She had looked away from him. 'Right. Was there something else?' he said.

'Yeah,' she said, not quite making eye contact. 'I think so. I don't know. Well . . . '

Phil waited.

She looked up at him. 'I've got an idea. Just . . . an idea.'

'Do tell.'

She began to look uncomfortable. 'I'm not sure I should. Like I said, it's just an idea. Something I want to work up from the films we've been watching. I don't want to tell you what it is yet in case I'm wrong and I get your hopes up. And I wouldn't want that. No.'

Phil smiled. 'OK. You do what you feel you have to.'

'Thank you, boss.'

She looked uncomfortable once more, as if she'd found the physical interaction taxing and overwhelming. 'I'd better . . . '

'Don't let me stop you. Look forward to hearing from you.'

'Yes. Right. Oh,' she said, nodding at the printout in his hands. 'The teams.'

'My next job.'

'Right.' She nodded, gave an embarrassed smile and disappeared.

Phil turned. Cotter was standing there grinning.

'What?' said Phil.

'Elli's a one off,' she said. 'I'm sure you're discovering that.'

'Every office has one, I think.'

'True.'

'She's got a hunch she wants to work through. But she won't tell me about it until she's got results.'

'That's Elli,' said Cotter. 'She's good, though. Her hunches are usually right too.'

'I look forward to it.'

Cotter glanced round before speaking again. 'How is everything?'

Phil's eyes narrowed. 'How d'you mean?'

'The case. The team. How are you settling in now we're in the middle of a big investigation?'

'Fine,' he said, aiming for circumspection.

'No conflict?'

'A few feathers ruffled,' he said, 'but nothing I can't handle. We'll see how it turns out.'

Cotter nodded. 'We'll see.'

They both stood there, silence speaking volumes between them.

'Right,' said Phil. He looked at the papers in his hands. 'I'm off to organise the teams.'

He turned and left. Feeling Cotter's eyes on him, watching him go.

Judging him still.

48

Phil didn't get far. DC Imani Oliver waited until he reached his desk before crossing over to him.

'Sir,' she said. 'Could I have a word?'

'Course you can,' he said, and sat down. DC Oliver pulled up a chair at the opposite side of the desk. 'Hear you've had a fun time watching home movies,' said Phil.

Imani shuddered. 'Not the best way to spend a Saturday afternoon,' she said. 'But it could be worse. I could have been watching the Villa.'

Phil thought he was just going to smile at her joke but found himself actually laughing. And it felt good. Imani Oliver saw his reaction, smiled.

'Long day, boss, and it's only lunchtime. Anything's funny.'

He noticed for the first time a bundle of papers in her hand. 'What you got there?'

She put them on the desk. 'I've been going through the letting agency agreement for the house Glenn McGowan rented,' she said. 'And there's something not right about it.'

'Like what?'

'Well, you'd expect the house to have been rented out to McGowan personally. Or even the company he worked for. That's what usually happens in these kinds of cases. Or there's an agency that sorts out property on behalf of the company for its employees to stay in.'

'But?'

'Nothing like that here. Glenn McGowan was doing this on his own. Not through his work. So it should be in his name.'

'And it's not?'

Imani Oliver shook her head. 'It's in a company name. Seems to be a holding company, from what I can gather. An umbrella. And guess who one of the directors is?'

Phil shrugged. 'Surprise me.'

'Ron Parsons.'

Phil leaned forward. 'I'm interested now.'

Imani Oliver smiled. 'Thought you might be.'

Any further discussion was suddenly curtailed. The office, chugging along on coffee and overtime, burst into life. Something had happened. Sperring put the phone down, almost ran to Phil.

Phil stood up. Imani Oliver stayed sitting. 'What's happened?'

'Murder,' said Sperring. 'Another one. One of the posh houses in Edgbaston. Two people dead. Very nasty, apparently.'

'They all are.'

Sperring shrugged, looked down at Oliver, not bothering to hide his distaste, then back at Phil. 'You're the senior officer here. You'd better get going.'

'Had I?'

Sperring's eyes were hard and bright. 'Unless you need someone to show you the way.'

Once again Phil wanted to punch him. Instead he swallowed his anger down. Tried to react calmly. 'No,' he said. 'I won't need that.'

'You know the way, then?' asked Sperring, unable, or unwilling, to keep the sneer from his voice.

'Doesn't matter,' said Phil. 'I'm not going.'

Sperring frowned.

'No. I'm not going,' Phil reiterated. 'Know why? You are.'

'What d'you mean?' Suspicion creased Sperring's features.

'You're a detective sergeant, that's a high enough rank; why don't you do it? I'm sure you're perfectly capable of running a murder investigation.'

Sperring stepped in close to Phil so no one else could hear. 'What you doing? Eh? What you playing at?'

'Me? Nothing,' said Phil. 'Does this conflict with anything you're doing?'

'No.'

'Then the case is yours. Go to it.'

Sperring stepped back, looked at him. Sizing him up, playing down his suspicions for the time being, but letting Phil know he was on to him. Phil didn't care what Sperring thought.

'I want to take Khan.'

'Take who you like.'

Sperring looked at Imani, back to Phil. 'I'd better get going, then. Real police work to do.'

'Don't let me stop you,' said Phil.

Sperring turned, left.

Phil was aware of being watched by Imani Oliver. He looked at her. 'DS Sperring and I seem to be encountering communication difficulties.' He kept his face as impassive as possible while speaking.

'Not surprised,' said Imani. 'The man's an arrogant, boorish prick.'

Phil stared at her. 'Do I have to give you a lecture on insubordination, DC Oliver?'

She shrugged. 'If you like. But he'll still be an arrogant, boorish prick.'

Phil smiled. 'You busy?' he asked.

'Was going to watch more hardcore S and M porn. Why, you want to join me?'

He laughed. 'Just wondered if you fancied a ride out to see Ron Parsons.'

She smiled. 'Better than watching the Villa,' she said.

49

Marina kept her hands wrapped round the cup of coffee on the table in front of her. It was too hot to drink, too milky and watery to taste. But she still held on to it. She stared at the surface of the liquid, the steam rising off it, curling away. How easy it was to slip from one state to another. All it took was the right conditions.

She looked round, blinking away thoughts too deep for where she was. A Little Chef restaurant on the A14 near Kettering.

She knew it wasn't a particularly original view, but Marina had never liked service stations. She found them depressing places to be in. The larger ones, with their overlit atriums and overpriced food, seemed like high-end prisons. They gave the illusion of freedom and allowed a modicum of movement, but in reality there was nowhere to go. Travellers milled around the chairs and tables, went in and out of the toilets, tried to convince themselves that the shop held things worth buying. She often wondered about the people who worked there, manning the food stations and tills, maintaining the buildings. Local, static. Even more imprisoned than the temporary travellers.

That was the large stations. The small ones were even

worse. This Little Chef had been made over in the aftermath of a well-publicised visit from a famous TV chef. It had been refurbished in primary colours, mainly red, with low-hanging lighting and minimalist seating. The window booth that Marina was sitting in was bright red upholstered plastic. Despite the changes, she got the sense that the makeover was an effort to maintain.

She looked at the coffee and waited. She was early. She had time to relax, bring herself down and question her actions, tell herself she was being stupid, that what she was doing wasn't rational behaviour. Then the opposite opinion would creep in and she would confirm for herself that she wasn't imagining things or overreacting, that she was definitely doing the right thing. Definitely.

After leaving Gwilym's house she had made a phone call, dropped Josephina off with Eileen, got in the car and driven straight here. She deliberately didn't allow herself any time to think things through in case she changed her mind.

The person she had phoned hadn't thought twice and had offered to meet straight away.

And here she was.

Marina saw her come through the door, look round the room. Marina waved. Tried to smile. The woman crossed the floor to join her. She had the looks, attitude and confidence to carry off anything she wanted to wear. Figure-hugging jeans and big boots, sweater and jacket. Dyed blonde hair contrasting with her black skin. Big smile for Marina and genuine warmth in her eyes.

Marina stood up, hugged her. 'You haven't changed a bit,' she said.

Detective Constable Anni Hepburn smiled. 'Neither have you. And it's been so long.'

They both laughed. Marina out of relief.

Anni sat down in the opposite seat. Looked around. 'Well, this place has gone up in the world.'

'I think it may be temporary,' said Marina.

Anni nodded and smiled.

'So how's Mickey?'

'He's fine, bless him,' Anni said. 'Sends his love.'

'Send mine back. And Franks?'

Anni's smile gave nothing away about her DCI. 'He's exactly the same. I doubt you'll want me to send him your love.'

'You doubt correctly.'

Anni gave a small laugh accompanied by another smile. Then the smile gradually disappeared. 'So what did you want to see me about that was so urgent?'

Straight down to business. Anni was a detective on the team Phil used to run and on which Marina used to be staff psychologist. The two women had always got on well on a personal level but had really clicked on a professional one. When Marina had needed someone to turn to, Anni was the first person she had thought of.

'Well . . . ' She didn't know how to begin. 'Thank you. For coming to see me.'

Anni shrugged. 'You said it was important. And it *was* you. I wouldn't have given up my Saturday afternoon for just anyone, you know.'

Marina smiled, touched. She realised in that moment just how much she had missed Anni. 'I appreciate it. Really I do.'

'So what is it, then?'

Marina took a deep breath. 'Well . . . '

And she told her. About the departmental dinner. About Hugo Gwilym's behaviour. Her suspicions about the wine. What happened afterwards. The blackout. The meeting at the café, the underwear return. The confrontation at Gwilym's house, the near confession. Phil's appearance. Gwilym's triumphant dismissal of her.

She sat back, exhausted. She looked at her hands. They were shaking as she attempted to pick up the coffee cup.

'Jesus Christ . . .' said Anni. 'Wait a minute. Hugo Gwilym. I know that name. Is he the one off the TV?'

Marina nodded.

'Oh wow. Looks like we've got another Savile.'

Marina felt so tired. Just talking about it all had forced her to relive it. She felt like crying again. Anni, sensing that, reached across the table, held her hand.

'Hey. Come on.'

Marina didn't speak, just held on to Anni's hand.

'What does Phil say?'

Marina took her hand away, rummaged in her handbag for a tissue, blew her nose. She had just about managed not to cry. Just about. 'I . . . I haven't told him . . .'

Anni looked at her, surprised. 'Why not? I'd have thought he'd be the first person you would have told.'

Marina shook her head. 'I . . . I couldn't. Anni, what if it was true? What Gwilym said? What if I did go back with him, of my own free will, what if I slept with him consensually? I couldn't remember. I couldn't have told Phil that, could I?'

'Yeah, but what were the chances of that happening? You should have told him.'

Marina looked her straight in the eye. 'Would you have told Mickey? If you'd been in my place? Would you? If there'd been even a shadow of doubt, would you have told him?'

Anni thought. 'OK, I see your point. But you can tell him now, can't you?'

'Soon,' said Marina. 'Hopefully. I need to ask a favour of you. A really big one. That's why I wanted to see you. Why I couldn't have just done all this on the phone.'

245

'Go on,' said Anni.

Marina delved into her handbag once more. She brought out the glass she had taken from Gwilym's kitchen, still wrapped in cling film, still holding the amber liquid. She slid it across the table to Anni.

'What's this?' Anni asked.

Marina told her where she had taken it from. 'I think it might be, I don't know, Rohypnol or something.'

'You want me to get it analysed?'

Marina nodded. 'Please. I know it's a big ask. But as I said, I can't get Phil to do it.'

Anni nodded. Took the glass.

'I'll pay if I have to,' said Marina. 'If it has to be done privately.'

'Leave it with me.'

'I just ... I have to know. If it's, if he ... ' She sighed. 'I know that you're busy and you gave up your day off to come all the way here and see me. But I wouldn't ask if it wasn't important.'

'Don't worry. I said I'll see what I can do. I'll call in some favours. Get it done as quickly as possible.' Anni's features hardened. She was suddenly all copper. 'If you're right about this guy, then it's not just you he's done this to. We've got to get him off the streets.'

'Thank you. It means ... I just ... ' Marina sighed. 'Thank you.'

Anni's hand returned to the table, took hers. 'No problem.'

Marina smiled.

'So,' said Anni. 'When you coming home, then?'

50

'There's one for you,' said Phil from the passenger seat of his Audi A4.

DC Imani Oliver looked to where he was pointing. A white bed sheet had been draped and tied to the side of a footbridge over the road. Painted on it was:

Jack, are the Villa really more important than our marriage? It's over, Jess.

Imani smiled. 'Don't blame her,' she said.

'Thought you were a fan?' said Phil.

She shook her head, eyes back on the road. Lips still pulled up in a smile. 'My dad was. Long-suffering. Any time anything exciting happened he always said the same thing. Better than watching the Villa. I picked it up from him. It still applies. Although these days just about anything's better than watching the Villa.'

Phil had decided to let his DC drive. He could have allowed the sat nav to give him directions, or he could have been stubborn and pig-headed and tried to find his way without it. Or he could let Imani drive. It didn't mean he had given in to Sperring, let the bastard win. It just meant they would get to their destination as quickly as possible. That was all. He nodded. Yes, that was all.

'You OK, sir?'

He became aware that DC Oliver was looking at him.

'Yeah, fine. Why?'

'Just . . . nothing, sir. You were talking to yourself. Your lips were moving.'

'I'm fine, DC Oliver.'

He cleared his throat, looked round. They were headed eastbound on the A41. Phil watched urban areas become suburban. Balsall Heath and Sparkbrook were all old terraces and small estates, the houses crammed together and overspilling on to the streets. The extensions, columned porches, gated fronts and concreted-over front gardens with parked cars made it seem as if an area twice as large had been squeezed in. The grocers' shops were similarly expansive, awnings and stands taking over the whole pavement. Too many cars and not enough road.

'Khan's house is down here,' Imani Oliver said as they passed the end of another crammed-in terraced street in Sparkhill.

Phil looked where she indicated. 'Surprised,' he said. 'Not what I was expecting.'

Imani frowned. 'What d'you mean?'

'I thought he'd have some place in the city centre. A flat overlooking the canal, something like that. A bit more *Grand Theft Auto*.'

She smiled. 'He's a good family boy, is Nadish. Still lives with his mum.'

'His dad was a copper, wasn't he?'

'Yeah. He's dead now.'

'Sperring said the job claimed him.'

Imani gave a snort. 'Yeah, you could say that.'

'What d'you mean?'

She immediately looked like she had said too much. 'Oh, you know . . .'

248

'No, I don't. But I think I should.'

'OK then,' she said with a sigh. 'It was all a bit before my time, but I know the story. Nadish's dad was a good copper. At first. Then he went over to the dark side. Got caught.'

'What happened?'

'Short story? Attached a hosepipe to the back of his car, stuck it through the window. And that was that.'

'Jesus.'

'Yeah. And now Nadish is the family's main breadwinner. Pushed himself to do his dad's old job, looks after his mother.'

'I wasn't expecting that.'

Imani risked a glance at him. 'No such thing as a stereotype,' she said.

They drove on. The cramped houses began to develop space between them as they reached the more suburban environs of Acocks Green.

'What about you, then?' Phil asked. 'What's your story?'

'What makes you think I've got one?'

'Everyone's got a story.'

'Or a journey. Makes it sound like *X Factor*.'

They both laughed.

Imani shrugged. There was a coolness to her, a composure that Phil liked. She weighed words out before answering him. She was guarded, only letting him see what she wanted to. It might make her difficult to get to know, but it would make her a damned good copper.

'What about your name?' asked Phil. 'Where's that from?'

'Imani? It means "faith" in Swahili.'

'Oh, right,' said Phil. 'You're ... what? African, then?'

'I'm from Druid's Heath,' she said, emphasising her Birmingham accent.

They laughed again.

'My family's from there. On my mum's side. My dad's

249

family's all Jamaican. I'm a hundred per cent Brummie.' She shrugged. 'Everyone's got to come from somewhere.'

They lapsed into silence. Phil wished he had put some music on when they got in, or even the radio. But out of deference to his DC he had given her the choice. She had opted for nothing.

The roads widened once more. Greenery became more abundant. Phil sensed they were nearing their destination.

'Ron Parsons,' he said. 'Tell me about him.'

'What d'you want to know?' she asked.

'I know nothing about him. Everybody clams up when his name's mentioned. Why? He's a villain, isn't he?'

'Yeah, one of the old firm,' she said. 'Before my time. Bit of a legend, by all accounts. The usual stuff, prostitution, protection, clubs, the lot. If it was bent and there was money to be made, especially through violence, he was involved.'

'And then prison?'

'Well, it was a bit more than that. You see, the West Midlands force had a bad reputation at the time. Corruption. And Ron Parsons was right in the middle of it. He got caught and went down. But he made sure he went down with casualties.'

'What d'you mean?'

'Tried to take half the force with him. If he was going to do time, he wasn't going to do it alone. Was going to name names.'

'I don't remember much of a fuss. Was there one?'

'A bit. It was hushed up mainly. Most of them took early retirement or were moved where they couldn't cause trouble. There was a lot of bad feeling. Coppers protecting their own and all that. Some wanted it all out in the open, the guilty named and tried. Everyone was tarnished.' She sighed. 'All ancient history now, though.'

'Was Sperring involved?'

She shook her head. 'No. But he's often talked about it. Came in on the tail end.' She looked at Phil, then quickly away, weighing her words again. 'But you know who *was* involved.'

'Let me guess. Khan's old man.'

'Exactly. He was caught. Given a choice. Turn evidence on Parsons and his lot, or go to jail for a long time.'

'What did he do?'

'Neither. Killed himself. Couldn't live with the guilt.'

'Jesus . . .'

'Yeah. I know. Didn't matter really. Not to the case. Parsons still went down.'

Phil rubbed his chin. 'Wow,' he said. 'And now he's back. How does Khan feel about that?'

'I wouldn't know,' she said. 'We're not close.'

'Right. But Parsons is working legit. Does that strike you as odd?'

'A bit,' she said. 'From what I hear, he still thinks he's got his empire. I mean, while he was away, there were others came and took his place. He created a vacuum. The Pakistani gangs and the Yardies moved in and filled it. And Parsons can't accept that.'

'Like a king who doesn't reign any more but still wants to be treated like one,' said Phil.

'King Lear,' said Imani. 'But without the madness and the daughters. Well, without the daughters. We'll see about the madness.'

Phil gave her a sideways look. 'You're not like the rest of the team, are you?'

Again she weighed her response before giving it. 'No,' she said eventually. 'I was fast-tracked. Graduate programme. I think I'm good at what I do – not being immodest; I just wouldn't be able to do it if I didn't think that – but some people don't agree.'

'You mean Sperring.'

She nodded. 'Just because I didn't come up through the ranks. The hard way. I didn't pay my dues, apparently. And he mistrusts me because of that. Told me so.'

'It's not because of that,' said Phil. 'It's because you're going to have his job one day.'

She pulled the car to a halt. Phil looked at her.

'We've arrived,' she said.

51

The house, like its owner, had seen better days.

It had been opulent once, but that was when Bucks Fizz were riding high in the charts. And it had last been decorated then too, Phil thought. He had heard of people discovering their self-defining memories and basing the rest of their lives round them. But he'd never heard of it happening to houses before. This one seemed to have reached its full potential thirty years previously and not developed subsequently. It was a large semi, with wrought-iron scrollwork round the windows and supporting an upstairs balcony. The windows looked like they needed replacing and the stuccoed front wall was mildewed. The drive was gravel, dotted with clumps of weeds. It looked like it had once been the best house in the street but while it was resting on its laurels every other house had come along and overtaken it.

Solihull was a pleasant suburb, thought Phil, if you liked that sort of thing. They had driven in past a wooded park and a golf course. Most of the houses were trim and conservatively but expensively maintained. Four-by-fours and prestige saloon cars sat on the driveways. A few Minis and Fiat 500s, presumably first cars for teenage offspring.

They had parked next to a Mini on the driveway. Pulled up

to the garage doors was an MG. It looked as well looked after as the house.

Phil and Imani exchanged a glance. Phil rang the bell, waited. The door was answered by a middle-aged blonde woman. It took Phil a few seconds to place her. Cheryl, the secretary from the letting agency.

He held up his warrant card, announced himself. 'Hello again, remember me? I just want to have a few words with Mr Parsons. Won't take long.'

Her eyes darted from side to side and she opened her mouth to give out a lie, but Phil saw a shadow move behind her.

'Is that him? Mr Parsons?' Phil stepped over the threshold. 'Mr Parsons? Sorry to trouble you at home. Could we have a quick word, please?'

Ron Parsons tried to move away, but seeing that Phil had already entered, he stopped. Phil went towards him. He noticed that the hallway was large, a curving wrought-iron staircase dominating. The glass in the door frames was bevelled and obscured. Panes that had been broken and replaced more recently didn't match. An ancient Chinese rug covered the wooden block floor.

'Come in,' said Parsons, clearly not happy.

He led Phil and Imani to a sitting room. The nondescript armchairs and sofa looked modern but didn't fit in with the rest of the room, which was, in keeping with the rest of the house, like a museum to eighties design. Like Parsons had been forced to buy something more recent but was so stuck in the past that he didn't know what would go. He crossed to a gold-plated drinks trolley, the kind that would sell for a small fortune in a Custard Factory vintage shop, poured himself a whisky. A large one. He didn't offer them anything.

While he was doing that, Phil's eyes were drawn to a row of photos on the wall of the alcove behind the drinks trolley.

They showed two young men, one large and ebullient, one slighter and more studious. The way they were arranged, the ebullient young man seemed to be the centre of the display.

Ron Parsons sat down in an armchair. Phil studied him. He looked different to the person he had met the other day. Smaller. Older. Less intimidating. He was dressed in jogging bottoms and T-shirt with a mismatching hoodie over the top. Old trainers on his feet. Unshaven. Red-faced.

'Been working out,' he said. 'Reach that age. Got to keep yourself in condition.'

'Absolutely,' said Phil, for something to say. Parsons could just be making conversation, but from the look in his eye Phil thought it was more to do with being ashamed to be discovered in anything other than a suit. He was old-school. His suit was his armour.

Parsons took a sip of his drink. Cheryl bustled in, but Parsons waved her away. She left looking sour, dejected. 'The wife. Checking up on me. Probably wanted to make you tea.' He shook his head. 'What d'you want? This is Saturday. I'm at home. There are rules.'

'I know, Mr Parsons,' said Phil, 'but I just wanted to run a couple of things by you.'

'What?'

'To do with the house you let to Glenn McGowan.'

Parsons looked irritable, if not angry. 'Couldn't it wait till Monday? Monday's a work day. Weekends are for family. It's not the done thing turning up here. Not the done thing.' He pointed a long, bony nicotine-yellow finger. 'You should know that. Time was you knew where you were in this town.'

Phil remembered the conversation he and Imani had had in the car: *Like a king who doesn't reign any more but still wants to be treated like one.* A perfect description.

'What d'you want to know?'

'There's a discrepancy in the paperwork,' said Imani.

Parsons stared at her, not bothering to hide his distaste. Phil didn't know whether that was because she was a woman, black, a police officer or all three. 'So what.' Another mouthful of whisky. 'It can wait till Monday.'

'No, Mr Parsons, I'm afraid it can't,' said Phil. 'We're in the middle of a murder investigation and we have to explore every avenue. It's our job. And I'm afraid murder inquiries don't keep office hours. Because murderers don't.'

Parsons muttered something under his breath, took another pull of whisky. The glass was empty. He stood up, went to the trolley, poured himself another one. Sat down again sighing. Waved his hand at Phil. Continue. The gesture managed to look both regal and defeated at the same time. Imani leaned forward.

'There's a discrepancy between what you told us and what the papers show, Mr Parsons.'

'Discrepancy, what discrepancy?'

'The house you let to Glenn McGowan,' she said. 'That wasn't to the company he worked for.'

'So?'

'It wasn't to him personally, either. It was to a holding company. An umbrella company.'

Parsons shrugged, knocked back the whisky. 'So? Why's that important?'

'Because you're one of the directors,' said Phil. 'It's your company.'

'No it's not,' said Parsons quickly, then looked at them, realising his mistake. His eyes darted to the photos on the wall, as if he found them suddenly interesting. 'Well, all right. What if it is? So what?'

'Why didn't you think to mention this before, Mr Parsons?' said Phil.

Parsons shrugged. Said nothing.

'We did some more digging,' said Imani. 'It turns out that you – or rather Shield Holdings, the company of which you're a director – actually own the property. Care to explain that?'

'What's to explain?' Parsons squirmed in his chair. Phil felt waves of heat coming from the man. Anger. 'The holding company owns the house. It's entirely separate to the letting agency. The letting agency lets it out. We make a profit.'

'Well, yes,' said Phil, 'you would. If you weren't leasing out your own property to yourself. Where's the profit in that?'

Parsons said nothing.

Imani continued. 'We found another couple of interesting names on the board of directors of Shield Holdings. Cheryl Parsons.' She looked towards the door. 'I believe we've had the pleasure?'

Parsons said nothing. Just stared at them, drained the whisky.

'And Grant Parsons. That your son?'

Parsons's expression changed. His cheeks, already flushed, turned beetroot. He looked like he was about to have a coronary. But Phil noticed that there was something else mixed with the anger in his eyes. Fear. Parsons's eyes flicked over to the photos once more.

'Leave my son out of this,' he said. 'You've got nothing . . . He's got nothing to do with this.'

'To do with what, Mr Parsons?' Phil felt his stomach flip. He was on to something. He knew it.

Parsons tore his eyes from the photos, stood up. 'To do with . . . ' He gestured with the hand holding the whisky glass. 'This. Anything. You leave him out of it.'

Phil remained seated. 'Can I ask—'

'No. No, you can't ask. You can't ask anything. If you want to talk to me, from now on, you make an appointment and do

257

it in office hours. And I'll have my brief with me too. He'll answer your questions for you.'

'Mr Parsons—'

He cut Imani off. 'Coming here to a man's house on a weekend, like he's a . . . a . . .'

'What, Mr Parsons?' said Phil. 'Witness? Suspect? Criminal?'

Anger flared once more in Parsons's eyes. No fear this time; he was on home territory. 'Get out. Both of you. Out. Now.'

They got out.

Didn't speak until they were in the car and driving away.

'See the way his eyes went straight to the photos on the wall?' Phil said.

'I did. Two of them there, though. Wonder which one's Grant.'

'I'm sure we'll find out.' Phil leaned across, switched on the radio. 'Better than watching the Villa?'

Imani smiled. 'Definitely.'

52

'Jesus Christ . . . what a fucking mess . . . Bloody savages . . . '
Sperring looked round the remains of Keith Burkiss's living room. Khan stood at the door, decoding messages from his stomach, deciding whether it was safe to enter.

'It looks . . . ' the DC swallowed hard, 'like an abattoir . . . '

The forensic scene investigators were just finishing up. Trying to glean all they could from what was left of the room. Which wasn't much. There was a body half in, half out of a wheelchair. A man, or what was left of him. Another body lay by the door. Or most of it did. A woman.

'If you're going to spew your ring, do it outside. I need you here working,' Sperring said, not looking round. Khan turned, left the room quickly.

Sperring stared at the carnage before him. Being squeamish wasn't something he had any time for. Khan had the makings of a good detective, but if dead bodies upset you, go work Traffic. He didn't want bleeding-heart liberals on the job feeling sorry for whoever was dead. Not like fucking Brennan. Wouldn't be surprised if the DI got little crystals out and started trying to commune with the dead. Fucking hippy. Sperring realised he was letting his anger at his boss cloud his judgement. He took a few seconds, got Brennan's face out of his head.

No, as far as Sperring was concerned, he wasn't looking at people. Not any more. He was looking at a crime scene. And it was his job to catch whoever had done it. Plain and simple. That was what he told himself; that was how he dealt with it. He didn't like post-mortems, it was true. But that, he rationalised, was different. That was the aftermath. This was a crime scene.

But Jesus, what a crime scene. Jo Howe and her FSIs had tagged, bagged and numbered as much as they could. Little yellow markers dotted the floor of the room. Sperring, in his paper suit, was careful not to disturb any of them, walking in and out only on the common approach path laid out for him.

He looked down at the first body, the woman, and felt himself gag. No, he told himself. I won't do it. I'm harder than that. He swallowed, ignored the sudden lightheadedness he felt and glanced again at the body. She looked like she was dressed up for a night out. A short, tight party dress was still on her torso. Torn and bloodstained, it was revealing more than she had anticipated, he thought. Her high-heeled shoes were partially on her feet, one heel snapped off, the straps still round her ankles. But it was her face, or what was left of it, that drew his eye and repelled him at the same time.

'Worked out what's happened?' said Jo Howe, crossing over to him. 'I can see the cause of death.'

Sperring nodded, didn't look up. 'Stevie bloody Wonder could see the cause of death.'

The living room wall looked like a gigantic meat painting. From the remains of the woman's face, it was clear that someone had taken her by the back of the head, probably holding on tight to her hair, thought Sperring, and smashed it repeatedly into the wall. Until she was dead. He looked again. No, he thought, long after that.

There were other marks on her body too. Cuts. Burns. She didn't go easy.

He turned away from her, studied the dead man. He looked shrunken. That was the first thing Sperring noticed. Not the lack of legs; the fact that it seemed as if he'd recently lost a lot of weight and his body hadn't caught up with the fact. His skin was used to being stretched and the abrupt contraction meant it had no elasticity. It hung in folds around his arms, his neck.

His death had been different to the woman's. Sperring could see that much. No blood at all. A pillow lay nearby. He knelt to examine it. Careful not to touch, he scrutinised the surface, looked at it from different angles, let the light catch it. He found what he was looking for. Dried saliva.

'Smothered,' a voice said from behind him.

He turned, stood. Esme Russell was there, similarly suited.

'You looked already, have you?' he said.

'A cursory once-over. Smothered. Most probably with that pillow.'

Sperring nodded. Jerked his thumb to the doorway. 'And her over there?'

'A much more unpleasant ending. It looks like it was the repeated bashing that finally killed her, but her body is covered in marks. I won't know if those were made before or after her death until I've properly examined her, but my instinct says before.'

'He played with her, then killed her,' said Sperring. 'Took his time.'

Khan re-entered. Sperring turned to him. 'Nice of you to join us. What you brung to the party?'

Khan took out his notebook, opened it. He knew how Sperring would react if he came in empty-handed, especially after his embarrassing retreat. So he had dug up some information.

261

'House belongs to Keith Burkiss. He has an ex-wife, Kelly, but they had a bit of an on–off relationship, apparently. Divorced, but she was back living with him.'

'Well it's permanently off now,' said Sperring. 'Who told you this?'

'Next-door neighbour. Apparently the wife divorced him when he got cancer. And diabetes. Said he had to have his . . . ' Khan trailed off, looked at the body. 'Oh yeah.'

'His legs amputated, you mean. Keep going.'

Khan managed to drag his eyes away from the scene and back to his notebook. 'She came back, the wife, Kelly. Well, ex-wife now. Don't know when. And . . . ' he shrugged, 'that's it.'

Sperring thought for a moment. Scrutinised the room. Took in the carnage. The place had been destroyed. Not just the bodies, but the furniture, the TV, ornaments. He turned to Khan.

'You're probably too young, but can you remember the Manson Family?'

Khan frowned. 'Was that a TV series? Did they play instruments?'

Sperring shook his head. Maybe Khan wasn't such a good copper after all. 'No. They were a cult in California in the late sixties. Manson would tell them what to do and they'd break into some rich Hollywood type's house, cause as much damage as possible and rape and murder whoever was there. Looking at this, all this, that's what I think it must have been like.'

'Right,' said Khan. 'So you think this is a cult, yeah? Some ritualistic murderer?' His eyes were glittering with excitement.

'Is it bollocks,' said Sperring. 'It's just some mental-case druggie who broke in, found him at home, thought he was an easy target, then was disturbed by her. Then lost his shit. That's what I reckon. That's what it looks like.'

Khan looked disappointed. Then a sudden thought struck him. 'Hey, d'you think it might be connected to that transvestite murder?'

Sperring stared at him. 'Why? What can you see here that could possibly link the two?'

Khan looked round, then back to Sperring. Defeat in his face. 'Nothing.'

'Right. Nothing. Mental druggie. We'll ask around. He'll turn up sooner or later. Bragging about what he's done. Trying to flog off what he's nicked. Going mental somewhere else. We'll catch him.'

Khan nodded. 'Right. But shouldn't we, you know, check other stuff as well?'

'Like what?' Sperring was irritated now.

'Well,' said Khan. 'Burkiss was suffering from cancer. We should find out if it was terminal, and if it was if anyone had anything to gain from his death. Financially, I mean. Did he have a will, you know. Like that. All that kind of stuff.'

Sperring sighed. Saw work piled up ahead for him. 'Yeah, all right. Do that. Let's examine all the avenues.'

'Isn't that what DI Brennan would say?' said Khan.

Sperring turned to him. 'Fuck DI Brennan.'

Khan laughed. 'Yeah,' he said. 'Fuck DI Brennan.'

Sperring smiled. 'Good lad. Glad we agree on something.' He turned to Jo Howe and Esme Russell. 'Thank you, ladies. All yours.'

He turned and left the room. Khan scurrying after him.

53

The Arcadian hated this time of day. That crepuscular transition between the dying day and the not-yet-born night. It was the heavy trudge home, the missed opportunities of the day, the optimism that had arrived with the morning now transformed into failure and sadness. Or maybe it was just him. Maybe everyone else liked it. Thought it contained the possibility of fun, adventure. Looked forward to seeing what the night brought.

Maybe.

He looked at the doll's house once again. The figure of the doll, his beautiful firstborn, still looked lonely. Her smile more painted on than ever, her hair sticking out and unkempt from where he had repeatedly stroked it. She looked worn from being carried. The grinning idiot with the cut-off legs beside her did nothing to help either. The Arcadian had added the blonde bimbo doll to the scene. But it still wasn't right. He had tried to make her fit in, taken a knife to her features, carved and cut away. Stabbing her in the face at the end. But it still wasn't right. He looked again. And felt nothing but sadness at the house, sinking down into depression.

The phone call hadn't helped. He had thought he had done the right thing. Disguising his tracks by making it look like a burglary. He had thought he was being clever. Apparently not.

He had run from the Bullring Centre, back home, where he had pulled down the hatches, locked them behind him and just sat on the floor, giving himself over to despair. He had cried and screamed and sobbed. Once he was all cried out, once he was empty, despair had eventually given way to anger.

He had stood up then, begun to pace. How dare he talk like that, say what he had said. To him. *To me. Who the fuck . . . who the fuck . . . I'll show them*, he thought. *Teach them a lesson. Go in there, confront them. Tell them what's what.* Eventually his anger had subsided too and he had slumped to the floor once more. Drifted off, staring. He didn't know how long for.

No butterfly. That was the thing that upset him the most about his work at the big house. No butterfly from either of them. He hadn't been surprised at the man. Wouldn't have expected it. But the woman . . . He had thought he would have seen hers leave her body. After all, he had spent a long time on her. Worked her up into the kind of state where the butterfly should have appeared. But it hadn't. He sighed. Sometimes he wished he had never heard from the voice. He had been happy enough before. In his own way.

The club had been everything to him. He had loved it. Lived for it. Before that . . . nothing. *He* was nothing. His *life* was nothing. *Nothing*. Just a mass of directionless energy. Uncontrollable. And that lack of control got him into trouble. With others, with himself. And worst of all, with the law.

Prison. He had hated prison. Especially the wing they had put him on. The Vulnerable Prisoners Wing. That was the official name. But everyone called it something else. Something more accurate. The Weirdos and Paedos. Nonces and Ponces. That was where they had put him. Where he had to stay.

The rest of the prison hated them. Hated *him*. He knew that. It was an open secret even amongst the screws that they were the lowest of the low. And they all hated each other too.

He was stuck with some right head cases. Real nut jobs. One man had taken a machete to his five-year-old daughter after she threatened to tell her mother what he was doing to her. Another told everyone he was in love with his fourteen-year-old niece, saved up all his phone time to call her, tell her what kind of love he was going to give her when he got out. Another was a screw who'd gone bad. The Arcadian heard the other screws talking about what he had done to his son. He reckoned he was the worst of all.

All fuck-ups. But not him. He was too clever for them. He wouldn't be coming back. Not that he was rehabilitated. No. He hated that word. He just knew how to be clever. Not get caught. He had spent a long time thinking about what had got him in there in the first place. And it wasn't what he was doing. No. Plenty of people did what he had done and got away with it. It was how he was doing it. No control. That was it. What he had to do. Learn control. Do that, and he would be unstoppable. Untouchable.

Because prison, the Arcadian knew from first-hand experience, didn't rehabilitate. It didn't correct, wasn't correctional, like they said in America. It incarcerated. It *hid*. Took the most damaged and dangerous and put them in the shadows. Hiding. Waiting. Biding. The shadows provided nourishment, kept them away from the light, toughened them with hatred, strengthened them with anger. Then released them. Hiding no more. Out of the shadows and into the light.

He took as many courses as he could, used the prison library all the time. Power. That was what he wanted. And knowledge was the best power of all.

When he was released, he kept himself to himself. Didn't

meet up with any of his previous or known associates, as the coppers called them. He knew they would be watching him. Waiting for him to step out of line. One wrong move . . . He wouldn't give them the satisfaction.

But what to do instead? He needed release. An outlet. He came to Birmingham, hit the gay scene. He sold his body to rich old perverts. That kept him going for a while, even bought him somewhere to live. He didn't enjoy it but he did all right. Then one of those rich old perverts told him about the club. Not just any club, *the* club.

And his life changed. For the better. For ever.

He was scared at first. Didn't know what to expect. But he soon got the hang of it. Soon fitted in. Because he understood the ethos. Knew what it was about. It wasn't just a place for deviants to go and get off and have the strength to go about their boring nine-to-fives once more. You could find that any-where. No. It was more than that. It was about honesty and desire. It was about admitting who you really were. To others, to yourself. And acting out those urges.

He loved it. It felt like coming home.

He could be as uncontrolled as he liked in there. Nobody minded. Even encouraged him. So he was. And he loved it. He also discovered that it was enough. He didn't let his activ-ities at the club spill over into the rest of his life. Didn't need to. He had balance. He knew who he was.

He had been noted. Spotted. Because of that, he was asked if he'd like to take things further . . .

And look where he was now.

The Arcadian opened his eyes. The doll's house was still in front of him. He studied the dolls once more. Maybe they didn't look so bad, he thought. Maybe it would all work out.

Maybe.

He felt something like a shaft of sunlight pierce his body.

That was the only way he could describe it. Like the windows had been opened and everything was much warmer, brighter. The clouds had gone. He didn't know where this sudden burst of optimism had come from, but he was pleased to feel it. He smiled, stood up.

He would go out. Yes, that was what he would do. Get dressed up, go down to Hurst Street, see what – or who – he could find. Take his mind off things. Get a workout. Sport sex, someone had once called it. Yeah. That was it. Just what he wanted.

And fuck the voice. Fuck the lot of them.

Feeling almost happy, his burden temporarily lifted, he began to plan his evening out.

Looking forward to seeing what the night brought.

54

Maddy was impressed. Very impressed. She had eaten in Indian restaurants and balti houses before, what student hadn't? But this one seemed different. A bit more upmarket. A bit flash. No, not flash. Sophisticated.

She looked round the place, tried to see it more rationally. It wasn't that upmarket, not fine dining, but it was certainly a lot higher up the scale than the normal student eateries she went to with her friends. Chain pizza restaurants in town and cheap baltis in Selly Oak and Ladypool Road.

This place had understated decor. Tables decorated with Indian fabrics. Comfortable contemporary leather dining chairs. Traditional wall hangings and shelved metal antiques sat alongside suffused modernist lighting panels. It was, to her, a lot more than just a local eatery in Moseley village.

And they were drinking cocktails. *Cocktails*. She had had cocktails before, of course. But that was on party nights with the girls, celebrating end of term or Christmas or exams or something. But never as a prelude to dinner. And never with someone else buying. No, correct that: a handsome young man buying.

Ben sat opposite her, smiling. He had scrubbed up well. Good hair. Nice shirt. Eyes locked on hers. Unflinching, unmoving. A long red drink in front of him. She stifled a giggle. He looked like an elegant vampire.

He held up his glass. Cranberry chiller, that was what he had asked for. He waited. She realised she was supposed to raise hers too. She did so.

'Here's to ... ' He lifted an eyebrow. 'What?'

She gave a small shrug and immediately regretted it. She felt so silly and girlie doing it. But that was how he was making her feel. She was trying to be cool and distant, sophisticated and grown up, but it wasn't working.

'Don't know,' she said. 'Friends?' *Us.* That was what she wanted to say. *Us.* But she didn't want to sound presumptuous. Forward.

'Us?' he said.

She giggled again. 'You read my mind.'

They clinked glasses. Drank. The French martini, all pineapple and raspberry and vanilla, was very sweet. Deceptively sweet, in fact. She realised her glass was nearly empty.

'Another?'

She didn't have time to answer. Ben was already calling the waiter over, asking for another drink for her. She noticed his was barely touched.

He leaned forward. Still looking at her. Took her hand in his. It was warm, there was strength in it. Smiling all the time.

'Thank you for the flowers,' she said.

He looked away as if shy or embarrassed, but turned quickly back to her. 'Were they OK? Did you like them?'

She nodded. 'They were ... lovely.' She felt his grip on her hand tighten. His smile increase in wattage. 'They were the first ... No one's ever bought me flowers before. Not like that.'

'I can't believe that.'

'It's true, honestly. They were ... ' she felt a thrill of pleasure run through her at the thought, 'lovely.'

Her drink arrived. She took a sip. Then a longer one. Just as good as the first. She blinked. 'I'll have to be careful,' she said. 'Wouldn't want to end up drunk.'

Another raised eyebrow. 'Why not?'

She opened her mouth to answer, but no words, no argument came. She smiled to herself. Why not indeed?

The food arrived. Ben had ordered for her. She wasn't confident in working her way round an Indian menu. She told him what strength she liked things to be – not too spicy – what she liked to eat, and left the rest up to him. They – or rather Ben – had decided to share a starter. 'It's all so good here,' he had said. 'You should try a bit of everything.' Maddy had agreed.

A big plate of lamb, chicken, kebabs and other things she didn't know the names of was placed on the table between them.

'Use your fingers,' said Ben. 'I won't mind.' She did so. They both did. The meat was some of the finest she had ever tasted.

'OK?' he asked.

She nodded. Definitely OK. He smiled once more. His taste, his opinion validated.

Maddy took another mouthful of martini. She felt happy. Properly happy, for the first time in ages. She couldn't believe how quickly her life had changed. She felt giddy, almost, like she was walking on a cloud.

She reached over for her napkin and caught sight of her wrist. She had worn a long-sleeved top to cover up the damage, and as it rode up slightly she became aware of it for the first time that evening. Ben had made her forget. Wow, she thought. She couldn't believe she was the same girl. In the space of twenty-four hours her life had been transformed.

They finished the starters. Her glass was empty once more.

'No, I'd better . . . '

Too late. Ben had already called for another refill.

'So,' he said, once the drink had arrived and Maddy had started on it, 'how are you?'

'Fine,' she said, aware that she was beaming like an idiot. She didn't care. Ben, the restaurant, the drink was all making her feel lightheaded. Pleasantly so.

'I'm glad it's me you're here with,' he said.

'So am I.'

'And not Hugo Gwilym.'

And suddenly, at the mention of his name, she didn't feel lightheaded any more.

55

Phil and Imani hadn't been back in the office more than twenty minutes when Sperring and Khan turned up. Phil felt rather than saw Sperring's arrival. He was sitting at his desk, writing up his visit to Ron Parsons, when he felt eyes on him. He looked up. Sperring was sitting at his own desk, staring straight over.

Phil returned the look. Showed he wasn't scared or cowed by his junior officer.

'How did it go?' he said.

Sperring leaned back in his chair, put his hands behind his head, affecting nonchalance. His features were implacable, giving nothing away. 'B and E that went wrong. Made a right mess. Some chavvy scrote off his tits, probably. He'll give himself away. Sooner or later. We'll have him.'

'Glad to hear you've got it covered,' said a voice from behind them. They both turned. DCI Cotter had come out of her office. She looked as happy as the rest of them to have been called in on her day off. 'You can handle the paperwork, Ian, and that means I can redeploy DC Khan.'

Sperring's hands came down as he turned in his chair to face her. 'What?'

'I'm sure a bit of overtime wouldn't go amiss, would it, Nadish?'

273

'Definitely not, ma'am,' said Khan, standing up from his desk.

'No plans for Saturday night?' she asked, crossing over to where he stood.

He shrugged. 'Nothing that can't be changed, ma'am.' He smiled. 'Work comes first. You know me.'

Phil caught Sperring shaking his head slightly. He agreed: Khan was ladling it on a bit thick.

Cotter smiled. 'Good. I want you and DC Oliver to get down to Hurst Street.'

Khan's expression changed. 'What? What for?'

'To distribute pictures of the tattoo or mark we saw in that video. There's a good chance that someone who frequents the bars down there might know the owner.'

Khan's face reddened. He looked round the room to gauge everyone else's reaction. No one was making eye contact with him. 'That's . . . ' He shook his head.

Cotter stepped up close to him. 'Problem, DC Khan?'

'Down there with the benders and shirtlifters? On a Saturday night?'

Cotter moved right into his face. Her voice dropped, her eyes didn't. 'Do you have a problem with people of different sexual orientation? A prejudice that might impair your ability to do your job?'

Khan wisely curtailed his first reaction. He closed his mouth, shook his head. 'No, ma'am.'

'Good. I've already informed the City Neighbourhood policing team who work down there that you'll be coming to join them. They've been doing what they can and they'll be able to give you a heads-up on the best places to go and who to talk to.'

Khan gave an abrupt nod, said nothing. Imani Oliver had risen from her desk, come to join them.

'We need to find the owner of that tattoo, or someone who

knows the owner. And that's the best place to start.' Cotter looked between the pair of them. 'Casual clothes too. Look like you're on a night out together.'

Khan and Imani shared a look. Phil, watching, almost smiled. A night out together was obviously the last thing either of them wanted.

'Good,' said DCI Cotter. 'Any questions?'

They both shook their heads.

'Then off you go.'

They turned and, with Khan walking like a condemned man off to the gallows, left the office. But not before he had given Phil the kind of stare he usually got from some criminal who had been found guilty as a result of his evidence given in court. The kind that was usually accompanied by a threat of vengeance.

Cotter watched them go, then looked at Phil and Sperring. 'You two may as well get off home. Get some sleep.'

'Yes, ma'am,' said Sperring. 'Just finish this report.'

'Of course,' said Cotter. 'But I want you both back in tomorrow. You'll have to give up the Lord's day.'

'No problem,' said Phil. 'Never was much of a churchgoer.'

She returned to her office, closing the door behind her.

Sperring waited until there was silence from behind her door, then leaned across to Phil. 'Well played,' he said.

Phil looked at him. 'What d'you mean?'

'You know fine well what I mean.'

'Pretend I don't,' said Phil, turning away from his screen towards Sperring. He could already feel his hands bunching into fists. 'Enlighten me.'

'It was a bastard trick you just pulled.'

Phil raised his eyebrow, inviting Sperring to continue.

'Getting the DCI to choose Khan to get down with the benders.'

'Nothing to do with me.'

'Like fuck it isn't. You threatened the boy with that already. You know somebody else could have done it. You didn't have to make it him.'

Phil leaned in close and low. 'I had nothing to do with it. The DCI chose. I haven't even spoken to her.'

Sperring stared at him.

'Maybe,' said Phil, 'it's only you who rates the kid. Maybe you only think you run this place.'

Sperring struggled to keep his fists down at his sides. Phil kept staring at him, not backing down.

'Problem?'

Neither of them had heard the door open behind them. But they recognised Cotter's voice straight away.

Phil sat back in his place. 'No, ma'am.'

'Good. Keep it that way. Get those reports done, then go home. Both of you.'

The door was closed once more.

Phil finished his report, then left the building. Feeling Sperring's eyes on him as he went.

56

Maddy's stomach turned over at the mention of Hugo Gwilym's name. Like she had just eaten a bad piece of meat. And she had been having such a good time. Ben saw the look on her face. Reached across for her hand once more.

'Sorry. I didn't mean to . . . to upset you.'

She shook her head. 'It's . . . it's OK. Really. Sorry, I should just . . . I shouldn't be so touchy. It's all . . . all in the past now. Over with. Draw a line underneath it and move on.' She realised she was nodding her head a little too hard. She stopped.

'Good,' Ben said. 'Good. I hope so.'

'Why wouldn't it be?' she said. 'Course it is. Yes. I don't want . . . don't want to be reminded of him.'

'I'm sure you don't,' said Ben as the waiter removed the starter dishes. 'I know exactly what he's like. I've heard all about him. He's . . . ' He shook his head. 'No, I'm sorry. I'll not go on. Let's forget him.'

'Right,' said Maddy. She took a sip of her drink. It tasted slightly sour. 'He's what?' she said.

'What?'

'You said you know what he's like. You've heard all about him. What d'you mean?'

Ben shrugged. 'Let's not spoil the evening talking about him.'

'No.' Maddy took another sip. 'Just tell me what you mean, though. What you've heard. And then . . . that'll be it.'

'Maddy . . . '

Her wrist was suddenly throbbing, hurting. 'I just want to know, that's all. Tell me and then . . . we can talk about happy things. He'll be gone.'

Ben looked down, round at the restaurant. Like he was reluctant to part with the words, like they would have to be torn out of him.

'Please.'

He sighed. 'OK. Wish I'd never mentioned him now.' He leaned in close to her, like they were conspirators in some secret plot. 'I've heard some things about him, that's all. Bad things.'

'What kind of things?'

He sighed once more, looked round. 'The kind of things that . . . He does them quietly. I found out. And it makes me hate him for it. Can't look at him on TV without thinking about what he's done.'

'What, like Jimmy Savile?'

'Yeah. Sort of . . . ' Ben shook his head, as if trying to dislodge what was there. 'Well, you know this better than me, what he did to you . . . '

'He's done it before? Tell me. Please.' Dread in her heart as she asked. But she couldn't stop herself, she had to know. 'Please.'

The reluctance to go further was visible on his face, in his posture. 'Well . . . OK. Right.' He sighed again and, mind made up, continued. 'He's done it before. He's a manipulator.'

'I know. Is that it?'

'No, I mean . . . more than that. Manipulation, that's him. That's his . . . what he does, what he gets his kicks from, what he gets off on. His life's work.'

Maddy said nothing. Her heart was hammering. Fearing what he had to say, but waiting for him to continue.

'It's not just manipulation, it's the psychology of manipulation. That's what he gets off on. The total capitulation, the subjugation of another.'

The waiter arrived with the main courses. They stopped talking while the dishes were laid out. The food smelled delicious, but Maddy didn't feel hungry any more.

'And,' he said, once the waiter had finished up and moved away, 'I've seen him do it.'

'You've seen him?' Her heart hammering even harder. 'Tell me.' She was almost shouting in her desperation.

Again Ben seemed reluctant to speak, but eventually he found the words. 'OK. See if this sounds right. If it rings a bell. He takes a young girl. A student, usually. This is him, what he loves to do. That girl, she . . . it's probably her first time away from home. She might be a bit innocent, naïve, even.' He saw the look on her face, gave her an apologetic smile. 'No offence, sorry.'

She nodded. Said nothing.

'So he'll take this young girl and . . . ' He looked round the restaurant, checking for eavesdroppers. Found none. 'Corrupt her. Wilfully corrupt her.'

Her heart flipped once more. She felt it was going to flutter away to nothing. She wanted him to continue but didn't want to hear what he was going to say next. Like poking a wound to make it hurt.

'He starts easy with them. Simply. Flirts a bit, makes them feel special. Like this guy who could have anyone he wants is taking an interest in her. At first she can't believe it. *Me? Why would he be interested in me?* But he keeps going. And she starts to realise that yeah, he is interested in her. It is her he wants. And she goes along with him.' He shrugged. 'I mean, if someone gave you that kind of attention, why wouldn't you?'

'Right,' said Maddy.

'He'll take them for drinks. Get them drunk, all the while talking about how wonderful they are. And then have sex with them. I've even heard that ... ' He stopped, shook his head.

'What?'

'Well, I don't know. I can't say for definite, but ... I've heard that he might even drug them. Rohypnol or something. Have sex with them while they're out of it.'

Maddy's hand went to her mouth. Last night. Gwilym's house. The blackout. *No ...*

57

DC Imani Oliver pulled her coat tight round her body. December was biting hard. Her face was chilled just from getting out of the car; the wind was numbing. And now it was raining. It had started while she and Khan had been driving down to the Southside Quarter and was now hitting so hard it was like a freezing blanket had been thrown over her.

Khan hadn't spoken since they left the station. At least not to her, not aloud. His lips had been working and his face twisting, but no sounds had emerged. The steering wheel had taken an occasional hit too. She knew what was wrong with him. She said nothing, letting him work it out in his own head.

They parked opposite an ornately facaded Chinese restaurant and walked up Hurst Street. Past the queuing clubbers waiting to get into Oceania, their enthusiasm undiminished by the rain, their underdressed bodies internally heated by an evening's worth of bar-hopped alcohol.

The City Neighbourhood policing team were round the corner up ahead of them on Queensway, on a Code 99, police jargon for tea break. They were huddled inside a late-night fast-food café, hands wrapped round cups of tea and coffee.

The presence of the three of them, uniforms bulked up by hi-vis jackets, kept anyone else out. The Middle Eastern guy behind the counter was polite and tolerant. Imani and Khan joined them, shaking off the rain as they got inside. One of them broke off from the group, turned to them. He was young, white, with short ginger hair and an easy, ready smile. Imani could see immediately that he would be good at community work.

'Lovely, eh?' he said, his accent broad and Brummie. 'You'd think it would put people off coming out, all this. No such luck.'

'Well, it is Christmas,' said Imani, returning his smile. Infectious, she thought. 'Imani Oliver. DC.' She stuck out her hand.

He shook. 'Mike Pierce. Constable.'

Khan introduced himself also, in as few syllables as possible. Pierce introduced the other two, Constables Dalton and Craig. Formalities concluded, he turned back to Imani.

'So what's going on, then? Where's the fire?'

Imani produced a stack of photocopies in a clear plastic folder from inside her coat. 'This mark,' she said, pointing to a blow-up of the tattoo from the DVD. 'We're looking for somebody with this.'

Mike Pierce studied it. 'Bit ornate. What is it?'

'A double helix,' she said. 'DNA genome.'

Mike raised his eyebrows. 'Very highfalutin. Your boss told me it was to do with a murder?'

'We think this tattoo belongs to the murderer,' said Khan. 'He killed a . . . ' he paused, bit back what he had been about to say, 'a transvestite. We thought someone down Hurst Street might know him or have seen him.'

'Right. Well, it's possible. We could ask round.'

'That's what we're here to do,' said Imani. 'Go round the

bars, show the picture. What d'you think the general response will be like?'

'Hard to tell. This area's come a long way as far as we're concerned, but it's still pretty closed to uniforms.' He smiled. 'Unless, you know, it's done for a reason.'

Imani shared his smile. She liked the way his eyes crinkled up at the corners.

'But they'll want to turn a murderer in,' said Khan, unsmiling. 'Even that sort wouldn't want a killer left on the streets.'

Imani saw the change in Pierce's eyes at Khan's words. The atmosphere became suddenly chilly. 'Probably,' he said. '*That sort* are the same as you and me.'

Khan gave a snort, turned away. Imani looked at Pierce, felt like she should apologise on Khan's behalf. He didn't give her the opportunity.

'Right then,' he said to the other two uniforms, 'tea break's over, lads, back on your heads.'

They binned their cups, set out into the rain.

Mike Pierce told them which bars to start in, who to talk to. 'We'll familiarise ourselves with the design and have a look around out here. You get the cushy job. You're inside.'

'Come with us,' she said.

'Maybe later,' he replied.

Imani and Khan set off. The rain showed no sign of letting up.

'Should have brought an umbrella,' she said.

'Yeah,' said Khan, 'then you and the ginger could have stood underneath it together.'

She turned to him. 'What?'

'I saw the way you were looking at him. Flirting.'

'I was not ...'

Khan gave another snort, resumed walking. Imani strode along until she had caught up with him.

'Brennan planned all this, you know.'

'What?' she said.

'This. All this. He planned it. Sending me off down here with you. Punishment. That's what it is. Punishment. He's such a prick.'

She knew that all his silent conversations in the car were tumbling out now. 'Punishment? For what?'

'We don't get on,' said Khan. 'Not like you two, eh?'

'What d'you mean?'

'You and Brennan. I saw you. Everyone saw you. Got your feet under the table with the new boss, haven't you? Sucking up to him. Smiling at him. Bet he doesn't know you've been flirting with the ginger.'

'What are you on about? That's absolute bollocks.'

'No it's not. I saw it with my own eyes.'

'The new DI seems like a decent bloke. Give him a chance.'

Khan gave another snort. The subject, apparently, was closed.

They reached the first bar. Music, light was spilling out on to the street. Imani opened the door. 'After you,' she said.

Khan, looking like he wanted to hit her, entered.

58

Ben took a sip of his drink. Maddy watched him, thinking about what Gwilym might have done to her while she was unconscious.

'Like I said,' Ben continued, 'I don't know for definite, but I've heard rumours. Lots of them. I've seen him do worse than that, though. As soon as you told me what had happened, about the . . . '

'Abortion.' Her voice small, fragile.

'Right. I knew. I knew it was him up to his old tricks again. He gets the girl pregnant. Forces her to have unprotected sex with him, knowing what's going to happen. Then, when she's pregnant, forces her to have an abortion. Manipulation, see? Controlling not just her mind but her body. And her dead baby's body.'

'And then . . . and then . . . ' Maddy felt tears welling up inside her.

'That's not all, though. There was a girl I knew. Friend of mine at uni. Nice girl. Really nice. Lovely.' Ben sighed, trailed off, his eyes taking on a sad cast.

Maddy waited. Eventually he came back to the room, back to her, continued.

'This girl.' He sighed. 'She was lovely until Gwilym got hold of her. She had to leave uni in the end.'

'What happened?'

'Started off like I said. *Who, me? He likes me?* . . . all that. The drink, the sex, the drugs. Oh yeah, the drugs . . . He got her hooked on heroin. Proper full-blown junkie.'

'But . . . why?'

'Because he could. Because he wanted to. He takes innocent girls and corrupts them. For fun.' He looked straight at Maddy, eyes full of honesty.

Maddy tried hard not to let the tears fall.

Ben reached across, took her hands. 'I'm sorry. I'm sorry . . .'

She shook her head. Wiped her eyes with the napkin. 'Sorry . . .'

'Don't be. It's my fault for mentioning him. I shouldn't have.'

'No, no, you should. I've got to . . . got to face it.'

Ben nodded, sat there. His turn to say nothing, to wait.

'So . . . when this girl, these girls . . . when he's done this, then what?'

'Nothing,' said Ben. 'He drops them. Lets them go. Moves on to the next one. Cut adrift.'

She nodded. 'Yes. Yes, that's right.'

'Sorry. I shouldn't have said anything. I've ruined the evening.'

'No, it's . . .' Maddy felt something hardening inside her. Crystallising. Her sadness, her fear turning to cold, bright anger. 'What about the university?' she said, her voice shriller and more abrupt than she had intended. 'Don't they do anything? Don't they know?'

'Oh, I'm sure they know.'

'Well? Why don't they do something?'

'You mentioned Jimmy Savile before. Why didn't anyone do anything about him? People knew what was going on, what he

286

was like. But they did nothing. Why? For the same reason the university do nothing about Gwilym. He's a cash cow, a money-spinner. A prized asset. What's a few unhappy students compared to the good he does for them?'

Maddy said nothing. Shaking inside. With what, she could no longer tell.

'He was ready to drop you, Maddy. Cast you adrift.' Ben smiled, gripped her hands harder. 'You met me at just the right time, didn't you?'

'How do you ... how do you know all this? About Gwilym?'

Ben sighed, took his hands away. At first Maddy thought she had upset him, gone somewhere he was unwilling to follow, but she soon realised she had misjudged him. He was rolling up his sleeve.

'The girl I told you about, the one Gwilym got hooked on heroin,' he said. 'She was my ... ' He sighed again. 'We used to be close.'

'Where ... where is she now?'

He couldn't meet her eyes, looked down at the cooling food. 'She's ... gone. Dead.' The last word whispered.

'Oh God. I'm sorry. I'm so sorry ... '

He shook his head. 'Don't be. It's not your fault.' He pointed to her wrist. 'You're not the only one. Gwilym's victims take different forms.'

He rolled his sleeve right the way back, showed her his inner forearm. The scar was still vivid. Red and ridged.

'What ... you tried to ... '

He nodded, rolled his sleeve back down, looking round once more to see if he had attracted attention. He hadn't. 'Like I said, his victims take different forms.'

She said nothing. Just stared ahead, eyes glazed.

'The question is,' said Ben, 'what d'you want to do about it?'

Her eyes came back into focus. 'What d'you mean?'

'Well, it looks like we met just in time.'

'For what?'

'Revenge,' he said.

'Revenge?' she echoed.

'Yeah,' he said. 'Don't you think it's time Hugo Gwilym got his comeuppance? A taste of his own medicine? Don't you think it's time for payback?'

'Well . . . '

Ben leaned in closer. 'Don't you think he should suffer for what he's done? Really suffer? Not just for what he's done to you or . . . ' His eyes darted to his scarred forearm. 'But for all the other girls. All the ones who came before you. The ones who'll come afterwards.'

'Yes, but I don't see how we can do anything . . . We *can't* do anything.'

'We can,' he said. 'And we will. We have to. If we don't, we'll be letting him get away with it. We'll be no worse than those bastards in the university who sit and do nothing, knowing exactly what he's about.'

Maddy thought. She realised that her answer could be the most important thing she had ever said.

'Yes,' she said eventually. 'Yes, you're right, we have to do something. We have to stop him. Yes. But how?'

Ben smiled. 'That's the spirit,' he said. Then he looked at the cooling food before them. 'Hey, you'd better eat up. You'll need your strength for what we've got to do.'

Maddy did as she was told. The food was delicious. As she ate, she suddenly realised that her appetite had returned.

With a vengeance.

59

The Arcadian made the black woman as police as soon as she entered the bar. The young Asian behind her was a copper also. He looked again at the Asian. He was terrified. He smiled to himself. Wanted to go up to the young copper, whisper in his ear, 'The opposite of love is not hate, it's indifference. If you hate something, and fear it, it's because you're secretly scared that you might love it.' But decided against it. He didn't want to draw attention to himself.

He watched as they went up to the bar. Talked to the Irish barman. Showed him something.

The Arcadian got up from his seat, made his way nearer to the bar, tried surreptitiously to see what was on the paper. He only caught a glimpse of it, but knew straight away what it was.

The helix.

Shit. I've got to get out of here.

He turned away from the two coppers. Tried to make his way as quickly and unobtrusively as possible across the bar. He almost reached the door.

'What's your hurry?'

The Arcadian stopped, turned. A tall, bearded bear of a man was in his way. Smiling.

'Off to a better party?'

The Arcadian looked back at the bar. The police were still talking.

'No,' he said. 'Well, maybe.' He smiled.

'Maybe we could go and find one together,' the bear said.

The Arcadian looked back at the bar. The police had finished talking now and were making their way to the front door. Towards him.

'Yeah,' he said, pressing himself up against the bear. 'Let's.'

They left the bar seconds before the police officers did.

'What's your name?' said the bear.

The Arcadian, he was about to say, but stopped himself. 'Are names important?' he said instead.

The bear shrugged. 'Suppose not. Got anywhere in mind?'

He turned, saw that the two officers were walking away from them.

'This way,' he said, heading in the opposite direction. The bear smiled, walked with him.

60

The first thing that hit Imani was the heat. After the cold and the rain of the night outside, she felt like she was steam-drying.

The music was deafening. The bar was rammed. Men crowded all around her, trying to hold conversations over the noise, buy drinks. Apart from her, there were no women in the place. The smell of aftershave, all mixtures, blends and price ranges, along with the alcohol, was pummelling her senses. That and the acrid chemical tang of something else that she couldn't immediately place. Poppers.

She noticed Khan had got inside the door and frozen. He stood, eyes wide, as if this was somehow his first adult experience. She felt a momentary pang of sympathy for him. But only momentary. It soon went.

'Let's go to the bar,' she shouted, and made her way there. He followed her. 'And let me do the talking.'

She was aware of eyes on her the whole time. Not a pleasant scrutiny. As the only woman in the place she would have expected that. But if she had been identified as a copper, that was doubly the case.

She reached the bar. Asked for Brendan. A short, stocky, middle-aged bald man came over to her.

'I'm Brendan,' he said. 'And what can I do to aid our boys and girls in blue?' His Irish accent was soft, tempered by years of living in Birmingham.

'Am I that obvious?' she said.

He nodded. ''Fraid so.'

He wasn't unfriendly, just wary. Imani didn't want to say or do anything to antagonise him. She wanted him on side. 'I got your name from Mike Pierce, the community officer.'

Brendan gave a smile at that.

'He said you're the one to talk to.'

'Did he now. What about?'

She produced one of the photocopied sheets. Told him what it was about. Brendan took it from her, studied it. 'Doesn't ring any bells,' he said. 'Something like that . . . '

'Exactly. Let me leave it with you. In case it jogs your memory. There's a phone number on there. We really appreciate this.'

'No problem.' He smiled again. 'I love a man in uniform.' He looked over at Khan. Smiled even wider.

'We'll be off, then,' said Imani and turned, ushering Khan out of the door.

The cold and the rain seemed welcome after the heat of the bar.

Khan turned to her. 'Did you see that? Hear what he said? Fucking hell . . . fucking hell . . . '

Imani didn't reply.

'And while we were in there, all the time you were talking, they were eyeing me up. All of them.'

'Lucky you.'

His expression became murderous. 'What? *What?* Lucky you?'

'Yeah,' she said, trying to make light of it. 'I wish I had that amount of blokes ogling me.'

He looked as if he was about to explode. Calmed himself down. But not without effort. 'It's not right. Not natural, what they do.'

Imani wondered whether to give him a lecture on gender and tolerance. Decided against it. 'I think you need some LGBT awareness training. I'm sure there's a course you can go on.'

He stared at her.

'Come on,' she said, walking off towards the next bar.

He followed along behind her, reluctant.

This one was a much camper affair than the first. A drag queen was up on a small stage, lip-synching to show tunes. The audience were whooping along, cheering when she showed a well-turned thigh in her split skirt, laughing as she camped up the lyrics with a Les Dawson-like rearrangement of her false breasts.

Imani realised Khan was mesmerised.

'Good legs,' she said.

He didn't reply.

'Did you know,' she said, leaning in close to him, 'that when you see a pair of legs on a packet of tights or stockings, or on a billboard ad, it's probably a man?'

He turned. 'What?'

She pointed to the drag queen on the stage. 'He's got good legs. TVs can make quite a bit modelling. Think on that the next time you see a picture.'

They drew a blank, left a couple of flyers, left.

Outside, the rain was easing up slightly. Mike Pierce came towards them. 'Any luck?'

Imani shook her head. 'We'll keep trying, though. Where would you suggest next?'

He looked up and down the street. 'Couple more bars, few restaurants and clubs, but we could do those for you if it's just the flyers. If it's actual eyeball-to-eyeball you're looking for, chancing your arm, making an ident, then . . . ' He shrugged. 'It's up to you.'

'What about in there?' Imani pointed to an unremarkable storefront. It could have been a grocery shop if not for the blacked-out windows and the sign above: *HUSTLER CINEMA XXX*.

Pierce smiled. 'Good luck. Be a bit of an eye-opener.'

'How d'you mean?' asked Khan. He looked like he wanted to be anywhere else but there.

'Let's just say the clientele don't go there to watch the films. Or they may do but that's usually secondary.'

'Oh,' said Imani.

'However,' said Pierce, 'it's a sleazy little pit. You never know.'

Imani looked at Khan. He had gone beyond anger now. He just wanted to get it over and done with. 'Come on then. We'll make this the last call of the night.' She looked at Pierce. 'Then we might sit in your van and just watch, if that's OK with you.'

Pierce smiled. 'Fine by me.'

Imani, with Khan trailing behind, entered the cinema.

61

It was late when Phil pulled up in front of the house. Not his own house. He didn't want to go home just yet.

He could see the rented place he shared with Marina and their daughter just along the street. A light was on in his bedroom window. Marina was either awake, reading probably, or had gone to sleep, leaving his bedside light on to help him find his way. But he wasn't going there. Not just yet.

He locked the car, walked up the driveway. It had once been a garage or coach house but a previous owner had converted it to a one-bedroom flat. It was where Eileen now lived.

Phil rang the bell, stepped back, waited.

'Who is it?' A voice from behind the door.

'It's me. Phil.'

A chain was removed, a bolt released, a heavy lock cracked. The door opened. There stood the only woman Phil had ever called mother.

'Thanks for waiting up.'

'I was up anyway. Watching something on BBC 4. One of those miserable Scandinavian crime series where they all have personality disorders and can't seem to find a light switch.' She gave him a brief smile. 'I suppose your day must have been like that.'

He smiled wearily in return. 'Stumbling in the dark with mentalists? My day's always like that.'

He entered. She turned off the TV. He sat down on the sofa. She had wasted no time in claiming the place as her own. Where Phil felt he was only a temporary fixture in his house, Eileen looked like she had been in hers for years. She had surrounded herself with as many familiar objects as she could, taking her home with her. It still wasn't that long since Don's death. Phil thought she was coping well. Or seemed to be.

She sat down in her armchair. The one that used to be Don's, Phil noted.

'Can I get you a tea? Coffee?'

'I'm fine.'

'Beer? I know you like a beer when you come in from work. I've got some in the fridge.'

He knew she was trying to be useful, not feel redundant, so he went along with her. 'A beer would be great, thanks.'

She tried to rise.

'I'll get it,' he said.

'Stay where you are. I'm not an invalid.'

She went to the kitchen, returned with a bottle of beer, the cap removed. Handed it to Phil. He thanked her, took a drink. Cold and refreshing, it went down well.

Eileen sat back. 'So what did you want to talk to me about? It sounded like it was serious.'

Straight to the point as always, he thought. 'Yeah ... ' he said, trying to find the right words. 'It's ... Marina. She's ... I don't know.'

He took another mouthful of beer, Eileen waited.

'She's being funny with me.'

'In what way?'

'Well ... I don't know. She's ... distant. No, that's not

right. She's . . . It's like she doesn't want me to . . . to be close to her.'

Eileen leaned forward. 'Has she said anything?'

'Not directly, no. But when I go towards her, she pulls away. And this morning she . . .' His eyes dropped to his bottle. He had always been able to tell Eileen anything, but he still felt embarrassed talking about sex with her. 'I went to join her in the shower, and she screamed. Actually screamed. When I touched her. Pulled the curtain across, said she wanted privacy. Said . . .' he thought back, tried to find the exact words, 'oh it's just you. Oh it's you. Something like that.'

'She was expecting someone else?'

'I don't know,' he said. 'Maybe in her mind she was. And there's a . . . barrier between us. She's put it up.' He shook his head.

'I see,' said Eileen. 'Has she mentioned anyone else's name recently? Started talking a lot about someone? From work, maybe?'

'I know what you're thinking,' said Phil. 'Talking about someone I've never heard of before is an indicator that she's having an affair.'

'*Might* be having an affair. It's not definite.'

'No, but . . .' He shrugged, took another drink. 'There is . . . Well, I don't know.'

'There is someone? Someone she's been mentioning?'

'Well, sort of. I don't . . . Hugo Gwilym.'

'What, from the TV? That Hugo Gwilym?'

Phil nodded. 'He's come up in the course of this case I'm working on. He's a colleague of Marina's at the university, same department. I asked her about him. Just to check, you know, that there was no conflict of interest. That he wasn't a friend.'

'Right. And?'

'She said she didn't know him. Had hardly met him, or spoken to him. But she didn't like him. Got quite angry about him, even. And then I went to talk to Gwilym. To do with the case. And . . . he mentioned her.'

'In what way?'

'In a . . . creepy way. Said something like, I enjoyed having your wife the other night. Something like that. Then said, for dinner. He'd had her for dinner. What he meant was he'd been at the departmental Christmas dinner with her.'

Eileen nodded.

'Marina said she didn't know him, but he made it seem that they were quite close.' He took another pull of beer. Found the bottle drained. 'She came in very late that night.'

Eileen waited, made sure he had finished talking. 'I see.'

He looked at her, expecting answers. Knowing how unreasonable that was.

'So you think she's having an affair with Gwilym?' Eileen said eventually.

'Well, that would be the logical thing to think, wouldn't it? Saying she didn't know him at all, doing the reverse thing of talking about someone a lot. Double bluff. Saying she hated him. Maybe he's found someone else. Dumped her. Hurt her in some way.' He sighed. 'I don't know . . .'

'But screaming when you tried to touch her,' said Eileen. 'Don't forget that. That's not the action of a woman hiding an affair.'

'What is it, then?'

Eileen sat back, looked thoughtful. 'When Don and I used to foster kids – you might even remember this – we were always careful with them. Some of them wanted hugging. Needed it. Some of them wanted it but didn't know to how to ask. They might have thought it was sexual, because that was

298

how they'd been brought up, and that's how they responded, but they wanted affection. They were kids, after all. But some of them couldn't bear to be touched.'

'Abused?'

Eileen nodded. 'They'd all suffered some kind of abuse. And it affected them in different ways. But the ones who didn't want to be touched, that was because it reminded them of their abusers. Of what they had been through.'

'So . . . you think Gwilym might have . . . touched her? Been inappropriate with her?'

'Oh I don't know, Phil. I'm just saying that's how the kids were. That's the behaviour they used to exhibit.'

'But if that's the case, then why hasn't she just come out and said it? Why hasn't she told me?'

'I don't know, Phil. You'll have to talk to her. Have you tried talking to her?'

'Yes . . . '

'Really tried?'

'I have, but . . . Well, she's been like she's been. And also . . . ' he sighed, 'what if she says yes? What if I talk to her and she says she was or is having an affair with Gwilym? What do I do then?'

'You deal with it, Phil. Like an adult. It'll hurt. Things like that are never easy to cope with, but you can both get over it if you try and if you want to.' She shook her head. 'Marina's the last person I would expect to do something like that.' She shrugged. 'But, people . . . Look. It might not be that at all. There might still be some other explanation.'

'I know, but . . . '

Eileen looked directly at him. Pity and compassion in her eyes. 'Talk to her, Phil. Just talk to her.'

62

Inside the cinema, behind a makeshift counter, sat a failed genetic experiment, a cross between a man and a toad. He was huge and fat, his skin greasy and warty. He had a shaved head and wore chunky gold jewellery that may have been expensive and genuine or may have been Argos. It was so tasteless Imani had no way of knowing. He wore a brown leather jacket that looked as greasy as his skin and a stained T-shirt pulled tight across his expansive belly. He looked half asleep, staring at a porn mag spread out before him, but Imani wasn't fooled. His round eyes missed nothing. He perked up when they entered.

'What can I do for you?'

'Here's what you can do for us,' said Imani. She showed him the photo, explained what it was about.

The toad's round eyes became hooded, hidden. 'Murder, you say?'

'Murder,' said Khan, as bluntly and emphatically as he could.

The toad rubbed his stubbly chin. 'Never seen that before.' He handed the flyer back.

'Hang on to it. You never know,' said Imani. 'We've got plenty more.'

The toad shrugged, put it under the desk. Went back to his magazine. When he noticed that the two police officers hadn't left, he looked up.

'What?'

'Mind if we take a look inside?'

'Why?' Eyes hooded and hidden again. 'We're licensed. By the council.'

'That's not why we're here,' said Imani. 'The tattoo?'

The toad clearly didn't want to let them in. He was weighing up whether it would be better to go along with them or cause a fuss by refusing them access when Khan made his mind up for him.

'Come on,' he said, pushing past Imani, 'let's get it over with.'

Imani smiled at the toad. 'Two minutes,' she said and followed him.

Going through the doorway from the front of the cinema she was immediately thrown into darkness. The light hadn't been particularly bright outside, but her eyes still took a while to get accustomed to it. She stood still, blinked. There was no sign of Khan. Ahead of her was a narrow passageway. Cheap plywood painted black. She saw a doorway at the far end, leading off to the left. She walked towards it.

She heard the film before she saw it. Overdubbed grunts, sighs and screams. She reached the doorway, looked inside. The room was the size of a combined living and dining room. Seating had been placed in rows in front of a large screen. On the screen two hugely tooled men were servicing each other. Their bodies were hard, hairless, slick and shining with oil and sweat. Their eyes were closed, their faces expressionless. They bore as much resemblance to real people as an episode of *The Simpsons*. It was the opposite of erotic. It was like watching heavy pneumatic machinery at work.

But most people weren't there to watch the film. They were too busy with each other. The room wasn't full but the clientele were all men. Middle-aged, most of them, Imani reckoned, and not particularly attractive. But they all had something that someone else wanted. Oral sex. Anal sex. Everything in between. A couple of transvestites being anything but ladylike. Even as a police officer Imani had never seen anything like this. She felt as if she had stepped into another world.

She looked round. No sign of Khan.

She left the room, continued down the corridor. It ended in a set of stairs. She could hear more overdubbed grunts and groans coming from down there. The hallway turned to the right. She looked down it. A silhouette of a couple in an embrace was etched against the weak covered lighting at the far end. Both male, neither needing the stimulus of the screen. Both in a state of undress. She turned, went downstairs.

It was the same set-up as before. The same kind of film, the same kind of audience. But somehow being in the basement made it feel even sleazier than above, like there were fewer or even no limits to what went on.

She found Khan. Standing mutely at the doorway, staring into the room, mouth open like he had been hypnotised. He had been noticed. Imani was aware of at least one seated man waving his erect penis at him, trying to attract his attention. Imani came and joined him.

'There you go, tiger,' she whispered in his ear. 'Don't let me stop you.'

He turned, anger jumping into his features, crowding out whatever confused emotions were already there.

Imani smiled, looked at the man who had been waving his penis. Young, dressed in jeans and an unseasonable T-shirt. Only his fly was undone. He saw Imani looking at him and immediately lost interest.

But Imani was suddenly interested in him.

'Look,' she said to Khan, still whispering, 'his arm.'

Khan looked where Imani told him to. The willy-waggler had bare forearms. On the inside of one was what appeared to be the tattoo they were looking for.

Imani couldn't believe her luck. She felt her heart race, fought to keep it down. Forced herself to remember her training. Khan shared a glance with her and they both moved towards the seated man.

'Excuse me,' said Imani, going for her warrant card, 'could we—'

She didn't get any further. The man jumped up and, penis still sticking out of his jeans, pushed her backwards into Khan. While the two police officers were trying to untangle themselves, the man ran past them towards the stairs.

'Stop!' shouted Khan. 'Police!'

The man didn't stop.

Imani and Khan ran after him.

63

Marina heard Phil coming in. She had thought of pretending to be asleep to avoid a conversation but couldn't bring herself to do it. Couldn't bring herself to lie any more to the man she loved. She had been lying awake, waiting for him. She had made a decision. She was going to tell him. Everything. Gwilym, the drugging, the testing. Everything. Then work it through, see what they could do about it.

She heard him downstairs, expected him to go to the fridge, get himself a beer, sit down. That was all right, she thought, heart tripping heavily, she could wait. But he didn't do that. She heard him coming straight upstairs.

She knew what he would do next, knew his routine as well as he did. Sure enough, she heard the door to Josephina's room creak open slightly, knew he would be checking on her, watching her sleep. He did it every night. They both did.

She heard him creep across the landing, booted feet moving as lightly as he could. She heard him in the bathroom. She heard the bathroom light going off. The bedroom door opened. He came in. Her stomach somersaulted.

'Thought you'd be asleep,' he said.

She was sitting upright in bed, the paper propped before her. She hoped he didn't notice her hands shaking. 'Nope.'

He sat on the edge of the bed, began to get undressed.

Now, she thought. *Tell him now.*

'How was your day?' he said.

'Oh, fine, you know,' she said. 'Didn't do much. Took it easy.' *Apart from meeting Anni, asking for a clandestine drugs test.* 'Went shopping for Christmas presents, that kind of thing.' *Please don't ask about the presents. Please don't ask to see them.* She paused. *This is it*, she thought. *This is the time. Tell him.* She opened her mouth to speak again. 'How was your day? How's the case going?'

'It's ... interesting. I'll tell you all about it if you like.' He yawned.

'You look done in,' she said. 'Tell me in the morning.'

He got into bed next to her. She could feel him looking at her.

She put the paper down.

'Marina ...'

'Yes?'

He stopped talking, became thoughtful. *Now*, she thought. *Do it now. Just tell him and get it over with.*

'I need to talk to you,' he said.

She opened her mouth to speak, to respond. But she was frozen. The words wouldn't come.

'Marina ...'

'I'm tired, Phil,' she said. 'It's ... it's been a long day. I ... I ... I'm tired.'

'But ...'

She turned over on her side. 'I'm tired,' she said more firmly. 'Let's ... let's talk in the morning.' She put the light out.

She closed her eyes. Aware of Phil still lying on his side, still staring at her. Willing her to move, to speak, to turn over and face him. She wanted to do so as well. But couldn't. She was a coward and she hated herself for it, but she couldn't.

Eventually Phil sighed, lay down. Marina kept her eyes closed, tried not to move. To convince him she was sleeping.

Hating herself for not being able to speak.

She lay like that for hours, pretending to sleep. Knew he was doing the same. Knew he was as terrified as her of what the other would say if they spoke.

64

The toad man said something. Imani didn't wait to hear what it was, just kept running. She heard Khan clattering up the stairs behind her.

The T-shirted man reached the doorway of the cinema and, knocking over a couple of prospective punters, turned left, ran up Hurst Street.

'Come on!' she shouted, and followed. She knew the words were meaningless, just something to key her up.

The man ran towards the Hippodrome. Evening theatregoers were just emerging. Imani knew that if they got caught up in that crowd they would lose him. She ran all the harder.

The T-shirted man saw the crowds ahead of him, risked a glance behind. Saw Imani and Khan were still after him, turned left and ran down a side street, away from the crowds, past the stage door. Imani gave chase. She heard Khan shouting something behind her, turned. He was making a call, giving their location, explaining the situation, requesting backup. Good. She ran all the harder to make up for his lack of pace while he was doing it.

Down past the snooker hall, pavement smokers jumping out of the way. The man reached the end of the cut-through, looked round, turned right. Imani kept chasing.

He ran along the pavement, dodging pedestrians, upsetting a few, towards the Holloway Circus roundabout. Looked round again. Imani felt her chest burning, her heart pumping. She was getting tired and wanted to stop, but she knew if she did that he would be gone. She pushed herself all the harder.

Found herself gaining on him. Pushed herself more . . .

He reached the corner, turned right. Down Smallbrook, past the all-night cafés, kebab shops and Turkish minimarts.

He's heading back to Hurst Street, she thought.

She willed her feet to run faster. Chest burning, legs aching. Each breath tore her throat red raw. Faster . . .

And there he was, an arm's length away from her.

She reached out, hand ready to grab him, pull him to the ground.

He sensed what she was doing, turned. Stopped.

And punched her square in the face.

Imani, shocked as well as hurt, went down. He didn't wait around, just ran on.

She put her hand to her face. It came away dark and wet with something more than rain.

'Bastard . . .'

She became aware of Khan running past her, not stopping. Groaning from the pain in her legs, her chest, her face, she pulled herself to her feet. Gave chase once more.

She knew from the direction Khan was heading where their target had gone. Down Hurst Street once more.

She ran past the Ming Moon restaurant and casino, left on to Ladywell Walk, past the cheap hotels and the even cheaper Chinese restaurants. Their quarry hesitated at the corner of Wrottesley Street, decided against running down there. *He knows the area*, thought Imani, still running. *He knows that's a dead end.*

Khan was running as fast as he could, calling for help – or

rather shouting – at the same time. Imani gave chase behind him.

The man ran on to Pershore Street. It was darker here, away from the bars and theatregoers. The market and the corner of the Bullring shopping centre towered above them on one side. Below was an occasional oasis of sodium street light against a huge stretch of darkness.

He ran towards the city centre. He showed no sign of slowing down.

Bastard's fit, thought Imani.

Queensway went over the top of them. Underneath were arches and alleyways. A car park.

He ran into that.

Khan followed. Imani, a few seconds later, did likewise.

The smell of exhaust fumes hit as soon as she entered. She was lightheaded enough from running and the punch; she didn't need that too. Cars were dotted about. The lighting was sporadic, episodic. Fluorescent tubes guttered and spat overhead. Slow-motion strobes.

Khan was standing just inside the doorway. Out of breath, hands on knees. Doubled over, but his eyes were roving.

'Came in here and I lost him,' he said through gasps of air.

'Is this the only way out?'

He pointed along to his right. 'Exit's there.'

'I'll get over there.'

Khan looked at her. His eyes widened in shock. 'Jesus Christ . . . '

'What?'

'He's done a number on your face.'

'Thanks.' She didn't know if Khan was going to apologise for his words or laugh at her. She didn't wait to find out. 'I'll go to the exit.'

She moved as quickly as she could. Got there. Waited. She

looked along at where Khan was, saw him start to edge his way in further. Head moving from side to side, eyes scanning the whole time.

'Here!' he shouted, and was off.

Imani looked towards the exit, then back the way Khan had gone. Gave chase. She saw him run into the depths of the garage. Saw a shadow detach itself from the wall behind a parked Nissan, come at him. One dark arm bigger than the other. Khan didn't have time to see that their assailant had found a weapon. He only had time to feel it connect, take him down.

'Nadish!' Imani ran towards them.

The figure saw her, turned. She saw that the weapon was a heavy metal car jack. She ran towards him, trying to remember her training. She wasn't going to get caught the same way again.

Reason with him, she thought. *Stall him, play for time.*

She opened her mouth to speak. He ran at her, the jack held above his head. She managed to get most of her body out of the way, but the jack connected with her forearm. She screamed, went down on her side.

He ran.

She pulled herself up to her knees, her body almost singing in pain. She saw her quarry reach the main door. Her heart sank as she realised he had got away.

Then . . .

A quick burst of light and he fell to the ground.

She got to her feet, made her way to the door. Mike Pierce was there, out of breath, with a handful of uniforms. One of them holding a Taser.

'Response team turned up,' said Pierce. 'Just in time, too.'

Imani looked down at the man lying there. Knelt down, checked his forearm. That was the tattoo, all right. And something else. His penis, deflated now, was still sticking out of the front of his jeans. She stood up again.

'Thank you,' she said.

'No problem,' said the officer with the Taser. He noticed the front of the man's jeans. Shook his head. 'Didn't even have time to tuck himself in.'

'My God,' said Pierce, looking away from the prone man and properly at Imani for the first time. 'Let's get you an ambulance.'

Imani nodded. 'You should see the other fella,' she said.

Then sank to the ground.

65

The rain had started up again, turning the night even darker, murkier. The Arcadian and his new friend walked through the Mailbox, not stopping to window-shop in Harvey Nichols or for a drink or something to eat at one of the many chain restaurants at the far end. They went out the other side, down the ramp on to the towpath at the side of the canal at Gasworks Basin.

Neither had spoken much. Neither needed to. They both knew what they wanted. And it wasn't conversation.

This would be an experiment, thought the Arcadian. Taking someone back to his while the doll's house was set up. Wondering if they would notice it, what they would make of it. It was his way of showing off, he thought. Letting the world – or one person in the world – see what he had done. He had to tell someone but he couldn't be obvious. So he would regard it as a puzzle for them to read. And if they did manage to work it out and, even worse, want to do something about it . . . Well, the doll's house might have another tenant.

'Wonder what the police wanted,' said the bear, stooping to avoid the low bridge they were walking under.

'Druggie, probably,' said the Arcadian. 'Pickpocket. Nothing important. No one important.'

The bear smiled. 'Best not to get involved.'

They had both seen the police chasing a man with his cock out down Hurst Street. They hadn't hung around to find out what would happen next.

'Is it much further?' asked the bear. 'I need to warm up.'

'Not much further,' the Arcadian said. 'Just round this bend.'

'And then we warm up?' Another smile, his eyes glittering from more than the rain.

'Yeah,' said the Arcadian. 'That's right.'

He needed it. The contact, the friction. The force. The high. It was the next best thing and he needed it. And the guy with him, big, strong-looking, muscular, seemed like just the man to supply it.

The bear stopped walking, pulled the Arcadian's arm, made him stop too.

'What?'

The bear looked around, saw that they were alone, made a grab for the Arcadian's cock.

'Not here,' said the Arcadian, angry at not being in control. 'We're nearly there.' He walked on. The bear, not disappointed in the slightest, followed.

The towpath curved round. New buildings – the Symphony Hall, the Sea Life Centre, the National Indoor Arena – replaced the older, brick-built ones. Canalside apartment blocks towered all around. Houseboats and narrow boats were moored along the banks. It looked like the future and past had collided.

The Arcadian walked up a ramp, crossed a bridge, down the other side. It brought them down by another towpath. A sign on the block of flats nearby said *King Edward's Wharf*.

'Nice,' said the bear.

Several houseboats painted in traditional primary colours

were moored alongside, their chimneys smoking, steam rising from their roofs as the heat inside evaporated against the cold night air.

The Arcadian walked past the moored craft. At the corner of the wharf was an ancient, run-down boat, the kind of thing a family might have taken a holiday in on the Norfolk Broads in the seventies. Mildewed and rusting, it was badly maintained and inexpertly repaired. It looked like it was barely watertight. The Arcadian stopped in front of it.

'You live here?'

The Arcadian turned to him, angry again. 'What's wrong with it?'

'Nothing ...'

The Arcadian took out a key, fitted it in the padlock on the door, opened it, went in. The bear followed.

Inside was cramped and dark. It smelled of damp and various kinds of uncleanliness. He put the light on. The squalid surroundings matched the smell.

The bear was wrinkling his nose. The Arcadian turned to him. 'You don't like it?'

The bear looked round the tiny space, back to the Arcadian. Found a smile. 'It's fine. It'll do.' And then he noticed the doll's house. 'What's that?'

The Arcadian smiled. 'A hobby.'

The bear nodded, laughed. 'Right.' He turned to the Arcadian, the doll's house forgotten. 'But this is more important.'

He grabbed hold of the Arcadian, kissed him roughly on the mouth. The Arcadian responded. He felt the bear's hands digging into him. His face pulled away. The bear looked at him.

'D'you like it rough?' Almost a whisper.

'Yeah,' the Arcadian nodded, 'I do.'

He didn't see the punch coming. It connected with the side of his face, spun him round, sent him reeling into the side of the cabin.

He staggered, put his hand to his mouth. Winced from the pain. It felt like his jaw had been dislocated.

'What the fuck's wrong with you?' he shouted. He noticed the bear was wearing latex gloves. He hadn't seen him put them on.

'I like it rough too,' said the bear, and swung at him again.

The Arcadian ducked, but the blow still connected with his ribs. The air went out of him and he fell to one knee, spilling old pizza cartons and plastic bottles off the table as he did so.

'I'm . . . supposed to be in charge . . .' said the Arcadian, getting to his feet. 'Me . . .'

The bear was no longer smiling. He said nothing. Just punched the Arcadian again in the face. His head snapped back and he was down. The bear didn't let him get up this time. He was on him again, punching him repeatedly. The Arcadian tried to fight back but the blows were too fast, too strong to respond to.

'This what you want?' the bear asked, pulling open the Arcadian's belt, yanking down his jeans and underpants so that he was exposed. 'This better?'

Another punch. The Arcadian could no longer see out of one eye.

He made another attempt to get to his feet, fighting the pain that had taken up sudden sharp residence in his body. The bear slapped him down. As he fell, he made a grab for the doll's house, brought it down with him.

The bear pulled the Arcadian's belt from his jeans, looped it round his neck. Pulled hard.

'You fucked up,' he whispered in the Arcadian's ear. 'Badly. Terminally.'

He pulled the belt tighter.

'Should have left it to the professionals. Not some sad little wannabe like you. You shouldn't have been anywhere near this.'

The Arcadian processed the words as quickly as he could, realised what was happening. He tried to talk, to argue. It was no good.

The belt was pulled tighter.

This couldn't be happening, he thought. Not now. Not to him. He was the Arcadian. He was better than this. It was him who should be doing this, not receiving it. It made him so angry. So impotently angry.

The belt was pulled as tight as it could go.

The Arcadian gave up struggling.

Through his one working eye he saw the doll lying on the floor next to him. She was smiling. He smiled back.

Beyond that, in his mind's eye, he saw a little red fire engine.

And beyond that, nothing.

No butterfly.

PART FOUR

BLACK SABBATH

66

When his iPhone rang, Phil felt as though he had hardly been asleep. He checked the clock on the phone. He was right.

'Phil Brennan . . .' His words were slurred. He rolled over on his side, away from Marina, who had jumped when the phone rang but seemed to be drifting back off now.

'Sorry to disturb you, sir. Constable Pierce here. City Neighbourhood. We've got a suspect in custody in connection with the case you're working on.'

'That's nice,' Phil said, still barely awake.

Pierce continued, patiently, 'He has the tattoo you were looking for.'

That opened Phil's eyes. He sat up. 'Really? The tattoo? Is he . . .'

'He's in custody, as I said, sir. The two detectives who brought him in are a little shaken up. And it looks like you're the best bet for the interview.'

'Shaken up? How?'

'He didn't want to come quietly, sir. DCs Oliver and Khan, they're a bit the worse for wear.'

'Don't suppose this'll keep till the morning? Clear head and all that.'

'He's been booked, sir. The custody clock's ticking.'

Phil rubbed his eyes with his free hand. 'Right. I'll be along as soon as I can get there.'

He hung up, put the phone back on the bedside table. Looked at Marina. She opened her eyes.

'What's up?'

'Got a suspect. The murder I'm working. Need me to do the interview.'

Marina nodded. 'OK. Good luck.'

'Thanks.'

He paused, kept looking at her. Wondering if she was going to say anything more. Wondering if he should say anything more. Her eyes closed again. The moment, if it had ever been there, passed.

Phil threw the duvet back, felt the cold immediately. Put his feet to the floor, stumbled off to the shower. He checked his phone again. Nearly five o'clock. He wondered how much sleep he had actually had.

Marina waited until she heard the shower running before sitting up. She checked the time. Jesus.

She hadn't slept much either. Every time she had drifted off, Gwilym had been waiting in the darkness, that sneering smile in place, hands outstretched ready to touch her. She had jumped awake every time those dream fingers made contact. They made contact a lot.

She heard Phil coming back into the bedroom, lay down, closed her eyes once more. She stayed that way until he dressed and left. Once she heard the front door go, she sat upright again. Grabbed her phone.

Time had barely moved. Damn.

She was relieved. Or at least she thought she was. Relieved that Phil had to go out, that circumstances had spared her once again from having the conversation. The confrontation.

320

She sighed. No. She wasn't relieved. She hadn't been spared, it had just been postponed. Yet again. She still had to talk to him. And the longer she left it, the harder it became.

After she'd spoken to Anni. Yes, that was when she'd talk to him. Once Anni came back to her with the results, she could talk to Phil. Tell him everything. Let the whole lot tumble out. Await his reaction. Take it from there.

Anni. She checked the time again. Too early to call. And she doubted that Anni would have had time to make any progress. Or to get her friend to make progress for her.

She lay back down again. Knew she would be lying there staring at the wall until the sun came up. Just waiting for the results to come back. A dark, unpleasant ripple ran through her. *Waiting to get the results back.* That was exactly what it felt like. A pregnancy test. An STD or HIV test. Cancer screening. Something that would have a potentially life-changing impact on her.

Oh God, she thought. STDs, HIV. She would have to be tested for them too . . .

No. She wasn't going to just lie there and wait. She had to do something.

She grabbed her phone again. Too early to call, yes. But not too early to text.

She found Anni's name. Left her a message.

Tell them to get a move on. Please . . .

67

'How do I look?'

'Wait till you see the other fella.'

Imani smiled politely at the joke. And winced. Smiling made her face ache.

Mike Pierce was sitting next to her. Once the suspect had been pulled to his feet after his Tasering, had had his rights read to him and been bundled away in the back of a van, Pierce hadn't left her side. He was there when the paramedics turned up, gave them an account of the injuries sustained by both herself and Nadish Khan, waited while she received treatment.

'Back to base?' he had said then. 'You really should go home.'

'And let the paperwork fairies take over from here? I'd love to.'

He had made sure she and Khan got safely back to Steelhouse Lane. Being in the MIU office in the middle of the night gave it an eerie, half-haunted, time-out-of-joint feel. The right place at the wrong time. As if being there at that hour was disturbing the ghosts.

He brought her a cup of what passed for tea, sat down next to her.

'Thanks,' she said, putting down the ice pack the paramedic had given her, bringing the cup to her lips.

'Don't thank me yet. You haven't drunk it.'

She smiled. It hurt. 'Not just for the tea. You and the boys, tonight ... thanks.'

He shrugged. 'No problem. That's what we do in Community.'

Imani put the cup to her mouth once more, felt the steam warm her face. She looked at Pierce. He had a strong jaw, good profile. Rugged features, but kind eyes.

'Listen,' she said, putting the tea down, 'I was wondering. You've been really great tonight and everything, but ... I mean, you don't have to ... but I just wondered if you fancied maybe having a drink one night ...'

Pierce smiled, eyes momentarily downcast.

He's married, she thought. *Shit. Or he doesn't date black girls. Racist.*

He turned to her. 'That would be lovely, thank you, but ...'

She waited.

'There's ... a reason I work where I do. Southside. Hurst Street.'

Imani frowned. Then got it. 'Oh. Right.'

He made a helpless, what-can-you-do gesture, gave a weak smile. 'Sorry.'

'No problem. Sorry for asking.'

He laughed. 'Don't mind at all. Shy kids get nothing, as my mother used to say.'

'What have they brought you back here for?'

Imani looked up when she heard the voice. DI Phil Brennan was walking towards them. He stopped when he saw her face.

'Jesus Christ ...'

She tried to smile. 'That bad, eh?' She looked up at him.

There was nothing but concern in his eyes. He knelt down beside her, studied her injuries. 'Who did that to you? Our suspect?'

'Yeah. I put my face in the way of his fist. He won't do it again.'

'You're damn right.' He nodded, still studying the damage. Then noticed that there was someone else there. Looked at him. 'Phil Brennan.'

'Mike Pierce. We spoke on the phone.'

They shook. Pierce got Phil up to speed. Phil thanked him, looked again at Imani. 'What did the paramedics say?'

'That I was lucky. Nothing broken. Least my nose won't have to be reset. But I'm going to have a pair of gorgeous black eyes in the morning. We got him. That's the main thing.'

Phil straightened up, looked round. Nadish Khan was sitting along from her, holding his side. Imani watched as Phil walked over to Khan, sat by him. 'Same guy?'

'Came at me with a bar or something in the car park.' Khan moved, flinched. Screwed his eyes closed in sudden pain. 'Paramedic reckons I've broken a couple of ribs.'

'Jesus.' Phil straightened up, looked between the pair of them.

'I'm sorry,' he said to them both. 'I had no idea this would happen.'

He means it, thought Imani; he really is anxious about us. 'Might have been a lot worse if Mike hadn't been there,' she said.

'And the response team,' said Pierce. 'Can't take all the credit.'

'Thank you anyway. All of you.' He looked again at Imani and Khan. 'I'm really proud of you both.'

They thanked him. Imani glanced at Khan. He seemed to be genuinely thrilled by the praise.

Phil was about to speak again when Khan's phone rang. He looked at the display. Whatever he had been feeling after Phil's praise quickly drained from his face.

'Sorry,' he said, 'I've got to get this.' He turned away so the rest of them couldn't hear the conversation.

Imani threw a quizzical glance at Phil, whose features remained impassive.

Khan finished the call, turned back to the group. From the look on his face he had been given some bad, or worryingly unpleasant, news.

'Everything OK?' asked Phil.

'Yeah,' said Khan, unconvincingly. 'Fine. I've, er ... got to go. For a bit. That OK?'

'Sure,' said Phil, still concerned. 'I think the pair of you should go home. You've done enough for one night.'

'Thanks, yeah. Cheers.'

Khan turned, left them. His walk was contradictory, thought Imani. Brisk yet reluctant. Like he had to be somewhere he didn't want to go.

Phil turned back to her and Pierce. 'So,' he said, 'where's this guy I've got to question?'

68

Marina didn't feel like she had been asleep. She must have been, though, because the noise of her phone, sharp, insistent, startled her into wakefulness. She scrabbled for it on the bedside table, found it.

'Hello?' Her voice anxious, breathing fast, heart hammering. Anticipating bad news.

'D'you know what time this is?'

Marina smiled, relaxed slightly. Anni.

She looked at her watch. 'Just gone six.'

'Yeah. Just gone six. In the morning. Sunday morning. When we should all be sleeping off our hangovers.'

'That what you're doing?'

'I was trying. But this woman keeps texting me in the middle of the night.'

'Sorry.'

Anni sighed. 'It's OK. I know you would do the same for me if things were the other way round.'

'You know it, sister.'

Anni laughed. 'That accent was terrible.'

Just hearing Anni's voice was making Marina feel better. 'Sorry.' She sighed.

'How you feeling?'

'No better, if I'm honest.'

'What did Phil say?'

Marina didn't answer straight away.

'Marina . . . '

'I didn't tell him, Anni. I tried, I . . . couldn't.'

'Oh God, Marina . . . '

'I'm sorry, I did try. But the words wouldn't come. When he came in last night was the perfect opportunity. And I opened my mouth and . . . He was exhausted. Just in from doing overtime on a long shift. Should have been his day off. If I'd said something, what if he'd taken it the wrong way?'

Anni said nothing.

'I'm going to tell him, though. Definitely.'

'Where is he now? Can't you do it now?'

'He's back at the office. Got called in. Has to question a suspect.'

'Right. So when?'

'When you get the lab results back. When I've got something concrete to take to him. So he'll know it's not just me being hysterical or making excuses for shagging some bloke when I was pissed.'

'Marina, he won't think you're being hysterical. You know that. And he definitely won't think you've shagged some bloke when you were pissed. He knows you better than that. And you know it too.'

'Thank you,' said Marina.

'No problem.'

'So . . . look, I hate to sound like I'm obsessed or anything, but . . . '

'When will the results be in?'

'Yeah. Sorry. Am I that transparent?'

'No. Like I said, I would be doing exactly the same as you if I was in your position. I'd be in a state too.'

'Yeah. Every woman would.' She paused, waited. 'So. The results . . . ?'

'It's Sunday. Nobody works on a Sunday.'

'Nobody's supposed to be working on this at all.'

'I know. Look, I spoke to my guy. Told him it was urgent, on the hush-hush, all of that. He said he understood and that he'd get back to me as quickly as possible.'

'When will that be? Today?'

'Marina . . . '

'Sorry. But I'm, you know. Anxious. Everything's on hold. Phil. Work. My life. Until I hear back from you.' She sighed. 'Look, I know I'm being demanding and unreasonable, but . . . ' she felt tears well up, 'I'm falling apart here . . . '

There were no words from the other end of the phone, just the sound of movement. Marina heard a door close, the atmosphere change. When Anni spoke again, her voice was echoing.

'OK. That's better.'

'Where . . . What happened?'

'I'm in the bathroom. Thought it best that Mickey didn't hear any more.'

'He's there?'

Anni laughed. 'He's always here. Can't get rid of the bastard. Bless him.'

Marina gave a small laugh too. It quickly died.

'Listen,' said Anni, 'I'll get in touch with my contact at the lab again. Ask him if he can go in today, see what he can do.'

'Thank you.' Marina felt relief wash over her. Or a certain amount. It was a start.

'But this is a really big favour. I want you to know that. Not that you're not worth it, but . . . ' Anni sighed. 'He's an old boyfriend. I think I may have to make it up in some way.'

'Oh.' Her words sank in. 'Oh. I'm sorry, Anni.'

'Don't worry. I'll buy dinner, peck on the cheek. That should do him. I just thought it best that Mickey didn't hear me say that.'

'Quite.'

'I'll see if I can get him to do it today.'

'Thank you. I really ... I can't tell you how much ...' Marina felt herself welling up once more.

'Hey. Don't worry. We'll get the bastard. I won't let him get away with what he did to you. You can be sure of that.'

The tears came. 'Thank you, thank you, Anni ...'

'Right. Now stop that. You've got a little girl to look after. Think of her.'

'Thank you.'

'Stop thanking me. I'm your mate. Just try and forget about it until I call.'

They made their goodbyes; Anni hung up.

Marina put the phone back on the bedside table. Stared at the ceiling.

69

Phil entered the interview room. The young man at the other side of the table looked up. He was affecting boredom, ennui, but Phil knew that something hissed and fizzed behind his eyes. The machine seemed to be running smoothly. But somewhere the circuits were shorting out. He was wearing a short sleeved T-shirt and jeans.

'No jacket?' said Phil. 'Cold outside.'

'Didn't have time to get it when I was pulled in here.' His voice laced with sarcasm.

Phil sat down opposite him. Put the manila folder he had been carrying on the table. Introduced himself. 'And you are?'

'Martin Trotter.' The man spoke his name slowly and clearly, a hint of sarcasm remaining.

Phil checked a piece of paper in front of him. 'You live in Ladywood, by the reservoir . . . ' He read down. 'You work in marketing. Oh. You're unemployed.'

Trotter bristled. 'Between jobs at the moment.'

'Know why you're here?'

''Cos your lot pulled me in. I've done nothing. I was attacked.' He rubbed the back of his neck where the Taser had hit him. 'Defended myself.'

'D'you want a solicitor?'

'Not now,' Trotter said. 'Later. When I sue your fucking arses off.' He laughed, sat back, arms folded.

Phil, relieved, ignored the comment. 'Arm,' he said.

Trotter frowned. 'What?'

'I want to see your arm.'

Trotter stretched out his right arm. Phil took a photo from the manila folder, checked the image of the tattoo against the one on Trotter's forearm. A good match. He put the photo away, sat back.

Trotter retracted his arm, looked puzzled. 'Happy now?' he said.

'Ecstatic. Right.' He looked up, straight at Trotter. Face professionally blank. 'What were you doing in the cinema?'

Trotter gave a snort, tightened his arms round his chest. 'What d'you think?'

Phil didn't reply.

Trotter leaned forward. 'Fucking.' He said it with relish, like a little boy challenging his parents with a naughty word. He sat back, pleased with himself, clearly thinking he had the upper hand. Phil kept eye contact with him as he asked the next question.

'Where'd you get the tattoo, Martin?' His voice light yet authoritative.

Trotter's attitude changed. His cockiness slipped as a shade passed over his features. 'Why d'you want to know?' His voice suddenly cagey, hollow. 'D'you want one or something?' Aiming for bravado. Missing.

Phil resisted the urge to smile. Contented himself with doing it inwardly. He had made a hit. 'Don't see many like that,' he said.

'You should move in more exciting circles, then.' Something passed across Trotter's face. He immediately regretted his words but didn't want his regret to show.

Phil knew he was on to something now. *Coppers in interviews are like lions bringing down wildebeest,* his ex-DCI Gary Franks had once said. *Any weakness, you just pounce on it. Go in for the kill.*

'Really? What kind of circles are those, Martin?'

Trotter said nothing.

'Come on, Martin. If your life's more exciting than mine, tell me about it.'

Trotter flinched, but he still said nothing. Phil decided to change his line of questioning. 'What's so special about that design?' he asked. 'Just looks like a twisted cage.'

Trotter gave another snort. 'Shows what you know,' he said, trying to regain the upper hand once more.

'Really?' said Phil, eyes wide in mock-ignorance. 'What is it then?'

Trotter looked smug. He lifted up his arm, admired the design. 'A DNA double helix. The symbol of life itself.' He shook his head, gave another snort of laughter. 'Twisted cage . . .'

'I want to see it again,' said Phil.

Trotter's skin was cold to the touch. Phil angled the desk lamp over the tattoo. Examined it closely. He looked up.

'This isn't real.'

Trotter looked slightly embarrassed. 'Never said it was.'

'Just temporary. Printed, not inked.'

'So?'

'Can't afford a proper one?'

Trotter stared at him. 'Fuck you.'

Phil leaned across the table. 'How do you know Glenn McGowan?'

Trotter stared at him, his brows knitted, his features puzzled. 'Who?'

Phil continued. 'Glenn McGowan. You might know him

332

better as Amanda.' He took some photos from the folder, displayed them in front of Trotter.

Trotter inclined his head forward, studied them. It didn't take long. His head snapped back, eyes on Phil once more. 'Her. Yeah, I know her.'

'He, or she, was murdered.'

'Murdered?' A light came on in Trotter's eyes. 'Is that the one they're talking about on the TV?' He smiled. 'A TV on the TV.' He laughed.

'Hilarious,' said Phil. 'So where did you know her from?'

'The—' He started to speak, stopped. His lips coming down fast, abruptly cutting off the words.

'Where?' Phil's voice calm, inquisitorial.

Trotter put his head back. His eyes were hooded, unreadable. He shrugged. 'Here and there. Around. Bars and that. Clubs.' His eyes slid away once more.

'Which ones? Which clubs?'

His lips came together. His eyes stared at the tabletop.

'Which clubs, Martin?'

Trotter looked up, a light coming on in his eyes. 'You think I murdered her? Is that what this is about it? You want to pin it on me?'

'So tell me why I shouldn't charge you.'

'Because I barely knew her.' He sat back, arms folded. Smiled. 'Changed my mind. Here's me waiting for my solicitor.'

Phil pretended he hadn't heard the last bit. 'If you barely knew her, how do you explain the fact that you were seen at her house?'

'What? I wasn't.'

'You were. Not only that, you had sex with Amanda.'

'What? This is ... this is a stitch-up ...' His eyes darted desperately round the room once more.

333

Phil remained calm. 'We've got it on DVD, Martin.'

He began to shake his head wildly. 'You can't have ... You're lying, you're fucking lying ... I swear, it wasn't me ... '

'Really? Here's a couple of tips, Martin. If you want to video yourself having sex, don't do it with someone who then ends up dead. And try to hide any distinguishing marks or features.'

Trotter looked puzzled. 'What?'

'The tattoo, the temporary one that looks like you've inked it in again when it started to fade. The symbol of life itself,' said Phil. 'How appropriate. Life is what you're looking at now, Martin.'

Then Trotter did something that Phil hadn't been expecting. He laughed.

'Something funny?'

'Yeah,' said Trotter. 'What you've just said.'

'You've just been identified from your tattoo. There can't be many of them around.'

'You think?'

Phil felt like a winter pond skater who had underestimated how thin the ice was. 'You're saying there's more?'

'Oh yeah,' said Trotter.

'How many?'

Trotter looked at his arm, then back at Phil. Something dark and ugly danced in his eyes.

'Loads,' he said.

70

Dawn had arrived. And with it more rain, grey skies and cold.

Nadish Khan sat on a soaking wet bench in Victoria Square, waiting. He looked round. The square – and the whole of New Street – had been given over to the wooden sheds of the German Christmas market. Although there wasn't much that was German about some of the stalls: a nail bar was in front of him, next to a stall selling winter Pimm's, the Mumbai Grill on its other side. The market was supposed to give a boost to the local economy, and it did. But, as he knew from being on the force, it also brought its own set of problems, street robbery, pickpocketing and drunkenness being the main ones. He had to admit, at night when it was lit it up it did have a lovely festive air to it. But not on a bleak, overcast Sunday morning in the pouring rain. It just looked like a whole shanty town of depressing wooden shacks.

He looked round again, checked his watch, pulled his coat around his shoulders, kept his head down. The rain still hit him. He wished he hadn't come. But he knew he had no choice. Or he had felt he had no choice. A debt of honour, the caller had said. Although Khan thought there was very little that was honourable about it.

He heard him before he saw him. Wheezing and groaning as he walked slowly, making a big production number of sitting down next to him. Bundled up against the cold and the rain, hat pulled down, scarf wrapped round the lower half of his face. He unwrapped the scarf, looked at Khan, smiled.

Ron Parsons.

'You got here before me,' Parsons said. 'Good. Punctual. I admire punctuality. Something sadly lacking in most people these days.'

'Just say what you have to say,' said Khan, looking round once more, this time to see if there was anyone he knew watching him, 'then go.' There was no one there. No one that he could recognise, anyway.

Parsons looked affronted. Offended, even. 'Is that any way to speak to an old friend of the family? Really? Is it?' He stared at Khan as he spoke, willing the younger man to make eye contact.

Khan was aware of the look he was being given. It was hypnotic, drawing his head round, but he tried to resist it. He settled for a quick glance at Parsons, then away again. He was repulsed.

'You're no friend of mine,' he said, talking to the wind and rain.

Parsons shook his head. Drops of water fell from the brim of his trilby. 'If your dad could hear you now . . . '

Khan turned to him. 'Yeah, well my dad's dead, isn't he? So he's not likely to hear me.'

'Nadish . . . '

Khan ignored him. 'And we all know how. We all know why, don't we? We know what he was when he was alive. What you made him.'

Parsons turned to him. His cheeks were red, his eyes too. His features suddenly ugly with anger. 'Now listen to me, you little shit. Don't think you're any better than me or your dad. Because you're not. So don't go getting all high and mighty with me.' He sat back, breathing heavily. The anger seemed to have exhausted him.

'What d'you want?' asked Khan. 'Why did you want to see me? Just say it and go. I haven't got time to sit in the pissing rain with the likes of you. I've got work to do.'

Parsons's hand was clenched into a fist. He had drawn it back ready to strike. His eyes were dancing, raging. This time Khan looked at him full on.

'You wanna hit me? Yeah? Go on then, old man. Take your best shot. I'm here.'

As he spoke, he was aware of a shadow detaching itself from the steps behind the bench. Huge and bearded, blank-faced. A body that moved like it was used to casual violence. Parsons's minder. Khan sat back.

Parsons managed to get himself under control. It took some effort. *Hasn't been spoken to like that in a long time*, thought Khan. *Good. Teach the old fucker a lesson*.

He got his breath, restored his equilibrium. 'I had a visit yesterday,' he said at length. 'From your DI Brennan.'

Khan, despite what he thought of Parsons, rolled his eyes. 'Oh. Him.'

Parsons spotted the gesture, pounced on it. 'Don't you like him, then?'

Khan realised he had given too much away. What he thought of Brennan was none of Parsons's business. 'What did he want?' he said.

'He's investigating something – or someone – I'd rather not have investigated.' He looked at Khan again, those hypnotic eyes burning into him. 'Do you understand?'

'What's it got to do with me?'

'What d'you mean, what's it got to do with you? He's your

boss. You're working with him. You're probably working on the same thing.'

Khan shrugged. 'So?'

'So, I'm giving you a job to do.'

'I've already got a job.'

'And now you've got another. Don't worry, I'll make it worth your while. And your mother's as well.'

Khan felt his hands shake. He was baring his teeth in anger. 'Don't ... don't mention my mother ...'

'Every little helps. That's all I'm saying. Things can't have been easy after your dad topped himself. What am I saying? I know they weren't. Your lot turned their backs on your mum. Buried him in more ways than one. No pension, nothing. She had to fend for herself. Bringing up a family, must have been hard.'

Khan frowned. 'What are you saying?'

'Just that.' Parsons's eyes bored into him. 'Good job she had someone on hand to help with the bills. The housekeeping. Someone who values loyalty. Rewards it.'

Khan understood. 'You bastard ...'

'I've been a good friend of your family. Gave her the money that brought you up. So show some respect, you little shit.'

The bearded shadow hovered on the edge of Khan's vision. Khan sat on his hands.

'That's better,' said Parsons. 'Now, all you have to do is make sure this investigation is looking in the opposite direction. The way I want it to look. You give me updates, I'll tell you where not to look. Simples.'

'Yeah? And how much are you going to pay me for this?'

Parsons shrugged. 'A grand.'

'A grand? That's an insult, you cheap old bastard.'

'Five, then.'

Khan turned to him once more. 'For a so-called friend of

338

the family. Five grand. To become everything I hate, everything my father was. Five grand.'

Parsons sighed. 'Ten, then. Can't say fairer than that. You can do a lot with ten grand. Your mother did.'

Khan didn't answer him. He felt like he had been stabbed in the heart.

Parsons said nothing. Waited.

Khan opened his mouth to reply. Couldn't. Instead he stood up. Walked away.

He heard Parsons's voice behind him. 'I'll take that as a yes, then.'

He didn't answer.

'I'll be in touch, Nadish. I'm sure you will be too. Soon . . .'

There might have been more words but Khan didn't hear them.

They were lost to the rain.

71

Maddy had been smiling since she opened her eyes. She thought she must have been smiling in her sleep. She knew why. Ben was lying right next to her.

She turned on her side, watched him. He was still asleep, breathing shallowly. She didn't blame him. It was still early. The weak morning light was only just daring to creep round the thin curtains that came with the rented house. Maddy was only awake because she was too excited to sleep. For a few reasons. All of them to do with Ben.

He was sleeping on his side, his face towards her. She could feel his breath on her skin. She closed her eyes momentarily, enjoyed it as a purely sensual experience. She opened them again, resumed watching him.

I'm not weird, she thought. *I'm not obsessed. I just love watching him sleep. What's wrong with that?*

She turned on her back, still smiling, glancing at him from time to time. She felt safe with Ben in her bed. Just next to her, even. Or just somewhere in the same house. If he was near her she felt that nothing and no one could get to her. That everything was going to be OK.

And the fact that he was going to help her give Gwilym his comeuppance made things even better.

She wasn't usually a vindictive, vengeful person. Live and let live, and all that. She could usually see the good in someone, even someone who had done horrendous things. But after the previous night's conversation with Ben, after hearing that she wasn't the first, that Gwilym had done even worse things to other girls before her . . . she knew that giving someone the benefit of the doubt wasn't always the best thing to do. Sometimes you just had to take a stand. Do something for the common good. And that was just what they were going to do with Gwilym. She wanted to make sure that no more girls went through what she had been through. And she was so happy that Ben was there to do it with her.

She moved the duvet back, turned away from him. Careful not to disturb him or wake him. She slowly slid out of bed, grabbed her thick terrycloth dressing gown, wrapped it round her naked body, put her feet into her furry slippers. If Ben hadn't been in the bed with her she would have been wearing pyjamas and even bed socks. The house was cold. But she had him to keep her warm. Besides, she liked to feel his naked body against hers. No, she *loved* it.

Another night and he still hadn't pressed her for sex. He knew she was still sore from her termination so he hadn't pushed her. 'When you're ready,' he had said, kissing her shoulders. 'It'll feel all the better because we've waited.'

She smiled at the memory. There was something about him that was so old-fashioned. Gallant, even. Or maybe she had just never had a boyfriend who treated her decently.

She made her way downstairs to the kitchen, put the kettle on. Boiled up enough water, made two mugs of tea. She put milk in, not knowing how he took it, and went back upstairs.

There was nothing worse than cold tea, she thought, but she didn't want to wake him. *Should have made it with lemon,* she thought, *instead of milk*. That way if it went cold it would still be drinkable.

She crept over to the bed. Stood looking down at him. He was still sleeping peacefully. She smiled again. Felt something intense flutter inside her that she had never experienced before.

She placed his mug of tea carefully on the bedside table. Straightened up again. As she did so he moved, turned over. The scar on the inside of his wrist caught the light. She reached out tentatively with her free hand, stroked the ridges.

And suddenly couldn't breathe.

Ben had woken suddenly and sat up, his hand going straight to her throat, grabbing her, squeezing and twisting. She tried to scream, to let him know it was her, that it was OK, but the only sound she made was a guttural gargle. Tea was being splashed and spilt everywhere. She looked him straight in the eye, imploring. But his eyes, those usually kind, soulful eyes, were nowhere to be seen. Instead, two dark, angry coals were staring at her like something from a horror film.

And then he realised who she was.

His grip relaxed, his hand pulled away. His eyes returned to normal.

'Oh my God,' he said. 'I'm so sorry . . .'

He jumped out of bed, enfolded her in his arms. He looked at her, his features now the soft, familiar ones she was used to seeing. His eyes were brimming with compassion.

'I've . . . I've spilt the tea . . .' They were the only words Maddy could find.

'Doesn't matter,' he said. 'Come on. Let's get back into bed.'

They did so, Maddy slipping out of her dressing gown and beneath the now damp duvet. She was shivering. Ben kept his arms tight round her.

'I'm so sorry,' he said. 'I do that when I wake up some-times, I've been told. Ever since I was little.'

'It's OK,' she said.

'No,' he said, 'it's not. Maddy, that was awful. I should never have done that to you. Never.'

'It's OK . . .' The words just tumbled out. She kept repeat-ing them like a mantra, every time he apologised. She didn't know what else to say. She thought he didn't either.

'Here,' he said eventually, leaning over to the bedside table, coming back to her. 'Here's my tea. Let's share . . .'

They did so, Ben putting the mug to Maddy's lips, letting her drink as if feeding a small child or a wounded animal.

The tea was finished. Ben replaced the mug. They lay together, Ben with his arms wrapped protectively round Maddy, for a long time. Neither spoke.

'You OK?' he said eventually.

She nodded.

He shook his head. 'I don't know what gets into me some-times. Hitting out at you, Jesus. Now doing that to somebody like Gwilym I could understand. But not you.'

'Gwilym,' she said.

'Yeah,' said Ben. 'You still up for it? Getting your own back on him?'

She nodded.

'Good. Good to hear it.'

'When . . . when shall we do it?'

'No time like the present.'

'Today?'

'Why not?'

'How?'

He smiled. 'I've been thinking about that. I've got a plan . . .'

He told her. She tried to listen, to pay attention to his words. Tried not to stare at his scar as he spoke.

72

Marina was in the kitchen, clearing up after giving Josephina her breakfast. Her daughter had gone off to watch TV while holding intense conversations with her stuffed toys and dolls. Marina was wiping down the surfaces, thinking about another mug of coffee. The phone changed all that.

It was in her jeans pocket. She had checked it every few minutes, just in case she had missed a call or somehow hadn't heard it or felt it vibrate. It was only when she had taken her mind off it and got on with other stuff that it had rung. Typical.

She checked the display, saw who it was. Anni. Her heart began to hammer once more.

'Hello?' She was out of breath just from saying that one word.

'Got the test results.'

Every single possible answer began to pinball through Marina's mind. This was what she had been waiting for. This was what she had been dreading. 'That was quick.' She knew she was stalling, playing for time, trying to compose herself. She didn't know whether she wanted to hear. Which would be worse.

'Yeah, well, I told him it was a rush job. Told him a bit about what had happened. Couldn't do it quick enough.'

Marina waited.

'Positive. Flunitrazepam. Rohypnol to you and me.'

Marina felt her legs give way. She had to sit down before she collapsed on the kitchen floor.

Positive . . .

'It was easy, really. I told him what to look for. He found it. Said it must have been an old batch, that he must have had quite a stock of it from a while ago. It was clear. Nowadays they put something in it to turn the drink a different colour so you know you've been spiked. Means you're not the first.'

Positive . . .

'You there?' Anni's voice light, solicitous.

'Yeah,' said Marina. 'Yeah, I'm here.'

'Well stay where you are. I'm coming over.'

'You're . . . what? What for?'

'Because you haven't told Phil. Because you've got no one else to talk to about it. And because we have to decide what we're going to do next.'

'What . . . we're going to do next?'

'Look, Marina, I know this must be a bit of a shock to you. But not that much of a one, really. This is what you were expecting. What you thought the test would show up. And it has. Give me a couple of hours. I'm on my way.'

Marina looked round her kitchen. Seconds earlier the biggest thing in her life had been deciding whether to have another coffee. Now it was trying to decide how best to bring a serial rapist to justice.

No. That wasn't true. The coffee had just been a distraction. It had always been about Gwilym.

'You there?' Anni's voice again.

'What? I'm . . . yeah. I'm here.'

'OK. Good. Look, you took that glass illegally, so it might not be admissible in court. But we'll find a way to get him. Don't worry. Hang in there. I won't be long.'

She rang off.

Marina put the phone down. Sat down.

Maybe she would have that coffee after all.

73

Detective Constable Patsy Yardley had had enough. And it was still early morning.

She pulled the hood of her anorak tight round her head, looked along the towpath that stretched from the back of the Mailbox all the way past the Gasworks Basin, right to the Sea Life Centre, and wished, not for the first time that morning, that she was still in bed.

'Think of the overtime,' said her partner, Detective Constable Pam Chapman.

'Normally I would. But that's not much compensation this time.'

'Think of the glamour, then.'

Patsy ignored her partner, kept walking along the towpath. The rain battering them. Patsy could barely see through her glasses. Both of them wore padded anoraks to keep out the cold and the wet, and they were glad of them. But there was another reason Patsy was glad she was dressed like that. It made her look as sexless as possible.

They had been given the task of tracking down violent sex offenders from the list that Elli had generated. The two they had visited the night before could be struck off the list. One was morbidly obese – nowhere near a match for the photo –

and also a ponytailed biker. He protested that he shouldn't have been on the sex offenders register, that it was all a mistake. He'd been stitched up by someone from a rival gang. Been set up with an underage girl who lied about her age. That was all. And yeah, he'd been violent. But only to the person who'd set him up. *Wouldn't you be the same?*

But all the time he was talking to them, proclaiming his innocence, Patsy had been aware of him trying to mentally undress her. Aware of something dark and twisted lurking inside him. They questioned him about Glenn McGowan. From his answers, whatever else he might have been, they knew he wasn't involved. Another one off the list.

The next one had been getting ready to go on a date. Pam had asked him who with. He became cagey, reticent. When she persisted, he became angry. They knew he had done time for child abuse and spousal abuse. He was a predator, a planner. He played the long game, insinuated himself in the life of a single mother, got to know her, moved in on her kids. Got them where he wanted them, then started to have his fun. He had nothing to do with the murder of Glenn McGowan. They were sure of that. But they did make a note to check up on him, find out who he was seeing. They didn't want him to repeat his patterns of offending. They didn't want him to find a new victim.

They kept walking along the towpath.

'Is it much further?' asked Pam from beneath her hood.

'Are we there yet? Are we there yet?' Patsy replied in a childlike, sing-song voice, mocking her.

'Piss off.' Pam walked faster. Eager to get it over with. 'Where's this next one?' she added. 'Wouldn't want to miss it.'

'King Edward's Wharf,' Patsy replied. 'Just along here.'

'Always fancied a houseboat,' said Pam. 'Something romantic about them. You know, pootling along, parking up here and there, some handsome lock keeper wearing an Aran sweater looking like Liam Neeson popping up to help you . . . '

'You'd never be able to stand upright, Pam. You're nearly six foot. Get real.'

'I know.'

'And your lock keeper might be wearing an Aran sweater, but he'll look sod all like Liam Neeson. More like Brian Blessed.'

'Yeah, all right. It was just a little fantasy, that's all.'

They reached King Edward's Wharf. A block of new flats contrasting with the brightly painted houseboats moored below.

'Which one is it?'

Patsy checked her list. 'Along here.'

They walked along the side of the wharf, counting the berths. The houseboat chimneys were smoking, roofs steaming where the rain hit and met the warmth from inside them. Patsy had to admit they did look nice and cosy. But then anywhere would on a day like this.

'Here it is.' Pam stopped walking. The berth they wanted was on the opposite side of the flats. It was next to a set of crumbling Portakabins, fenced off from the path by a sad-looking mesh barrier. In contrast to the rest of the well-maintained wharf, the path here was covered in weeds and rubbish. The boat matched its surroundings. It wasn't as old as the other houseboats but it was in much worse condition. Rotting and rusting, its roof and walls mildewed and leaking. Curling gaffer tape had been used to temporarily patch up holes that were now letting in water. Its windows were rattling and ill-fitting.

The two women shared a glance.

'Someone lives here?' asked Pam. 'Looks like it's ready to sink.'

'Let's get it over with, then,' said Patsy. 'What's the name?'

'Scott Sheriff,' said Pam, looking once again at the list. 'Let's get this done and go and find a café on Broad Street. I'm soaked through.'

Patsy put her hand on the door to knock. It was open.

They exchanged another glance.

'Mr Sheriff?' she called. 'Hello?'

No reply.

'Mr Sheriff?' she called again. 'It's Detective Constable Yardley and Detective Constable Chapman, West Midlands Police. Could we have a word, please?'

Nothing.

Another shared glance.

'We're coming in, Mr Sheriff, just want to see that everything is OK . . . '

Patsy pushed open the door and immediately recoiled. The smell coming from inside complemented the exterior completely. 'Jesus . . . '

She stepped inside. And hurriedly came out again.

'What . . . what's the matter? What's there?'

'Call it in,' said Patsy. 'We've got a body.'

74

'L oads?' That wasn't the answer Phil had been expecting. Trotter allowed himself a small smile. *Gotcha*, it said.

'Why are there so many?'

Trotter was immediately cagey again. 'Can't say.'

'Yes you can. Or I'll think you're making the whole thing up and charge you with the murder of Glenn McGowan.'

Trotter sat back in his chair. Puffed out his cheeks, his lips. Leaned forward again. 'OK,' he said. 'Here's the thing. If I tell you what you want to know, about the tattoos and that, I want something in return.'

'And what might that be?'

'Immunity.'

Phil frowned. 'From what?'

'Everything. Immunity from everything you could do to me with what I tell you. And everything *they* could do.'

Phil looked directly at him. There was no one else in the room. The interview wasn't being recorded. Someone from the team might be listening in, but he didn't think that was a problem. 'OK,' he said. 'Immunity. Talk to me.'

Trotter nodded in acknowledgement. 'It's a club.'

'I know that much,' said Phil.

Trotter looked upset. 'How?'

'The thing on your arm. It's the kind of stamp you'd get in a club. It must mean something special; you haven't washed it off. And you've inked over it.'

Trotter looked aggrieved. 'But you don't know what kind of club, do you?'

'A fetish club,' said Phil. 'Something like that. Loads of them around.'

'Not like this one,' said Trotter, the darkness dancing in his eyes.

'What's so special about this one, then?'

Trotter leaned forward, arms on the table. 'It's extreme. Extreme passions. Extreme behaviour.'

'Right,' said Phil. 'So it's an extreme fetish club. Big deal.'

Trotter slammed his hand down on the table, anger in his eyes. 'You think you're so clever, don't you? Think you know it all? You know nothing.'

Phil leaned in to him, eyes unflinching. 'Then make me understand.'

Trotter nodded. 'There's loads of clubs around. Fetish, BDSM, whatever. Some of them call themselves extreme. But they're not. None of them. It's just dressing up. They're safe places with safe words in safe environments. Mutual respect. What's extreme about that?'

'So how is this place different?'

Trotter gave a sickly smile. 'It's the opposite. No safe words. And it's definitely not a safe place. You go there, you take the consequences. If you've got passions that you can't control, that need an outlet, *crave* an outlet, that's where you go.'

'Passions?'

'Kinks. Desires. Dreams. Whatever. Not your run-of-the-mill shit. You like being beaten up, enjoy inflicting pain, dress up as a woman or a baby, there's places for you. But this is if your thing's further on than that.'

'And what happens there? What d'you do?'

'Anything to anyone. And fuck the consequences. Because there aren't any. Might not even be consensual. Might not even be with adults.'

'What, rape? Murder?'

'Anything.'

'Then you'd be arrested.'

Trotter shook his head slowly. When he spoke, it was as if he was explaining something to a very simple child. 'You're not listening. There are no consequences. Nothing will happen to you. You're perfectly safe. The law doesn't apply.'

'I find that hard to believe,' said Phil.

Trotter shrugged. 'Believe what you like. I'm telling you the truth.'

'So where is this club?'

'Digbeth. In an old factory. The place looks derelict from the outside. But it's not. Got a big red door. Can't miss it.'

'Street?' asked Phil.

Trotter shrugged. 'Dunno. I'll draw you a map.'

Phil kept going. 'How do people find out about it?'

'All over the place. Fetish events, word of mouth, internet forums, wherever. Some are invited along, some enquire. They all know the score. But the club's very choosy. They don't take just anyone.'

'When's it open?'

'Whenever. There's always something going on there. Like I said, it's not like a nightclub. It's where people go when they want something. And somebody always wants something.'

'Who runs it? Who owns it?'

'He's called Ben, bloke in charge,' said Trotter. 'All I know.'

Phil felt a jolt of electricity jump through him at the name. He opened his manila folder once more. Took out a couple of photos, slid them across. Screen grabs of Glenn McGowan as

Amanda having sex with the person who called himself Ben. 'Is this Ben?'

Trotter looked at the photos. Phil watched Trotter. 'Might be.'

'This tattoo,' said Phil, pointing to a blown-up photo. 'Like yours. But real.'

The words made Trotter angry, as Phil had intended. 'I'll get one soon enough.'

I doubt that, thought Phil. He continued. 'What's behind the tattoos, then? You get a stamp like yours if you're . . . what? A newbie, or something?'

'Yeah,' said Trotter. 'Then you work your way up.'

'Why a tattoo?' asked Phil. 'What does it mean?'

'Like I said. People go there to do things they can't do any-where else. You've got to have insurance. The tattoo's a reminder. Of what you've done, what you owe the club. The deal you made. You keep quiet, the club keeps quiet. Loyalty. Then there's the next level,' said Trotter.

'Next level?'

Trotter nodded. 'The brand. That's for the hardcore, the real elite.'

'So what d'you have to do to get one of them?' asked Phil.

'Show commitment.'

Phil shook his head. 'Right.' He pushed across the photo of Glenn McGowan and Ben having sex. 'What's so extreme about this?'

'Well, they're both getting what they want.'

'Then Glenn McGowan was murdered.'

Trotter shrugged. 'Yeah. So they both got what they wanted.'

Phil sat back, thinking. An idea coming to him. 'Hold on. You mean . . . ' He tried to order his thoughts coherently. 'Whoever killed Glenn McGowan, they got what they wanted. They murdered someone. A transvestite.'

Trotter nodded.

'And ...' he frowned, 'Glenn McGowan, as Amanda, he ...'

Trotter finished the sentence for him. 'Wanted someone to kill him.'

Phil said nothing, processing the information.

'When I said desires,' said Trotter, 'you just thought I mean the murderer. You didn't think I meant the victim.'

'So people go to this club who want to be killed? Is that what you're saying?'

'People go to do things they can't do anywhere else. And I think that's about as much as I have to say on the subject. The person in the photos may or may not be Ben. I don't know. So, if you have no further questions ...'

Phil leaned forward. 'What do you go there for, Martin? I'm curious.'

Trotter smiled. This was the moment he had been waiting for, the one question he wanted to answer. He was an actor taking the stage to deliver his grand soliloquy. 'I'm HIV positive,' he said, and sat back, arms folded, as if that explained everything.

'So?' said Phil.

A wistful look came over his features. 'I like to spread the love around.'

Phil's stomach turned over. 'You mean you go there to have sex, knowing you're going to infect people?'

Trotter pointed his thumb and finger into the shape of a gun. 'You got it.'

'That's a crime,' said Phil.

'Is it?' said Trotter. 'For one thing, you've given me immunity for what I've just said; for another, it's entirely consensual.' He smiled. It wasn't pleasant. 'The people I meet there want to be infected, I assure you.'

Phil said nothing. He could find nothing to say.

Trotter made to rise. 'So if you don't mind . . .'

Phil looked up. 'Where are you going?'

Trotter pointed to the door. 'Away. Off. Free.'

'Sit down, please,' said Phil.

Trotter stared at him.

'Sit down.'

He sat.

'You were promised immunity from anything that arose concerning your testimony about the club,' Phil said. 'But there's a bit more to it than that.'

Trotter was getting angry now. 'Like?'

'Resisting arrest. Assaulting two officers in the course of their duty. Causing affray. You were engaged in oral sex in the cinema, so we can add deliberately trying to infect another person with HIV.'

'You can't—'

'And also, due to the fact that you were caught willy-waggling in public, I think we can add indecent exposure to the list.' Phil stood up. 'Have a good day.'

He left the room. But didn't get far. A uniform was running towards him.

75

Marina rang the doorbell, stood back and waited. It was exactly the kind of house she had been expecting. It couldn't have said 'students live here' any more clearly if they'd painted those words on a bed sheet and hung it from the upstairs windows.

It sat in a row of century-old terraced houses in Selly Oak. Most of the others in the street had replacement windows and doors, block-paved areas in front for cars instead of gardens, and some had even been pebble-dashed. But not this one. It had a shabby air of impermanence and transit. Just passing through.

Marina hadn't been able to wait for Anni. She had had to do something, get out of the house and do something positive towards bringing down Gwilym, feel like she was making progress. Recruit an ally. So she had left Josephina with Eileen and phoned Joy Henry. A quick trip into the university's psychology department and a riffle through the student files and she had what she needed.

The girl from the café. The one who had come to talk to Gwilym when she was there. The troubled-looking one. Marina had worked out what was happening, knew she couldn't have been the only one Gwilym had assaulted. The state the young girl was in made her think that they would have something in common. Or a common enemy at least.

She made to ring the bell again, wondered if it was actually connected. As she stretched forward, the door was opened. It was the girl from the café. The first thing Marina noticed about her was how much happier she looked since the last time she had seen her. She was wearing a thick terrycloth dressing gown and slipper socks, and no make-up. She looked at Marina quizzically, then realisation came into her eyes.

'Madeleine Mingella?'

'Maddy. Yes . . . '

'Maddy.' Marina smiled. 'I'm Marina Esposito. From the psychology department?'

'Yes,' she said, 'I know.' Fear was creeping into her voice, her posture. She held on to the door, ready to close it on hearing the wrong word.

Marina's voice dropped, confidentially. 'I wanted to have a word with you. About Hugo Gwilym.'

The light went out in Maddy's eyes. Marina knew she had to keep talking or she would lose her. 'I think we've had . . . a similar experience. I think we should talk. I think it might help. Both of us.'

Maddy looked torn. She glanced behind her, looking wary, as if expecting someone to appear. No one did.

'Can I come in, please? It's easier to talk inside. And warmer.'

Maddy opened the door, let her in. Closed it quickly behind her. 'Come into the kitchen,' she said.

Marina followed her down the hall. Posters for bands and clubs were Blu-Tacked over the plain wallpaper. A poster of Justin Bieber Marina presumed was there ironically. It was covered in graffiti that, while not complimentary, was to her mind not actually inaccurate.

The kitchen was at the back of the house. An old wooden table that bore the scars of decades of student living stood in the centre of the room. Maddy indicated for Marina to sit down at it. She did so. Maddy put the kettle on.

'Sorry about the mess,' she said.

The kitchen wasn't as bad as Marina had been expecting. 'It's fine,' she said. 'Looks just like mine when I was a student.'

They both smiled politely. Maddy made tea for Marina, served it in the least brown mug she could find, sat down opposite her. She looked apprehensive, like she was steeling herself for a blow.

'Your housemates around?' asked Marina.

'No, they're . . . I don't know. Not here.'

'Partied out. Didn't get home.' Marina smiled once more. 'Look. It's about Hugo Gwilym. After I'd seen you in the café the other day, the state you were in, I guessed what had happened. I knew he was responsible.'

'How did you know?'

'The way you looked and acted.' Marina's eyes went to Maddy's bandaged wrist. She said nothing. Maddy covered the bandage with her dressing gown sleeve. 'The thing is, Maddy, he did something similar to me. Drugged me. And then . . . ' She couldn't bring herself to say the next few words. She closed her mouth, not trusting herself. She could feel tears beginning to well. She fought them back. She took a deep breath, another. Wiped the corners of her eyes, aimed for a smile. 'Well, you know the rest, I'm sure. The thing is, we can't let him get away with it. We've got to stop him.'

Maddy glanced at the door once more, but there was no one there. She looked back at Marina. 'I know. That's exactly what . . . ' Another look round. 'Exactly what I've been thinking.'

'Good,' said Marina. 'We're not the first that he's done this to.'

'I know,' said Maddy, excitedly. 'I heard about what he did to another girl before me. It was . . . horrible.' It was her turn to hold back the tears now.

'Look, my husband's a detective in the police.' Maddy's eyes widened at the statement. 'And I've got another friend, she's a police officer too. She's coming to meet me. They'll help. But I can't do it on my own.'

'What . . . what d'you want me to do?'

'I need you to give a statement to my friend. I know it'll be difficult, but she'll help. She'll make it the best it can be for you. We can stop him. But only if you help me. Will you do that?'

Maddy thought about it, glanced at the doorway again and nodded.

Marina smiled. 'That's brilliant, thank you, Maddy.'

Maddy smiled shyly. 'We were already going to do something,' she said.

'We? Who's we?'

'My boyfriend and I. We were going to—'

'She doesn't need to hear all that.'

The two women looked up. Marina saw a tall, dark-haired young man standing in the doorway. Handsome, well-dressed. He was smiling, but Marina didn't get a friendly vibe from him.

'Oh,' said Maddy, as if she had been interrupted doing something she shouldn't have been. 'This is Marina Esposito. She's a lecturer at the university.'

Marina stood, extended her hand. He took it. His smile flicked at the corners of his mouth like blades catching the light. 'And you are?'

'My name's Ben,' he said.

'Marina's going to help us,' said Maddy. 'With Hugo. Her

husband's a police officer. He's going to stop him.' She smiled. 'So we can all work together.'

Ben kept his smile pinned in place. 'Well thank you,' he said, 'but we don't need any help.'

Maddy looked upset. 'But Ben, he did the same to her. She can help . . .'

Ben looked straight at Marina, ignoring Maddy. His voice was soft, low, like the slithering of a snake through a jungle. 'I said we don't need any help. The matter is in hand.'

Marina looked at Maddy. Saw pain, disappointment and confusion vying for space behind her eyes. *Poor kid*, she thought. *Has she just got away from one manipulative man to go straight into the arms of another?*

'I see,' she said. She turned away from Ben, faced Maddy directly. Tried to stop her looking at him before answering her. 'Look, Maddy, it would help if you came with me. Please.' She glanced at Ben, aware of his presence; back to Maddy, her voice low once more. Co-conspirators. 'Please, Maddy. What I'm proposing is for your own good.'

'She's not interested,' said Ben, moving round, blocking Maddy from her.

'I'd like to hear Maddy say that herself,' said Marina.

Ben turned to Maddy. Stared at her. Maddy looked between the two of them, genuinely torn. Eventually she wilted. 'I'd better do what Ben says,' she said.

Marina shook her head. Handed her a card. 'Here. My number. If you ever change your mind. If you find you want to talk to me.'

She took it. Ben stared at her.

'I'll see myself out.'

Marina walked out of the house into the street and away. The sky was dark and oppressive. Even that felt lighter than the atmosphere between Ben and Maddy, she thought.

76

Phil stepped over the threshold, on to the boat. Focused. Processed. Assessed the situation.

A mess. A dead body in the middle of it. But more than that.

Before he went any further, he spoke to one of the two anoraked women standing on the jetty. Both of them looked drained. 'Which one of you found the body?'

They looked at each other. One wanted to speak more than the other. 'DC Pam Chapman,' she said. 'We both did.'

'Has he got a name?'

'Scott Sheriff,' she replied. 'He was on the list of local violent sex offenders. We were checking him out.'

'I'll bet he'll be the last call you make today.'

She smiled slightly.

Phil thanked her and went inside, crossing to Jo Howe, the FSI team leader. 'What have we got, then?'

'White male, short, stocky, bit paunchy. Looks like an attack.' She pointed to the body. 'Or a sex game that went wrong. Look.'

Phil looked. The man's jeans and underwear were down round his ankles. A leather belt was pulled tight round his neck. It looked like he had been attacked, half his face resembling raw mince. The eye that wasn't swollen shut was bulging, face turning purple. His fingers were at his neck.

'Leave the body for Esme,' said Phil. 'See what she makes of it. What about the rest of the place, what have you got?'

'Well,' said Jo, 'looks like he lived alone. And looks like he let his attacker in. No sign of a forced entry. The area of struggle was here' – she indicated the main living area – 'nothing on the kitchen, bathroom, anywhere else. Localised.'

'That should help,' said Phil. He thanked her, turned to the shelves. Scanned the book spines. Mostly non-fiction. True crime. Life stories of famous serial killers. A couple of encyclopedias, a dictionary. *Wanted to better himself*, he thought. Then looked at the serial killer books again. *Maybe not better himself. But he might have had an ambition for something.*

He scanned further, gently removing tattered magazines with his gloved fingers. Extreme bondage. Mainly gay. Looked well read. He went back up to the top of the shelf, picked off a serial killer book at random. It was about Ted Bundy. The spine was heavily creased. He allowed it to open naturally. He looked at the page. It was heavily annotated. Notes in the margins, passages underlined. The section dealt with Bundy stalking and selecting victims. The notes questioned his techniques, offering variations, suggesting improvements. One comment said quite simply: *More rope. Bigger KNIFE.* The last word underlined so heavily the pen had gone through the paper.

Phil put the book back, took down another one. The same thing. He got the picture. Felt a prickling on the back of his scalp.

He looked round the room again. Something caught his eye. A doll's house, lying on its side, furniture spilled out.

363

Curious, he knelt, examined it. It was old, well-used, made of cheap, heavy plastic. It had been cleaned up, the felt-tip pen marks scrubbed away, the dirt erased, but it would never look good again. The furniture was in a similar condition.

Then he saw the doll.

Lying beside the man's head, blonde, smiling. It looked familiar. Or the clothes looked familiar. He had seen someone wearing something similar recently . . . He placed it. It looked like Glenn McGowan. Or rather Amanda. In the DVDs, in the flesh.

The prickling disappeared. He felt a fizzing inside him. He was on to something. He pushed the doll's house back with a gloved finger, looked underneath. There were two other dolls there. Different to the first one. One was a male doll with its legs cut off. The other was similar to the first, female, blonde, but this one looked like it had been stabbed repeatedly. Frenziedly.

He replaced the house, stood up. Thought. Something jarred about those two dolls. Something very specific. He closed his eyes. It was fairly recent . . .

He opened them again, feeling like he had just had an electric shock. He took out his phone, called Sperring. Waited for the man to answer.

'Phil Brennan,' he said. 'Listen. That double murder in Edgbaston you're working. Tell me about it.'

'What d'you want to know?' Sperring couldn't have sounded more reluctant if he'd had his tongue removed.

'Victims. Details. What they looked like, what they had done to them, that kind of thing.'

A sigh. 'Keith Burkiss. Male. Mid forties. Lost both legs to diabetes, had stage four cancer—'

'What did you say?'

'Stage four cancer.'

'The bit before. Lost both legs to diabetes?'

'That's right.'

'How was he killed?'

'Smothered with a pillow, it looked like.'

'And the other one?'

'His wife. Well, estranged wife. Kelly Burkiss. She was a right mess.'

'Was she cut?'

'Yeah. Loads of times. Whoever did it didn't like her.'

'Thanks.'

'What's this about?'

'Tell you when I see you.' He hung up. Looked back at the dolls. Then round at the room again. 'Have the cupboards been gone through?' he asked Jo Howe.

'Not yet,' she said.

'Fine.' He crossed to a small chest of drawers placed up against one wall. Began pulling them out in order. The top two contained clothes, but the ones nearer the bottom didn't. Restraints. Dildos. Big black ones. Whips. Nothing wrong with that, thought Phil, not in and of itself. And not proof of anything. He pulled open the next drawer. Smiled. A knife.

'A big knife,' he said aloud. 'Bigger than Ted Bundy's.'

He knew better than to touch it. He tried another drawer. His smile got wider. A black wig and moustache. Identical to the ones in the video.

'Gotcha,' said Phil.

There was one more thing he had to check. He crossed to the body, knelt beside it. Pulled back its right sleeve.

'Careful,' said Jo Howe. 'Leave that for Esme.'

'Oh I'm being careful, don't you worry,' said Phil. He peeled back the sleeve a little more. And there it was. A double helix tattoo.

365

He let the sleeve drop back into place, stood up. Or as much as the cramped interior would allow him to.

'I think we've got our man,' he said. Then looked round the room again, taking everything in one more time. The books, the doll's house, the wig, the knife . . . Perfect.

Or at least that's what someone wants us to think . . .

77

Maddy walked up the pathway to Hugo Gwilym's front door, trying to remember all the things Ben had told her she should be. Strong. No bullshit. In charge. She kept trying, saying those words over and over in her head like a mantra, but other thoughts kept creeping in, getting in the way.

The way Ben had behaved in front of Marina. The way he had made her behave. She had felt useless when Marina left, pathetic and weak. She had also felt like she had done the wrong thing. Or been persuaded to do the wrong thing. And she disliked herself because of it.

But Ben had talked her round. 'Don't listen to her,' he had said. 'We don't need her. I've got it all sorted out. It'll be fine.' He had taken her face in his hands then, turned it up so she had no choice but to look at him. It was the first time she'd realised just how strong his grip was. He had smiled. 'You just do as I say, and everything will work out for the best. OK?'

And Maddy had nodded and agreed.

But now she felt anything but OK. Doubts were hammering at the certainty Ben had tried to instil in her. She thought she should listen to them. Even act on them, maybe. But as she approached Gwilym's front door and felt her hand go towards the bell, she realised she wasn't going to. It was easier to do what Ben wanted. Less trouble. Safer. For her.

She kept her hand on the bell. He could ignore it at first, but if she was insistent, he would have to come down and see who was there. He did so. Opened the door wearing his dressing gown and an angry expression. Which changed to shock and bewilderment when he saw who it was.

'Maddy? What are—'

She didn't give him time to finish, just swept past him, down the hall and into the living room.

'Maddy, you can't just . . . ' He followed her in.

She stood in the centre of the room, turned to him. 'I need to talk to you, Hugo. Urgently. Now.'

He looked round. His hair was unkempt, his stubble a little more than designer, coming in very grey. His eyes darkrimmed, sunken. *He looks old*, she thought. *What did I see in such an old man?*

'Maddy, it's . . . it's not convenient right now. Come back . . . Look, why don't we—'

'Not convenient?' she said, finding the strength to go with her words. 'You mean you've got someone here, is that it? Didn't take you long.'

He began to make a half-hearted protest but soon stopped.

'Now, Hugo. It has to be right now. Say no and you'll be sorry. Very sorry.'

He saw something in her eyes, her manner, and knew he would have to do what she said. 'Give me . . . give me a minute.'

He left the room, going back upstairs. Maddy went into the hall, unlocked the front door, left it on the latch, went back into the living room where she had been standing. She heard voices from upstairs, a woman's raised, his placating. Soon, a young woman came hurrying down the stairs, still fastening her clothes. She looked into the living room, saw Maddy. Wasn't happy.

'You're well out of it,' said Maddy.

The young woman grabbed her coat and left, slamming the door behind her.

Gwilym re-entered the room. 'This better be good.'

'Oh it is, Hugo.' She knew what she had to say next. Ben had rehearsed her. 'I'm going to go to the police, Hugo.'

'The police? Why?'

'Tell them you raped me.'

'Oh Maddy, that's just rubbish. There's no need to do that.'

'Yes there is, Hugo.'

'Look . . .' He crossed towards her, smile in place, arms outstretched. 'Let's talk about this. It ended badly, I know, but—'

'I've got proof,' she said, cutting him off.

His mood changed suddenly. 'Proof? What kind of proof?'

She smiled. She enjoyed seeing his reaction. Enjoyed having the upper hand with him for once. 'Proof that you were the father of our child.'

'You can't prove that. It's . . . it's gone.'

She remembered the lines she had rehearsed. 'It's not, Hugo. I couldn't go through with it.'

Gwilym's face had drained of colour. He looked like he had aged ten years in as many seconds. 'What d'you mean?'

'I kept it, Hugo.'

'You're . . . you're lying.'

'No I'm not.' She rubbed her stomach, advanced towards him. 'Here it is, Hugo, here's your child . . . Want to feel?'

He backed away from her, letting out a moan that sounded like the final breath of a wounded animal.

'A simple DNA test,' she said, still advancing. 'That's all

it'll take. I'll show them the marks on my wrist. I'll tell them that you raped me.'

Gwilym looked round frantically, like he was trapped.

'And I wasn't the first, was I, Hugo? You like to do this. Take a young woman, seduce her to get her pregnant, or worse . . . ' Maddy kept advancing. She could feel anger rising within her. Rage at what he had done to her, at how she had been so stupid as to let him. She wanted to lash out, hit him. Hurt him.

'What . . . what are you going to do?' he said. 'What d'you want from me?' His voice small and pathetic. Defeated. 'What d'you want me to do?'

'Hand over all your research about deviant personalities for that book you've been working on,' said a male voice.

78

Marina drove. She had her iPhone set for hands-free, and called Anni. It went to voicemail.

'Hi, Anni, listen, it's me. I know you're on your way but I just wanted to get the ball rolling. I didn't want to sit around waiting and do nothing, it would have driven me mad. So I decided to pay a call on Maddy Mingella, another of Hugo Gwilym's . . . I don't know, victims? I could be polite and say girlfriends or conquests, but, you know. Anyway. Long story short, she wanted to help but her boyfriend didn't. Said they had something already in place. I didn't like him, Anni. Got a very bad vibe from him. So I stuck around afterwards. Just in case.' She laughed. 'You taught me well. Always follow a hunch. So I'm following them. And he's driving a very unstudenty car, which makes me even more suspicious of him. No one I was at college with drove a Lexus four-by-four. I'm rambling again and I'm sure this is going to cut me off, so, to the point. Judging from the route they're taking, they're on their way to Gwilym's place. I'm going after them. We can't let them mess things up, or tip him off. So. I know you're on the way. I'll meet you at his. I'll text you the postcode when I'm there and you can stick it in your sat nav. See you soon . . .'

She hung up. Kept driving.

79

Gwilym turned. The voice had come from the doorway to the living room. Ben was standing there, leaning against the door frame. He smiled. Maddy thought she should have been glad to see him, but she didn't feel that way. She thought this would have gone better if he hadn't been there. Or even if Marina had been here.

'Hand over . . . what?'

Ben detached himself from the frame, walked into the room. 'Every copy. Every note. Every laptop, every memory stick. All of it. The whole lot. So you're not left with the slightest trace.'

'Why?'

'Because I want it,' said Ben.

Gwilym's expression changed. 'Who are you, anyway?'

Ben smiled. It wasn't pleasant. 'Who am I? Don't you recognise me?'

'Should I?'

'Evidently not. Let's just say I'm with her.'

Gwilym looked between the two of them. 'Well,' he said, getting angry now, 'you're not having it. Definitely not. No. You're not going to pass my work off as your own. Not after all the effort I've put into that. No way.'

'Work? Effort? *Your* effort?' Ben moved nearer to him. 'My effort, you mean.'

Gwilym frowned. Confused.

'Yes, my effort. If you'd recognised me, you'd remember. I was one of your unpaid researchers. Though it was more than that, wasn't it? We did all the work for you. Everything. Then you stepped in, gathered it all up, took the credit. We don't even get a mention. And you, I don't know, get another best-seller, win another award.' He looked over at the mantelpiece. A heavy black obelisk, inscribed with gold lettering, sat on one corner. 'Awards like this one.' He picked it up, read it. 'Popular Science Book of the Year. I didn't even know there was an award for that.'

'There's an award for everything now,' Gwilym said, weakly.

'Clearly. But d'you think that's fair? We do all the work, you get . . . ' he held the award up, 'this.'

'That's . . . that's not how it is.'

'Oh yes it is,' said Ben. 'And we can't have that. Can we?'

'So that's . . . that's what this is all about? You want . . . you want my book.'

Ben laughed. 'Oh no. It's about so much more than that. Now hand everything over, or we go to the police. Right now.'

Maddy looked at Ben, confused. Surely that was the idea all along? That was what they had agreed. And all this bit about the book, that was just a side issue, not important. This wasn't going the way they had planned it.

She looked at Ben, tried to catch his eye. He ignored her.

'Go get it,' he said to Gwilym.

Gwilym, seeing he had no choice, left the room.

Ben stood by the mantelpiece, admiring the award. Maddy crossed over to him. 'What's going on? This wasn't what we agreed.'

'Slight change of plan,' he said without looking up. 'This way's better.'

'But Ben, we—'

He turned to her. 'Shut up. Just shut up.' His eyes were blazing, mouth snarling. Maddy stepped back. She wished she had never listened to him. Never met him. Either of them.

Gwilym returned to the room, a briefcase under one arm. He put it down on a chair. 'Here it is,' he said. 'Everything. Notes, laptop, the lot.' He stared at it, eyes full of sadness, like he was saying goodbye to his only child.

'Good,' said Ben. Then he strode across the floor, lifted up the award he was holding and brought it down heavily on Gwilym's head.

Maddy stared, too shocked to scream. Gwilym hit the floor hard, blood haloing out around his head. Maddy looked at Ben. Open-mouthed, in shock.

'What . . . what did you do that for? That wasn't—'

'Here,' he said, 'catch.'

He threw the award at her. She caught it instinctively. Then, realising what she had done, let it drop to the floor. She looked back at him. And noticed for the first time that he was wearing latex gloves.

'What's going on, Ben? I want to go home.' She could feel herself starting to panic. 'This isn't what we planned . . .'

Ben advanced towards her. As he did so, he pulled out a knife from his jacket pocket. That smile again.

'On the contrary,' he said, 'this is exactly what I planned . . .'

374

80

'OK, listen up, everyone . . .'

Phil scanned the room. The whole team looked tired but wired. The news of Scott Sheriff's murder had done that to them. It was up to him now to ride that adrenalin wave.

'Apologies once again for bringing you all in on your day off. But with Christmas coming we could all do with the overtime.' There were no complaints. 'The first thing I have to say is that there have been big developments in the case we're working on. It's by no means definite, but we think we may have found the killer of not only Glenn McGowan but Keith and Kelly Burkiss too.'

He waited while that news travelled round the room.

'As I say, at the moment, without forensic and DNA tests, not to mention a post-mortem and further investigation, it looks like we have our man. Or it seems that way.' He held up his notes. 'His name's Scott Sheriff, aged thirty-one, originally from Rotherham, and he has the double honour of being not only on the sex offenders register but also on the list that Elli put together of known sexually violent individuals.' He looked at Elli. 'So well done.'

She smiled, bashful. Today's T-shirt, he noticed, involved a scrapyard in Totters Lane owned by I. M. Foreman. He had no idea what that meant.

'The one thing that we won't be able to do is bring Scott Sheriff in for questioning. He's dead. Murdered.' Phil waited while the news sank in.

'I doubt we'll be on overtime looking for that murderer,' said Sperring. His reply was a ripple of laughter.

Phil ignored him, continued. 'It looks like – and again we haven't had time to do a full investigation – a sex game gone badly wrong. Or it's been made to look like that. He's been beaten up and strangled.'

'Maybe that's what whoever did it wants us to think,' said Khan. 'Maybe it's some victim of his getting his own back.'

'Maybe,' said Phil. 'At this stage we keep an open mind. However, he owned a load of serial killer literature, not to mention extreme bondage stuff, and we're bringing it in to be gone through. We don't want to jump to conclusions, but trying to link him not only to Glenn McGowan but also to Keith and Kelly Burkiss will be a priority. Let's see what we've got.'

He turned to the board behind him. Sheriff's badly beaten face had now joined the other dead up there.

'We believe Glenn McGowan was acting out his ultimate fantasy. He wanted to be murdered. Scott Sheriff, from what we've found in his boat, wanted to be a killer. We also believe Sheriff is the man in the videos with Glenn McGowan. Someone must have put them together. Introduced them. We think that happened at a place in Digbeth. A disused factory turned into a private club for extreme deviants to meet. We're still not sure how people find the place or each other, but we know it's there.'

Elli put her hand up. 'Yes, Elli.'

'I've been doing some research,' she said. 'And there are

some parts of the internet that are completely unregulated. Way, way down behind walls of code. The kinds of places most people never go. They could have met there.'

'Are there, I don't know, chat rooms there?'

'Everything. The bottom of the internet is like the bottom of the sea. All sorts of weird and wonderful monsters live there.'

'Right,' said Phil. 'Keep on it.'

She nodded. It looked like there was something else she wanted to say but didn't. No doubt she would later.

'Sounds like that German cannibal bloke,' someone said. 'What he did.'

'Armin Meiwes, good analogy,' said Phil. 'Can everyone remember him?'

Plenty of nods, a few shrugs.

Phil continued. 'Worth mentioning because I think it has some bearing here. He was obsessed with killing and eating someone, so he advertised for a victim, on the internet of course, and found one. He cut this guy's penis off first and they both ate it. Then he sat by him while he bled to death in the bath. Meiwes read a *Star Trek* novel while this happened.'

Phil saw the looks on everyone's faces as he spoke. It wasn't pleasant. 'This case always disturbed me. I'm sure it disturbed everyone. I read up on it after we found the body of Glenn McGowan and there are loads of similarities. Apparently Meiwes looked outwardly respectable but actually had a severe psychiatric disorder and an appetite for self-destruction. That seems to be the same with McGowan. His murder looks to have been premeditated, with McGowan fully complicit. Remember the photos we saw. What he allowed to be done to his body. Lot of self-hatred there. A victim who went looking for his murderer. Looks like he found him.' Phil waited while they took it in. 'So we think that connects Sheriff with

McGowan. But we don't know what connects Sheriff with the Burkisses.'

'Think I can help there,' said Khan.

All eyes were on him.

'When you phoned up earlier and said there might be a connection, I went and had a look on Keith Burkiss's computer. Found some interesting emails. Looks like he was making payments to someone.'

'For what?'

'To kill him. That's what it looks like. Keeps talking about wishing he could see the look on the bitch's face when she realises she's not getting a penny. How that'll be his only regret.'

Phil frowned. 'The look on the bitch's face?'

Khan nodded. 'Got me thinking. Maybe Kelly wasn't meant to be there?'

'Maybe,' said Phil.

'So did Burkiss know Sheriff? And if so, how?' asked Sperring. 'Doesn't seem the type to go to this club. Unless they have disabled access.'

More laughter. Phil ignored it.

'I don't know,' he said. 'That's what we need to work on. Establish a link. For now, the club might be the best place to look. It seems to be run – or owned – by someone called Ben. That was also the name of the man in the video who we now believe to be Scott Sheriff. So maybe calling him Ben was a joke. We don't know. Yet.'

'What do we do next?' asked Imani.

'We look into Scott Sheriff. Uniforms are out canvassing the area, asking if anyone saw him coming home last night. If anyone was with him. If they saw anything suspicious. Long way to go yet. In the meantime, I want everyone to keep working on this case. Find a solid link between Scott Sheriff and the victims, preferably one that ties in with the club. Go through his book collection, see if he's done anything like this before.'

'Should we read them in italics?' asked Elli.

Phil frowned. 'What d'you mean?'

Elli blushed. 'Well, it's just that all the books with serial killers in, they all have their inner monologue in italics.'

Phil smiled. 'Just the bad ones.'

She smiled too. Pleased that her joke hadn't completely fallen flat.

'And they always make them out to be superhuman,' said Imani.

'When in reality,' said Phil, 'they're just pathetic little nobodies. Right. In the meantime, I think it might be time to pay this club a visit. Let's get prepared for that.'

He looked round at the team once more.

'Again, thank you. You're doing a fantastic job.'

The meeting broke up. DCI Cotter approached Phil. 'Can I have a word, please?'

She walked into her office. Phil, not liking the tone of her voice, followed.

81

Maddy was too terrified to speak. Almost too terrified to breathe. Ben was still moving towards her, the light catching the blade of his knife, glinting in his eyes.

'The plan?' he said. 'This is the plan. This was always the plan.'

'No,' she said, finding her voice, shaking her head, 'no ... We ... we agreed to, to go to the police ...'

He shook his head, laughed. 'No, not at all. You might have got that impression. I can see how you would. Because that's what I told you. And you're so easy, so, so easy to manipulate. Piece of piss. God, if Gwilym could do it, I'd have no trouble ...'

'What?' Maddy wasn't sure what she was hearing now. Above the roaring in her ears, the thoughts and emotions tumbling through her, she was sure she could make out the sound of own heart breaking. 'What d'you mean?'

'Stupider than I thought. The plan to get Gwilym and you out of the way. You attack Gwilym, get him hospitalised at the very least. Or I make it look like you attack him. That award statue was just poetic justice, don't you think?'

Maddy said nothing.

Ben continued. 'And then, once you've killed him or whatever, you feel so remorseful over his death – this poor little innocent girl that the big bad man has chewed up and spat out, oh woe is you – that you kill yourself. Here. In his house. Over his body. Again, poetry. I planned that bit too.'

'But . . . why?'

'Because they'd believe it. You've already tried it once. Got the marks to prove it. They'll think you just dug in with a bit more conviction this time. Did it properly.'

Maddy shook her head. The torrent was raging inside her, making it hard to think. 'No, no . . . I mean, why? Why do this? Any of this?'

'I need that research. Too inconvenient. Too incriminating. And you've seen me, of course. You have to go.'

'But what about the girl?'

Ben frowned. 'Girl?'

'The other girl. The one before me. The one that Gwilym turned into a smackhead.'

He thought for a few seconds. 'Oh, her. Made her up. Never existed. Well, I'm sure she did. Or someone like her. Probably loads like her. He was very prolific, old Hugo. Because you're not the first. You got that bit right.'

'But Ben . . . ' She couldn't think of anything else to say.

'Just made her up. To tug at your poor little heart strings. Get you all sad. Get you to do what I wanted you to do.'

The torrent was slowing, her thoughts, emotions forming into something she could recognise. 'You . . . you used me . . . '

'Yes. I used you.' He pointed to Gwilym's body. '*He* used you. You see a pattern emerging here? Course you do. You're easy to use. Easy to manipulate. So why not?'

He reached her. The tip of his knife almost touching her skin. She could sense he was readying himself to grab her. She looked round, tried to work out what her best options for escape were. Couldn't see any.

He had her.

And then the doorbell rang.

82

'Sorry?' said Phil. 'What are you saying here exactly?'

He sat on a chair in front of Cotter, who was behind her desk. The DCI leaned forward, hands clasped. Like she was posing for a formal photograph. He wasn't angry, just disbelieving. Cotter spoke in calm, measured tones.

'Just what I said. Go carefully. Cross the t's, dot the i's. Don't rush.'

'But this club is the basis for everything we've been investigating. We don't know what it is, what it's like, who goes there. We have to find out.'

'Exactly,' she said, leaning back. 'We know nothing about it. I'm sure we've all got a different mental image of what goes on in there, and we need to make that a realistic one before we go wading in.'

'But surely if we go in, we'll find out.'

'Let's build an airtight case against Scott Sheriff first. That's our number one priority. I admit, the evidence is pointing towards that – strongly pointing – but we need to be certain. And we can't do anything else until we are. We need physical proof, DNA matches. We need more than circumstantial evidence and supposition. And when we've got all that, we put this to bed.' She stopped talking, looked at him, brows furrowed. 'You touched on something out there. About how convenient it all is. How everything's been nicely laid out to point us in the one direction. Towards Scott Sheriff. Very neat.'

'Which makes me think two things,' said Phil. 'Either he's responsible for the killings because he's a fucked-up wannabe serial killer and his death in a sex game gone wrong was just a coincidence.'

'Or?'

'That he's responsible for the killings because he's yada-yada, and he was deliberately murdered because we were on the verge of discovering his identity.'

'And which one do you believe?'

Phil folded his arms. 'Put it this way. I don't believe in coincidences. Not in cases like this one.'

Cotter sighed. 'I tend to agree with you.'

'Then let's go to the club. Look, if we delay, it gives them time – whoever *they* are – to clear out. Get wind of what's going on and disappear.'

Cotter sat back, scrutinising him. He didn't move, just waited for her to speak. When she did, she weighed her words carefully. 'Another way of looking at that would be good riddance.'

'What?'

'Well, we've got our murderer. End of. If they up sticks and leave, move to someone else's patch, then it's their problem, not ours. We keep our stats up. Hooray for us. And really,' she said, lowering her voice, 'does it matter?'

Phil frowned. 'What d'you mean?'

Cotter waved her arms expansively. 'Well, Glenn McGowan wanted to die. He got his wish. So did Keith Burkiss.'

'Kelly Burkiss didn't.'

'No, true. But . . . ' Another shrug.

'So what are you saying? That we let serial killers loose so long as they only kill people who want to die? Is that it? And anyone who gets in their way is just, what, collateral damage?'

'It's just a discussion, Phil. That's all. Hypothetical. It's not black and white, is it? What about people who campaign for the right to die? Who've got some terminal illness. They either have to get a doctor to look the other way or take themselves off to Switzerland for it. It's the same thing.'

'Not exactly,' said Phil. 'They've got terminal illnesses, like you said.'

'So did Keith Burkiss.'

'Yeah, but Glenn McGowan didn't.' Phil thought for a moment. 'Well, maybe a mental illness. But as I see it, those suffering from terminal illness just want to get some control back over their lives. The illness has taken it away. And these things have to be regulated. If not, what have you got? Harold Shipman.'

'I completely agree with you,' said Cotter.

'But it's not just about that,' said Phil. 'Not just about killing people. What about Martin Trotter? Infecting people with AIDS?'

'Well again,' said Cotter, 'he said they wanted to be infected. It was consensual.'

'I know,' said Phil, 'I mean, God knows why, but who's going to pay for their care when they're too ill to look after themselves? We are.'

'But then who already pays for alcoholics and the obese?' asked Cotter. 'We do. They do that to themselves. We can't stop this from happening just by closing down one club.'

'Yeah, yeah, I know,' said Phil. He rubbed his face. 'Everything's fucked. The system's fucked. But let's do our bit to try and stop one little part of it.'

'We will,' said Cotter. 'But let's do it properly.'

The conversation over, Phil got up and left.

He had a sudden, overwhelming need to talk to Marina.

83

Ben stopped moving, knife still in hand. Stood suspended animation-still. Like all his senses were heightened.

The doorbell rang again.

Maddy looked between the door and Ben. This was her chance. Her only chance. *Run*.

Ben came out of his trance, saw what she was doing. He grabbed her, fingers digging into her arms like metal claws, stopping her moving. The knife at her throat, his mouth at her ear.

'Don't.' Snake-hissed.

She didn't move.

'Don't move, don't scream. Don't do anything.'

She felt the blade on her skin. Like a razor of ice.

The doorbell rang again.

Maddy found her voice. 'You're ... you're going to do it anyway, aren't you? Cut me. What, what difference does it make when you do it?'

His hand moved from her arm, clamped down hard on her mouth.

'Look.' A voice through the door. Muffled but familiar. 'I know you're in there, don't pretend. I saw you both go in.'

Maddy felt Ben stiffen as the voice spoke, his breathing

increase. He shifted from side to side. Deciding what to do next. He tightened his grip on her and, the knife still at her throat, pushed her forward. Out of the living room, down the hallway towards the door. He took his hand from her mouth.

'Run!' Maddy shouted. 'Get the police! Run! Help me!'

Ben threw her to the floor. She didn't have time to put her arms out, stop herself. She hit the stripped boards with a thud, the wind knocked from her lungs. She saw Ben throw open the front door and pull the person in, slamming the door shut behind him.

Maddy looked up. Ben held Marina Esposito at knife-point.

'Inside, now,' he said. He pushed her along the hallway towards the living room, then bent to pull Maddy up from the floor. The knife was soon back at Maddy's throat. Marina stood where she was, staring, eyes wide. 'Now!' shouted Ben. He pushed the knife hard against Maddy's skin. 'Or I cut her.'

Marina walked slowly towards the living room. Then stopped.

'Oh my God . . .'

She had seen Hugo Gwilym lying on the floor.

Ben kept going, pushing Maddy, making Marina move backwards until they were all in the room. Marina was the first to speak.

'So what did you intend to do?' she said.

Maddy looked at her. She looked so calm, in control. But then she knew about Marina's history. Everyone in the department did. She had faced down psychopaths before.

Ben didn't reply.

'Kill me,' said Maddy. 'He was going to kill me. Make it look like I did that to Gwilym, then make it look like I killed myself.'

'A murder suicide,' said Marina. 'How original. And did you really think you'd get away with it?' She moved in towards him. 'Did you?'

'Shut up! Shut up!' Maddy could feel Ben's ragged breathing against her neck, feel him tightening his grip on her. He was getting frantic. Out of control. Not a good sign.

'It's not particularly original, is it?' Marina kept talking. 'Look.' Her voice was low, soothing. 'Give me the knife, Ben. We can sort this whole thing out without anyone else getting hurt. Come on. Give me the knife.'

Marina stuck out her hand. Maddy looked at it. *She isn't as calm as she's making out,* she thought. Marina's hand was shaking.

'Come on, Ben. You've got to abandon that plan. You can't do that now.' She edged even further forward. 'Come on. Give me the knife.'

Ben made a sound like a wounded animal. A scream of impotent rage. 'Shut up! Shut up, you stupid fucking mouthy bitch, shut up! I'm thinking . . . '

'Good,' said Marina. 'That's good, Ben. Come to the right conclusion. You can't do what you were going to do. It won't work. And you won't get away with it. Now come on . . . '

Maddy was aware of his head jerking up suddenly. She heard him bark a laugh in her ear.

'No,' he said, 'you're right. You're right.' She was aware of him nodding his head. 'I can't do what I planned to do. No. You're right.'

'That's good,' said Marina. 'That's very sensible. Now, just give me the knife . . . '

'I've got a better idea,' said Ben. 'See what you think of this. Maddy comes in, hits Gwilym, leaves him lying there. Why? Because she's found him with his lover, that's why. His older, married lover . . . ' He gave another bark of laughter. 'So she smacks him one, and before she kills herself, know what she does?'

He took the knife away from Maddy's throat, pointed it at Marina.

'She kills you. Perfect.'

Then Marina's phone rang.

84

Phil was standing outside the station, sheltering from the rain under a tiled porchway, not keeping noticeably drier. He had turned the collar of his jacket up, pulled it in. He didn't know why people did that. It didn't keep the rain off or make you any warmer. Maybe it was just one of those things you did so you felt you were doing something positive. Being in control of things.

That thought sent him back to his conversation with Cotter.

He took his phone out, looked at it. No calls from Marina. He sighed, pressed her number.

It rang.

He waited.

He looked round. Down at the Bullring and New Street, the streets would be full of Christmas shoppers. Here, the only people who came along were those that had a reason. Going to the children's hospital on the other side of the road, or the police station. Neither sounded like fun.

The phone was still ringing.

And ringing.

He heard Marina's voice. 'Hi, this is Marina Esposito. I'm sorry I can't take your call right now . . .'

Should he leave a message? He took the phone away from his ear, ready to terminate the call. But something stopped him. He replaced it.

'Hey, it's me. I'm ... ' He sighed. 'I want to talk to you. Just, just give me a call. Bye.' He was about to hang up but realised he had forgotten something important. 'Love you.'

He ended the call. Pocketed the phone. Made his way back inside.

At least it was warm and dry in there. If nothing else.

85

'Leave it,' said Ben.

Marina's hand had gone to her jeans pocket. She slowly removed the phone.

'I said leave it . . . '

She looked at Ben, tried to keep her breathing steady, her hand still. She didn't want him to see her shaking. Maddy seemed terrified, quite rightly, and Ben looked like he could lose it at any second and go berserk. It was down to Marina to keep calm and, despite what she was feeling inside, take charge.

She slipped the phone out, looked at the display. Phil. That gave her an idea.

'It's my husband,' she said. 'Look.' She held the phone out so he could see the display. 'Phil. My husband. Detective Inspector Phil Brennan, to give him his full title.'

'So?' Ben was trying to look uninterested but Marina had noticed a stab of fear behind his eyes. 'Why should I care what your husband does for a living?'

'Because he's been investigating Hugo Gwilym.'

Ben snorted. 'Bullshit.'

The phone kept ringing. Marina raised her eyebrows. 'Really? You don't believe me?' She held out the phone once more. 'Ask him. Go on, ask him.'

Ben looked at the phone, back to her. She knew he was thinking about it, weighing the odds. She decided to keep talking.

Calm, be calm . . .

'He knew I was coming here,' she said. 'To see Gwilym. I told him. Phil's already been to see him once this weekend. Again, if you don't believe me, ask him.'

Ben stared, breathing heavily. The phone kept ringing.

'He knew what I was coming to see Gwilym about. Knew what he'd done. That's why he's calling. He knows what Gwilym's like, what he's capable of. That's why he's investigating him. That's why I came round to talk to Maddy earlier.' She switched her look from Ben to Maddy. 'I said my husband was a police officer, didn't I? I said he would help.'

Maddy nodded her head. Her throat moved against the knife. A trickle of blood ran down her neck. She gasped.

Marina tried to focus, concentrate. *Don't let this go any further.*

'So if I don't answer, he'll know something's gone wrong.'

The phone stopped ringing. No one spoke. No one moved.

'Bullshit,' repeated Ben eventually.

'Really? You think so?'

'Absolute bullshit.'

Marina kept the phone in her outstretched hand. 'You want to take that chance?'

Ben didn't move.

'Why don't you call him back? See what he says?'

Ben moved his hand indecisively towards and away from Marina's outstretched one. Wanting to take it, not wanting to take it, gasping, his face contorted, as if in pain. There was anger there, Marina noted, but also something else. Indecision. And fear.

'Come on,' he said. 'Come on . . .'

Marina didn't speak. She didn't think the words had been directed at either her or Maddy.

'Come on, Ben ... Think, think ... What would you do, eh? What would you do ...'

Marina didn't move.

'Come on, help me here ... help me ...'

Marina barely breathed. Neither, she noticed, did Maddy.

Then Ben nodded, smiled, as if someone had given him wise advice. Or even told him a joke. 'Yeah,' he said. 'Yeah. Good idea.'

He looked straight at Marina, his grip tightening on Maddy's throat.

'I know what I'm doing,' he said.

'Come on, Ben,' said Marina. 'Don't do anything stupid now. Anything you might regret.'

'I'm not going to regret this. I know exactly where I'm going to take you, what I'm going to do with you. I know exactly what's going to happen.' He smiled. 'Oh yes ...'

Marina said nothing. She knew words could no longer reach him.

86

'Boss? Can I have a word?'

Phil had just walked back inside when Elli approached him. She looked excited, empowered. Without waiting for him, she went over to her desk, sat down, clicked her mouse.

'Here,' she said. 'I got curious about the DVDs.'

'Glenn McGowan having sex in his living room,' said Phil.

'Aha,' she said, holding up one finger. 'That's what I thought. That's what we all thought. That's what made me curious. Remember the discrepancies? The timing? When did he do this if he'd only just moved in?'

'Yeah, I do.'

'Well ... ' She began pointing and clicking at the screen. 'There's a program I've been toying with. A bit of measuring software, gives dimensions to rooms. Handy for computer re-creations and virtual simulations of crime scenes. You can build up 3D models with it. If you know what you're doing.'

More pointing, more clicking. The screen changed. A three-dimensional image of a room appeared.

'Here we are. This is Glenn McGowan's living room. I got a uniform to go and measure it for me. Now ... ' Another point and click and the screen image changed. It showed another room. 'This is the size of the room on the DVD.' She pointed with her finger. 'You can see that this wall is longer, this one shorter. The door comes in at a different point. And in photos of McGowan's house, you can see into the hallway from this door. On the DVD you can't. It's blacked out.'

She looked up at him, eyes shining with her discovery.

'So what does this tell us?'

She looked slightly deflated that he hadn't worked it out. 'That the DVDs were filmed in somewhere decorated identically to McGowan's living room. In fact, I think it's the other way round. McGowan's living room was decorated to resemble this place.'

'So the DVD was filmed a while before he turned up at the house?'

'Yep. All our timeline questions answered. The DVD was filmed first. The house was decorated to look like this place.'

'So where is this place?'

Elli smiled. 'I can't come up with all the answers. This club, maybe?'

'Maybe,' said Phil. 'Thank you, Elli. Fantastic work.'

She beamed. 'Thanks, boss.'

He didn't have time to say anything more as Nadish Khan was waving him over. He looked pale and jittery, Phil thought; not surprising after the night he'd just had.

'What you got for me?' said Phil.

'This,' said Khan, pointing to his screen.

'What's that, then?' asked Phil.

'Well, I went back to looking through Keith Burkiss's stuff.'

Phil noticed Khan glance across at Sperring, who seemed to not be listening. Studiously so.

'I just thought, you know. Because before, I found that connection with Keith Burkiss and the guy he paid to kill him. And that might be the guy we found.'

'Scott Sheriff, yes.'

'Yeah. Well, I went back into those emails. And I found something else. Some from Hugo Gwilym.'

Phil leaned forward, interested now. 'Go on.'

'Well, as far as I can tell, it looks like Burkiss was helping Gwilym with research as well. Like Glenn McGowan was.'

'That's quite a coincidence.'

'Yeah. What I thought. This deviant book he was doing.'

'Deviant psychopathologies.'

'Yeah. That one. Keith Burkiss was helping with the research.'

Phil frowned. 'What was deviant about Keith Burkiss?'

'That's what I wondered,' said Khan, a look of triumph on his face. 'So I read through all the emails. And there's one from Gwilym saying that he's deviant through rage.'

'Rage.'

'Yeah, rage. There's loads of emails like that, about how he wants to plan his own death, how he wants his ex-wife to get nothing, all of that. How the whole thing's been done just to piss her off.'

'He'd have himself killed just to piss her off?'

Khan pointed to the screen. 'What it says here.' He sat back. 'Then other ones start appearing. Asking if he's serious about what he's saying. If he wants to go ahead with it. And Burkiss says yes. The emails end by saying "one of our representatives will be in touch". What d'you think?'

'Very interesting. But that would mean that Gwilym was the link, not this club.'

Something shone in Khan's eyes that Phil couldn't read. 'So it's this Gwilym guy, yeah? Not the club or anything, anyone else?' He swallowed hard. 'Not Ron Parsons?'

'Well, we're keeping an open mind. But . . . ' Phil stood up. 'Good work.'

Khan looked relieved. 'Cheers, boss.'

Phil walked over to Imani's desk. Tried to ignore the fact that Sperring had been eavesdropping and even now was scrutinising Khan.

'I've found out who owns the building,' said Imani. 'The one the club's in.'

Phil looked at her. The DC's face was a mess. Her eyes were swelling, bruising underneath. Her nose was heavily plastered. 'You should be at home,' he said.

'Haven't got time for that,' she said. 'Look.'

Phil looked.

'They've tried to cover it up, but if you know where to look, it's easy.'

'And how do you know where to look?'

'A hunch. After Parsons tried to hide the ownership of McGowan's house, I thought he should be the first one to look at. Or rather the same company, Shield Holdings.'

'And they're the owners?'

'Yep. Hidden, but not unfindable. If you know what you're looking for.'

'So Parsons is involved.'

'There's a few names listed as directors, not just him. Cheryl Parsons, that'll be the current Mrs Parsons, I think, and Grant Parsons.' She looked up. 'That's his son, right?'

'Grant, yeah. Son of Parsons. Wasn't that his name?'

They kept talking. At the next desk along, Nadish Khan quietly picked up his mobile, sent a text. Waited. The reply was swift. He sighed, looked round again to see he wasn't being observed, sent another. Waited. Again the reply wasn't long in coming. With a heavy, resigned look on his face, Khan stood up and made his way to the door.

Phil, talking to Imani, hadn't noticed him leaving.

But Sperring had. He got up from his seat. And, at a distance, followed him.

87

Hugo Gwilym's house was in darkness when Anni Hepburn drove up and parked outside it. The winter night had cut in cold and black, the roads crammed with pre-Christmas shoppers seemingly stocking up for the apocalypse. It had taken her far longer to drive than she had thought it would and she was just relieved to reach her destination. But something, she felt, wasn't right.

She got out of the car, locked it, looked round. A Prius was parked one house down. Marina drove a Prius, Anni knew. Identical to the one parked there. She walked over, looked inside. Baby seat. That was Marina's.

She walked back over to Gwilym's house, went up the path, rang the doorbell. Waited.

Nothing.

Rang it again.

The house was in darkness, the curtains still open. She had a feeling no one was home. She walked to the front window and, making a visor from her cupped hands, peered in.

'Shit . . . '

There was a body on the living room floor. Male, middle-aged. Wearing a dressing gown and little else. A blood halo around his head.

She ran back to her car, opened the boot. She kept a crow-bar there for just such emergencies. She ran back to the front door, smashed in a pane of glass, put her hand in, turned the lock. She was in.

Straight into the living room, straight to the body. Her phone was in her hand ready to call an ambulance. She knelt down beside the prone man. Reached out and gingerly moved his head.

He groaned.

'It's OK,' she said, 'I'm a police officer.'

He groaned again.

'Don't try to talk or move. You've got a head injury. I'm going to call an ambulance.'

'No . . . '

His hand came up, grabbed her arm. There was a surprising amount of strength in the grip.

'No . . . ambulance . . . ' He shook his head to emphasise the point. The movement caused him pain, making him lie back down once more.

'Try not to move,' said Anni. 'Your skull might be fractured. You need medical help.' She looked at him again. She had a fair idea who he was now.

'No.' He gasped as he spoke. 'No ambulance. No hospital.' More gasping. 'No police.'

'Too late for that, mate,' she said.

He groaned once more.

'Who did this, d'you know?'

He started to shake his head again, but remembering how much it hurt, stopped. 'Can't . . . can't say . . . '

'Can't? Or won't?'

He didn't reply.

'You're Hugo Gwilym, aren't you?'

He smiled at that. 'D'you . . . d'you want an autograph?'

He's everything Marina said he was, she thought. 'No, you're all right,' she said. 'Just trying to make an identification. Can you please tell me who did this? Let's start from there.'

'No. Can't.'

'I'm police.'

'No ... don't want police ... '

'Not your decision to make.' Anni looked round the room, listened. They were definitely the only people there. 'Where's Marina? Marina Esposito?'

'I don't ... don't know ... '

'Was she here?'

'Marina? Don't know ... Has she been here? Was she supposed to be here?'

'Yes, she was. Did she do this to you?' *I wouldn't blame her if she had done.*

'No ... '

'What happened, then?'

Gwilym rolled over on his side, away from Anni. His hands came up and covered his head. 'Please, just leave me alone ... '

Anni stood up, looked round. Tried to think what to do next. She took her phone out, called Marina. Nothing. Voicemail. She left a message saying where she was and who she was with and to call her as soon as possible. As she ended the call, she had a feeling that something bad had happened. Something had gone very wrong.

Gwilym groaned. 'Will you go now, please? Just ... leave me alone ... '

Anni didn't even bother to reply. She had to do something, take some kind of action. She thought. Then, mind made up, she took out her phone again.

She would call Phil.

88

The weather hadn't kept people away. The German market was in full swing now that daylight had gone and darkness had fallen. The place had looked like a shanty town of wooden huts in the grey day. Now, all lit up, it made the area look festive and Christmassy. The mulled wine and beer stalls came into their own, as did the sausage stalls. People looked happy as they moved round the place.

All except Nadish Khan. He sat on the same bench he had occupied earlier. Stared down at his feet. He was cold and wet, tired and miserable. He felt like his life couldn't get any worse.

Ron Parsons sat down next to him. And Khan felt like his life just got worse.

'I want you to know,' Khan said, not looking up, addressing his shoes and his clenched fingers, 'that I'm doing this for my mum.'

'Whatever works for you, son.' Parsons lit a cigarette. Khan flinched from the smoke.

'It's not for me. I'm not my dad. Not like him at all. I'm better than that.'

'Course you are, son. Now what's happening?'

Khan told him. The killing of Scott Sheriff, the discovery

of the body. Blaming him for the murder of Glenn McGowan and Keith and Kelly Burkiss. Then Trotter's statement about the club. And the subsequent discovery of ownership. Finished, he sat back. He felt exhausted. Like he was a Catholic who had just undergone a long and arduous confession.

'Right,' said Parsons. 'You'd better deal with it, then.'

Khan stared at him. 'What? What d'you mean, I'd better deal with it?'

'What I say.'

'But ... ' Khan looked away. Saw the shadow of the bearded, plaid-shirted henchman lurking behind him. Looked back at Parsons. 'I told you. I found a connection between Burkiss and this university bloke. I've told them to work on that angle, forget the club.'

'You'd best make sure they do, then.'

'But ... ' Khan couldn't believe he was hearing this. In his mind, this wasn't how it should go. He would tell Parsons what he wanted to know, take the money, and that would be that. Not this. Not at all. 'What can I do? I've told you what's happening. I've warned you. That was what we agreed. That was my part of the deal. I'm finished.'

He stood up. The bearded henchman moved closer. Towered over him.

'Sit down,' said Parsons.

Khan remained standing.

'D'you want me to make you?' Parsons looked up at him. And for the first time Khan saw in the other man's eyes what must have made him such a feared gangster in his time. That mixture of anger, madness and the anticipation and uncaring consequence of violent action. It was still there.

Khan sat down.

'That's better.' Parsons put his cigarette beneath the sole of

402

his shoe. Ground it out. He turned to Khan. 'Now. The investigation is still ongoing. I don't want it to look at that club. Understand? And it's your job to make sure it doesn't.'

'That wasn't what we agreed.'

'It was what I agreed. You do your part, you get paid.'

'I want my money. My mother's money. I've done my part. That was the deal.'

Parsons shrugged. 'Only deal you're going to get is the one I just offered you.'

Khan stared ahead once more. His heart was hammering in his chest. Everything around him was brightly lit and coloured. People going about their lives. *Enjoying* their lives. But not him. He was presiding over what felt like the end of his. Or at least his career. His dreams. Everything he had believed in or wanted for himself. He looked at his hands. They were shaking.

He stood up.

'Sit down,' said Parsons.

'Fuck you,' said Khan.

'Sit down.' Louder this time, with much more menace.

'No,' said Khan. 'That's it. I'm not throwing away my career over a piece of shit like you. A piece of old shit. That's the end. We're finished.'

'We are not finished . . .' Parsons was nearly shouting. He stared at Khan, the full beam of his mad, angry eyes on him. 'We are finished when *I* say so.'

'I think you'll find,' said a voice from behind them, 'that you're finished when *I* say so.'

They turned. There stood Ian Sperring.

403

89

Marina could see nothing. Feel nothing. The blindfold was tight, the restraints on her wrists even tighter.

She had no idea where she was. She had been bundled into Ben's waiting car. He had held the knife at Maddy's throat the whole time. Threatened to cut her if Marina didn't co-operate. Marina had to swallow all her instincts and do as she was told. For Maddy's sake. She knew what Ben was capable of. Gwilym's body on the floor was proof.

Maddy tied Marina up at knifepoint. Then Ben did the same to Maddy. Ben's car was a 4x4. He put Maddy and Marina in the back, told them to lie down and covered them with something. Then he drove off. Marina tried to do that thing she had seen in films, where the captive remembers the route he's been taken by all the noises on the way. That and a combination of measuring. Eight seconds, car turns right. Thirteen seconds, car stops. Probably at a junction. Listen: noise of a pedestrian crossing. Seventeen seconds, car goes forward. Then round a corner, probably left. She soon became confused, not being able to tell one distance from the next, one pedestrian crossing from another. And then Ben started playing music, which disorientated her even further.

Eventually the car came to rest and Marina felt the blanket

being pulled back. Hands grabbed her, hauled her from the car. Made her walk. She barely had any balance and was terrified. She couldn't see, couldn't hear and had no idea where she was being led. Eventually she came to a standstill and the hands disappeared.

'Wait here,' a voice said. Then laughed. 'Like you've got a choice.'

She heard a door close.

Then nothing.

'Maddy?' Marina's voice was small, tentative. Just in case she was on her own. Or worse, left with Ben. 'Maddy? You there?'

'Yes . . . ' Maddy's reply was equally tentative. 'I'm here . . . '

Marina felt relief at that. At least he'd kept them together. That was something.

'Can you . . . can you see anything?' she asked.

'No. I'm still blindfolded. What about you?'

'Nothing.' Marina sighed. 'Have you any idea where we are? Where he might have brought us?'

'No, none. No idea. He's . . . he's not who I thought he was . . . Oh God, oh God . . . '

Marina heard sobbing. She didn't blame the girl, but she knew enough to know that crying wasn't going to be helpful in getting them out of there. 'Listen, Maddy, I know you're upset. I know this is . . . ' She sighed again. 'I know. But you've got . . . Listen to me . . . you've got to be stronger than that. We have to find a way out of here. We have to.'

'I kn-know, but . . . but . . . it's just . . . they never tell you, never prepare you, no one does . . . '

'What d'you mean?'

She spoke through her sobs. 'When I started university, they g-gave us all a lecture about b-being raped. And they said stuff, you know: if someone grabs you, s-stamp on their

405

instep, it b-breaks the little bones in their foot, and then run ... or, or head-butt them, bridge of the nose if you can ... ' She sighed. 'N-never anything about this ... '

'No, Maddy, no one can give you a lecture warning you about something like this. But come on. We have to get out of here. We *will* get out of here.' Marina hoped she sounded more confident than she felt. 'Now listen to my voice, can you hear me?'

'Y-yes ... '

'Good. Keep listening. And come towards me. Can you? Come on. Walk towards my voice.'

She heard movement. Slow and tentative, matching Maddy's voice when she had first spoken.

'Good girl, good. Keep on coming ... good ... '

She felt Maddy walk into her.

'Oops. Good. You're here. Well done. You made it. Now. We have to try and find a way out of these things. Can you do that?'

Maddy started to cry again.

'Maddy, please. Keep it together. Come on. We can do this. Now ... I know your hands are behind your back, but feel your way round me until you've got your back to me. Can you do that?'

'I'll ... Yes. I will.'

Marina felt fingers on her waist. Small movements, like mouse footprints, as Maddy made her way round her, until she eventually reached the position Marina wanted.

'OK. Good,' said Marina. 'Now. We don't know how long we've got. So what I want you to do is try and find my wrists. The restraints, they're leather and they've got buckles like a belt. I want you to feel where that buckle is on my wrists and undo it. Can you do that?'

'I'll ... I'll try ... '

'Good girl. Course you can.' Marina felt hands on her wrists. Scrabbling fingers working at the restraints. 'That's it, you can do it ...'

She heard Maddy grunting with the effort.

'You're doing great. Keep going ...'

She didn't know how long she stood there. It could have been seconds, minutes or hours. All she was aware of was Maddy's fingers working on her wrists. Her fingers trying to get a purchase on the leather, pull it out, pull it through ...

Then nothing.

'Maddy?'

She heard sobbing again.

'It's no good, I ... I can't do it ...'

'Yes you can, Maddy. You can. You can do it. Now come on, try again ...'

She felt fingers on her wrists, then they were violently pulled away. 'I can't, it's no good, I can't ...'

Marina swallowed down her first response, which wasn't very complimentary. Instead she kept herself calm, her voice steady. *Shouting's not going to help*, she thought. *Giving in to this isn't going to help*.

'Come on, Maddy, try again. Or let me try on you ...'

Maddy pushed her wrists up against Marina's. Marina tried to undo the clasp.

She sighed. It wasn't easy.

But she had to keep trying. Because there was no alternative.

90

Parsons's bodyguard moved forward when he heard Sperring speak.

'Don't, sunshine,' said Sperring, holding up his warrant card. The bodyguard looked at Parsons and then at Sperring again. Backed down. 'Clever boy.' Sperring stepped in front of Parsons. 'Now,' he said, 'what have we got going on here?'

Khan couldn't even bring his eyes up to meet his colleague's.

'Mr Sperring,' said Parsons, as if greeting an old friend. 'Been too long.'

'Not long enough,' said Sperring. He looked between Parsons and Khan. Eyes settling on Khan. He sighed, shook his head. 'I thought better of you, Nadish. I really did.' His voice held real sadness, genuine hurt.

Khan looked away.

'So you going to tell me what's going on, then?'

'It's him,' said Khan, jabbing his finger at Parsons, still not looking up. 'He wanted . . . wanted to know about the investigation. What was happening, where we were looking.'

Sperring stared at Parsons. 'Did he now. And what did you tell him?'

Khan sniffed. Sperring realised he was crying. 'The . . .' He sighed. 'Everything.' His voice had shrunk. 'The club. The building. Who owns it, everything . . . ' He shook his head like he couldn't believe those words were coming out of his mouth.

'And what did Mr Parsons have to say to that?'

'Look,' said Parsons, 'I'm sure this can all be settled—'

'Shut it, you,' said Sperring, with an angry look that almost matched Parsons's of a few minutes ago. 'I'll deal with you in a minute.' He turned back to Khan. 'What did he say?'

'He said to, to divert attention away from it . . . look somewhere else . . . '

Parsons was on his feet, furious. 'You little fucker . . . '

Khan looked up. Eyes red-rimmed, pain-filled. Face contorted through tears and self-hatred. 'He said he'd give my mum money . . . That's why I said I'd do it. Since my dad . . . ' He didn't finish the sentence. 'It's been really hard.'

'And you believed him? He said he'd give your mother money and you believed him?'

Khan's eyes couldn't meet Sperring's. 'Yeah. Why not? He gave my dad enough.'

Parsons was still on his feet. Sperring squared up to him. Stared straight at him. Their raised voices were attracting attention, but people gave them a wide berth. No one wanted their enjoyment of the evening to be tainted.

'I hate bent coppers,' said Sperring. 'But you know what I hate more? The scum that bend them. You're nicked, Parsons.'

Hearing those words, the bearded bodyguard moved forward. Sperring turned to him. Smiled. There was no happiness in it. 'You want to do this, son?' he said. 'Really?'

The bodyguard stared at Sperring, unblinking. But something in Sperring's gaze made him look away. He backed away again. Sperring nodded. 'Good lad.' He turned back to

Parsons. 'You're a piece of shit. But you're an old piece of shit. You wouldn't survive going back inside, which is where I want to send you. Not for long. And while I might get some enjoyment out of that, I have to ask myself, is it worth it? All the time-consuming bollocks I'd have to go through. All the paperwork, compliance, building a case for the CPS, not to mention dragging young Nadish's name through the shit.' He stared at Khan. 'Not that he doesn't deserve it for what he's done.' He turned back to Parsons. 'I'd enjoy seeing you rot in prison, make no mistake. Dying in prison, too. And don't get me wrong, I'd do it, but it's a lot of work. So.' He stepped in nearer, so that Parsons had no choice but to look at him. 'What can you tell me to make me change my mind?'

Parsons cleared his throat. Sperring looked straight into his eyes. Saw that the old man was beaten and he knew it.

Parsons sighed. 'It's ... it's about my son. All about my son.'

'Who, Grant?'

'Yeah,' said Parsons. 'Sort of. But mainly about Ben ...'

91

'Come in,' called Anni, 'it's open. Living room.'

Phil stepped over the threshold of Hugo Gwilym's house once again. This time it couldn't have felt more different.

He had been stunned, Anni's call completely unexpected. Even more so when she told him that she was in Birmingham and that he should come and meet her. He told her he was in the middle of a case and couldn't really spare the time. She told him that this was important, and he would have to make time. It was to do with Marina. He started to ask questions, but she told him everything would be answered when he got there. But he needed to get there right away.

And then she told him where to meet . . .

He walked down the hall into the living room. Anni was sitting in an armchair. She jumped up when he entered and crossed the room to him, made to hug him, stopped. Phil gave a small smile. He had thought of doing the same thing and had also stopped himself. Because he was still, technically, her boss. They settled for awkwardly shaking hands, both of them having the good grace to look embarrassed about it.

'Anni,' said Phil, once formalities had been dispensed with, 'what's going on?'

'It's about Marina,' said Anni.

'You said.'

'And him.' Anni jerked a thumb at the sofa. Hugo Gwilym sat in his dressing gown, his hair matted with blood, a tea towel full of melting ice held to his head. Anni looked back at Phil.

'Is he all right?' asked Phil.

'He'll live,' said Anni, 'unfortunately. Now, where shall I start?'

Phil shrugged. Felt that familiar tightening in his chest. 'Wherever you like.'

'Sit down, then. I think it's better if you sit down.'

Phil sat in the armchair Anni had recently vacated. Anni sat on the sofa with Gwilym. Careful not to touch him.

'Marina's been a bit off lately,' said Phil, before Anni could speak. 'Withdrawn, pulling away from me. Does this have anything to do with that?'

'You could say,' said Anni. She leaned forward, cutting out Gwilym from her focus. Like it was just her and Phil in the room. 'She . . . thought she had been raped.' Anni said nothing more, waited for Phil to process the statement.

'She . . . what? *Raped?* Who by?'

Anni jerked a thumb at Gwilym. He had his head down, avoiding Phil's stare.

'Him? He raped my wife?' Phil was on his feet, crossing over to Gwilym, who held the tea towel in front of him like a soggy shield. 'He actually raped my wife . . .'

'No, don't, don't hit me . . .'

'It's OK,' said Anni. 'It's OK.'

Phil stood there staring. Eyes never leaving Gwilym. 'Did you? Rape my wife?'

412

Gwilym shook his head. Slowly. He winced from the pain. 'No. I . . . I didn't.' His voice was small, broken. Like a shattered ornament dropped from a great height. It could be repaired, but it would never be the same again.

'Then why would she think that?' Phil and Anni both stared at Gwilym.

'Because I . . . I maybe let her think it.'

'*Maybe* let her think it?'

'All right . . . ' Gwilym held up his hands as if surrendering. 'I did. I . . . let her think I . . . that we'd had sex.'

'Why would you do that, Hugo?' said Anni, her voice dangerously calm.

'Yeah,' said Phil, more overtly angry, 'why?'

'Because I . . . I was jealous of her . . . '

Phil and Anni shared a look. 'Jealous?' said Phil. 'Why?'

'Because she . . . I wanted to wind her up. Get her to, to work with me. On my book.'

'Your book?'

He nodded. 'I've only ever written about deviants. Studied them. She had . . . Well. She's confronted them. Faced them. First hand. And yes. I was jealous.' His face twisted as his words became more bitter. 'She came into the department and it was like she was a star. Yes, a star. The real deal. And I was just . . . '

'A fake?' suggested Anni.

'That's what she made me feel, yes. Fake. So I thought, right. Right, you bitch. I'll have you.'

Phil felt unsteady. His vision was wavering, turning red-tinged. His anger was rising. 'And did you?' he asked. 'Have her?'

Gwilym looked down. Shook his head once more. 'No. I . . . I couldn't.'

'What stopped you?' asked Anni.

'She . . . she'd borne a child. Another man's child. Not

413

mine. And I . . . I couldn't do that. Not when . . . No.' His face twisted once more, in disgust this time.

Anni looked at Phil. Her face was as blank as her voice was calm. Both dangerous signs, he knew. 'Hugo has been explaining his little hobby to me while I was waiting for you to get here,' she said.

'Do tell.'

'He likes to groom a student, preferably an impressionable one, and have sex with her. Forcibly, if he has to. That's why Marina contacted me. She stole a glass from his kitchen. I had it analysed. Flunitrazepam. Rohypnol, to the layman. He likes to get a girl out of it and rape her. And if she gets pregnant, that's a bonus. Then he forces her to have an abortion. Then . . . ' Anni shrugged, 'he drops her. Seduces, rapes, manipulates, impregnates, then abandons. All because he can. What a charmer.'

'When you say it like that,' said Gwilym, tea towel back to his head again, 'it sounds horrible.'

'Whichever way you say it it sounds horrible,' said Phil. He moved across the floor so that he stood directly over Gwilym. 'You've never seen a deviant, is that what you said?'

Gwilym nodded once more. Winced.

'You never looked in a fucking mirror, then?'

Phil grabbed him so hard and so fast that he dropped the tea towel, ice bouncing all over the floor.

'Phil, don't . . . '

He grasped the front of Gwilym's dressing gown, screwed it so tight he had trouble breathing.

'It all makes sense now,' said Phil, to himself as much as to Gwilym. 'Everything makes sense. The way she's been recently. How she didn't want to be touched. By a man. By *me*. Because she thought she had been raped by a piece of shit like you . . . '

He twisted the dressing gown even tighter. Something ripped. Gwilym whimpered.

'Phil, boss, please . . .'

Anni's hands were on him, trying to pull him away from Gwilym's neck. Phil blinked and, as if seeing her for the first time, took his hands away. He pushed Gwilym back down on to the sofa. Gwilym shouted out in pain as his head hit the back of it.

'So,' said Phil, once he had regained control of himself, 'what's happened? Where is Marina? And why am I here?'

'I . . . I don't know where she is,' said Gwilym. He went on to tell him about Maddy and her boyfriend and how they'd taken his research material and his book. He seemed to be more upset by that, thought Phil, than anything else.

'And where's Marina?' he asked again.

'I don't know. Honestly . . .'

'She said she was on her way here, boss,' said Anni. 'Following those two. They do that to him' – she pointed at Gwilym's head – 'then disappear. And Marina's car is outside. Not good.'

'No,' said Phil. 'Not good.'

He took his phone out, called her number.

'I tried that,' said Anni. 'No reply.'

It went to voicemail. He left a message. Turned back to Gwilym. 'So who are these people? You said Maddy?'

'Maddy Mingella. My . . .'

'Your ex,' said Anni.

He nodded. 'Yes. My ex. And her new boyfriend, I presume.'

'D'you know him? Recognise him?'

'He was a student. I'd seen him before. He said he'd worked on the book. One of the researchers.'

'Name?'

Gwilym made a useless gesture. 'I ... I can't ... I don't know.'

'Who will know?'

'Joy Henry. Departmental administrator. The records should be in the department.'

'Then why are we still here?' said Phil, moving fast towards the door.

92

The Lost and Found on Bennetts Hill was just a short walk from where Khan had met Parsons. It was an imposing Victorian building, in an area that had once been Birmingham's financial district. The buildings had all been sold off to developers, and most of them had been turned into pubs and restaurants. This one was no exception.

It was divided up like a Victorian house. A conservatory, parlour, dining room-cum-library, complete with fake bookshelf wallpaper. The place was doing a brisk pre-Christmas, post-shopping trade. Sperring flashed his warrant card, told the waitress they needed somewhere a little more private.

She opened a massive wooden door with 'The Boardroom' stencilled on it in gold lettering. Inside was a long table made of highly polished wood with leather armchairs around it. A huge Victorian map dominated one wall. There were paintings and reclaimed knick-knacks around, giving the room an 'ironic' Victorian style.

Sperring waved away the waitress's offer of refreshments. He told Parsons's bodyguard to wait outside, told Parsons to sit down. He did so. Sperring sat opposite him. Khan, who hadn't spoken or been spoken to on the journey there, sat one seat away from Sperring.

'So,' said Sperring when they were settled, 'you were going to tell me about Ben.'

Parsons looked like a defeated man. A flash of desperation shot across his eyes as he briefly considered trying to lie his way out, but Sperring spotted it, stared him down. Parsons began talking.

'Ben,' he said, 'was my son.'

'You had two, as I remember,' said Sperring.

'Yeah, and now I've got one.' He sighed. Looked and sounded genuinely grief-stricken. 'Ben died. Murdered.' He looked up, anger back in his eyes. 'And none of you lot did a fucking thing about it.'

Sperring frowned. 'Wait a minute . . . Did I hear something about this? Yeah, think I did. Few years ago now?'

'That's right,' said Parsons.

'Yeah.' Sperring nodded. 'Remember now. Wannabe gangster. Threw his weight around. Got knifed. The thug life claims another one.'

Parsons slammed the table. 'He was my son! And my heir. I was grooming him. He was going to take over everything from me. Make his old man proud, he was.'

'You mean everything that was left of your bent empire,' said Sperring. 'I presume you're not talking about the letting agency. Or maybe you are. Maybe that's all you've got left.'

Parsons opened his mouth, ready to argue, but changed his mind. Looked down at the table instead. 'I had two sons,' he said, voice low and confessional. 'Ben and Grant. Ben was the loud one, everybody's mate, well loved . . .' He drifted off in a reverie for a few seconds, then came back. 'Grant, he's . . . quieter.' It was clear from the expression on his face that he didn't view his other son in the same way. 'Quiet, yeah. But clever, you know? University and that.' He spoke the word like it was as distant and foreign to him as Burkina Faso.

'Which one?' asked Sperring.

'Birmingham. Didn't want to go far from his family.'

'So what happened to Ben?' asked Sperring, with an expression that said he knew the story but was waiting to hear Parsons's version of it.

'He made somebody angry. There was a falling-out.'

'Way I heard it, he stiffed someone on a drugs deal.'

'Whatever,' said Parsons, anger simmering once more. 'It was a business deal that went wrong. I told him to make it up, put it right, be friends, be big enough to say sorry and move on, but he wouldn't. He was a . . . very proud boy.' Admiration shone in Parsons's eyes.

'And?' said Sperring, prompting.

'He was killed,' said Parsons, the words bringing an end to the wistfulness. 'Machete.' He stared across the table, finger pointing. 'And you did nothing about it. None of you.'

'And I'm sure you co-operated fully with the police. I'm sure you were a model citizen, trying to help us do our job. Told us everything you knew. Gave us every encouragement.'

Parsons fell silent.

'So this other son,' said Sperring, keeping the conversation going, 'what happened to him?'

93

Marina sat on the floor, exhausted. She didn't know how long she had been in the room. No one had come to see them, or if they had done they had been very quiet about it. And she was still trying to get Maddy's restraints off her.

Her nails had broken and her fingers felt raw from trying to work the thick leather strap free. But she had kept going until eventually she had to stop.

'Need a rest . . .'

They had taken it in turns, tried everything. Back to back; one sitting, one standing; one lying, one crouching on top. Anything and everything that might help. And nothing had. They were no further forward.

Marina was starting to feel as desperate as Maddy now. She wanted to scream, shout, kick out. But she had swallowed all that, tamped it down. For Maddy's sake. If she lost it, the girl would fall to pieces. And that was the last thing either of them needed.

Marina sighed. 'Wait,' she said, 'I've had an idea.'

Maddy didn't answer. Marina assumed she was listening, so continued.

'We've been doing this all wrong. Ben didn't take my phone off me. It's still in my jeans pocket.'

'So?' said Maddy, her voice holding no hope at all. 'You can't reach it. Can't see to call. You may as well not have it.'

'Can't see at the moment. But these blindfolds feel different to the wrist restraints. I think we might be able to get them off.'

'How?'

Marina caught the desperate note of hope in the girl's voice. Hoped she could back up her words with actions.

'Well, let's think about this. If I lie on the floor and you sit with your back to me and your hands level with my head . . . Let's try it.'

Marina lay on the floor. It felt cold, smelled musty, unpleasant. *If I could see it*, she thought, *I probably wouldn't do this*. She felt Maddy shuffle along the floor next to her, hands working their way up her body until they reached her face.

'You there yet?'

'Nearly . . . Yes. I can feel the blindfold.'

'What's it made of? Is it leather? Something like that?'

Marina felt hands probing her face. 'No, it's . . . some kind of cloth.' Working their way round the back of her head. 'Tight, though. He's tied it tight.'

'Yes,' said Marina, 'I know. Can you get it off?'

More probing. 'The knot, it's . . . I don't think so. It's too tight. I can't get my fingers in to undo it.' A sigh of exasperation. 'If I could see it . . . '

'Well you can't. Just get hold of it as best you can and pull it upwards. Over my head.'

'But . . . won't that hurt?'

'Yes, Maddy, it will. But lying here tied up in the dark, I think it's the lesser of two evils. Just dig your fingers underneath, hard as you can, and pull.'

'You sure?'

'Just do it.'

Marina felt the girl's fingers jab roughly against her skin.

'Ow.'

'What?'

'Snapped a nail. It hurts.'

'It'll grow back. Just get the blindfold off.'

The fingers were back again. Scratching and clawing at the side of her head. Pulling, tearing. Maddy was grunting with the effort, pulling as hard as she could. It felt to Marina like someone had twisted her hair up and was trying to pull it out from the roots. She tried not to scream.

More grunting from Maddy. More twisting.

Then Marina felt the blindfold begin to move.

'That's it, keep going. It's moving, it's moving . . . '

Her words encouraged the girl. She worked with renewed strength. It felt like Marina's head was being pulled apart. She could feel it in her eye sockets and closed her eyes as tight as she could so her eyeballs weren't pulled out too.

'Keep going,' she managed to gasp. 'That's it . . . '

With a final surge of strength, Maddy managed to pull the blindfold clear of Marina's head. The force of it knocked her face forward on to the floor.

'You did it! You did it! Well done . . . '

Marina was gasping, sucking in great lungfuls of air, eyes screwed tight shut, willing the pain to go. It did eventually. And once it had, she slowly opened her eyes.

It took a while for her to acclimatise, but once she did, she saw that they were in what seemed to be a cellar. It was dark, no overhead light. Stairs leading down towards them. The outline of a rectangle of light at the top.

'What . . . Where are we?' asked Maddy. 'What can you see?'

'Some kind of basement, I think,' she said. 'Let's just hope we have a signal.'

Maddy made her way back to Marina, who guided her into removing the phone from her jeans pocket.

'Well done,' she said, once she had managed it. 'We'll make the call first, then I'll get your blindfold off.'

It wasn't easy. Maddy knelt down with the phone in her hands behind her. Marina gave her instructions on how to open it; whereabouts to touch on the screen, which numbers to press, what they would activate. One good thing, she noticed: there was a signal.

There were two missed calls. One from Anni, one from Phil.

'Right,' said Marina. 'Let's return this . . . '

94

'He took it bad,' said Parsons. He'd always been a bit ... sensitive. But this sent him over the edge. Gave him a breakdown. Had to leave university. Couldn't cope. But we looked after him. Cheryl, she was good to him.'

Parsons spoke about his other son without warmth or conviction. Sperring could imagine what it must have been like for the boy. Ron Parsons was the kind of man who regarded a breakdown as a sign of weakness. The same with sensitivity, he reckoned. If the kid had been like that, his upbringing with a father like Ron Parsons would have been hell.

'Anyway,' said Parsons, 'he got better. Or started to. But there was something ... not right. He wasn't the same any more. Like part of him had died along with Ben.' He looked embarrassed that he had actually said that. He continued. 'But he wanted to do something, move on. So he set himself up in business.'

'You didn't want him to take over your empire?'

'He wasn't like that. He ... he said some bloke at university, some professor or something that he'd worked with, gave him the idea. Deviant personalities, he said. To be honest, I didn't have a clue what he was on about. But he said there was money in it. And that I did know about.'

'What did he mean?'

'He said he'd been doing his research and found a gap in the market. I mean, he already hung about in some dodgy clubs. Never told me what he got up to, but said it put him in touch with a potential clientele. So he worked from that.'

'Doing what?'

Parsons frowned. 'Well . . . say you want to . . . I mean, he was dealing with extremes here. Real extremes.'

'Deviants.'

'Yeah. Exactly. So. Say you had some fantasy that you wanted to act out. Like, I dunno, kill someone. He'd find someone who wanted to be killed. Put you together.'

'What?' said Sperring. His mind was racing. Glenn McGowan and Keith Burkiss running round in his mind. 'He would put them together?'

'Yeah. Like some sick internet dating site. That kind of thing. Look, I might think they're sick and you might think they're sick, but bottom line? There was money in it. That's why he started the club. Give them somewhere to meet. Mingle.'

'So how did he find this clientele? You can't put an ad in the *Birmingham Mail*. Where did they come from?'

'All over the place. He started with the university thing. That professor and his deviant book. He contacted the people he'd interviewed for it, the extreme ones. Asked if they were serious or just all talk. And if they were serious, he told them he could set it up. For a price.'

Sperring thought about Keith Burkiss again, the emails. The payments. He imagined that Glenn McGowan had had a similar arrangement. 'What about the house for Glenn McGowan?'

Parsons sighed. 'That was a mistake, but I didn't find out till afterwards. He used one of our houses. That was dangerous. It could be traced. I tried to cover it up, got Cheryl to make a paper trail. But it didn't work. Then I tried damage limitation.' He pointed at Khan, who refused to look at him. 'But I started too late.' Another sigh. 'So now I'm here.'

'So who killed Glenn McGowan?' asked Sperring.

Parsons shrugged. 'Just some wannabe serial killer who fancied himself. Sad little bastard living out his dream.'

'And this sad little bastard, did you kill him?'

Parsons gave a look of mock-effrontery. 'What, me? You should know better than to ask me that, Mr Sperring.'

'OK then,' said Sperring, hands on the table, attempting a tolerance he wasn't feeling. 'Let's put it hypothetically. Could you imagine why somebody might *want* to kill him?'

'Well, speaking hypothetically, Mr Sperring, and this is only guesswork, of course, I would say that because he was a sad little no-hoper and a bit incompetent, he must have messed up.'

'How?'

'Well, again hypothetically, if he was given a job to do, like, say, kill some legless bloke, then that's what he should have done. Left it at that. Not gone berserk and killed his wife as well. Made him unstable. A liability. And with a liability, you have to make an executive decision. Get rid of him.' He shrugged, a cunning look in his eyes. 'Hypothetically, of course.'

Sperring stared at him, face professionally impassive. 'So where's your son now?'

Parsons shrugged again. 'No idea. And if I had, I wouldn't tell you.'

'Is he at this club?'

'No idea.'

Sperring stood up. 'Let's go and see, shall we?'

Seeing Sperring's movement, Khan looked up. 'What ... what are we doing?'

'I don't know about you,' said Sperring, 'but I'm tracking down a killer.'

Khan looked at Parsons, back to Sperring. 'What about him?'

'What about him?'

'If we leave him, he'll warn his son.'

'Then we bring him with us,' said Sperring. 'Or have him arrested and taken to the station.'

Khan looked away. Sperring understood. 'Oh, I see. When you said what are we going to do about him, what you really meant was "what are we going to do about me"? Am I right? If I take him in, he'll stitch you up.'

Khan nodded.

'Yeah,' said Sperring, looking at his junior officer with distaste. 'So. What *are* we going to do?'

'His name was Parsons,' said Gwilym. 'Look under P for Parsons.'

They were in the psychology department's offices at the university. Gwilym had phoned Joy Henry, described the youth and been given a name and told where to look for the file he was seeking.

Gwilym had dressed in an old jumper and jeans and pulled on a woollen beanie to hide the congealed blood on his head. He looked, thought Phil, one step above a homeless person. *And I hope*, he thought, with understandable venom, *that when I've finished with him, that's what he'll be.*

'Something wrong with your arms?' said Phil. 'You look.'

Gwilym, opening the nearest filing cabinet, did so.

'Here,' he said eventually. He held out a file to Phil. Photo clipped to the top. 'This is him.'

Phil took the file. 'Grant Parsons. That's our boy.' He scanned it briefly, closed it. He was about to speak to Anni, plan their next move, when his phone rang. He took it out, checked the display. Looked at Anni.

'It's Marina.'

'Well, what are you waiting for? Answer it,' she said.

'Phil?'

She lay on the floor, her head on one side, the phone beneath her. It was the only way she could make the call. She had thought of putting it on speaker but thought that would attract attention.

'Where are you? What's happened?'

She felt tears form in her eyes, just from hearing his voice.

'I'm ... I don't know. I've ... been taken somewhere. I can't move. He bundled us into a car, tied us up, blindfolded us. I tried to work out where we were going, but ... I don't know.'

'Who's with you?'

'Maddy Mingella. She's a student. Her boyfriend, he went insane, he ... ' She felt the tears would come if she kept talking.

'Has he hurt you? Are you OK?'

'No, he hasn't hurt me. Not really. I'm OK. We're both OK.'

'Good.' She heard him sighing with relief. Then there was a pause.

'Hello?' Marina felt a hysterical edge creeping into her voice.

'I'm . . . I'm still here.' She could tell from his voice that he was struggling not to cry too. 'Listen, Gwilym said—'

'Gwilym?' A shudder passed through Marina. She felt like she was going to be sick. 'Hugo Gwilym? Is he . . . still alive?'

'Yeah. 'Fraid so.'

'You're . . . you're with him now?'

'Yeah. And Anni.'

'Oh.' Her heart was racing. She didn't know what to say next.

'Look,' said Phil. 'I know what happened.'

'Oh.' Marina felt the tears starting once more.

'Gwilym told me everything. Sack of shit.' Phil's voice changed direction. She could imagine him addressing those words to Gwilym himself. Despite everything, that made her smile. 'And you've got nothing to worry about. He didn't rape you.'

'He . . . didn't?'

'No. He didn't. Didn't touch you. He's told me all about it.'

'Then why did he . . . did he make me . . . '

'Because he's a piece of shit. So that's one less thing for you to worry about. You were lucky. But he's not going to be.'

Marina couldn't help herself. The tears started.

'Hey,' said Phil, 'come on. Don't cry. I need you to help me. You'll set me off too. And then neither of us'll be any use. Come on.'

She tried her best to sniff the tears away. 'OK,' she said, 'OK . . . I'm fine now.' She hoped he would believe her.

'Right. Listen. We need Maddy's help. What can she tell us about Grant Parsons?'

Marina frowned. 'Who?'

'Grant Parsons. Her boyfriend. The one who's taken you both.'

'That's not his name.'

'It's not? But Gwilym's identified him as the guy who attacked him. I've got his photo here.'

'No,' said Marina. 'His name's Ben.'

There was silence from the other end of the phone. Eventually Phil spoke. 'Ben.'

'Yes. That's what he said his name was. That's all we know him as.'

Marina was aware of Phil's heavy breathing down the phone. 'Ask Maddy,' he said, 'whether Ben's got a tattoo on his arm. Right forearm, inside.'

She asked her. Word for word.

'No,' said Maddy, still restrained, still blindfolded, shaking her head. 'Not a tattoo, no. He's got a mark there, though. He told me it's a ... Well, he told me it was where he'd cut himself. Like self-harmed. But it's all ridges and that. Red.'

'Did you hear that?' asked Marina.

'Yeah,' said Phil. 'Like a brand, you mean?'

'I ... I don't know ... '

'A burn?'

'Yes,' said Maddy, 'like a burn.'

'Jesus. Keep this line open. I'll try to get back to the station, see if we can get a fix with the GPS. Then we—'

The phone call was abruptly ended.

Marina looked up. Ben's booted foot had been brought down on her phone.

'You bitch . . . '

She stared at him. She tried to sit up, bring herself upright. He planted his foot on her chest, pushed her down again. She hit the floor hard, the air huffing out of her. She looked slowly up at him once more. Rage, and viewing him from below, contorted his features.

'Who were you talking to?'

Marina didn't answer.

'I said who were you talking to?' He sounded unstable, she thought. Like he was about to snap.

Still she didn't speak.

'I said who . . . ' he kicked her, hard, in the ribs, 'were . . . ' another kick, harder this time, 'you . . . ' and another; she felt something crack, 'talking to?'

Marina tried to breathe deeply. It hurt. 'My . . . my husband . . . '

With a scream of rage he turned away from her. 'Husband . . . husband . . . fuck, fuck . . . '

Marina looked over at him. Tried to ignore the pain in her side. 'Yes,' she said. 'My husband. The police officer. He knows where I am.'

'He can't.'

'He knows who you are too,' she said, struggling to get breath back inside her body. 'Grant.'

His face contorted even further. 'Grant? Fucking . . . Grant? I'm Ben. *Ben*. Not Grant.'

'No,' she said, voice as calm as she could make it, 'you're Grant. That's who you are.'

He shook his head violently enough to dislodge something. 'No . . . I'm not. I'm Ben. Grant, Grant's a . . . pussy. He's weak. Nothing. A nobody. Everybody hates Grant.' He gave a twisted approximation of a smile. 'Everybody loves Ben. *Everybody*.'

His raving had given her a way in. She pursued it. 'But why?' she said, trying once again to remain calm. 'Why does everybody hate Grant? What's he done wrong?'

He knelt down beside her, his face right up against hers to emphasise his words. 'He's weak,' he said slowly, an exasperated teacher explaining a simple point to even simpler children. 'Weak. He's nothing. What his father always said, always called him. Nothing. Nobody. Not like Ben. Ben was everything, Ben had it all. Grant . . . nothing.'

'So you became Ben.'

He nodded. 'I *am* Ben.'

'Good. Right. And he's strong.'

'He is.'

'And he makes you feel strong.'

'Yeah. Course he does. And everybody loves him.' He pointed at Maddy, gave her a kick. 'Even her. She loved him.'

Maddy began to cry. Marina kept going. 'Ben's upset her,' she said. 'Made her cry.'

'So?'

'That's not what you do to someone who loves you, is it? You do the opposite.'

He staggered away from her, hands to his head. 'Shut up, shut up . . . '

'If you love someone—'

He turned back to her, lifted her off the floor. Screamed into her face. '*Shut up* . . . ' Holding her head with one hand, he drew back his other, slapped her as hard as he could.

The force of the blow almost dislocated her jaw. She had never known a slap like it. Her whole face stung as badly as if she had just put her head inside a wasps' nest.

He was calming down now. His breathing was returning to normal. Marina tried again. 'Look, Ben,' she said, 'it doesn't have to be like this. You could let us go. That'll be the end of it. The longer you keep us here, the worse it gets for you.' Her voice dropped, became warm, consoling. 'Come on. Just let us go. You don't have to do this. Be bigger than that. What d'you say?'

Her only answer was a smile.

'You're letting us go?' She knew he wasn't.

He crossed to the corner of the room, rummaged around, found what he was looking for, came back. Marina saw that he was holding a ball gag. A big one. A well-used one.

'No . . . no . . . '

He ignored her protestations, pulled her head up and pushed the ball into her mouth. She couldn't breathe and tried to scream, her body going into involuntary panic. He pulled the gag tight round the back of her head, tied it.

'There,' he said, 'that should shut you up.'

She stared at him, wide-eyed, her heart hammering, thinking she would never get enough air into her body through her nose.

'Now,' he said, 'I've decided what I'm going to do with you. Both of you. And you're not going to enjoy it. But then you're not meant to . . . '

Marina stared at him. Her last weapon, her voice, her reason was gone. She was helpless.

98

'No, no, no, no, no . . .'

Phil stared at his phone, tried to call Marina back. Nothing.

'Phil?' It was Anni. 'What happened?'

'The line went dead. She . . .' He sighed, ran his fingers through his hair, turned backwards and forwards as if looking for a way out. 'It went dead. While she was talking.'

'You think someone got to it?'

'Ben. Or Grant. Or whoever he's calling himself.' Phil nodded. 'Yeah. Him. Shit . . .' He paced once more, feeling that familiar tightening in his chest. *Not now . . . I don't have time for it now . . .*

He kept hearing Marina's voice, over and over in his head. He replayed the conversation, went back over everything. Tried to pick out something – anything – he could use to find her.

'The club,' he said aloud. 'That's where she must be. It's the obvious place for him to take them. That's where we look first.'

'We?' said Anni. 'I'm off my patch here and you need to stand down.'

He stopped pacing, turned and stared at her. 'What?'

'I said, you need to stand down.' She swallowed. 'Boss.'

'Why? This bastard's got my wife.'

'Conflict of interest, that's why,' she said. 'You know the rules.'

Phil did know the rules. If an officer had a personal involvement in a case for whatever reason, he had to stand aside and let someone impartial take over. He turned to Anni, nodded. 'Yeah,' he said. 'You're right. I should.'

He still had his phone in his hand. He called Cotter.

'Situation's changed,' he said when she picked up. 'You know how you hoped whoever ran this club would pack up and leave to become someone else's problem? Well, two things. That person is Grant Parsons, Ron Parsons's son and he's taken two hostages and holed up in there.'

Silence on the line. Phil held his breath. After what seemed like an eternity, Cotter spoke.

'I'll get the helicopter in the air.'

Phil let out a sigh of relief. 'Thank you.'

He brought her up to speed. 'One of the hostages is Maddy Mingella. She's a student who had the misfortune to get involved with both Gwilym and Grant Parsons. I don't know who the other one is.' He turned away from Anni so he couldn't see her silent remonstration with him.

'Make sure the helicopter's got the thermal imaging equipment going,' he added. 'We'll need Firearms in their ARVs and we need the operational support unit for numbers.' He hung up, looked at Anni. 'We're good to go.'

'I'll deal with this one.' Anni jerked a thumb at Gwilym. 'What you doing? Go.'

'I will,' said Phil, keying numbers into his phone. 'One more call. If I'm going in there to get them, I need someone with me I can trust.'

99

Sperring was still sitting in the Boardroom of the Lost and Found, staring across the table at Ron Parsons and wondering what to do with him, when his phone rang.

At first he ignored it; then he checked the display. When he saw who it was, he was definitely going to ignore it. Reluctantly, though, he decided to pick up.

'Yeah,' he said, 'what d'you want?'

'It's me,' said Phil.

'I know. Your name came up. I can read, you know. What d'you want?'

'Someone I can trust,' said Phil. 'On my side.'

'Oh yeah?' said Sperring, gearing up for an argument. 'And who might that be?'

'You,' said Phil.

Sperring was taken aback. Phil explained to him what he wanted. As he did so, Sperring's face was split by a wide grin.

Conversation over, he ended the call, looked across the table at Parsons, then at Khan.

'Your lucky day, Nadish,' he said.

Khan looked up, eyes dazed. 'What?'

'You'll see.'

Sperring stood up. Khan, taking his cue from the older officer, did likewise. Parsons looked between the pair of them.

'What about me?' he said.

Sperring stopped, turned. Gave the old gangster his full attention.

'Know any good solicitors?'

100

A nni's first thought about the building was: *it's so different from the one I'm used to*.

Southway station in Colchester looked like an eighties prison. Or a hospital designed by someone who didn't want the patients to get well. This one, she thought, looked like a Gothic castle.

Nice. Wish I worked here.

She walked through the main doors, straight up to the desk. The sergeant looked up from the notes he was writing. She held her warrant card up to the glass.

'Detective Constable Hepburn,' she said. 'Anni Hepburn.'

He was young and anonymously blond, she thought. Good-looking in a bland way. She saw a squash ball on the counter before him. *Must practise his wrist-strengthening exercises during his shift*, she thought, and didn't know if that was a good thing, keeping healthy, or just too narcissistic.

He smiled at her, looked at the card, then back to her. 'Bit far off your patch, aren't you?'

'I've been visiting an old friend,' she said. 'Something came up while I was doing it.'

She looked at the figure standing next to her. So did the desk sergeant. Hugo Gwilym stood there looking dishevelled in his old clothes and beanie hat.

The desk sergeant frowned, leaned in towards Anni. 'He looks like that bloke off the telly,' he said, out of earshot of Gwilym.

'You mean,' she said, 'he looks like that bloke who *used* to be on the telly.'

'Eh?'

Instead of elaborating, she turned to Gwilym. 'Come on, over here.'

He moved forward obediently. He looked broken, like he no longer had the strength to argue any more. Like the fight had left him. He stood next to her at the desk. She looked at him. He stared back at her, eyes red-rimmed.

'Well?' she said.

He didn't move, didn't speak.

'Haven't you got something to say?' she prompted.

Still he didn't speak.

She leaned in to him. 'It's over, Gwilym,' she said. 'Finished. You're finished. If you don't do this now, you're only putting off the inevitable. You know that.'

He sighed. Opened his mouth. 'My name's Hugo Gwilym,' he said.

Anni saw the light of recognition in the desk sergeant's eyes.

'And why are you here, Hugo?' said Anni, as if she was leading a recalcitrant small child.

'I'm . . . here to . . . to turn myself in.'

The desk sergeant waited, looking perplexed. Anni leaned in once more, prompted again. 'And why are you here to turn yourself in, Hugo?'

He looked at her. One last, long, despairing, pathetic look. She stared back at him. As empathic as a rock. Realising that this really was the end, knowing he had no choice, he turned back to the sergeant.

'I'm here to ... turn myself in because ... ' he sighed, 'I'm a rapist ... '

The desk sergeant's eyes nearly popped out of his head.

Anni smiled. 'And get him a doctor for his head. Wouldn't want the bastard suing us.'

101

'Here we are . . .'

Grant Parsons pulled tight on the rope binding Marina to a chair. Her hands were still behind her back, still in the same restraints. Her arms and legs were now tied up too. And she was still gagged.

'I thought of putting the blindfold back on,' he said. 'But then I thought, no. Let her see what's happening. Hate you to miss the fun.'

After smashing her phone and gagging her, he had pulled her up the stairs with him, Maddy screaming as she was left behind. He dragged her along what seemed like endless corridors until they had emerged in what at first she took for a living room. She soon realised it wasn't real. With its pink walls and matching furniture, it seemed more like a stage or film set, like a doll's house room made human size.

Parsons dragged her over to an armchair by a dining table set for dinner, tied her to it. Then he left the room, came back with armfuls of files and papers. She noticed that the research material he had taken from Gwilym was amongst them. Gwilym's laptop, now smashed into uselessness, was also there. He piled everything up on the table, then pulled the chair she was tied to into the centre of the room, positioning it so that she faced the door.

She heard sounds going on, liquid, wet sounds. She tried to turn her head to see what was happening, but her restraints wouldn't allow it. She smelled something. The air took on a chemical tang.

'Hubby's on his way,' he said from behind her. 'My dad called to let me know. From the police station. Called me instead of a solicitor. Maybe he's not so bad after all. So, with that in mind, I've had to take precautions. You see that door? There. Ahead of you. That's the way your hubby's going to enter. The only way in. And the first thing he'll see will be you.'

She heard something being thrown to the ground. It clanged emptily. Parsons walked round until he stood in front of her, looking at her. He wiped his hands on his jeans. Knelt down so his face was at her eye level.

'No,' he said, 'that's not true. The first thing he'll see will be the fire, over there.' He gestured behind her. 'All the files about this place, about me, about everything I've done, they're all there on that table. And they're all going up in smoke. He'll look at that first. And then he'll see you. And he'll not be able to move. He'll stand there staring, struck immobile by indecision. Because he knows he'll only be able to save one thing. You, or the evidence. And it might be too late for the evidence.' He laughed. 'Might even be too late for you by then.'

Marina closed her eyes. Unable to move, to speak, all she could do was think. She tried to will herself away, be anywhere but here. Phil was on his way. He had to be. If he wasn't and Parsons was lying . . .

No. She couldn't think about that. He had to be. He *had* to be.

What if he didn't know where she was? What if he couldn't find her? What if . . .

She kept her eyes tightly closed. But it didn't work. The tears still ran down her face.

'Crying?' Parsons laughed. 'That's nothing. Wait till the smoke starts. You'll be crying plenty by then. But at least you'll have done your job. You'll have stopped them getting further. Stopped them reaching me.'

He walked to the door, turned, looked at her. 'I don't know what to say,' he said. 'I'm sure I should have a speech prepared, but really, I just want to get out of here and away. Bye.'

He slammed the door shut.

She heard the fire before she saw it or smelled it. Crackling, like white noise eating up everything in its path. She tried to scream, but the gag wouldn't let her. She pulled at the restraints but they were too tight.

She sat back, trying not to give in to panic. Trying desperately to find a way out.

There wasn't one.

No, she thought. *It can't end here. It can't . . .*

102

The circus had arrived at Digbeth.

The mobile operations van was parked a block away in the rubble-strewn grounds of a low-roofed sixties-built derelict factory. The armed response vehicles, unmarked Audis with the rear seats removed and gun safes in their place, were parked up next to them. The operational support unit had arrived. Sergeant Joe Cass and his team of seven officers. Tooled up, ready.

The street had been closed, the area evacuated.

Phil looked over the road at their target building, on the corner of Burchall Street and Cheapside. It looked like nothing from the outside, just another derelict factory or warehouse building with mesh and metal plates up at the windows, blackening brickwork. The double front doors were old and heavy-looking. Red paint had faded to flaking and peeling pink and it looked like they hadn't been opened for decades. There was no sign of life from within the building. Overhead, a helicopter circled and swooped, its beam lighting up the street as if they were at a film premiere.

Beside Phil were Sperring and Cotter.

'You have any more information on those hostages? Name of the second one?' asked Cotter.

Phil shook his head. 'She might be a lecturer. That's as much as I know.'

'This isn't the way I wanted to do this.' Cotter turned back to the building, sighed. 'Just . . . We'd better not mess this up.' She went back inside the mobile unit. Phil made to follow her.

'Can I have a word?'

Phil turned. Sperring ground out the stub of a cigarette under his heel.

'Only take a minute.'

Phil waited.

'You know who the other one is, don't you?' It was a statement, not a question.

'Yeah, I do.'

'Why didn't you tell the boss?'

Phil's voice dropped. 'Because it's my wife.'

Sperring's eyes widened.

'She went round to Gwilym's house. There was something she wanted to . . . ' He sighed. 'Parsons took her . . . '

'Then you shouldn't be heading up this team. And you shouldn't be going in.'

'I know.' He looked Sperring square in the eye. 'Do we have a problem here?'

'Is it going to get in the way of you doing your job as a copper?'

'Of course not.'

Sperring kept staring. Deciding. 'Then we don't have a problem. But if that changes, I knew nothing about it. We never had this conversation and you're on your own.'

'Thanks. That's fair.'

'Yeah,' said Sperring, rubbing his chin. He looked embarrassed. 'If it was me, I dare say I'd have done the same thing.' He laughed. 'Not with my ex, though. I'd have left the cheating cow to rot.'

Phil laughed. It felt incongruous but good. 'You ready?'

'One more thing. Why did you phone me about this? Tell me first?' said Sperring. 'You could have called Imani Oliver; you seem to be getting on well with her. Why me?'

'You're next in line,' said Phil. 'And like I said, I wanted someone I could trust.'

'And you think you can trust me?'

'Yeah,' said Phil, 'I do. We might not have a lot in common, but I'm not asking you out on a date. I'm asking you to back me up. You're a good copper. I know you'll do that.'

Sperring looked like he didn't know what to say. Phil didn't give him the chance.

'Come on,' he said, 'we've got a raid to organise.'

He went back inside the mobile operations unit. Elli was sitting at her laptop.

'What have you got?' he said.

'I've got the plans up for the building, but they're old. I'm sure it doesn't look like that in there now. And I've got the thermal images from the helicopter. Look.'

She pressed a button, showed Phil. Yellow and red blobs stood out against the blue/grey screen.

'There are people inside, but not many. One looks to be motionless, stuck in a room in the middle of the building. The room seems to be getting warmer.'

'What about the rest?'

'There's movement towards the back of the building. Looks like two people. There are other heat signatures around too. They seem to be positioned at the entrances.'

'Good.' He turned to Sergeant Cass. 'Your team ready?'

'Say the word,' he said.

'OK, then. Sperring? You good to go?'

'Bostin.' Sperring nodded. A look passed between them.

'I'll take that as a yes, then.' He looked round once more.

447

The armed response unit were ready and in place. Phil hated working with them. He never felt safe. He knew they were well trained and would not discharge their weapons unless they had to, and then only after giving prior warning, but it just took one mistake . . . He knew how much people played with a new phone when they bought one. Imagine what that was like with a gun.

The teams had all seem the thermal images, had sorted out the entrances. They knew where they were going. All Phil had to do was give the word.

'Boss.'

Elli was at the door of the unit, looking at him worriedly.

'What?'

'That room that I said was getting warmer. It's very hot now. I think there's a fire in there. As well as a person.'

Phil turned to the team.

'Go.'

103

Marina couldn't see. Smoke was clouding out her vision. She was having difficulty breathing, the gag stopping her from getting enough air into her lungs. She was beginning to feel lightheaded.

And hot. Very hot.

Like Bonfire Night. Like the ones she had gone to as a child. Standing too close to the flames, the heat coming off warmer than a hot summer day. Ready to take off her coat and scarf; why did she need them? Then a step away and you're back in the cold November night. And you're glad of the coat and scarf. Just like that. Except she couldn't step away now. Couldn't step anywhere. And the heat was getting closer.

Her mind slipped back again and she was in the present. She struggled, squirmed, tried to pull her arms free of the ropes, just succeeded in making them tighter. And all the while, the heat increasing, increasing . . .

Still seated, she tried to pull herself forward, towards the door, away from the flames. It was like trying to jump in the air wearing lead diving boots. But she had moved about a centimetre. She tried it again, grunting and gasping. Another centimetre or so. Then again. She had to stop, rest. It was so much effort. Even from that small amount of movement her stomach muscles hurt. Her head felt even lighter as her exertions depleted further the amount of oxygen reaching her brain. She was gasping, gagging.

The flames were still as intense. She didn't know how long she had.

Images flashed into her mind. She saw Phil's face. Smiling at her. Felt a knife twist inside her as she realised she would never see him again. Her daughter, Josephina. The tears started.

Screaming against the gag, she tried to push herself forward once more. Another centimetre. Then another. Then ...

She lost her balance. The chair fell sideways. She felt a searing pain in her arm as she landed on it. She tried to move. Couldn't.

This is it, she thought.

This is the end.

104

Phil stood back as the OSU prepared their battering ram. They brought it back, hammered it at the double doors. The doors didn't want to give. The OSU weren't going to take no for an answer. Eventually, with a creaking and splintering of ages-old wood, the doors opened.

'Move! Move! Move!'

They rushed in. Phil ran in with them. All was suddenly noise and commotion. The OSU surged into the building. Phil looked round. The inside was completely different to the exterior. The walls were stripped back to the bare brick, the floors polished concrete. It looked more like the entrance to a suite of Shoreditch artists' studios or some hipster internet company. *Like the rest of Digbeth*, thought Phil.

He tried to take bearings, decide where to go.

'Elli,' he said to his earpiece, 'I'm inside. Where should I go?'

'Straight ahead,' she replied. 'That's where the heat's coming from.'

'OK.' He set off down the corridor in front of him.

There were doors off on both sides. An indication of what was inside was given by the decoration around the frame. One had chains cemented into place. He glanced into the room. It looked like a prison cell. Or the stage set of a prison cell. The floor was flagged stone. The dried blood looked real enough.

Back into the corridor again. Looking round.

'It's on the first floor, I think,' Elli said. 'Head towards it.'

Phil did so. He passed other doorways. The next one along had rusted circular saw wheels pinned up. He didn't want to see what went on in there. The one after that a dried snake-skin. He focused. Kept going. Found a set of stairs at the end, took them two at a time.

'Are you still registering heat signatures?' he asked her.

'Yes, but it's getting much warmer.'

'How many?'

'There was just one. There's that many people in the building now, it's hard to tell.'

He didn't need Elli to tell him where the heat was coming from. He felt it himself now. He ran towards the far end of the corridor. There was a door in front of him. Doll's heads of varying sizes all around the frame. This was it. He pulled it open. And immediately felt and heard the roar of the flames.

He looked round, hand over his face. It was the room from the DVD. McGowan's living room writ large. He looked down. Marina was lying on the floor.

'Shit . . .'

His heart was hammering as he knelt down, began to pull her out. She was near to being unconscious. He tried to untie her, realised it was futile. He dragged her, chair and all, down the corridor.

'Get an ambulance!' he shouted into his earpiece.

'What have you found?'

Phil didn't reply straight away. He couldn't. He waited until he was far enough away from the flames, then looked at Marina.

Please don't be dead, please don't be dead, please don't be dead . . .

He reached round behind her head, wrenched off the gag. She gasped a breath. Opened her eyes. She looked round in panic. Then saw who it was.

'Hey ...'

'Hey yourself,' he said, smiling.

Any further conversation was cut off as she began coughing.

'We need the fire engines here, Elli. Quick as they can.'

'They're on their way,' she said.

He dragged Marina further down the corridor, then, when he was a safe distance from the blaze, started to pull at her bonds. They were tight, difficult to budge. But he managed to get most of them off, as well as the heavy leather restraints tying her wrists together.

'Can you stand?' he said.

She nodded numbly and he pulled her to her feet.

'Got ... pins and needles ...' she said. 'Oww ...'

He smiled. 'Come on. I'll help you.'

He put his arm around her, helped her to walk.

He reached the stairs and picked her up in his arms, carried her down. Marina opened her eyes, smiled.

'Carrying me over the threshold,' she said, managing a weak smile. 'Caveman.'

'Shut up,' he replied. He was smiling too.

They reached the front door. He carried her through. Imani Oliver ran over towards them. Phil set Marina upright.

'The ambulance is in its way. Don't worry. You're safe now.'

Marina put her arms round his neck. Began to sob. 'I thought ... I thought I'd never ...'

'I know,' he said, 'I know ...'

They held each other in the street, strafed by the light of the helicopter.

'Boss,' said Elli, 'I've picked up those other two heat signatures.'

453

'Where?'

'On the roof.'

Phil looked up. The flames hadn't reached the roof yet.

'There's an alleyway between that building and the next,' said Elli. 'If he can cross that, he might get away.'

'And he's got someone with him,' said Phil.

'Maddy,' said Marina. 'He's got Maddy ...'

Phil turned to her. 'Stay with Imani,' he said. 'You'll be fine.'

She frowned, clung on tightly to him. 'Wh-where are you going?'

Phil looked back at the building.

'Up there,' he said.

105

The flames hadn't reached the stairwell. Phil was grateful for that. He was unhappy about leaving Marina, but not as upset as she was with him for going back inside. But it was his job. She knew he couldn't have done anything else.

'Ben,' she said, 'he calls himself Ben. It's his . . . other personality, I think.'

'His dead brother,' said Phil. 'Thanks for the heads-up.'

'Let me . . . come with you . . . '

'You're not going anywhere. The ambulance'll be here soon.'

Marina nodded reluctantly.

One final kiss and he was off into the building again.

He took the stairs two at a time until he could go no further. Then he found a set of metal ladders bolted to the wall in front of him. He looked up. There was a hatch at the top. He started to climb.

Swinging the hatch back, he pulled himself out on to the roof. Looked round. The beam from the helicopter swung back and forth like a roving searchlight. He saw them. Two figures. One holding the other close. At the far side of the building, right at the edge. He walked towards them, the blades of the helicopter creating mini twisters all around him.

Grant Parsons saw him coming, turned. He grabbed

Maddy, held her in front of him like a shield. Phil kept walking. Slowly. Purposefully.

Parsons had a knife at her throat. A big knife, Phil noted.

'Get back,' he shouted. 'Get back . . . ' He pushed the knife against her neck.

Phil noticed she couldn't move, that her arms were pulled tight behind her back. Tied, he thought. Her eyes were wild, staring.

'Who am I talking to?' shouted Phil above the din of the 'copter. 'Grant or Ben?'

'Ben,' he shouted back. 'It's always Ben.'

From below, Phil heard the sirens of the arriving fire engines.

'OK, Ben,' he shouted. 'Why don't you put the knife down. Then we can talk.'

'I've got a better idea,' shouted Ben. He stepped up on to the parapet, put his feet right back against the edge of the building.

Phil ran forward. Ben brandished the knife once more. Maddy screamed.

'Back! Get back!'

Phil noticed that there was a plank of wood on the parapet. It stretched across the alleyway to the next building. Parsons's escape route. He must have planned it.

Parsons edged his way towards it, Maddy stumbling along with him.

'Your empire's burning,' said Phil. 'It's all over. Why don't you give up, eh? Then we can talk.'

Ben shook his head. 'No, it's better this way.'

'You can't get away. Look down there, look above you. You're surrounded. It's over. You're finished.'

'So?' he shouted. 'At least I'll be famous. At least they'll remember me. At least . . . '

Phil wasn't sure, but he might have seen tears in Ben's eyes.

'At least . . . I won't have been a failure . . . *He* won't think I was a failure . . . '

He moved even closer to the edge.

Phil heard a sudden noise from behind him. He turned. It was Sperring, opening the hatch, letting it clang against the roof. Ben had heard the noise too, turned his attention towards it.

This is it, thought Phil. *I won't get another chance.*

He readied himself to run forward, jump at Ben, grab Maddy and pull her to safety.

But Maddy had different ideas. She screamed. Primal, angry.

'Fuck you! Fuck you! I've had enough . . . being hurt, used, abused . . . fuck you . . . '

She stamped down hard on Ben's instep. He screamed in pain. Lost his footing. While he was disorientated, she brought her head forward, then let it fly back, hitting the bridge of his nose and his forehead with so much force that Phil heard the crack even above the blades of the helicopter.

Ben screamed once more, dropped the knife as he brought his hands up to his face. Maddy swung her leg forward and let it go backwards, hitting him in the shin. His footing became unsteady.

Phil ran, reached out, grabbed Maddy. Caught her by the arm. Pulled her forward, towards him, away from the edge.

Ben was weaving about in pain, eyes closed, blood fountaining from his broken nose. He staggered backwards. His heel hit the edge of the plank and he lost his balance.

'No . . . '

He put his arms out, windmilling, but he couldn't fight the momentum.

He disappeared over the side.

Screaming as he went down.

Phil held Maddy to him.

'It's OK,' he said. 'It's OK. I've got you. You're safe.'

PART FIVE

TOMORROW'S DREAM

106

The Christmas decorations were up. Phil and Marina's house was looking as warm and welcoming as any rental property could.

Phil stood at the doorway between the kitchen and living room, looked at all the people there. He hadn't realised how many people he knew in Birmingham. And here they all were, drinking his booze, eating his party food. He corrected himself. *Their* booze and party food.

The Christmas party had been his idea. He had surprised himself by proposing it, and was in turn surprised when Marina agreed. Boxing Day evening, when everyone had had enough of enforced proximity with their families and wanted to see other faces. The perfect time, he thought. Not all of them were fed up with their families. Some of them had brought their families with them. And that was fine by Phil and Marina.

They had been worried that the two lots of people, police and academics, wouldn't mix. But those worries had proved to be unfounded. Alcohol, the great social lubricant, had seen to that.

Just over two weeks had passed since that night on the rooftop in Digbeth. And they were still dealing with the fallout.

Marina had been taken straight to hospital and kept in

overnight, suffering from the effects of smoke inhalation. Luckily, her fall to the floor had been the best thing that could have happened. The air was clearer there, freer of smoke, and it was that that had probably saved her. She had been released the next morning. Phil had been waiting for her.

She had smiled when he turned up. Really pleased to see him. And in returning that smile he knew just how pleased he was to see her too. Relieved to see her up and moving. He had gathered her things, put his arm round her to help her out.

'So,' he said as they walked down the corridor towards the exit, 'are we good?'

She had burrowed into him. 'Yeah,' she had said. 'We're very good.'

They had held each other close all the way to the car.

Things hadn't gone so well for Grant Parsons. He was still alive, but the fall had broken his neck and shattered his spine. Paramedics had rushed straight to him and it was their prompt action that had saved him. His solicitor had argued that he was too ill to stand trial, so he had been transferred to a secure hospital, although he clearly wasn't going anywhere.

His father had claimed to be broken by grief and ignorant of his son's actions. When it was suggested to him that he knew a lot more than he was telling, he started plea-bargaining. His bearded henchman was offered up as the murderer of Scott Sheriff. The CPS seemed content to settle for that.

Most of the information regarding the club had been lost in the fire. Phil imagined there were some very relieved individuals walking around Birmingham that Christmas.

Cotter had had words to say to Phil too.

'You're telling me you didn't know your wife was in that building? Really?'

Phil had stood before her desk. He refused to feel like a

naughty schoolboy summoned before the head teacher, although he knew that was how she was trying to make him feel.

'Would it have mattered if I'd known? Or if I'd said I knew?'

'Of course it bloody would. You would have had to stand down from the operation. You know that.'

'I saved that girl's life. I saved my wife's life.'

Cotter sighed. 'I know you did . . . '

'I'm not sorry. It was the right thing to do.'

'We have procedures to follow.'

'And I followed them.'

'Yes, but . . . ' She shook her head. Looked straight at him. 'You got away with it this time. Don't do it again. I don't have that in my team.'

'OK.'

'You are staying with my team, aren't you?'

Marina was on the other side of the room, chatting with some of her work colleagues. She was aware of Phil watching her. He raised his bottle in a salute. She raised her glass in return. Both smiling.

She felt better than she had done in ages. She felt purged. Clean. She knew what had done it.

A week ago, Phil had arranged for her to see Hugo Gwilym in custody. The request was unorthodox, but then the whole case had been somewhat unorthodox. She had asked Maddy to accompany her. Maddy had been wary at first, but Marina had assured her that he couldn't hurt them in any way. And seeing him would do them both some good, put an end to the ordeal.

He was being held on remand in the old Winson Green prison, now renamed Birmingham Prison after being taken over by a private contractor. The staff wore brightly coloured ties and had the company's insignia on their shirts, a change from the usual prison officer uniform. But the visiting room was just the same as it had always been. Like hope had been checked in at the gate along with mobiles. It was where fathers watched their children grow away from them as they got older. The spark of recognition dimming with each visit. Their wives and girlfriends getting more and more vague about who they had nights out with.

But there would be none of that for Marina and Maddy.

Marina showed the letter signed by DCI Cotter that allowed them to visit, then they took their places at the table. While they were waiting, Marina turned to Maddy.

'You still OK about this? You don't have to go through with it.'

'No,' she said, nodding, 'I'll be fine.'

Marina had noticed the change in Maddy, even in such a short space of time. She sat more upright, looked people in the eye. Wasn't afraid to voice her opinions. More confident. Which could only be good, Marina thought. But there was something else about her that she'd noticed too. The new-found confidence came with an aggressive, antagonistic edge. She had found out how to fight back. Marina hoped she chose her targets carefully.

Hugo Gwilym entered. Marina couldn't believe just how bad he looked. He seemed to have aged by at least a decade since he had been in there. His stubble had become a grey beard and his hair, without the artfully tousled grooming, just looked a mess. But it was his eyes that showed the most change. They were scared, defeated. Sunk into his emaciated, hollow cheeks.

He sat, almost breaking down when he saw them.

'Thank you,' he said, 'thank you so much for coming . . .'

'I just wanted to see you,' said Marina. She kept her voice

464

as neutral and calm as possible. 'It felt like our business was never properly concluded.'

'Our business . . . ' He closed his eyes, shook his head. 'You make it sound so . . . It wasn't . . . ' He opened his eyes again. 'Business. It was anything but.' He looked across at Maddy. Stretched out his hand. She instinctively recoiled.

'Don't touch me,' she said.

Gwilym withdrew his hand. 'Like that. I see.'

Marina kept staring at him.

'Look,' he said. 'I . . . I realise I've behaved appallingly to you. Both of you. And being here . . . ' he gestured round the room, 'has given me ample time and opportunity for reflection.' He tried a smile. 'I'm a changed man. Really, I am.'

'Good,' said Marina.

Warming to his theme, he continued. 'Yes. Completely changed. I have behaved so . . . so badly. It would mean so much if you could find it in your hearts to forgive me.' Another smile. This one bashful, self-effacing. 'Could you perhaps do that?'

'Forgive you?' said Marina. 'For what you did to me? The worry, the anguish you put me through . . . ' She could feel her heart racing, her voice getting louder. She tried to control herself, lower her voice. 'Forgive you? For using rape as blackmail against me?' Her turn to smile. 'Fuck you, Hugo. You're exactly where you deserve to be.'

He recoiled from her words as if he'd been slapped. 'But . . . but that's . . . that's very harsh, a very harsh thing to say . . . '

'Is it? Really? Compared to what you did to me – and to Maddy – I'd say you're getting off lightly.'

'Lightly?' Fire entered his eyes. 'Lightly?' He leaned forward, conspiratorial. Eager for his words to be heard and properly understood. 'You have no idea what it's like in here. *No idea*. It's hell. Absolute hell. I'm on a wing with sex offenders. Can you *believe* that? I'm in with the child abusers and the—'

'Rapists?' said Marina.

Gwilym pretended not to hear. 'Vulnerable prisoners, they're called. They're vulnerable all right. The wing is over-crowded and hard to control and the rest of the inmates are all trying to get at them. At me too. Because I'm a celebrity. That's what it is, that's why I'm there. That's what makes me vulnerable. And I am. I'm living in fear of my life . . . '

The two women didn't respond, just stared at him. Maddy eventually spoke.

'Good,' she said.

Again, Gwilym looked as if he had been slapped.

'You're there because you're a rapist, Hugo. Not because you're a celebrity. You preyed on vulnerable young women and exploited them. For your own fun, your own kicks.'

He had closed his eyes and was shaking his head again. 'No, no, no, no . . . All wrong, Marina. All wrong.' He looked at Maddy. 'She's wrong, isn't she? That wasn't . . . wasn't what happened, was it? It wasn't like that.' Another smile. 'You're carrying my baby, aren't you, Maddy? Our baby . . . '

'No I'm not. That was a lie. I got rid of it.'

Gwilym recoiled.

'I wouldn't want your baby growing inside me.'

Gwilym looked like he was about to cry. 'No, no . . . Maddy, that's . . . No. She's wrong. You're wrong. Tell her the truth.'

'I don't need to,' said Maddy. 'Marina's just told it.'

He sat back. An ugly, unpleasant look crept on to his face. Understanding dawning. 'Oh, I get it. Like that, is it?' He looked straight at Maddy. 'She's poisoned your mind. Told you all those lies about me, made you believe them. I see what's happened. Oh yes.'

'Hugo,' said Marina, calm now. 'The only one telling lies is you. To yourself. And the sooner you face up to that and accept it, the sooner you realise that you are where you are because you brought it on yourself and you deserve to be here, the better.'

Gwilym said nothing.

The three of them sat in silence for a while. Gwilym eventually spoke.

'I thought you'd come here today to forgive me,' he said. When they didn't respond he continued. 'But I can see that isn't going to happen.'

'No, Hugo,' said Marina, 'the reason we came here today was for closure. Because we wanted to see you in this place. We wanted to see you punished, put somewhere you can't hurt any woman ever again. And we've seen that. I can't speak for Maddy, but I've got what I came for.'

'You can speak for me,' said Maddy. 'So have I.'

'I think we'll go now, Hugo, and leave you to get on with the rest of your life.' Marina stood up. Maddy followed.

'No, please, wait, don't go . . . '

They turned back to him. He looked so pathetic sitting there, Marina thought. She waited to see what he was going to say.

'Don't make me go back there, please . . . It's . . . it's . . . I can't describe it. The howling at night, the threats, the bullying, the . . . ' He shook his head. There were tears in the corners of his eyes. He blinked them away, looked at her again. 'I'm on suicide watch . . . '

'Good.' It was Maddy who had spoken. Gwilym stared at her. 'Now you know how you made me feel.'

'Well, goodbye, Hugo,' said Marina. 'I'm sure they do think of you as a celebrity. In the same way we think of Jimmy Savile as a celebrity.'

467

They left. Outside, Maddy became tearful. Marina put her arm round her.

'Was that as bad as you thought it was going to be?'

'Yeah,' she said between sobs, 'kind of.'

'The pain will go,' said Marina. 'Things will get easier.'

Maddy nodded, kept crying. 'I know . . .'

'But that's not much consolation at the moment. Right.'

Maddy smiled.

'What are you going to do now?'

Maddy took out a tissue, wiped her eyes, blew her nose. 'Go home. Back to Somerset. See my mum. She knows about what's happened. She's been great. I'll spend Christmas with her. And then . . .' She shrugged. 'Dunno. See about coming back. If I can face it.'

Marina nodded. 'I'm here if you need me. Whatever you decide. Always.'

Maddy hugged her, and Marina felt tears beginning in her own eyes.

She was glad she had gone, glad she had seen Gwilym. It had put the whole episode to rest. Made her able to move on. She felt Maddy's arms around her.

She's going to be all right, she thought. *I'm sure of it.*

And then: *I hope so.*

Marina jumped as someone spoke to her. It was Anni.

'Sorry?' she said.

'I said, are you enjoying yourself?' Anni smiled, shook her head in mock-admonishment. 'Jesus, woman, you're going senile.'

'Sorry. Miles away. I'm having a fine time. You?'

Anni looked over at Mickey. He was talking to Imani Oliver. 'Just keeping my eye on him, that's all.'

'I'm sure he's fine.'

'Oh, I know he is,' said Anni. 'But I do love to wind him up.' She laughed. 'I'll make him feel guilty for something he hasn't done. Or, knowing him, probably not even thought of doing. Might even get a present out of it.'

Marina joined in the laughter.

'I've missed you,' she said.

'Missed you too.'

Sperring had put aside his prejudices and attended. It was worth it to see the look of surprise on Phil's face as he walked in, bottle of whisky in hand.

'I was going to say I've brought me own, but this is for you. Happy Christmas.'

Phil looked amazed.

'Boss.'

He looked even more amazed. Sperring laughed and walked inside.

He knew Khan had been avoiding him all evening. He had been avoiding him for the last two weeks. And Sperring didn't blame him. But he had to talk to him.

He cornered him as he was coming out of the toilet.

'All right, Nadish?'

Khan nodded, tried to dodge past him.

'Want a word with you.'

Khan went pale. 'Can't it wait? Till—'

'Work? Next week? Never? No, it can't wait. We'll have it now.'

Resigned, Khan stood there.

'I want to tell you a story,' Sperring said, deliberately doing a terrible Max Bygraves impression that he knew would go completely over Khan's head. 'This happened in China. Years ago. In a village miles from anywhere. True story. There was this postmaster, ran the village post office. For about twenty years. It was discovered, long story short, that money had been disappearing. And it was him. He'd been doing this all the time he'd been working there. Someone would get a cheque, he'd have that. Bit of cash, he'd help himself to that too. Years this went on for. All the time he'd been there. Amassed millions, he did. Or hundreds of thousands, forget which. But a lot, anyway. And then he got caught.'

Sperring sighed, took a swig of his beer. Khan stood like he was on the scaffold waiting for the drop.

'Anyway, there was a big trial. He was found guilty because, obviously, he was. And d'you know what his punishment was?'

Khan shook his head.

'Go on, guess.'

'I . . . I can't.'

'All right, then, I'll tell you. They gave him his old job back.'

Khan stared at him.

'Honestly. True story, as I live and breathe. They gave him his old job back and made him pay back the money to the people he'd stolen it from, bit at a time. They said prison wouldn't have helped. And anyway, he'd been a good post-master, apart from that.'

'Right,' said Khan. 'Good for him.'

'Yeah,' said Sperring. 'Good for him. That was his punishment. He had to look at all the people he'd betrayed, every day for the rest of his working life. And he knew that they knew what he'd done. And you know what? He was the best postmaster they could ever have wanted.'

He finished, stared at Khan.

'D'you understand what I'm saying?'

Khan nodded. 'I think so.'

'Good.' Sperring looked round the room. 'Right, there's

470

this bird been giving me the glad eye. Better go and be charming.'

'OK,' said Khan. 'Thank you.'

'Don't thank me yet, Nadish.'

And off Sperring went to track down Joy Henry.

Marina found Phil. Smiled at him.

'Having fun?'

'I think so,' he said. 'You?'

'I think so.' She looked round the room once more. 'It's working, isn't it? This. Your lot. My lot. It's working.'

He looked directly at her. Into her beautiful dark eyes. 'Yeah,' he said. 'It's working.'

She leaned in close. 'But I'm looking forward to everyone going home.' She snaked an arm round his waist, squeezed his bottom.

He looked at her. 'D'you want me to throw them out? I'll get the OSU in to do it.'

They both laughed. Anni and Mickey wandered up.

'Not interrupting anything, are we?'

'And what if you were?' said Marina.

'I wouldn't care,' Anni said.

The four of them talked. Old times. Cases. War stories. Enjoying each other's company. Eventually Anni's expression changed.

'Look,' she said. 'I know I've asked already, but ... when are you two coming home?'

Phil and Marina looked at each other.

And smiled.